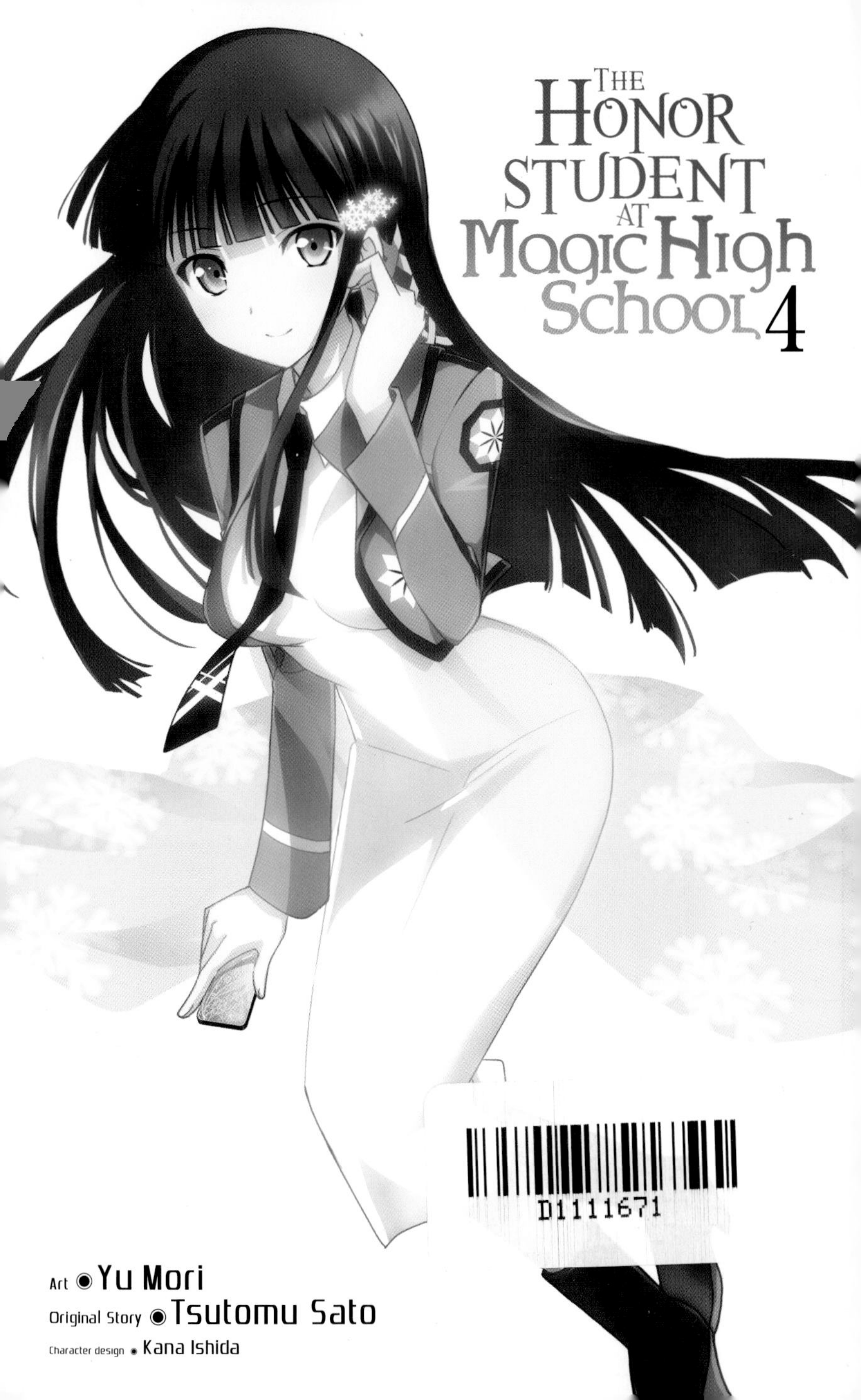

The Honor Student at Magic High School 4

Art ● Yu Mori

Original Story ● Tsutomu Sato

Character design ● Kana Ishida

CONTENTS

The Honor Student
at Magic High School

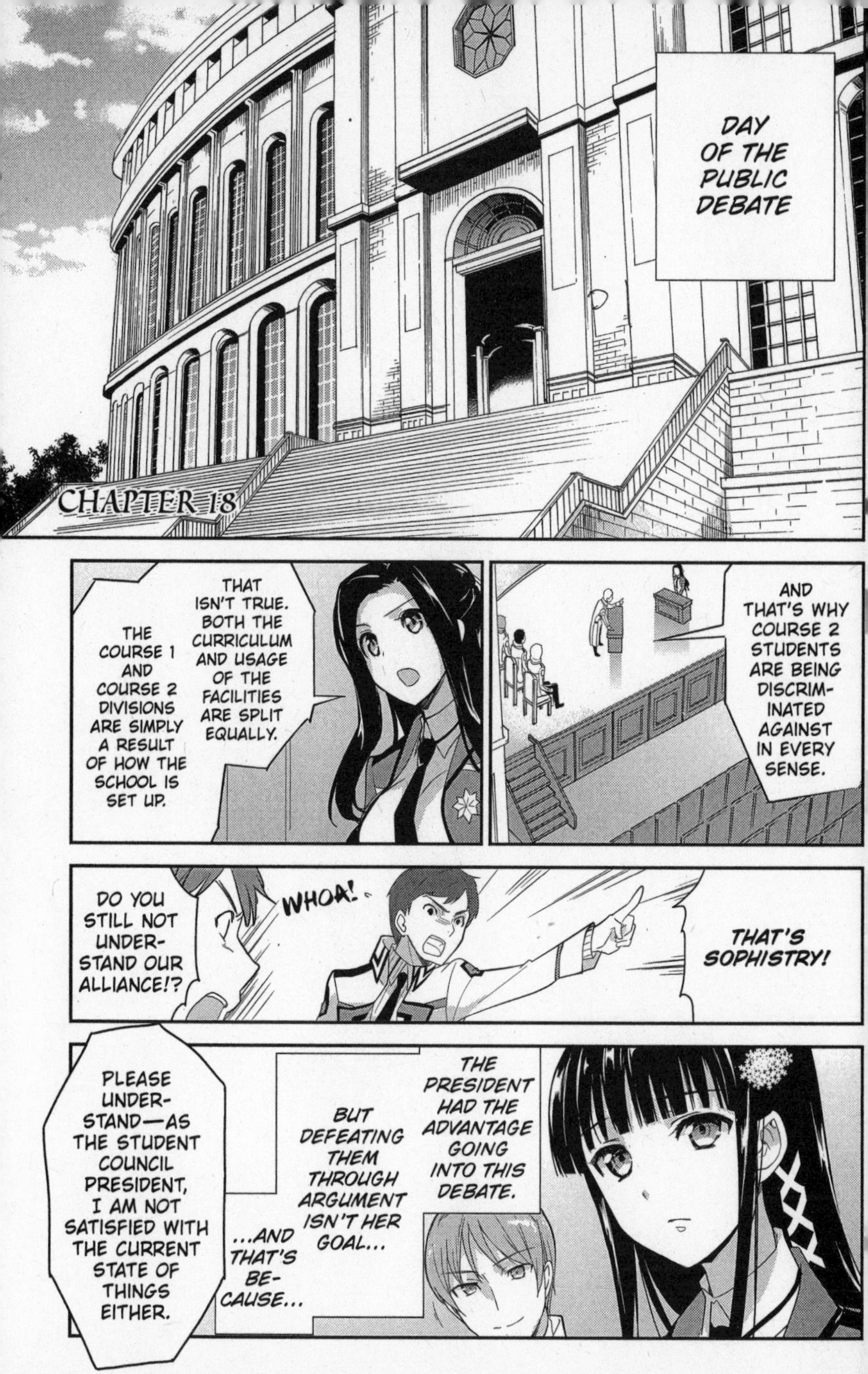
DAY OF THE PUBLIC DEBATE
CHAPTER 18
AND THAT'S WHY COURSE 2 STUDENTS ARE BEING DISCRIMINATED AGAINST IN EVERY SENSE.
THAT ISN'T TRUE. BOTH THE CURRICULUM AND USAGE OF THE FACILITIES ARE SPLIT EQUALLY.
THE COURSE 1 AND COURSE 2 DIVISIONS ARE SIMPLY A RESULT OF HOW THE SCHOOL IS SET UP.
THAT'S SOPHISTRY!
WHOA!
DO YOU STILL NOT UNDERSTAND OUR ALLIANCE!?
THE PRESIDENT HAD THE ADVANTAGE GOING INTO THIS DEBATE.
BUT DEFEATING THEM THROUGH ARGUMENT ISN'T HER GOAL...
...AND THAT'S BECAUSE...
PLEASE UNDERSTAND—AS THE STUDENT COUNCIL PRESIDENT, I AM NOT SATISFIED WITH THE CURRENT STATE OF THINGS EITHER.

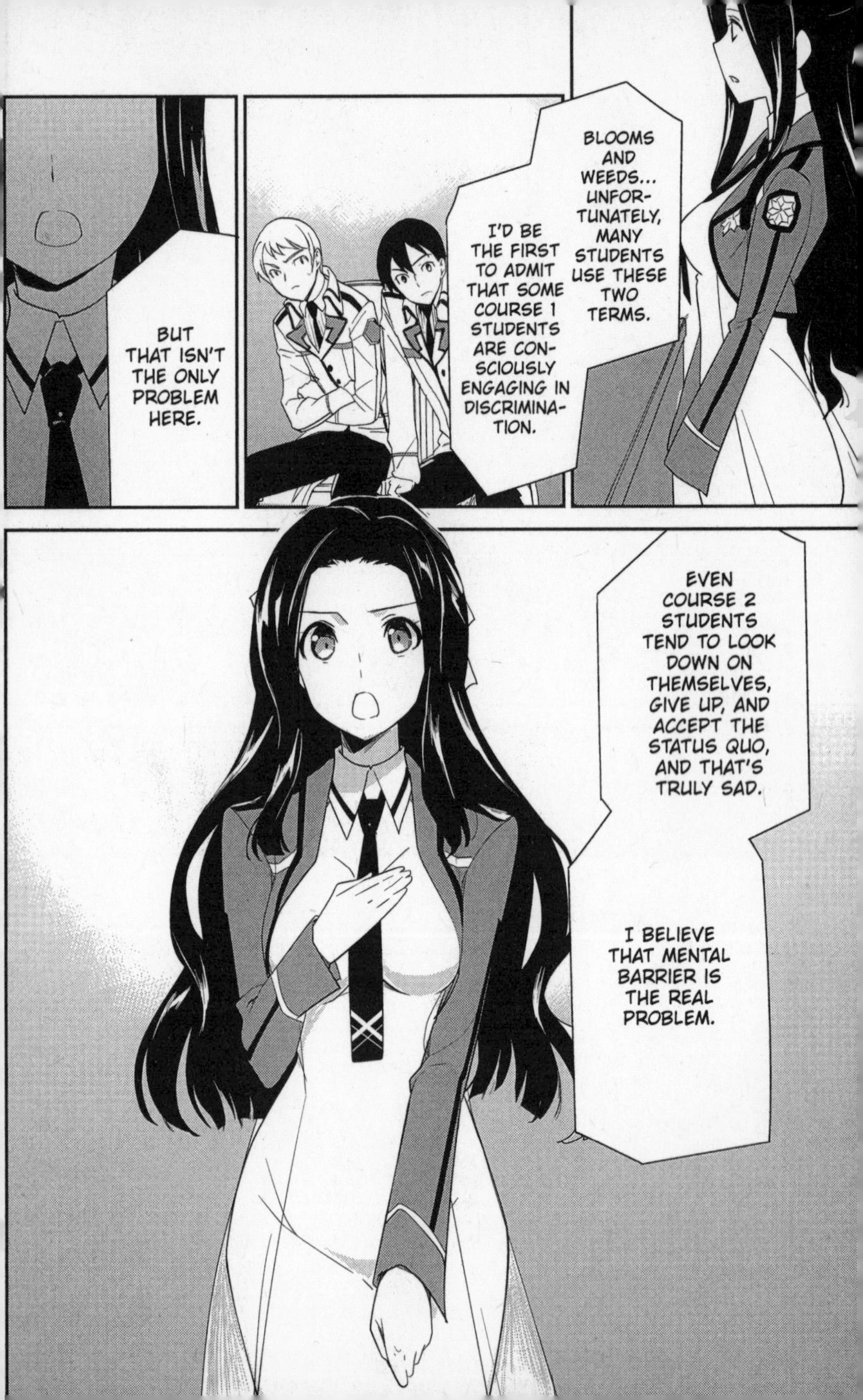

BLOOMS AND WEEDS... UNFORTUNATELY, MANY STUDENTS USE THESE TWO TERMS.
I'D BE THE FIRST TO ADMIT THAT SOME COURSE 1 STUDENTS ARE CONSCIOUSLY ENGAGING IN DISCRIMINATION.
BUT THAT ISN'T THE ONLY PROBLEM HERE.
EVEN COURSE 2 STUDENTS TEND TO LOOK DOWN ON THEMSELVES, GIVE UP, AND ACCEPT THE STATUS QUO, AND THAT'S TRULY SAD.
I BELIEVE THAT MENTAL BARRIER IS THE REAL PROBLEM.

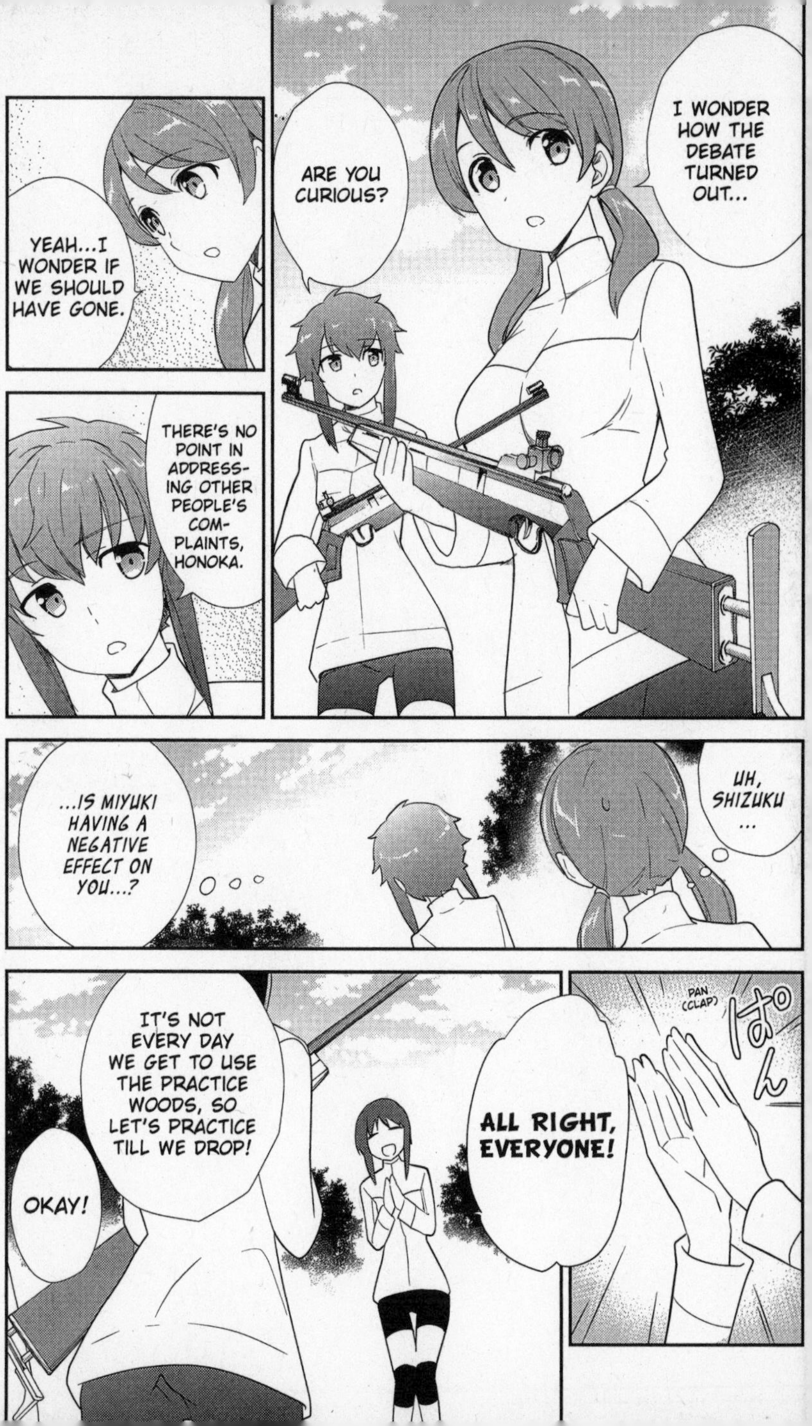
I WONDER HOW THE DEBATE TURNED OUT...
ARE YOU CURIOUS?
YEAH...I WONDER IF WE SHOULD HAVE GONE.
THERE'S NO POINT IN ADDRESSING OTHER PEOPLE'S COMPLAINTS, HONOKA.
UH, SHIZUKU...
...IS MIYUKI HAVING A NEGATIVE EFFECT ON YOU...?
PAN (CLAP)
ぱん
ALL RIGHT, EVERYONE!
IT'S NOT EVERY DAY WE GET TO USE THE PRACTICE WOODS, SO LET'S PRACTICE TILL WE DROP!
OKAY!

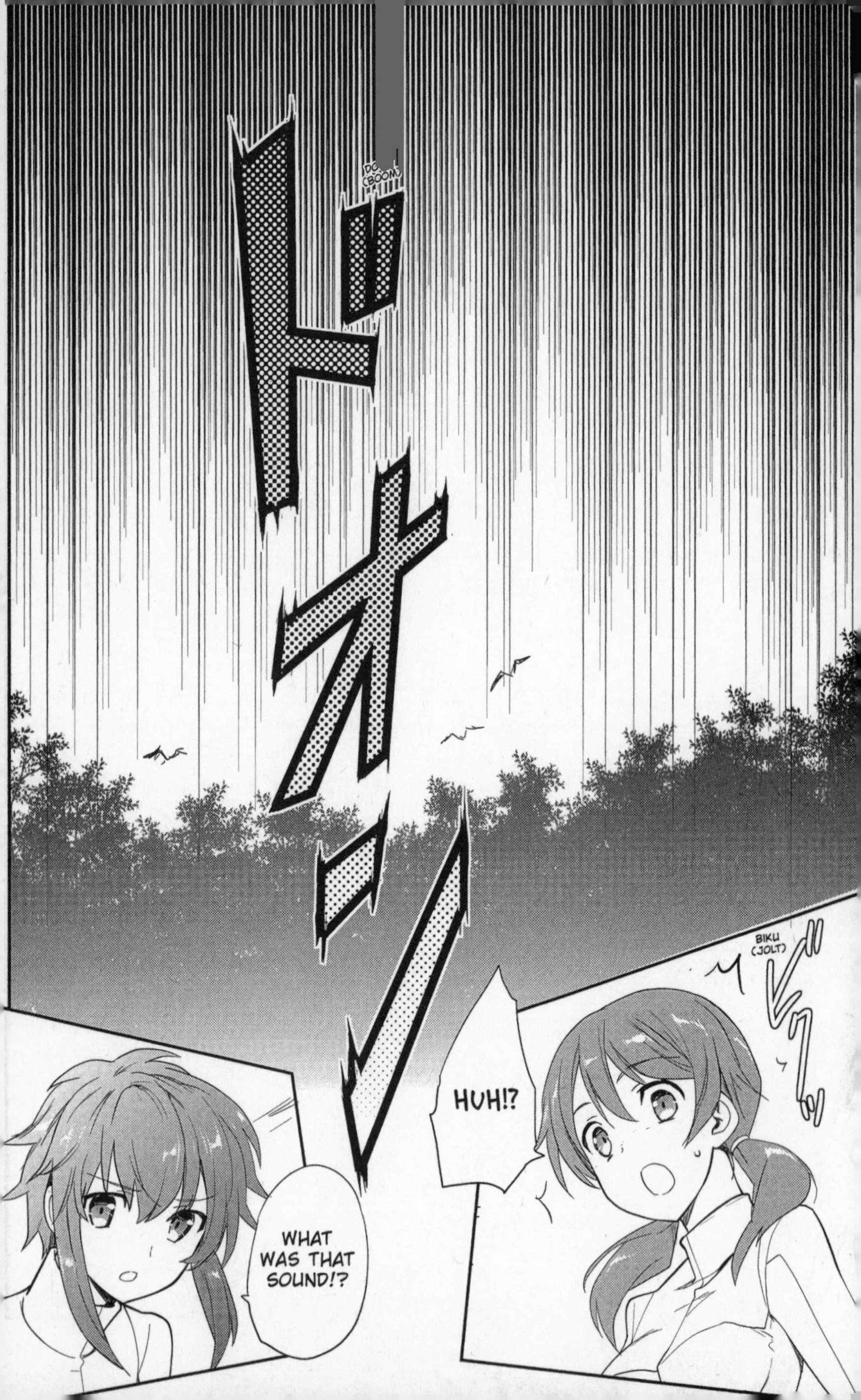
DO (BOOM)
BIKU (JOLT)
HUH!?
WHAT WAS THAT SOUND!?

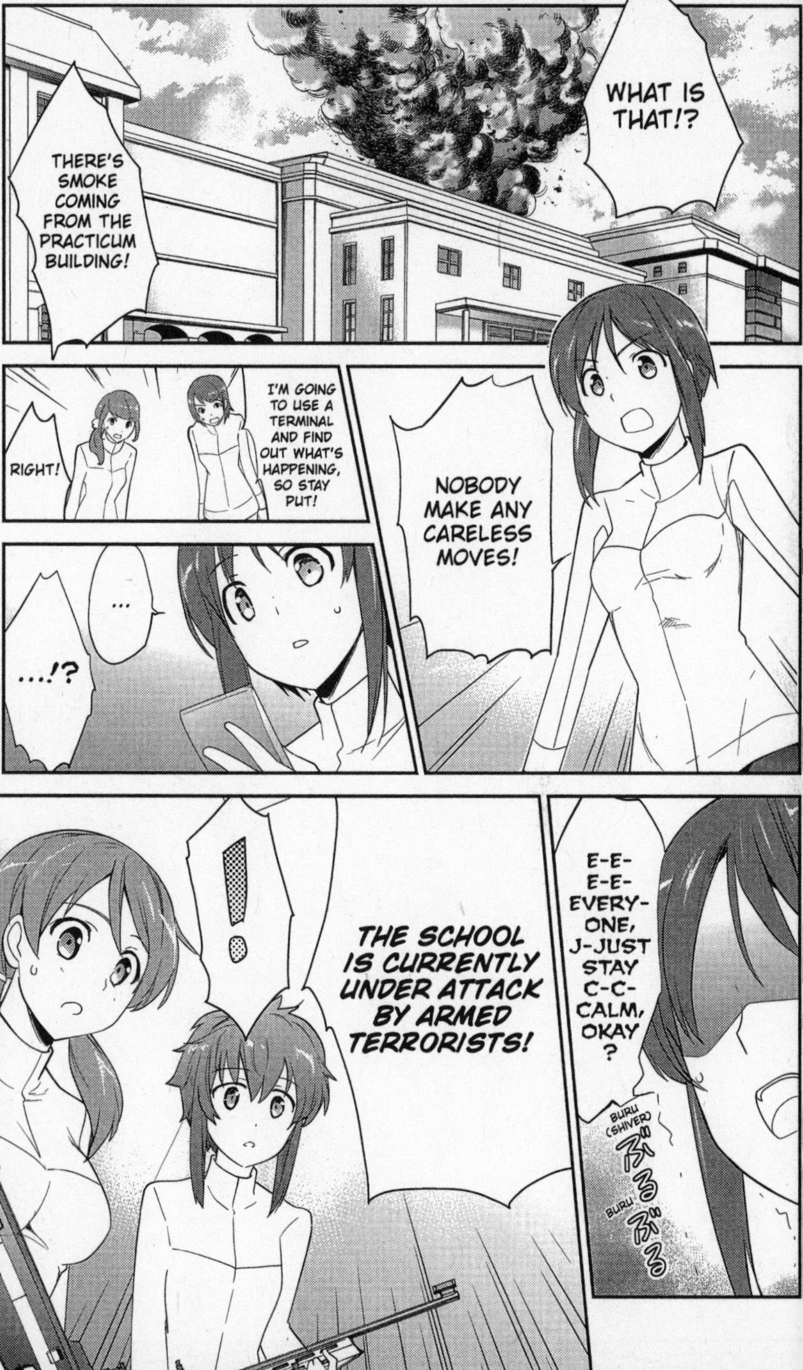

WHAT IS THAT!?
THERE'S SMOKE COMING FROM THE PRACTICUM BUILDING!
NOBODY MAKE ANY CARELESS MOVES!
I'M GOING TO USE A TERMINAL AND FIND OUT WHAT'S HAPPENING, SO STAY PUT!
RIGHT!
...
...!?
E-E-E-E-EVERY-ONE, J-JUST STAY C-C-CALM, OKAY?
BURU (SHIVER) ぶる
BURU ぶる
!
THE SCHOOL IS CURRENTLY UNDER ATTACK BY ARMED TERRORISTS!

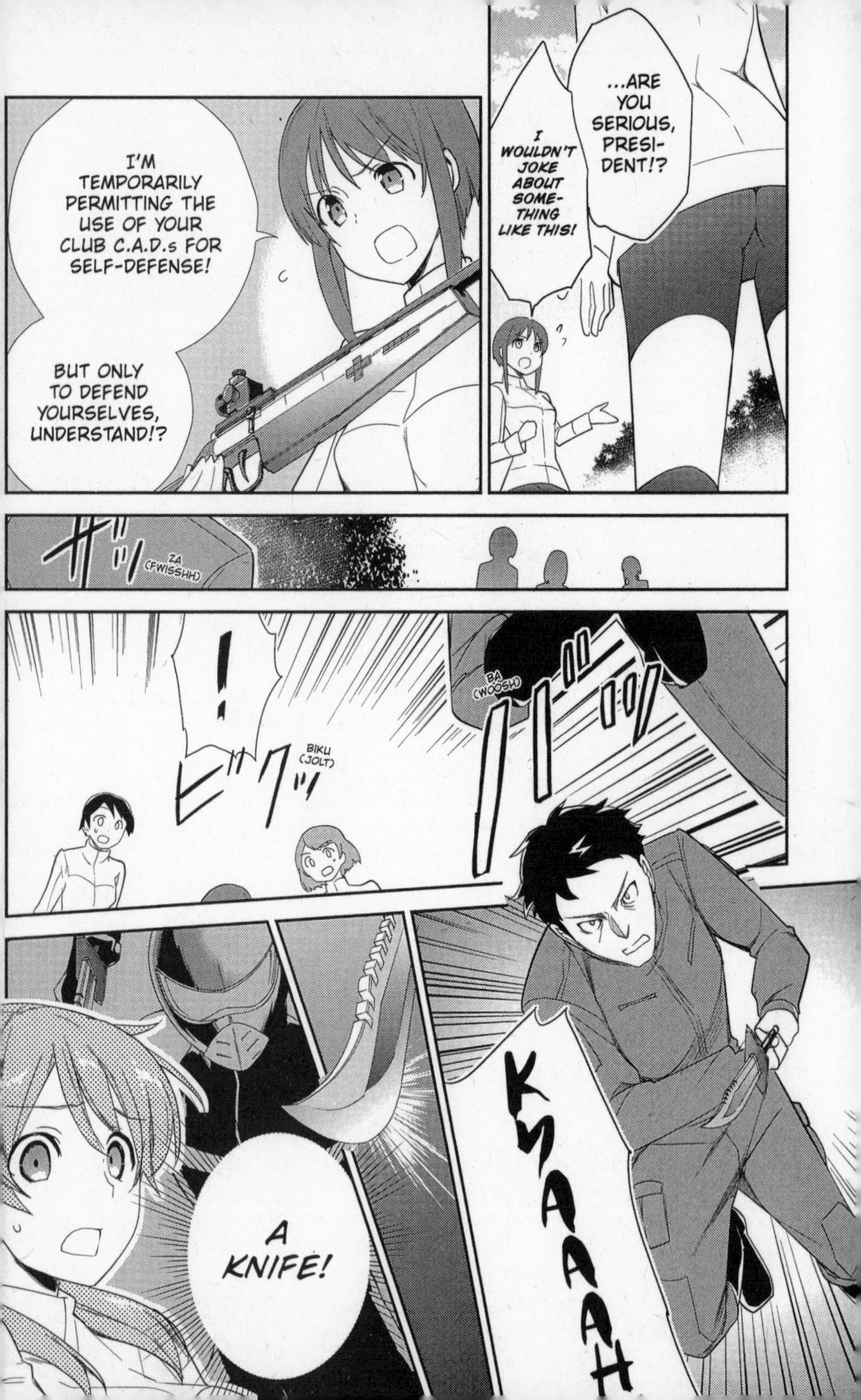
...ARE YOU SERIOUS, PRESIDENT!?
I WOULDN'T JOKE ABOUT SOMETHING LIKE THIS!
I'M TEMPORARILY PERMITTING THE USE OF YOUR CLUB C.A.D.s FOR SELF-DEFENSE!
BUT ONLY TO DEFEND YOURSELVES, UNDERSTAND!?
ZA (FWISSHH)
BA (WOOSH)
!
BIKU (JOLT)
KYAAAAH
A KNIFE!

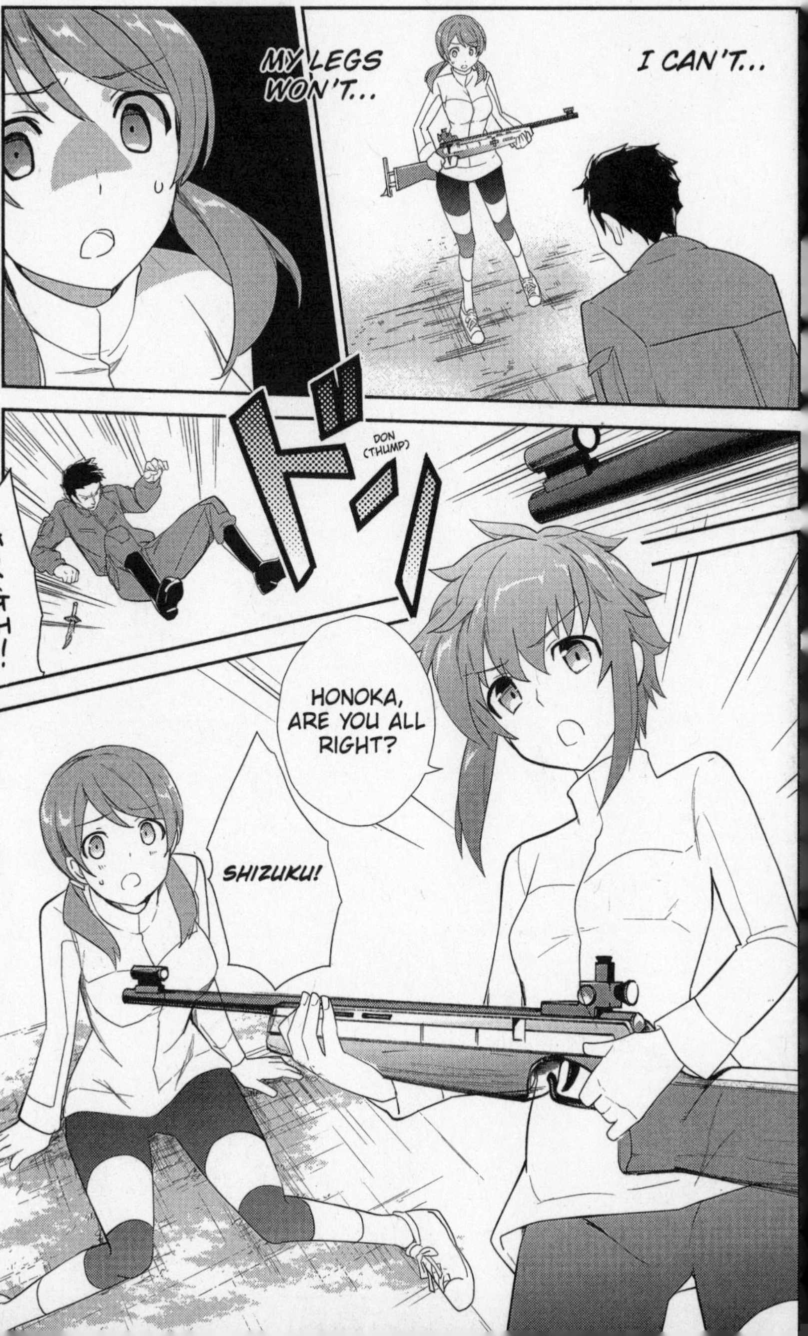
I CAN'T...
MY LEGS WON'T...
ドッ
DON (THUMP)
ARGH!
HONOKA, ARE YOU ALL RIGHT?
SHIZUKU!

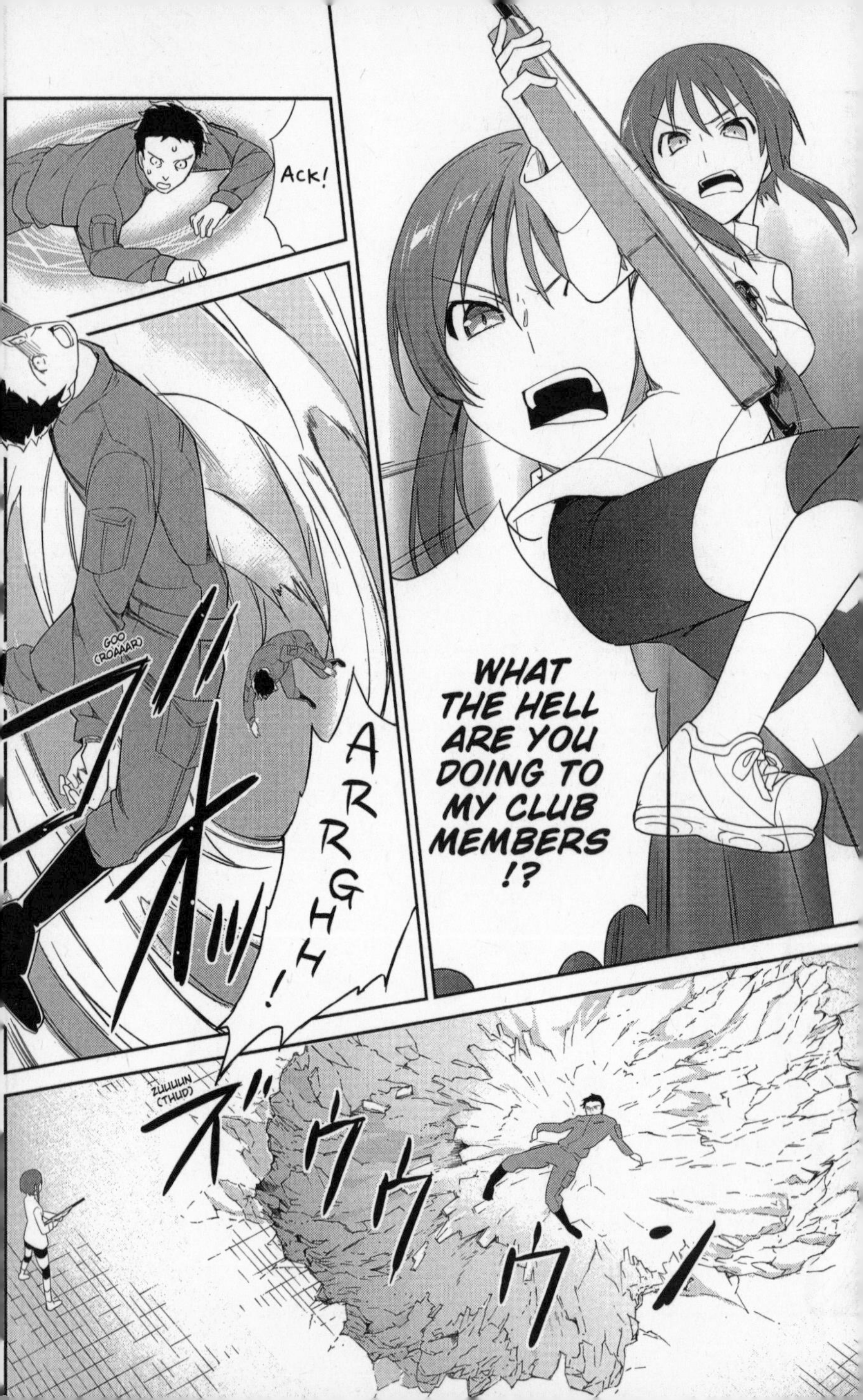
WHAT THE HELL ARE YOU DOING TO MY CLUB MEMBERS!?
ACK!
GOO (ROAAAR)
ARRGHH!
ZUUUUN (THUD)

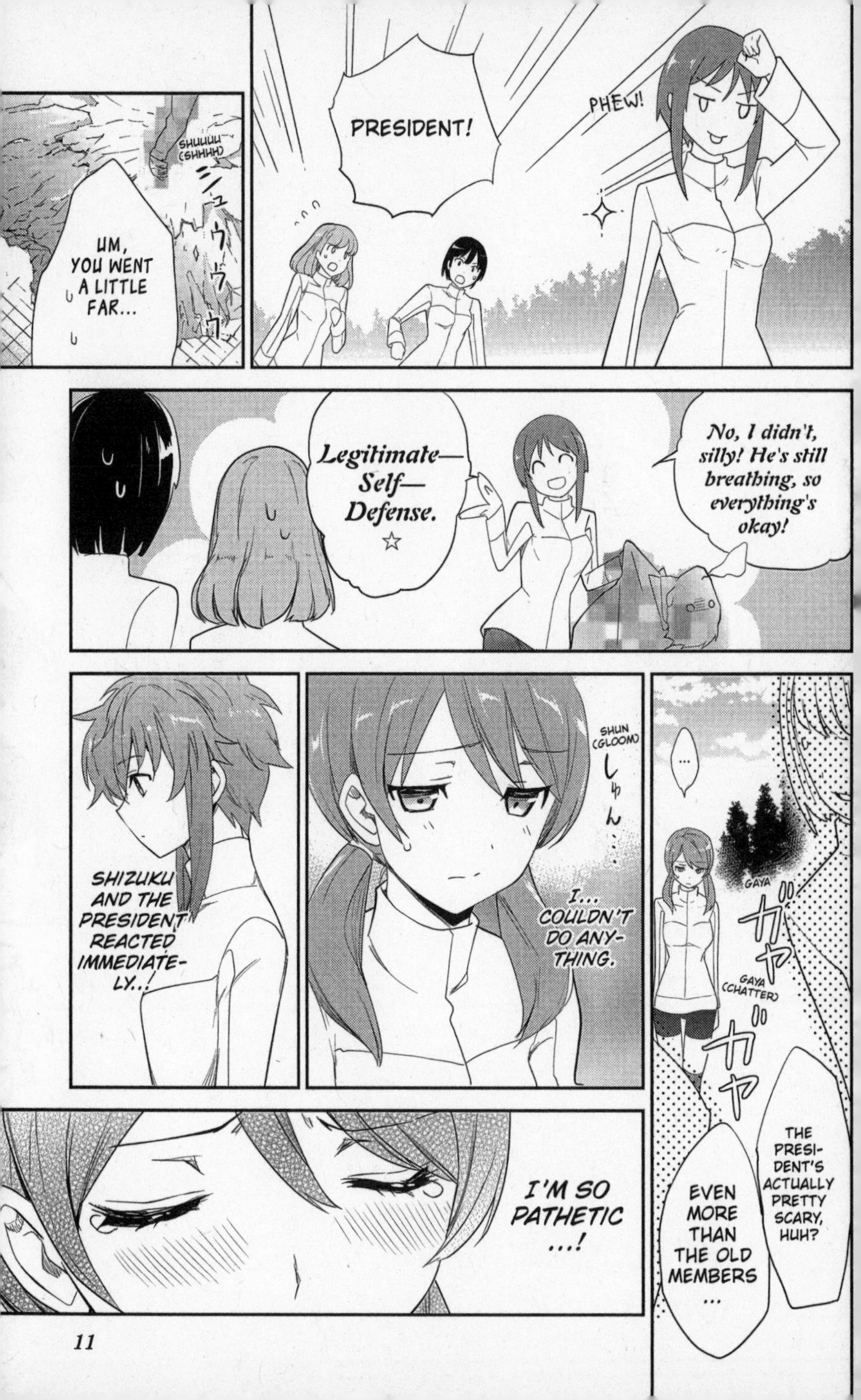
PHEW!
PRESIDENT!
SHUUUU (SHHHH)
UM, YOU WENT A LITTLE FAR...
No, I didn't, silly! He's still breathing, so everything's okay!
Legitimate—Self—Defense. ☆
...
GAYA
GAYA (CHATTER)
THE PRESIDENT'S ACTUALLY PRETTY SCARY, HUH?
EVEN MORE THAN THE OLD MEMBERS...
SHUN (GLOOM)
I... COULDN'T DO ANYTHING.
SHIZUKU AND THE PRESIDENT REACTED IMMEDIATELY...!
I'M SO PATHETIC...!

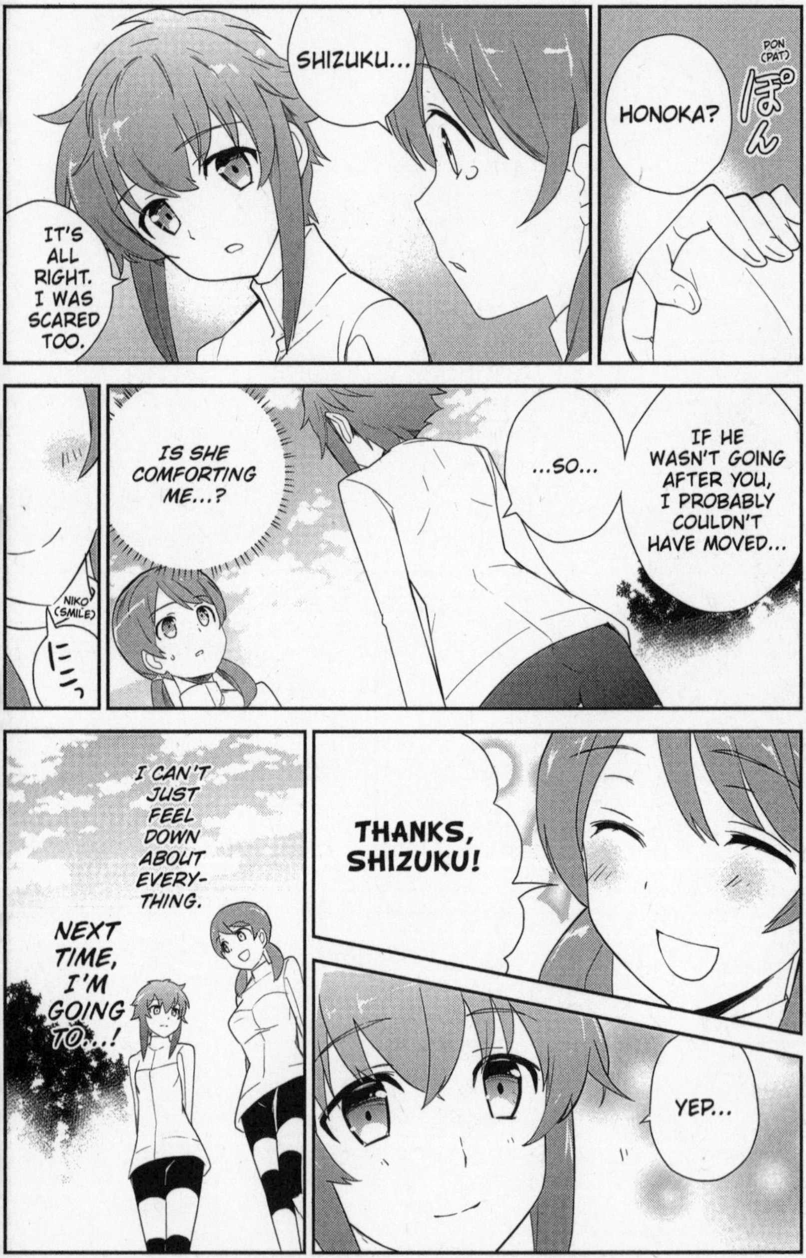
PON (PAT)
ぽん
HONOKA?
SHIZUKU...
IT'S ALL RIGHT. I WAS SCARED TOO.
IF HE WASN'T GOING AFTER YOU, I PROBABLY COULDN'T HAVE MOVED...
...SO...
IS SHE COMFORTING ME...?
NIKO (SMILE)
ニコッ
THANKS, SHIZUKU!
YEP...
I CAN'T JUST FEEL DOWN ABOUT EVERY-THING.
NEXT TIME, I'M GOING TO...!

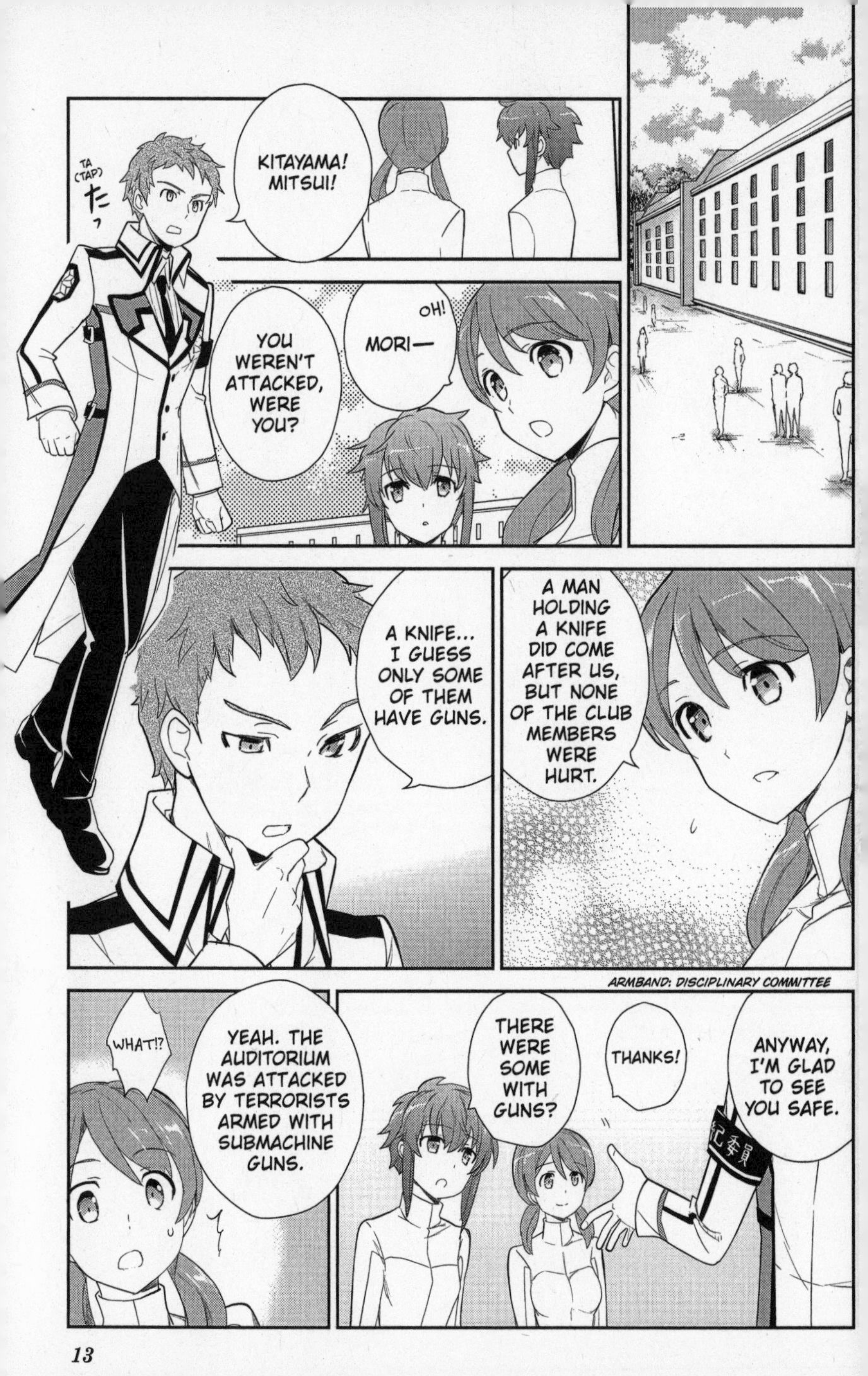
KITAYAMA! MITSUI!
TA (TAP) た
OH!
MORI—
YOU WEREN'T ATTACKED, WERE YOU?
A MAN HOLDING A KNIFE DID COME AFTER US, BUT NONE OF THE CLUB MEMBERS WERE HURT.
A KNIFE... I GUESS ONLY SOME OF THEM HAVE GUNS.
ARMBAND: DISCIPLINARY COMMITTEE
ANYWAY, I'M GLAD TO SEE YOU SAFE.
THANKS!
THERE WERE SOME WITH GUNS?
YEAH. THE AUDITORIUM WAS ATTACKED BY TERRORISTS ARMED WITH SUBMACHINE GUNS.
WHAT!?

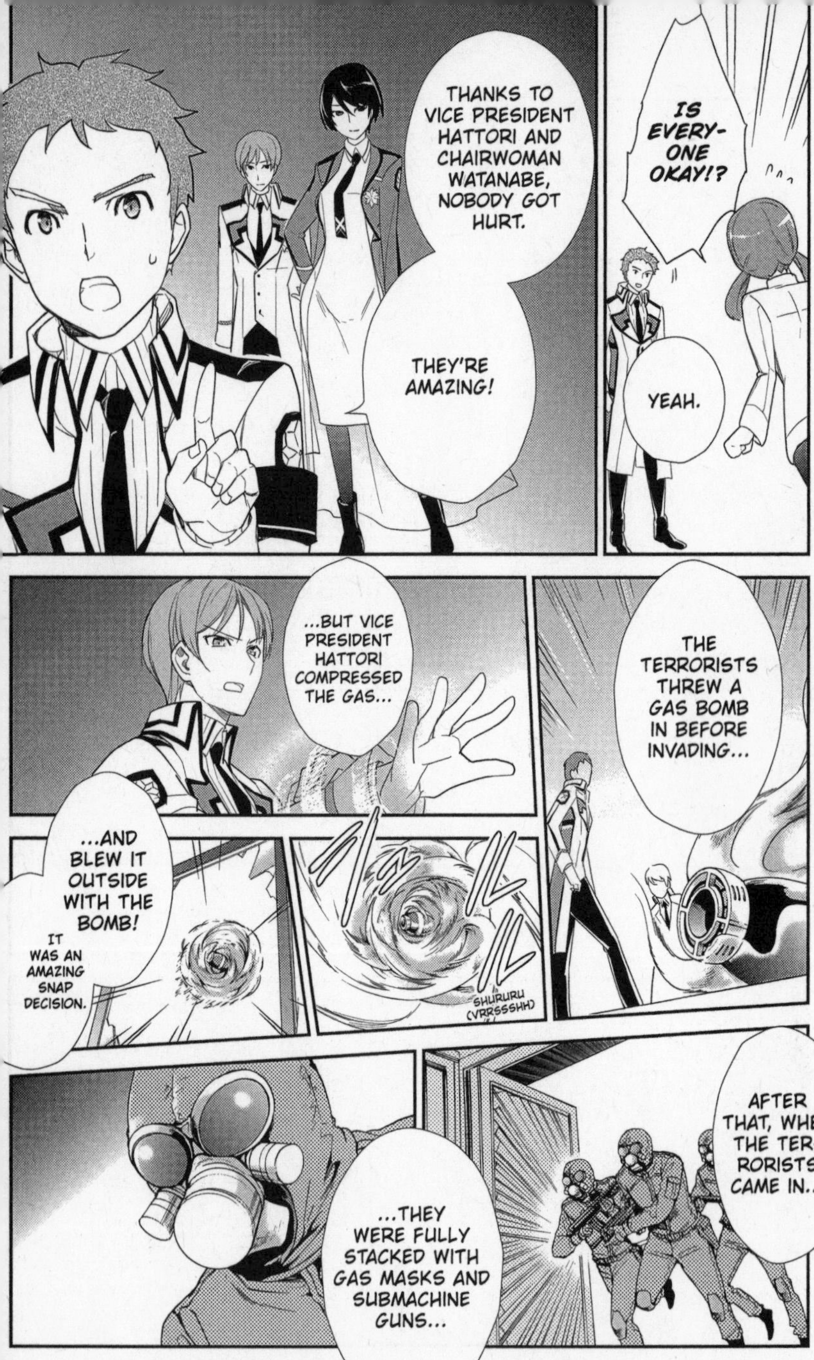
IS EVERYONE OKAY!?
YEAH.
THANKS TO VICE PRESIDENT HATTORI AND CHAIRWOMAN WATANABE, NOBODY GOT HURT.
THEY'RE AMAZING!
THE TERRORISTS THREW A GAS BOMB IN BEFORE INVADING...
...BUT VICE PRESIDENT HATTORI COMPRESSED THE GAS...
SHURURU (VRRSSSHH)
...AND BLEW IT OUTSIDE WITH THE BOMB!
IT WAS AN AMAZING SNAP DECISION.
AFTER THAT, WHEN THE TERRORISTS CAME IN...
...THEY WERE FULLY STACKED WITH GAS MASKS AND SUBMACHINE GUNS...

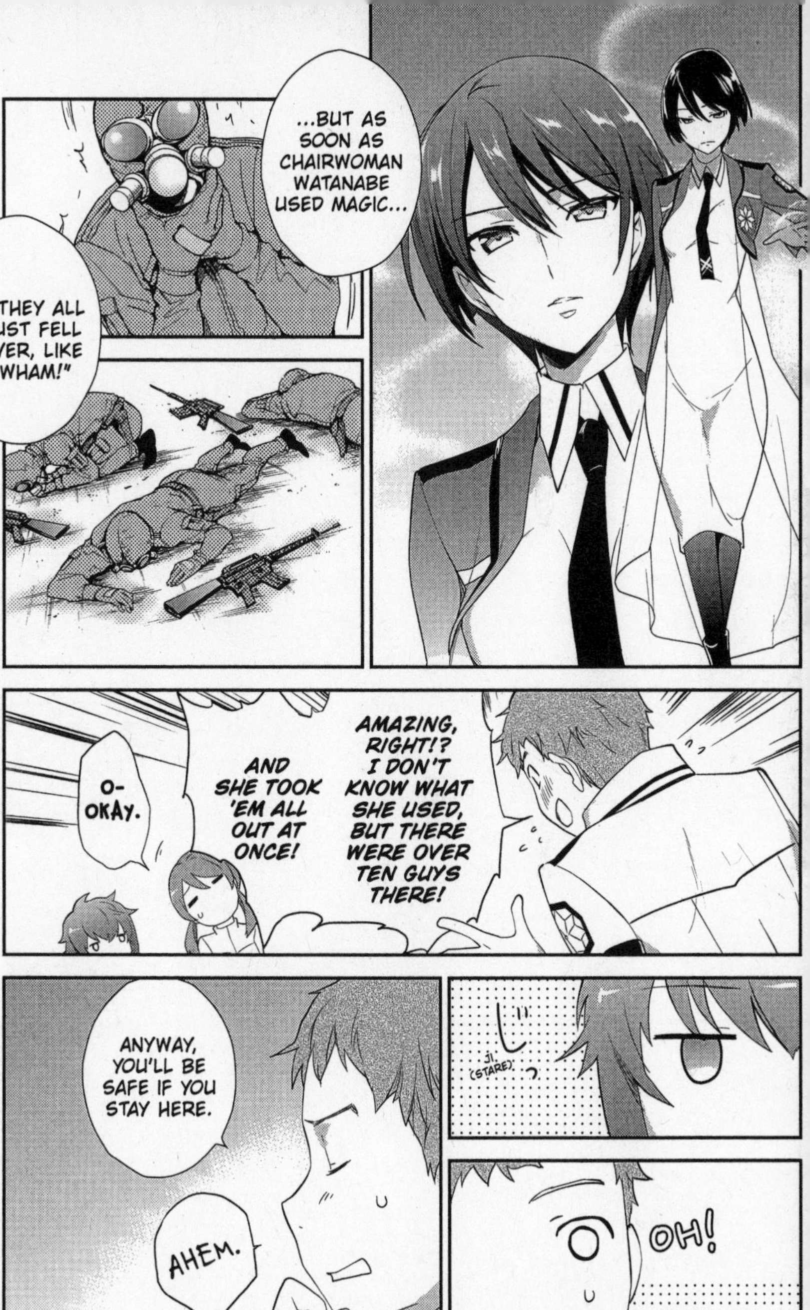
...BUT AS SOON AS CHAIRWOMAN WATANABE USED MAGIC...
...THEY ALL JUST FELL OVER, LIKE "WHAM!"
AMAZING, RIGHT!? I DON'T KNOW WHAT SHE USED, BUT THERE WERE OVER TEN GUYS THERE!
AND SHE TOOK 'EM ALL OUT AT ONCE!
O-OKAY.
JI. (STARE)
OH!
ANYWAY, YOU'LL BE SAFE IF YOU STAY HERE.
AHEM.

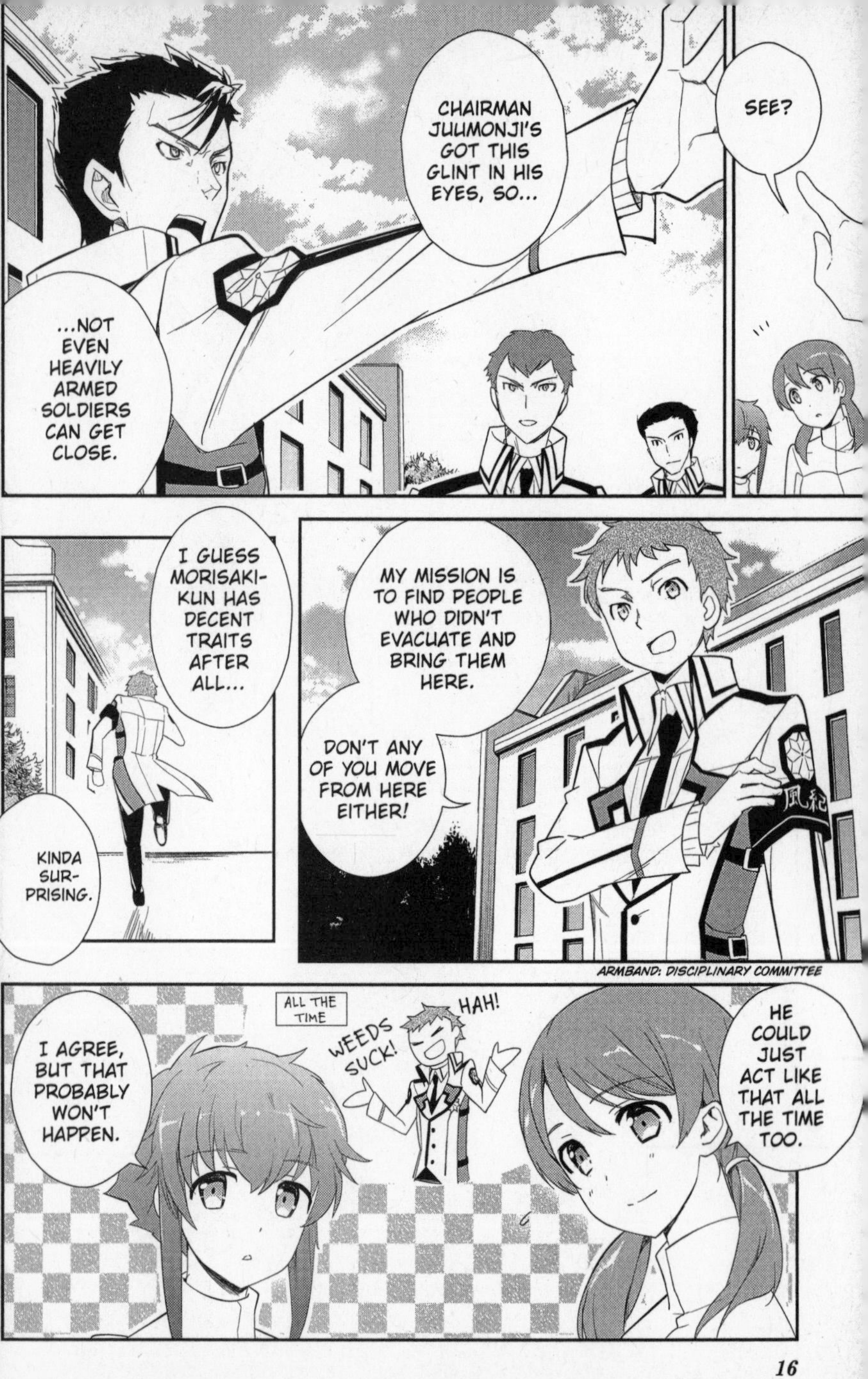
SEE?
CHAIRMAN JUUMONJI'S GOT THIS GLINT IN HIS EYES, SO...
...NOT EVEN HEAVILY ARMED SOLDIERS CAN GET CLOSE.
MY MISSION IS TO FIND PEOPLE WHO DIDN'T EVACUATE AND BRING THEM HERE.
DON'T ANY OF YOU MOVE FROM HERE EITHER!
風紀
I GUESS MORISAKI-KUN HAS DECENT TRAITS AFTER ALL...
KINDA SURPRISING.
ARMBAND: DISCIPLINARY COMMITTEE
HE COULD JUST ACT LIKE THAT ALL THE TIME TOO.
HAH!
WEEDS SUCK!
ALL THE TIME
I AGREE, BUT THAT PROBABLY WON'T HAPPEN.

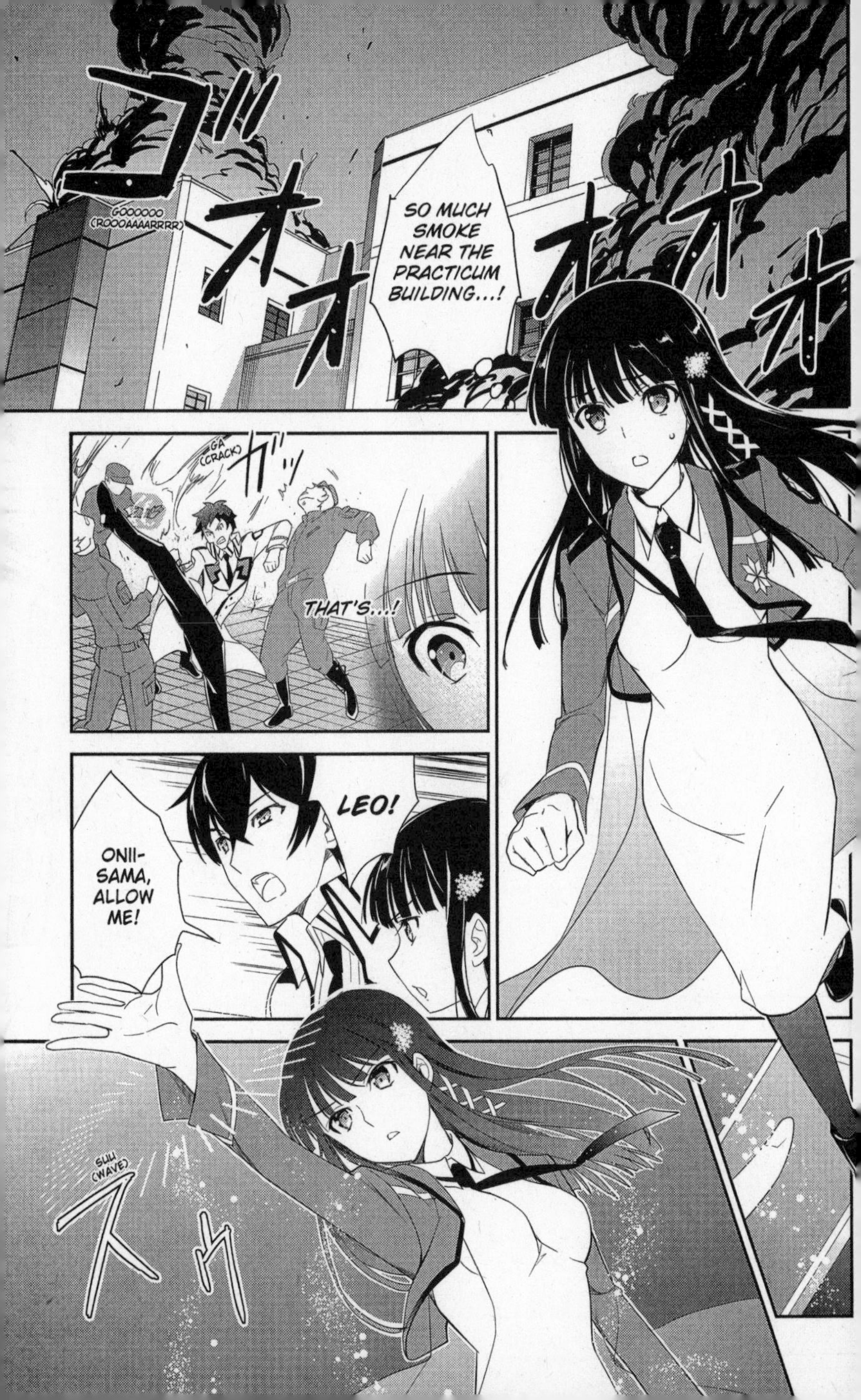
SO MUCH SMOKE NEAR THE PRACTICUM BUILDING...!
GOOOOOO (ROOOAAAARRRR)
GA (CRACK)
THAT'S...!
LEO!
ONII-SAMA, ALLOW ME!
SUU (WAVE)

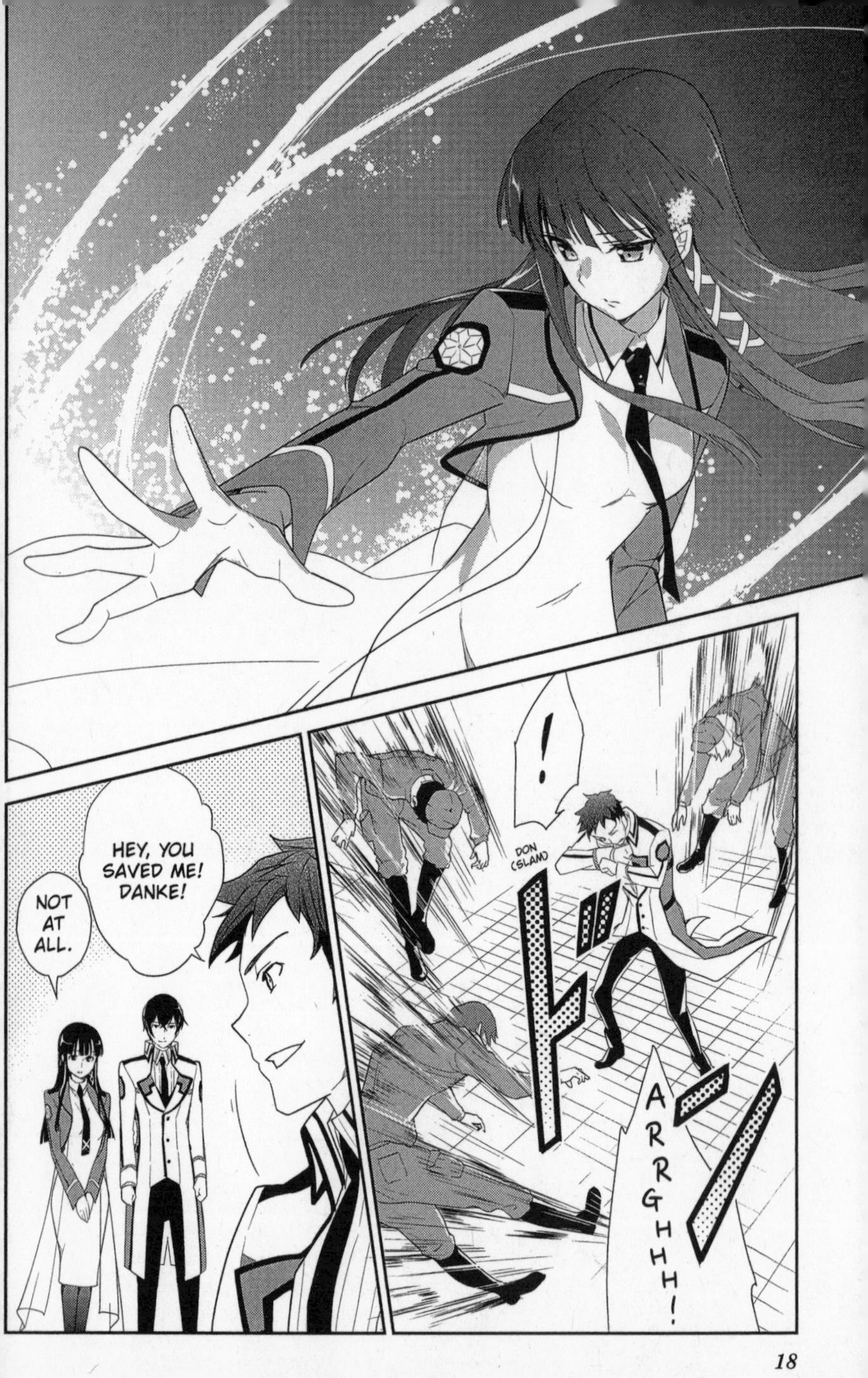
!
DON (SLAM)
ARRGHHH!
HEY, YOU SAVED ME! DANKE!
NOT AT ALL.

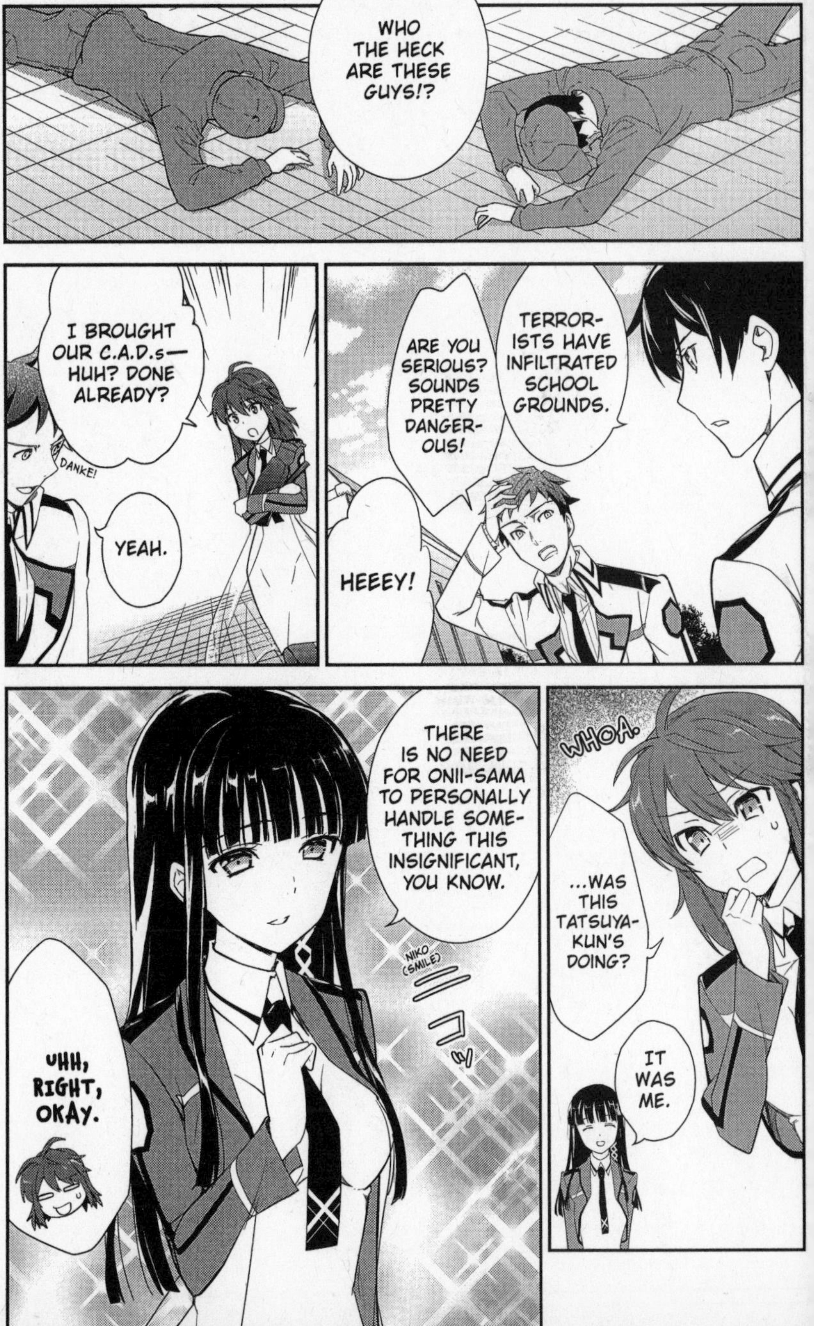
WHO THE HECK ARE THESE GUYS!?
TERROR-ISTS HAVE INFILTRATED SCHOOL GROUNDS.
ARE YOU SERIOUS? SOUNDS PRETTY DANGER-OUS!
HEEEY!
I BROUGHT OUR C.A.D.s—HUH? DONE ALREADY?
DANKE!
YEAH.
WHOA.
...WAS THIS TATSUYA-KUN'S DOING?
IT WAS ME.
THERE IS NO NEED FOR ONII-SAMA TO PERSONALLY HANDLE SOME-THING THIS INSIGNIFICANT, YOU KNOW.
NIKO (SMILE)
UHH, RIGHT, OKAY.

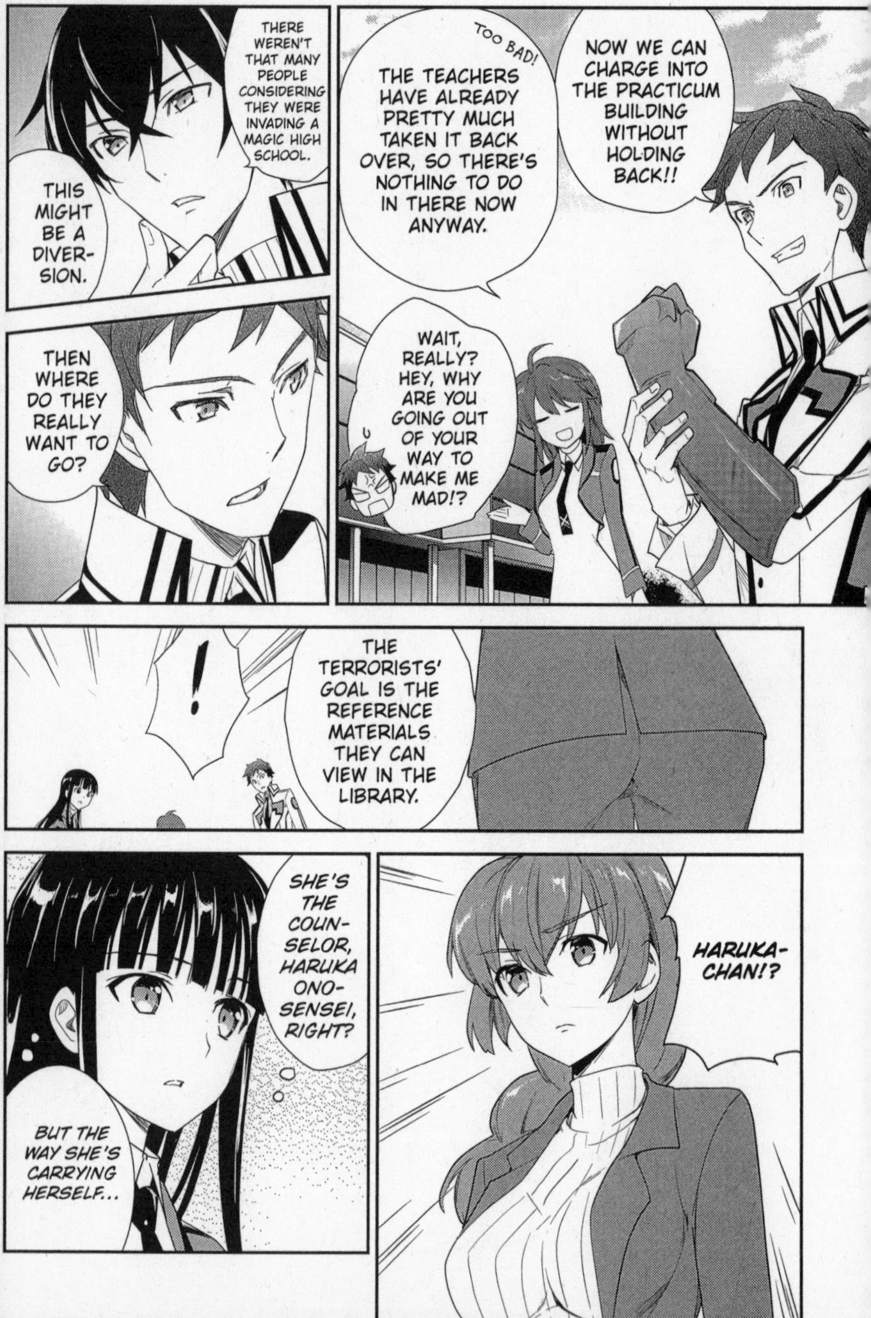
NOW WE CAN CHARGE INTO THE PRACTICUM BUILDING WITHOUT HOLDING BACK!!
TOO BAD!
THE TEACHERS HAVE ALREADY PRETTY MUCH TAKEN IT BACK OVER, SO THERE'S NOTHING TO DO IN THERE NOW ANYWAY.
WAIT, REALLY? HEY, WHY ARE YOU GOING OUT OF YOUR WAY TO MAKE ME MAD!?
THERE WEREN'T THAT MANY PEOPLE CONSIDERING THEY WERE INVADING A MAGIC HIGH SCHOOL.
THIS MIGHT BE A DIVERSION.
THEN WHERE DO THEY REALLY WANT TO GO?
THE TERRORISTS' GOAL IS THE REFERENCE MATERIALS THEY CAN VIEW IN THE LIBRARY.
!
HARUKA-CHAN!?
SHE'S THE COUNSELOR, HARUKA ONO-SENSEI, RIGHT?
BUT THE WAY SHE'S CARRYING HERSELF...

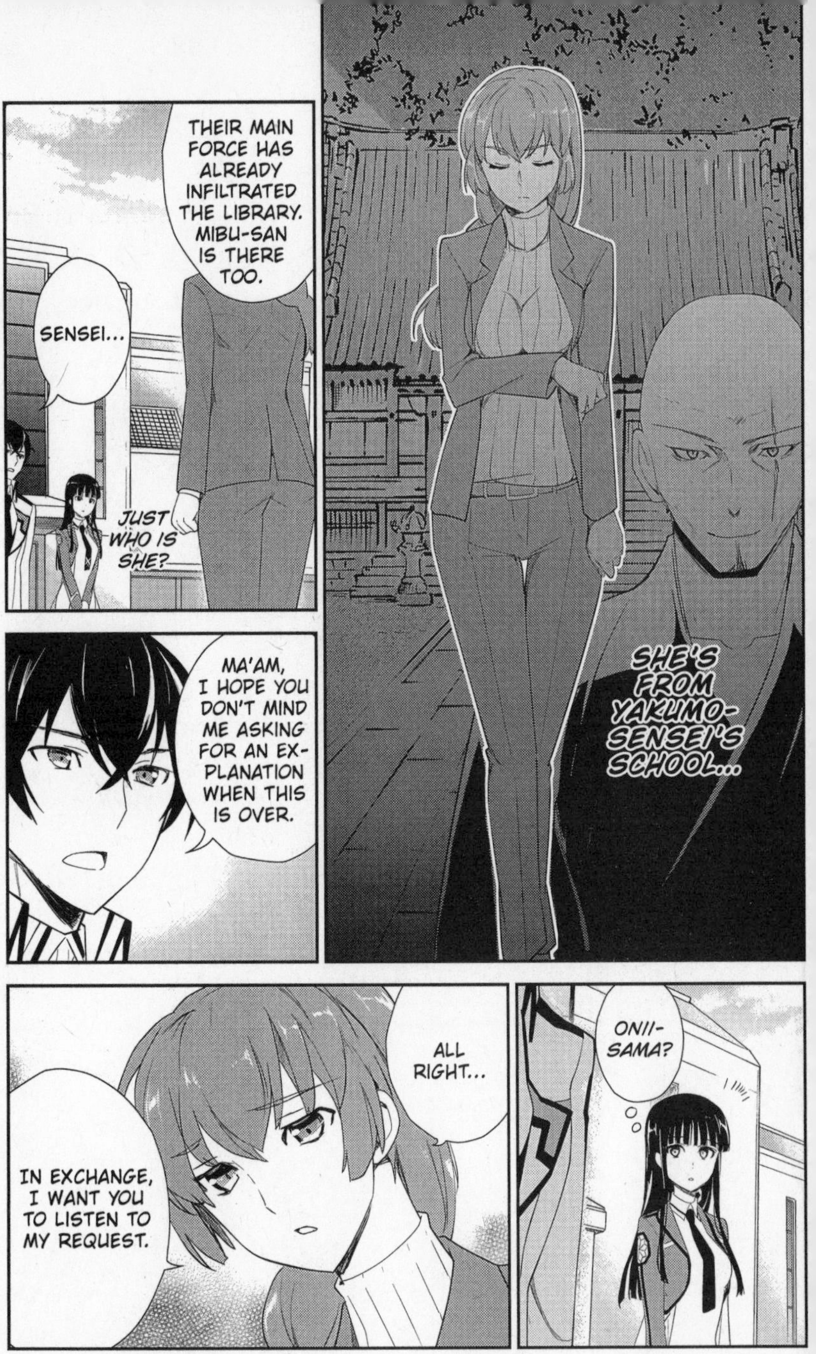
SHE'S FROM YAKUMO-SENSEI'S SCHOOL...
THEIR MAIN FORCE HAS ALREADY INFILTRATED THE LIBRARY. MIBU-SAN IS THERE TOO.
SENSEI...
JUST WHO IS SHE?
MA'AM, I HOPE YOU DON'T MIND ME ASKING FOR AN EX-PLANATION WHEN THIS IS OVER.
ONII-SAMA?
ALL RIGHT...
IN EXCHANGE, I WANT YOU TO LISTEN TO MY REQUEST.

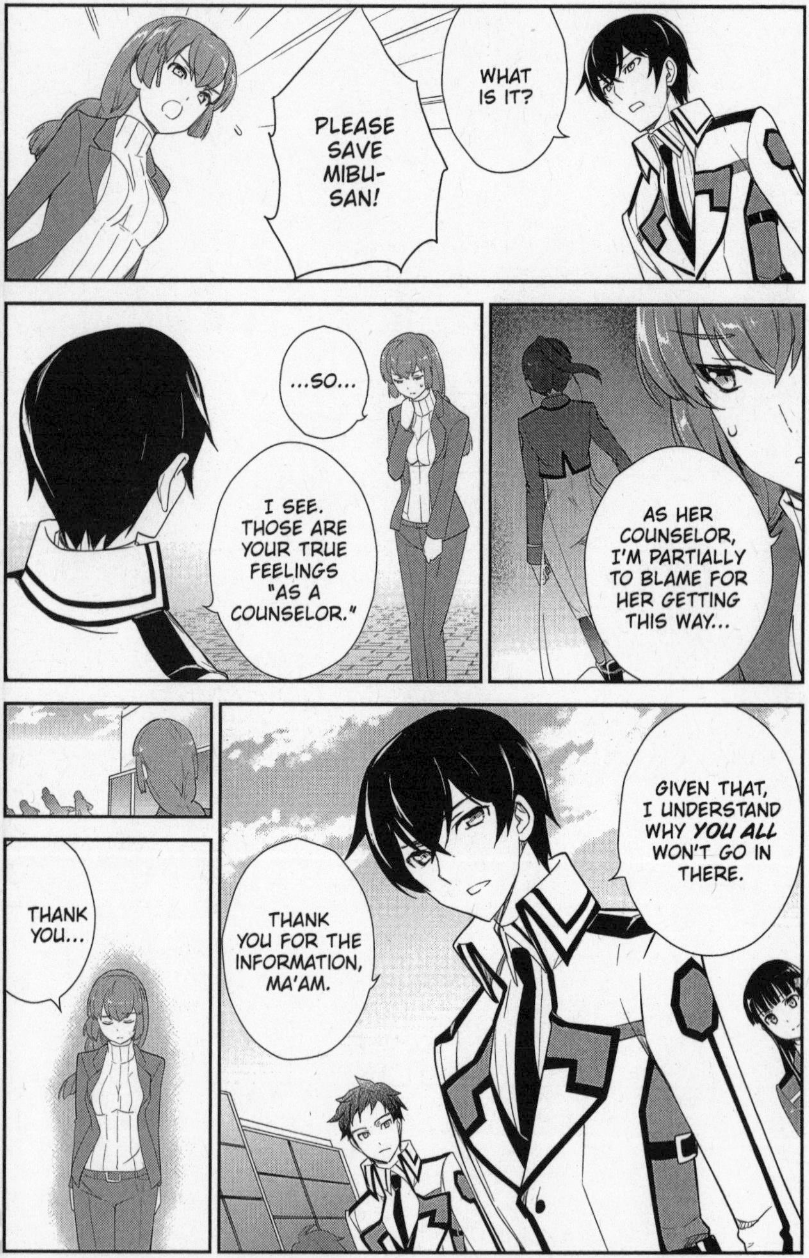
WHAT IS IT?
PLEASE SAVE MIBU-SAN!
AS HER COUNSELOR, I'M PARTIALLY TO BLAME FOR HER GETTING THIS WAY...
...SO...
I SEE. THOSE ARE YOUR TRUE FEELINGS "AS A COUNSELOR."
GIVEN THAT, I UNDERSTAND WHY *YOU ALL* WON'T GO IN THERE.
THANK YOU FOR THE INFORMATION, MA'AM.
THANK YOU...

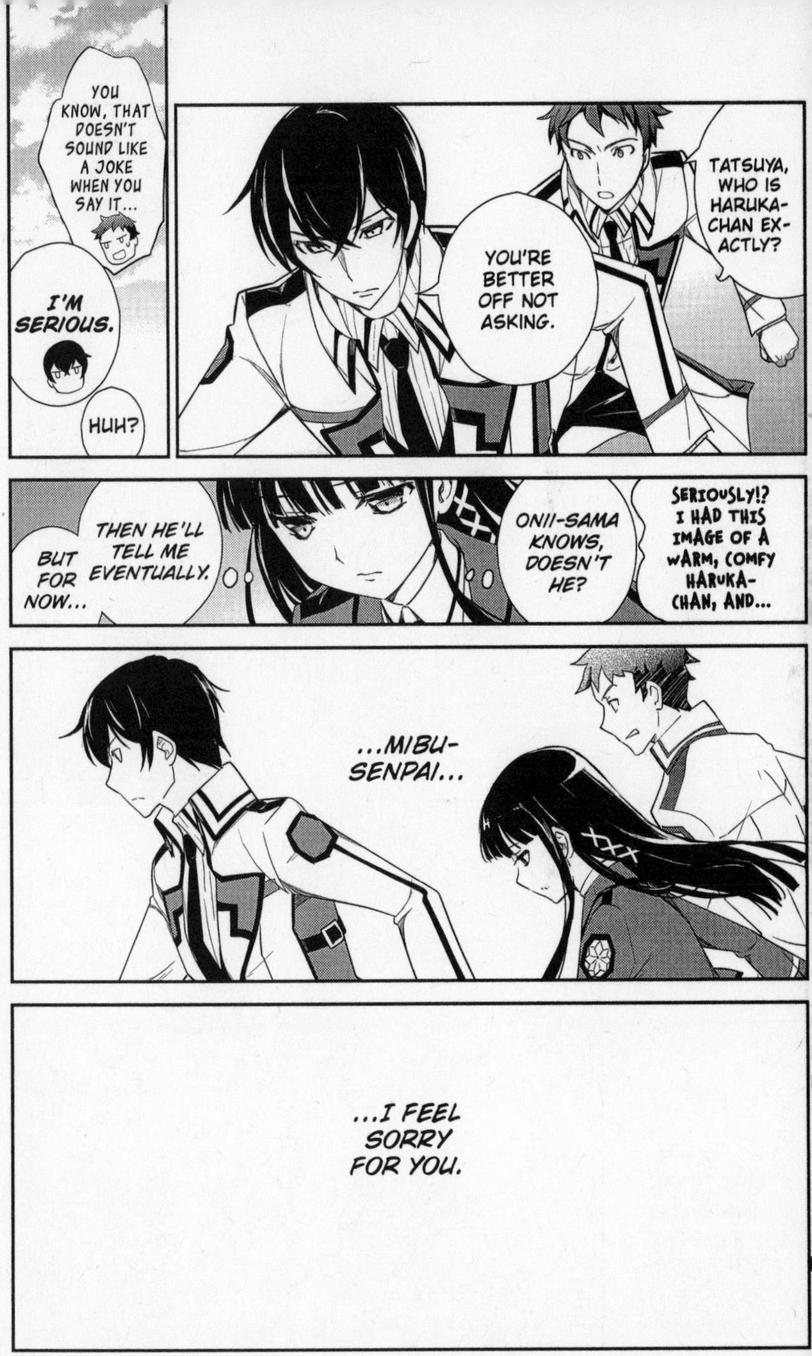
TATSUYA, WHO IS HARUKA-CHAN EXACTLY?
YOU'RE BETTER OFF NOT ASKING.
YOU KNOW, THAT DOESN'T SOUND LIKE A JOKE WHEN YOU SAY IT...
I'M SERIOUS.
HUH?
SERIOUSLY!? I HAD THIS IMAGE OF A WARM, COMFY HARUKA-CHAN, AND...
ONII-SAMA KNOWS, DOESN'T HE?
THEN HE'LL TELL ME EVENTUALLY.
BUT FOR NOW...
...MIBU-SENPAI...
...I FEEL SORRY FOR YOU.

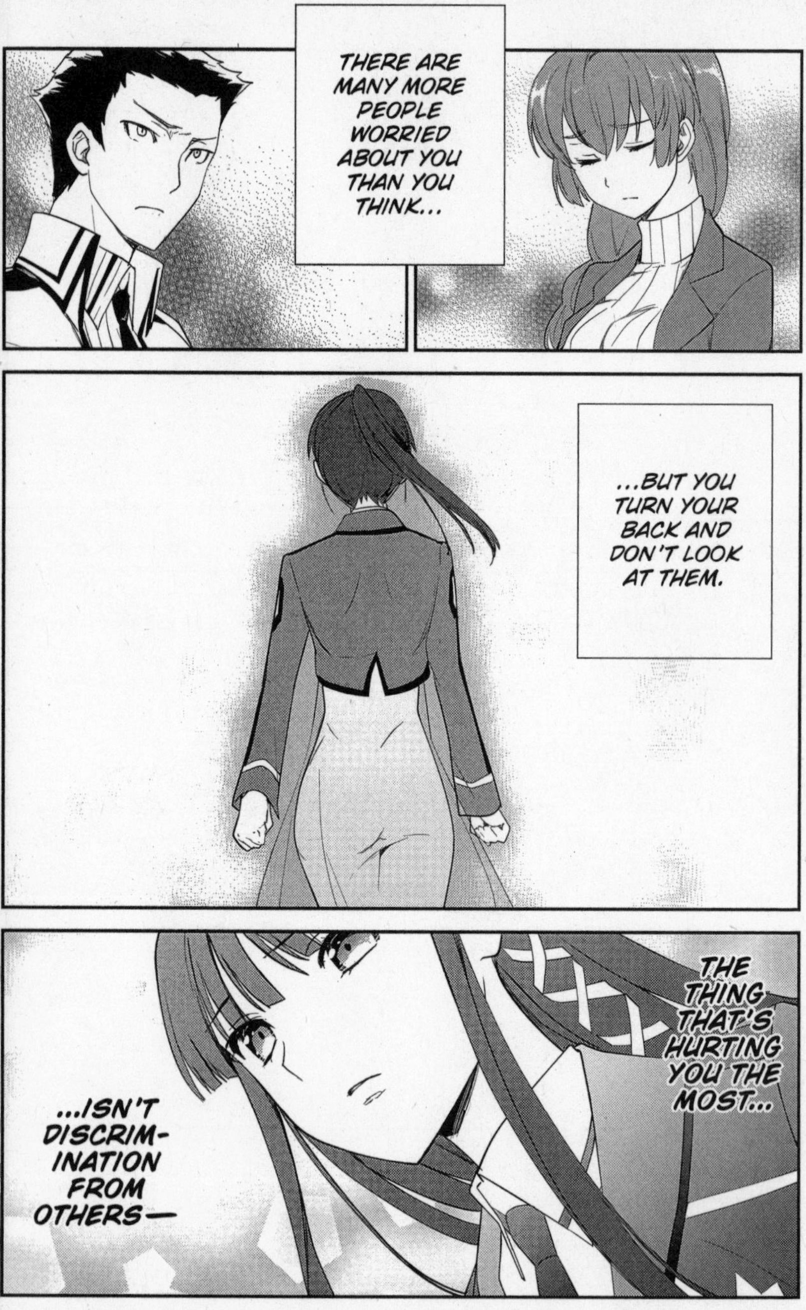
THERE ARE MANY MORE PEOPLE WORRIED ABOUT YOU THAN YOU THINK...
...BUT YOU TURN YOUR BACK AND DON'T LOOK AT THEM.
THE THING THAT'S HURTING YOU THE MOST...
...ISN'T DISCRIM-INATION FROM OTHERS—

LIBRARY SPECIAL VIEWING ROOM

≥BEEP≤

≥TAP≤
≥TAP≤
≥TAP≤

≥BEEP≤

≥TAP≤
≥TAP≤
≥TAP≤

ALMOST THERE.

HAVEN'T YOU BROKEN THE SECURITY YET?

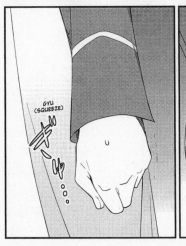

GYU
(SQUEEZE)

≥TAP≤
≥TAP≤
≥TAP≤

≥BEEP≤

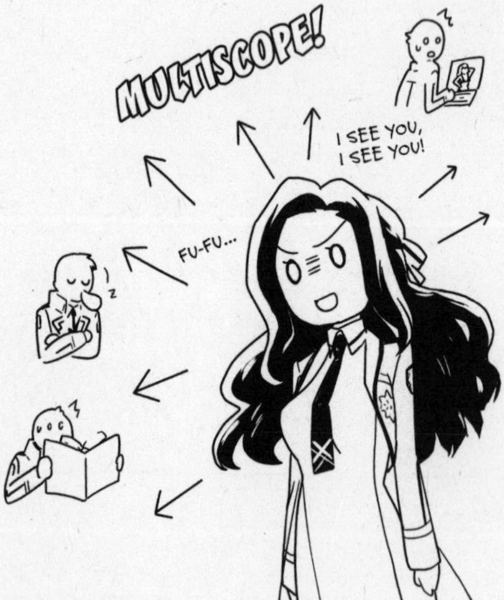
MULTISCOPE!
I SEE YOU,
I SEE YOU!
FU-FU...

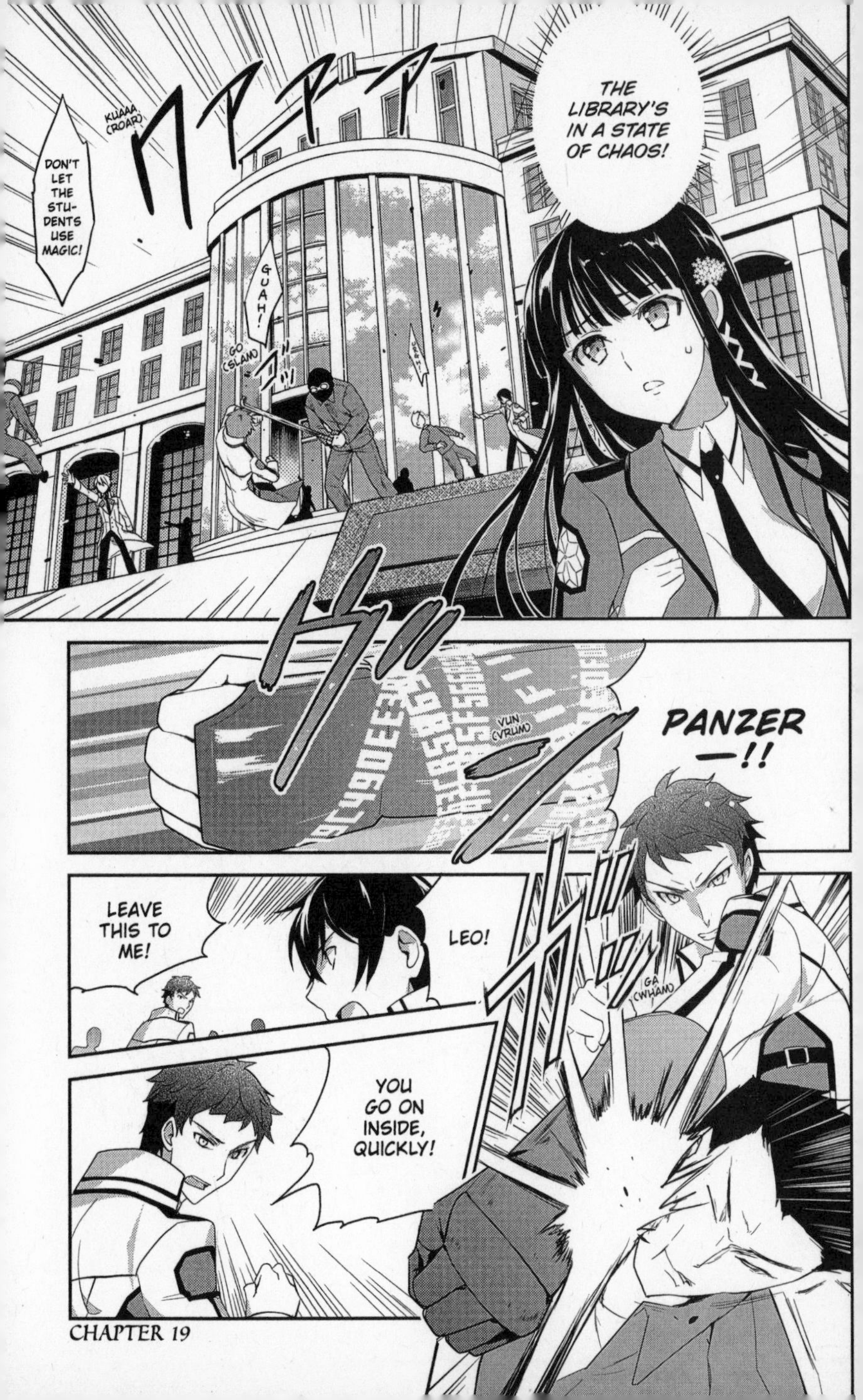
THE LIBRARY'S IN A STATE OF CHAOS!
KUAAA (ROAR)
DON'T LET THE STU-DENTS USE MAGIC!
GUAH!
GO (SLAM)
PANZER —!!
VUN (VRUM)
GA (WHAM)
LEO!
LEAVE THIS TO ME!
YOU GO ON INSIDE, QUICKLY!

CHAPTER 19

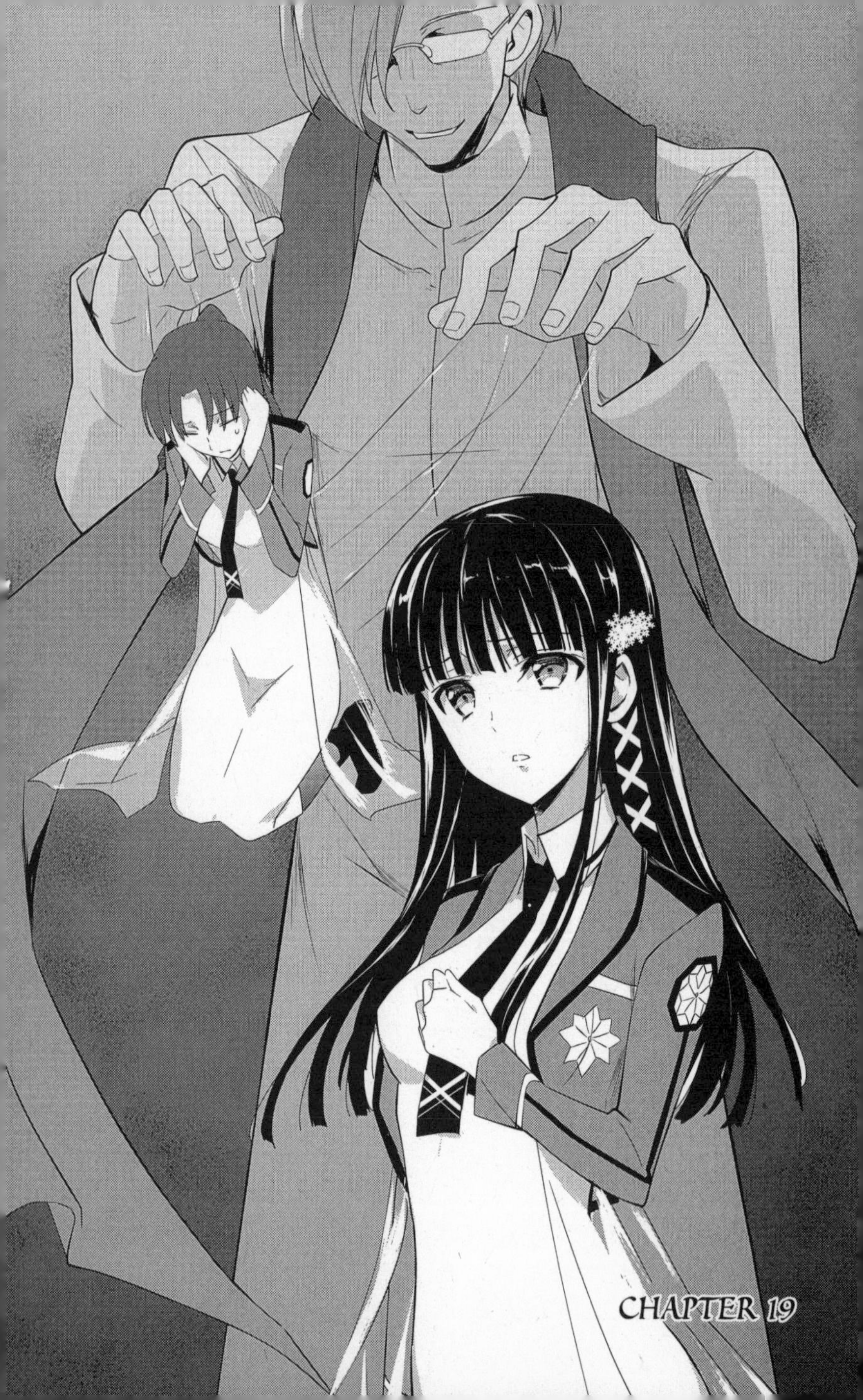
CHAPTER 19

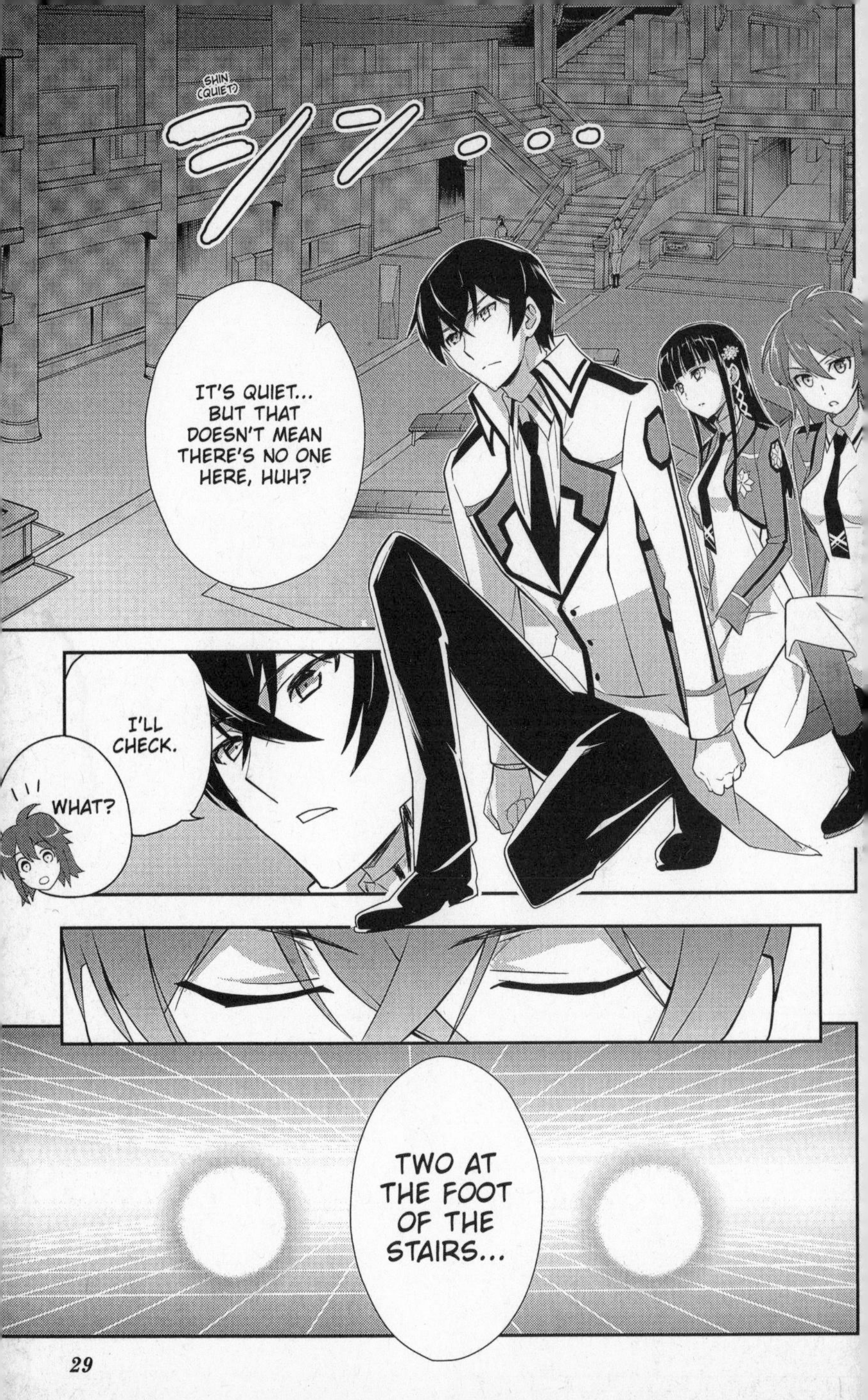
SHIN (QUIET)
IT'S QUIET... BUT THAT DOESN'T MEAN THERE'S NO ONE HERE, HUH?
I'LL CHECK.
WHAT?
TWO AT THE FOOT OF THE STAIRS...

...TWO WHEN YOU GET TO THE TOP OF THE STAIRS...
...AND... FOUR IN THE SPECIAL VIEWING ROOM ON THE SECOND FLOOR.
AMAZING! IT'D BE POINTLESS TO TRY TO AMBUSH YOU, TATSUYA-KUN!
THEY MUST BE IN THE MIDDLE OF STEALING DATA FROM THE VIEWING ROOM.
THEN WE GOTTA HURRY.
LET ME TAKE THIS ONE!
ばっ
BA (LEAP)
ERIKA!

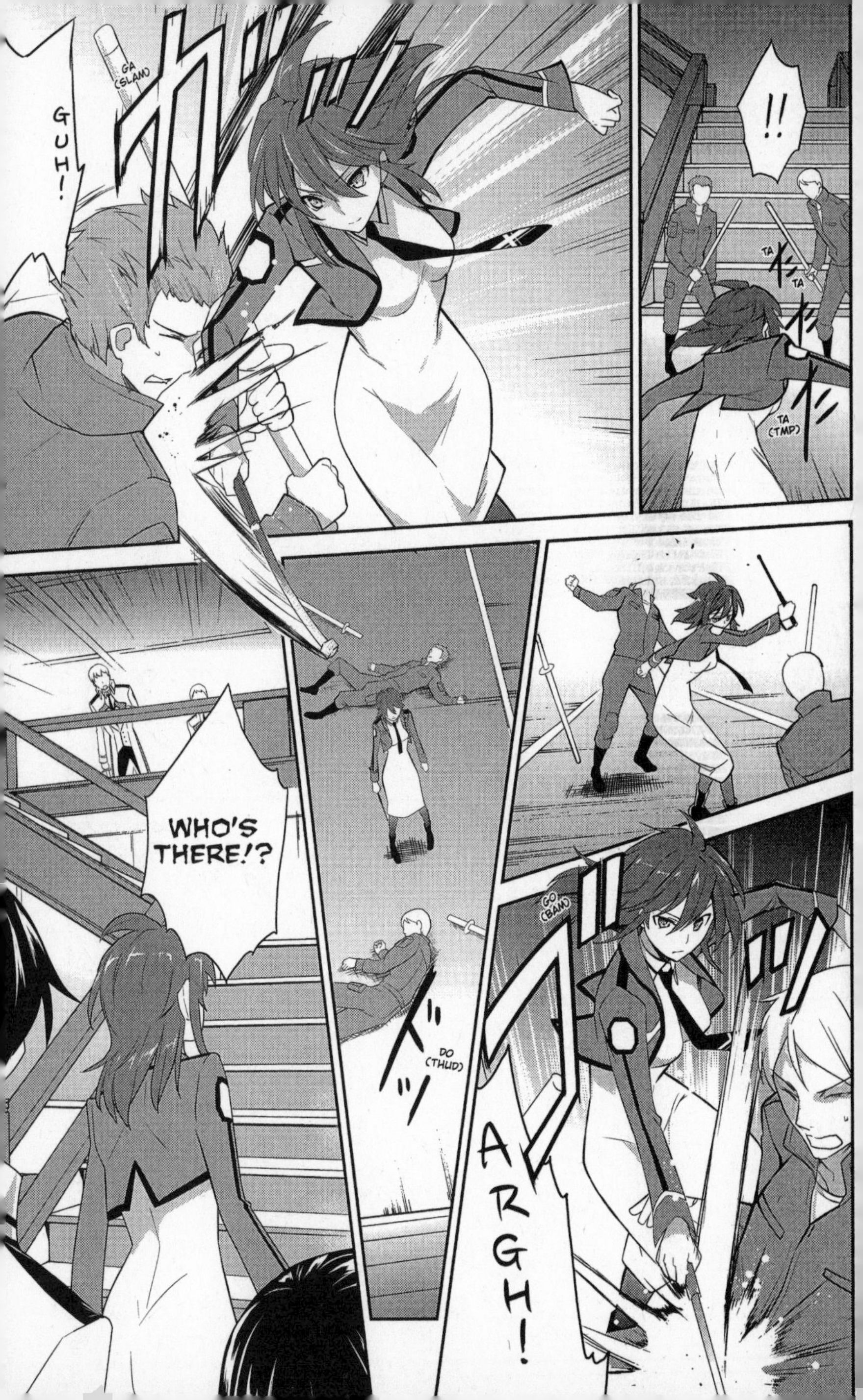
!!
TA
TA
TA (TMP)
GA (SLAM)
GUH!
GO (BAM)
ARGH!
DO (THUD)
WHO'S THERE!?

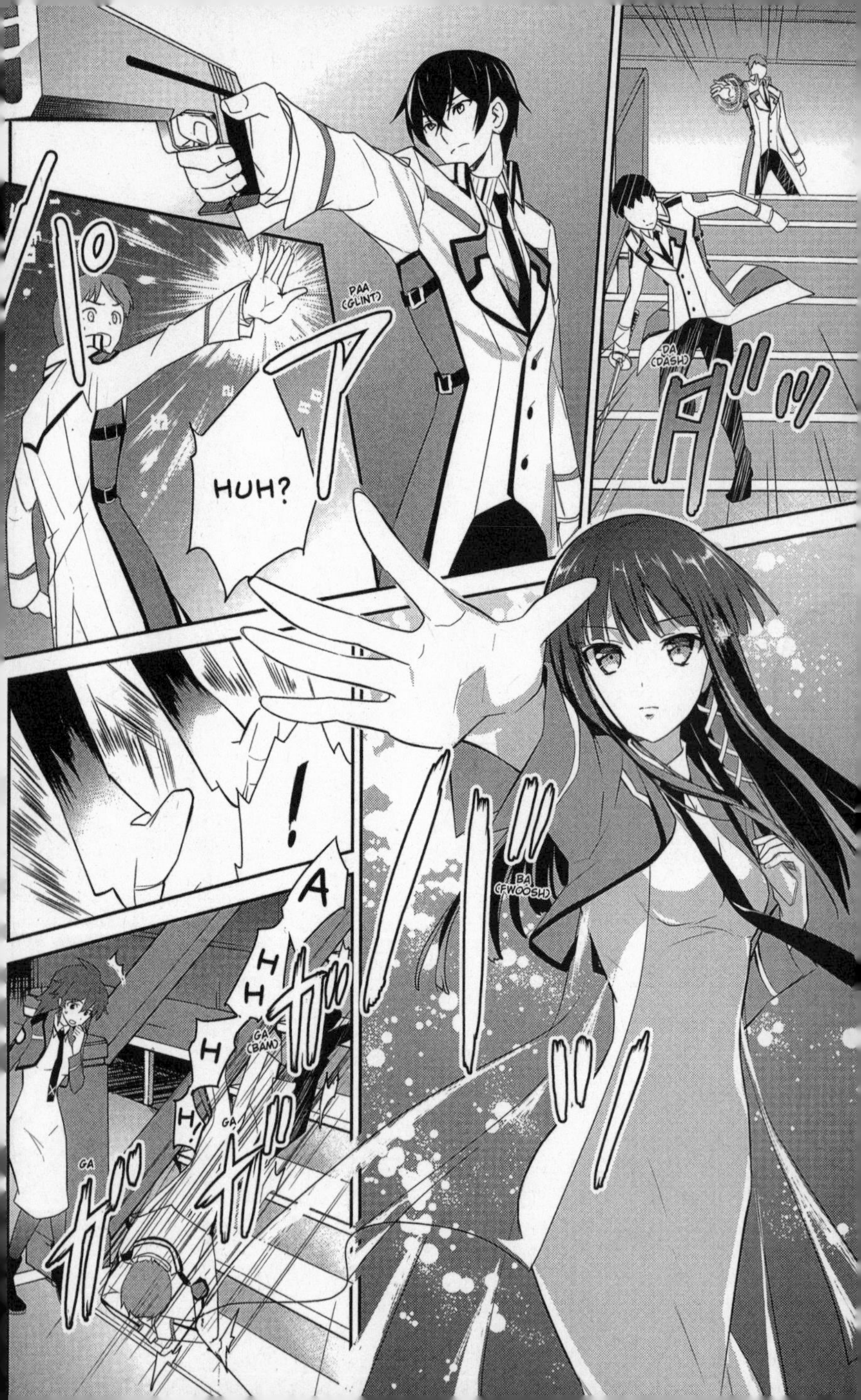
DA
(DASH)
PAA
(GLINT)
HUH?
!
BA
(FWOOSH)
AHHHH!
GA
(BAM)
GA
GA

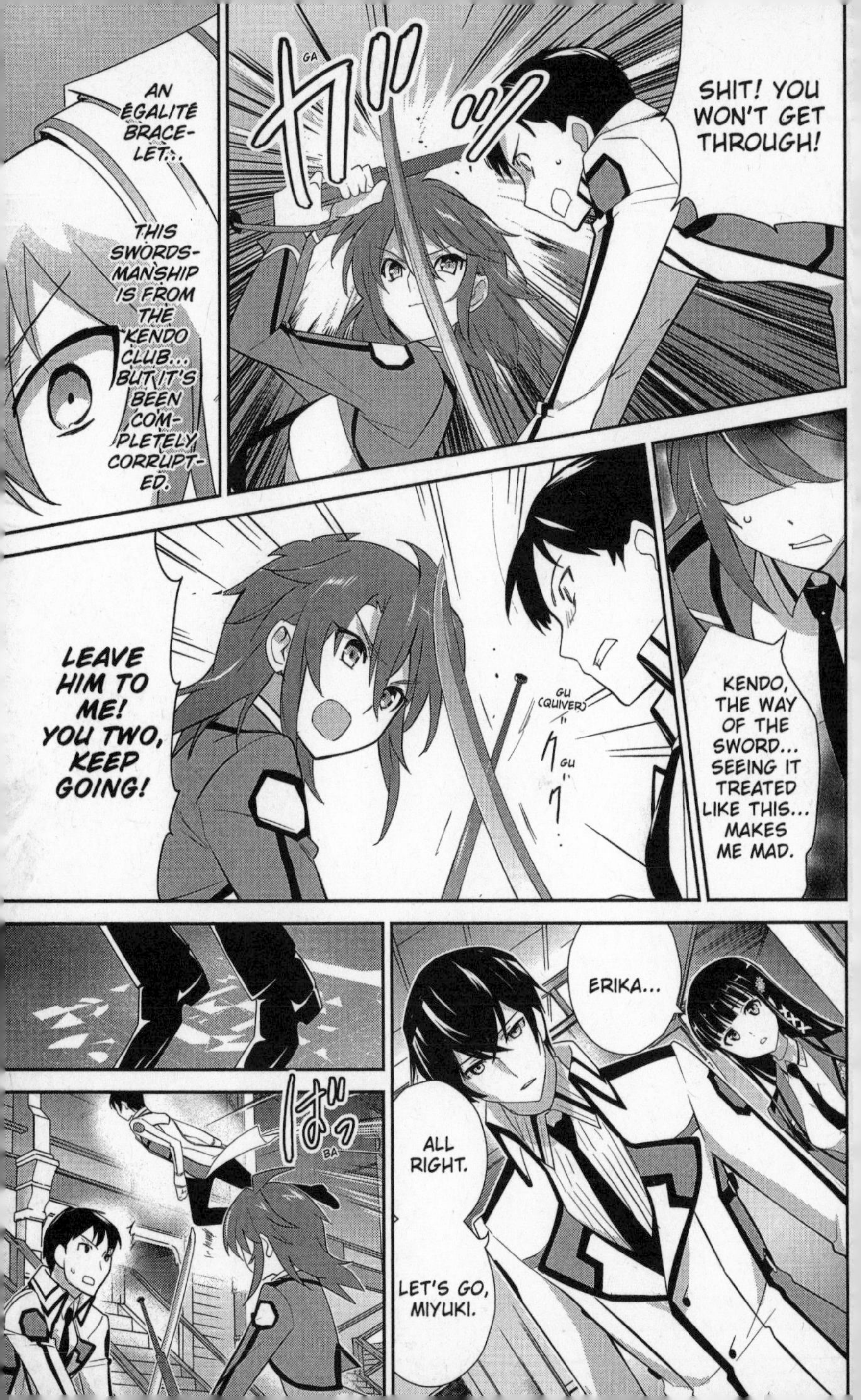
GA
SHIT! YOU WON'T GET THROUGH!
AN ÉGALITÉ BRACELET...
THIS SWORDSMANSHIP IS FROM THE KENDO CLUB... BUT IT'S BEEN COMPLETELY CORRUPTED.
KENDO, THE WAY OF THE SWORD... SEEING IT TREATED LIKE THIS... MAKES ME MAD.
GU (QUIVER)
GU
LEAVE HIM TO ME! YOU TWO, KEEP GOING!
ERIKA...
ALL RIGHT.
LET'S GO, MIYUKI.
BA

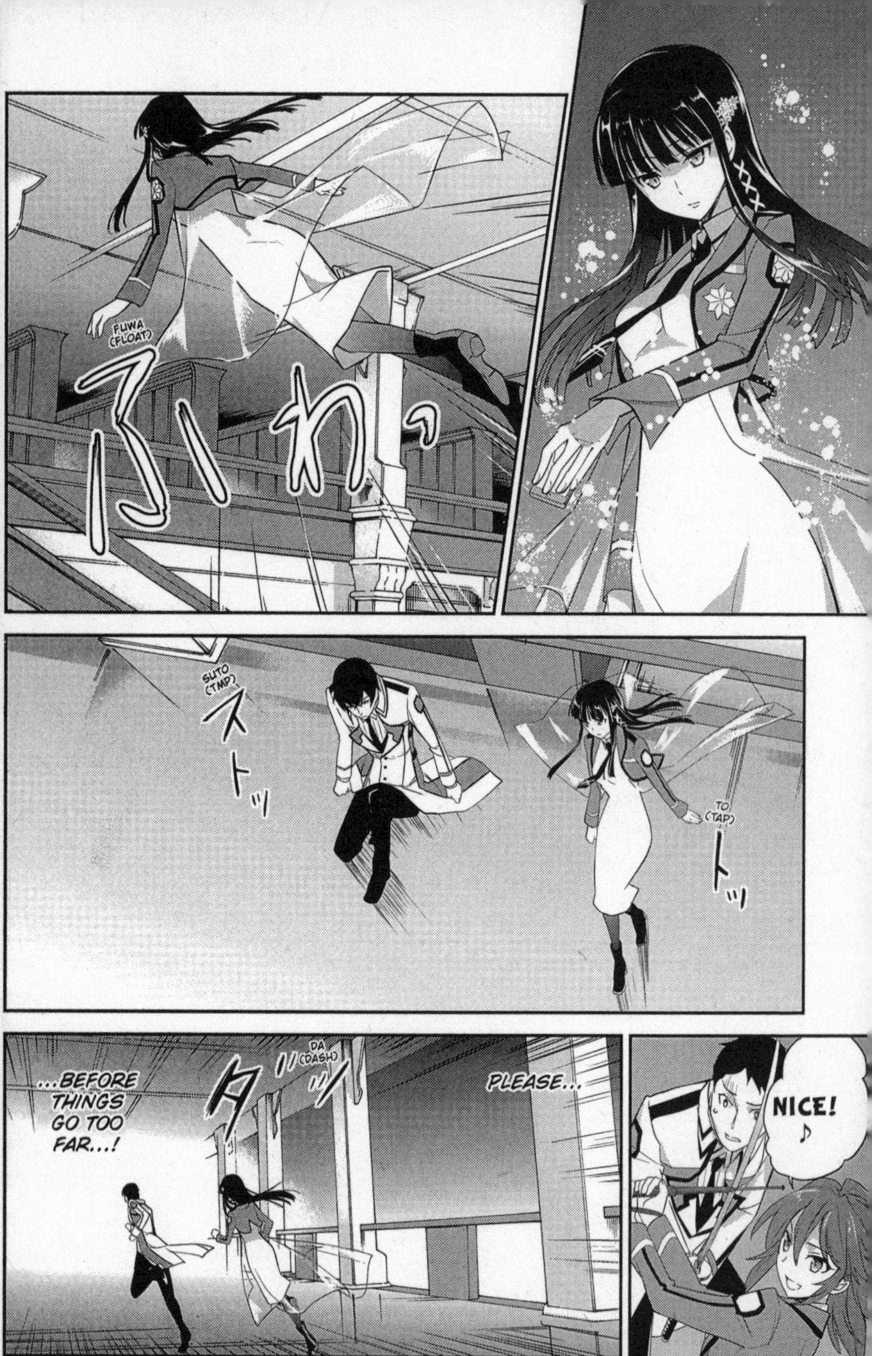
FUWA (FLOAT)
ふわっ
TO (TAP)
トッ
SUTO (TMP)
ストッ
NICE! ♪
PLEASE...
DA (DASH)
ダッ
...BEFORE THINGS GO TOO FAR...!

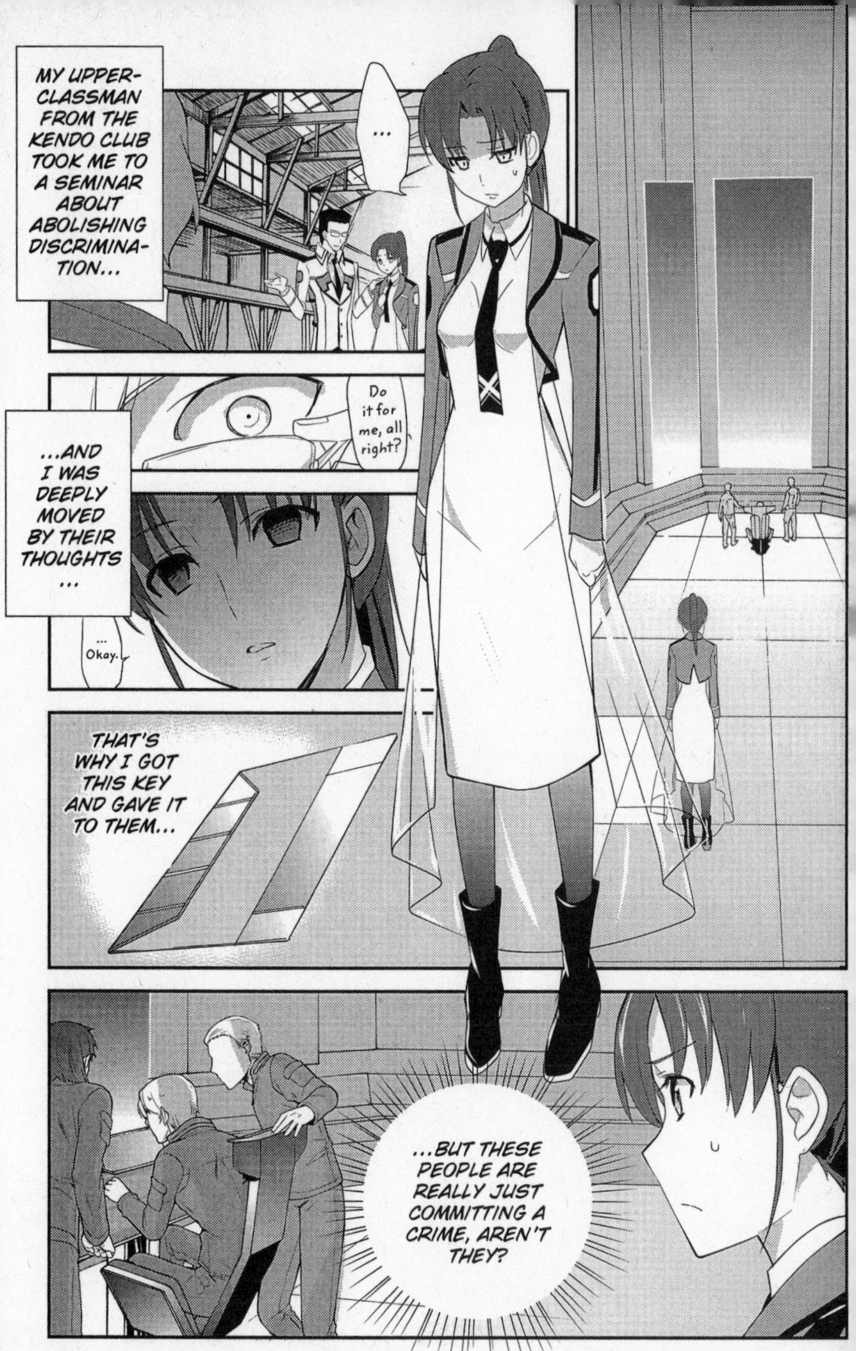
...
MY UPPER-CLASSMAN FROM THE KENDO CLUB TOOK ME TO A SEMINAR ABOUT ABOLISHING DISCRIMINA-TION...
Do it for me, all right?
...AND I WAS DEEPLY MOVED BY THEIR THOUGHTS ...
... Okay.
THAT'S WHY I GOT THIS KEY AND GAVE IT TO THEM...
...BUT THESE PEOPLE ARE REALLY JUST COMMITTING A CRIME, AREN'T THEY?

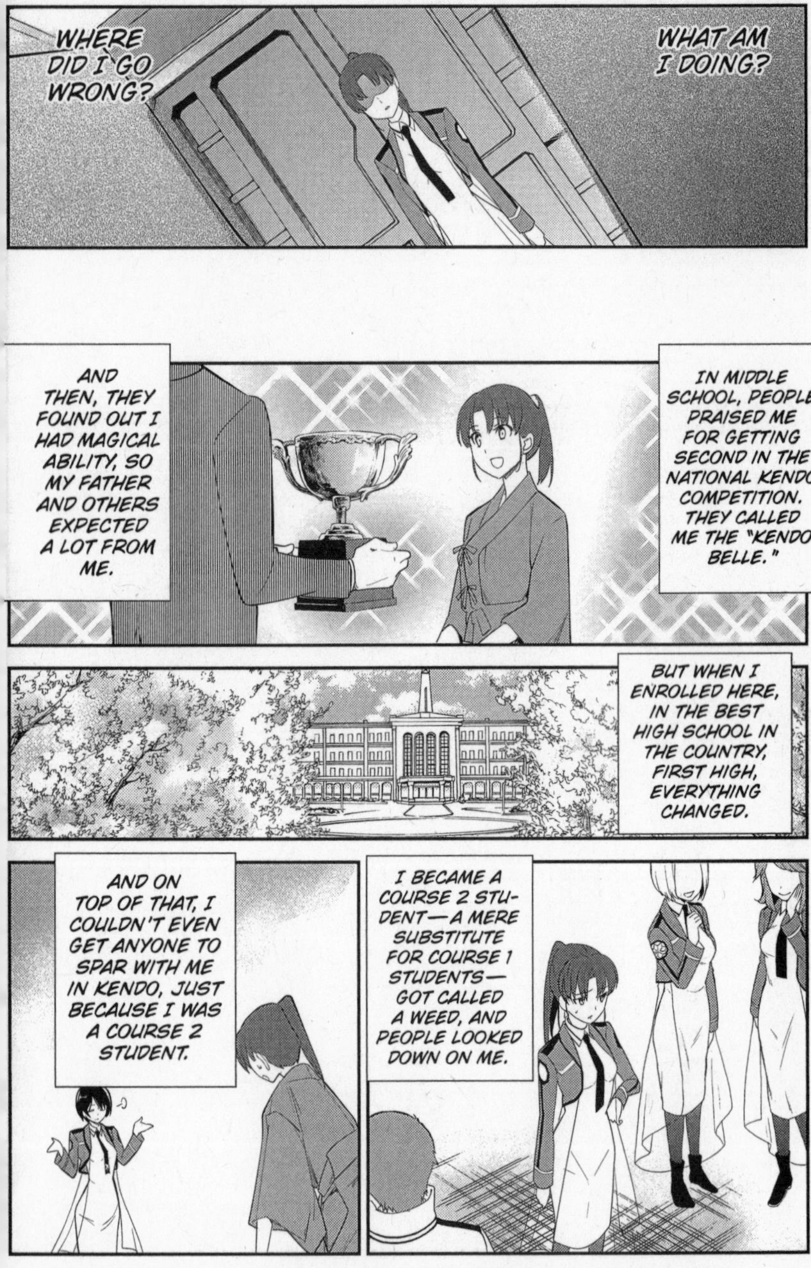
WHAT AM I DOING?
WHERE DID I GO WRONG?
IN MIDDLE SCHOOL, PEOPLE PRAISED ME FOR GETTING SECOND IN THE NATIONAL KENDO COMPETITION. THEY CALLED ME THE "KENDO BELLE."
AND THEN, THEY FOUND OUT I HAD MAGICAL ABILITY, SO MY FATHER AND OTHERS EXPECTED A LOT FROM ME.
BUT WHEN I ENROLLED HERE, IN THE BEST HIGH SCHOOL IN THE COUNTRY, FIRST HIGH, EVERYTHING CHANGED.
I BECAME A COURSE 2 STUDENT—A MERE SUBSTITUTE FOR COURSE 1 STUDENTS—GOT CALLED A WEED, AND PEOPLE LOOKED DOWN ON ME.
AND ON TOP OF THAT, I COULDN'T EVEN GET ANYONE TO SPAR WITH ME IN KENDO, JUST BECAUSE I WAS A COURSE 2 STUDENT.

MAGIC DOESN'T DETERMINE A PERSON'S WORTH.

SO WHAT...?

BUT WHEN I SAW MIYUKI SHIBA-SAN, THE NEW STUDENT, I FELT AN OVERWHELMING GAP BETWEEN US.

SINCE STARTING AT FIRST HIGH AS THE STUDENT REPRESENTATIVE, SHE'S GOTTEN INCREDIBLY HIGH MARKS. HER LOOKS AND BEHAVIOR—BOTH PERFECT. I COULD PLAINLY SEE THAT SHE WAS WHAT A TRUE HONOR STUDENT LOOKED LIKE.

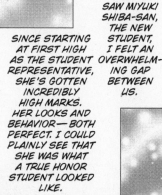

I SEE...

I'M A FAILURE ...

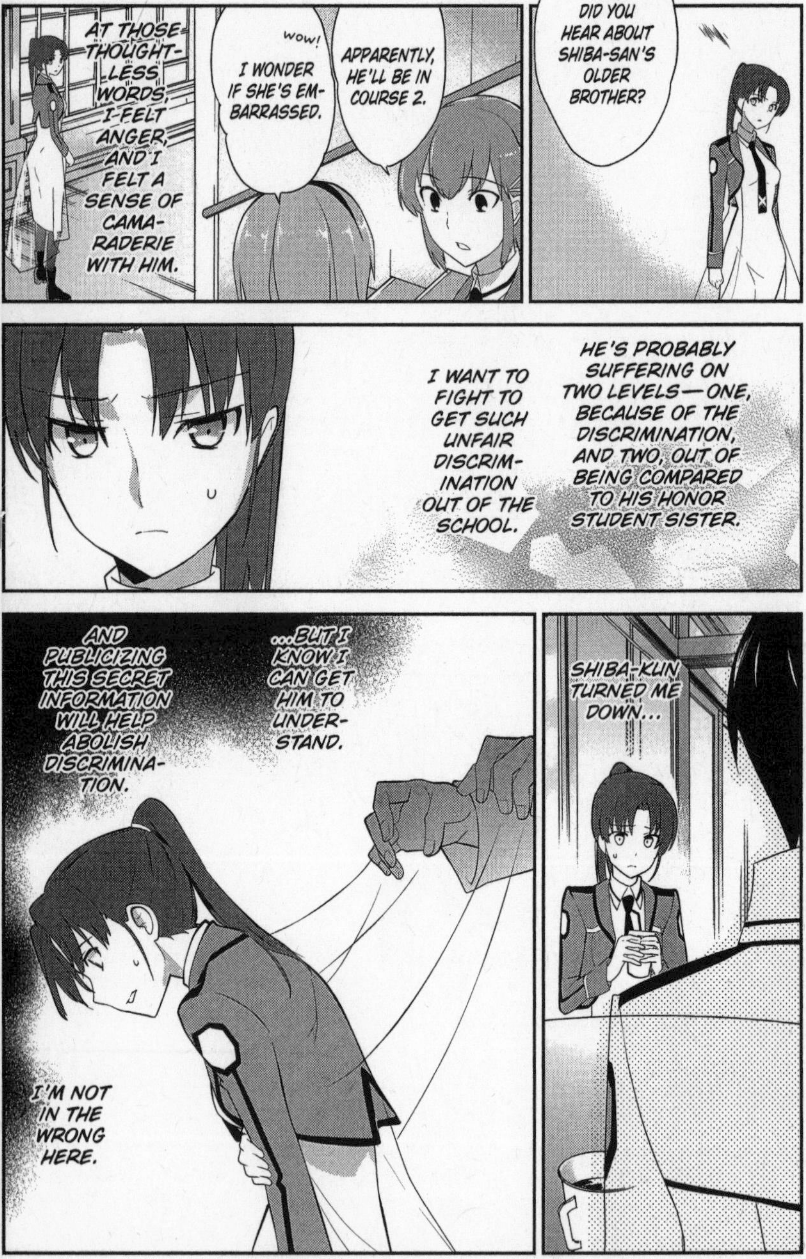
HEY, DID YOU HEAR ABOUT SHIBA-SAN'S OLDER BROTHER?
APPARENTLY, HE'LL BE IN COURSE 2.
WOW!
I WONDER IF SHE'S EMBARRASSED.
AT THOSE THOUGHTLESS WORDS, I FELT ANGER, AND I FELT A SENSE OF CAMARADERIE WITH HIM.
HE'S PROBABLY SUFFERING ON TWO LEVELS—ONE, BECAUSE OF THE DISCRIMINATION, AND TWO, OUT OF BEING COMPARED TO HIS HONOR STUDENT SISTER.
I WANT TO FIGHT TO GET SUCH UNFAIR DISCRIMINATION OUT OF THE SCHOOL.
SHIBA-KUN TURNED ME DOWN...
...BUT I KNOW I CAN GET HIM TO UNDERSTAND.
AND PUBLICIZING THIS SECRET INFORMATION WILL HELP ABOLISH DISCRIMINATION.
I'M NOT IN THE WRONG HERE.

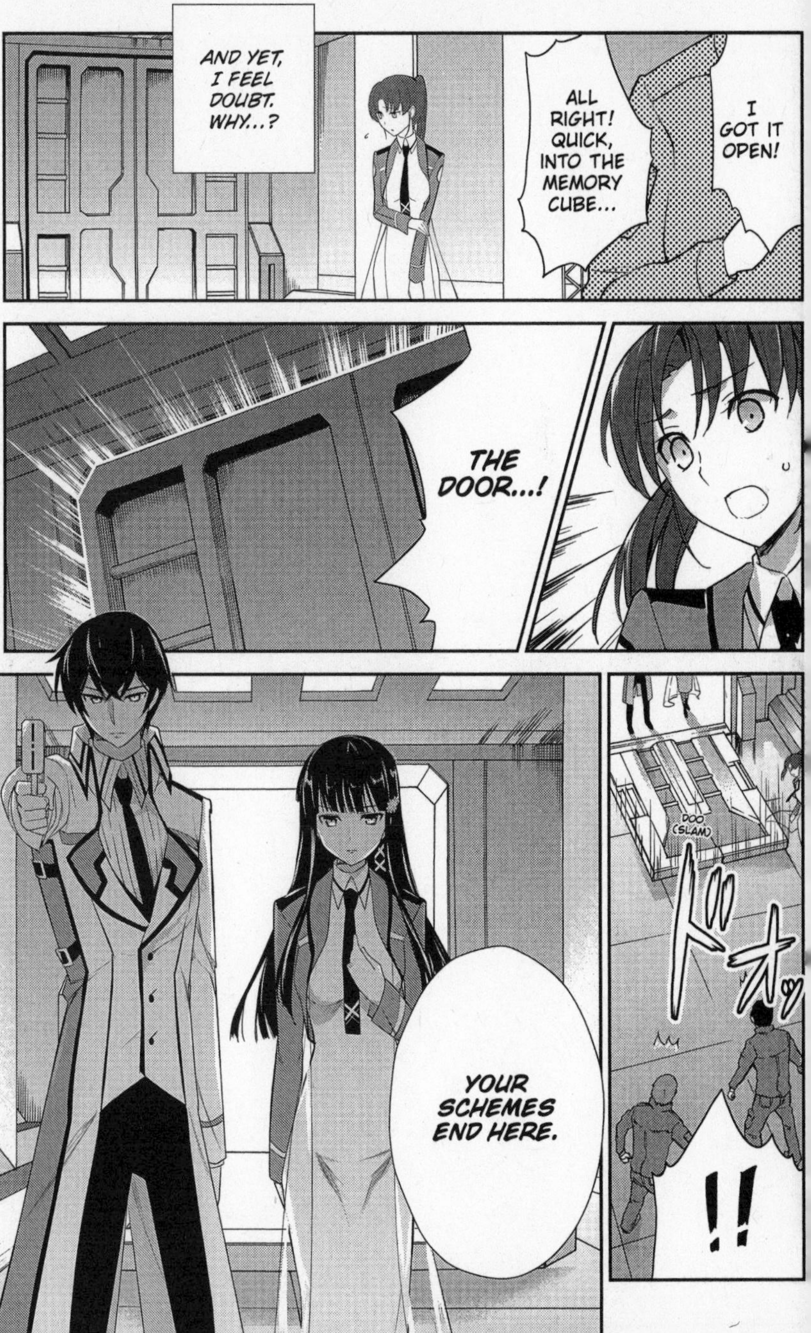
I GOT IT OPEN!
ALL RIGHT! QUICK, INTO THE MEMORY CUBE...
AND YET, I FEEL DOUBT. WHY...?
THE DOOR...!
DOO (SLAM)
ドオッ
!!
YOUR SCHEMES END HERE.

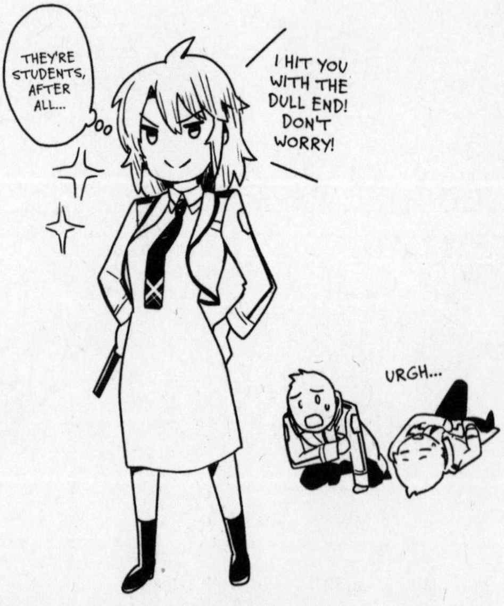
I HIT YOU WITH THE DULL END! DON'T WORRY!
THEY'RE STUDENTS, AFTER ALL...
URGH...

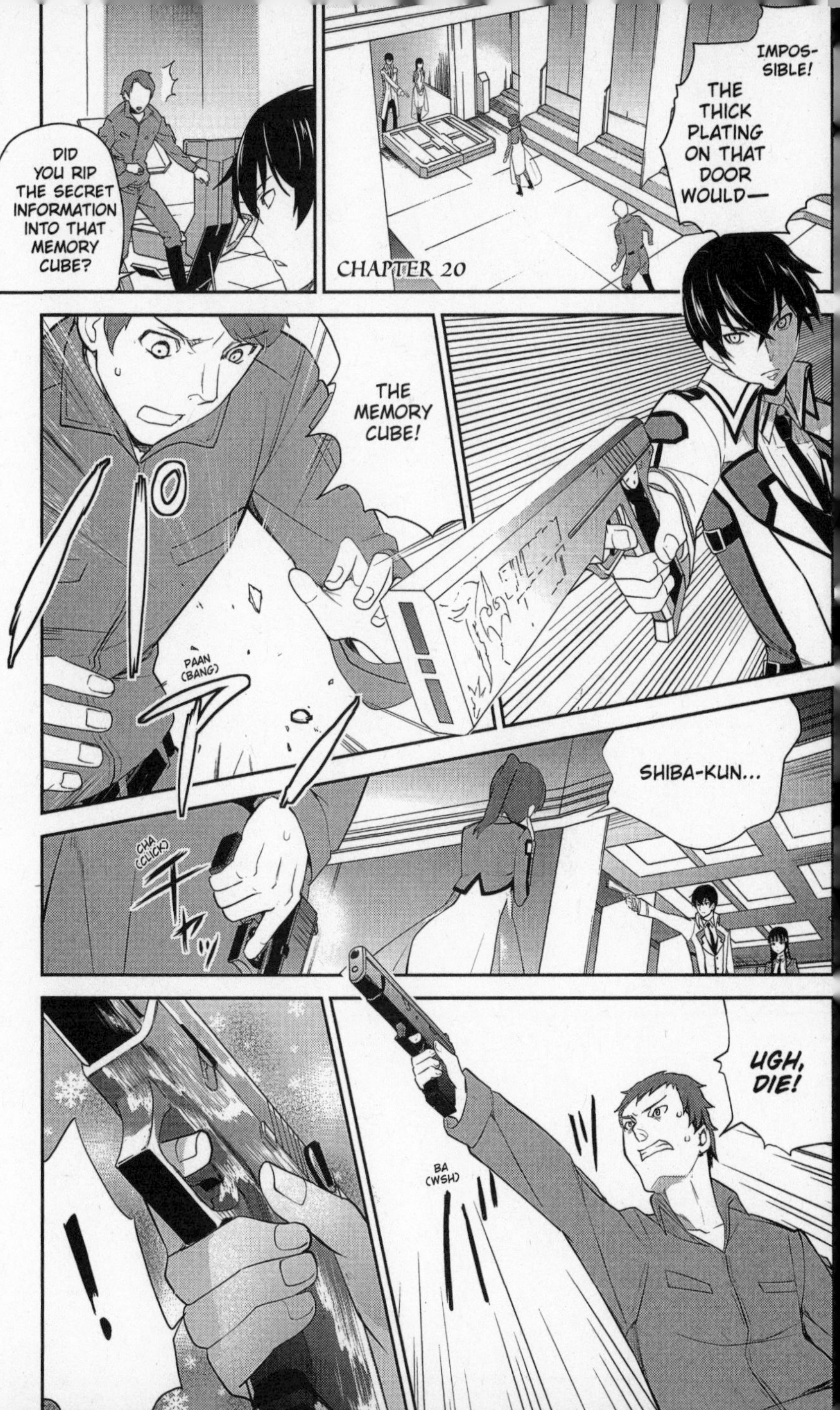
IMPOS-SIBLE!
THE THICK PLATING ON THAT DOOR WOULD—
CHAPTER 20
DID YOU RIP THE SECRET INFORMATION INTO THAT MEMORY CUBE?
THE MEMORY CUBE!
PAAN (BANG)
SHIBA-KUN...
CHA (CLICK)
UGH, DIE!
BA (WSH)

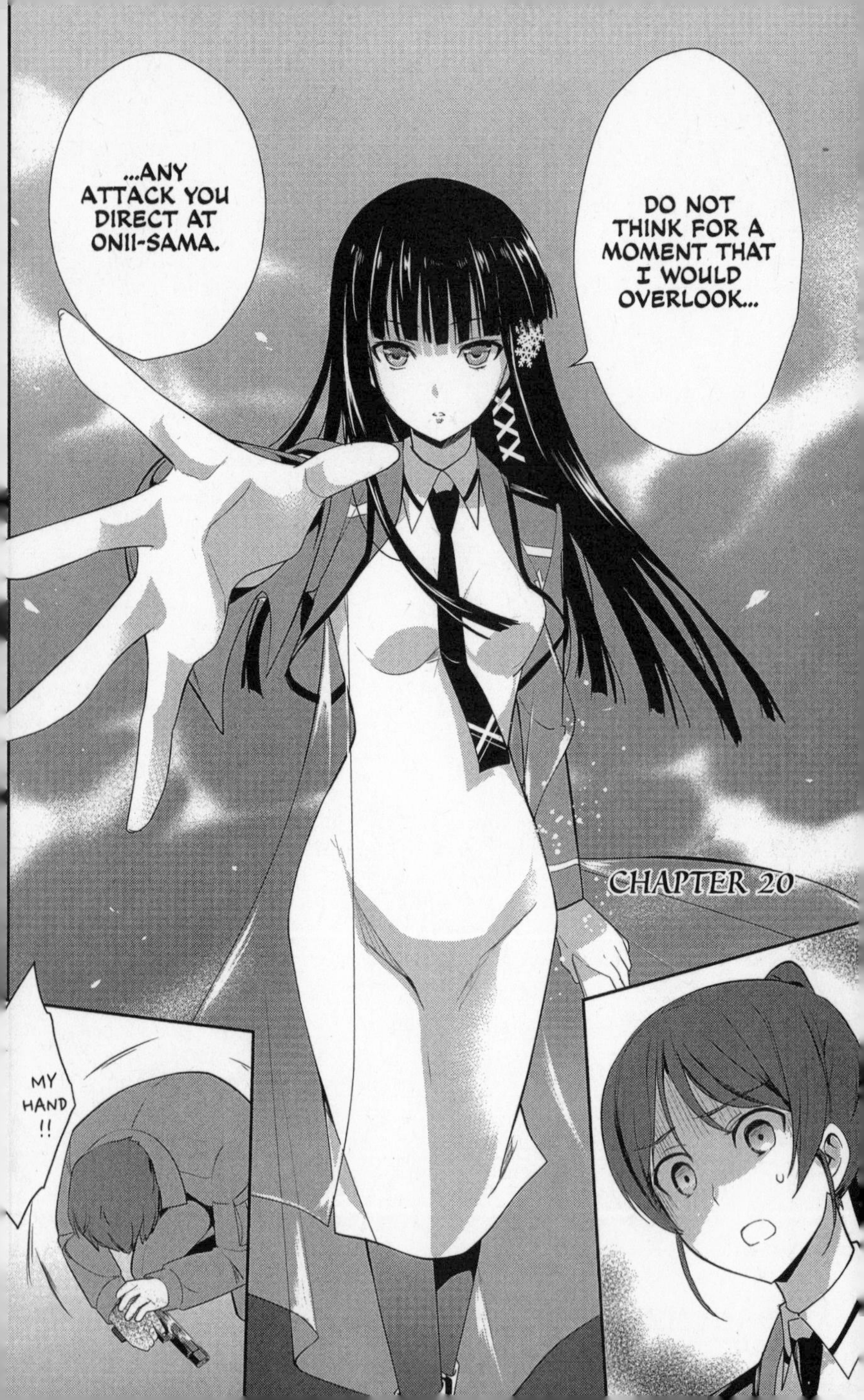
DO NOT THINK FOR A MOMENT THAT I WOULD OVERLOOK...
...ANY ATTACK YOU DIRECT AT ONII-SAMA.
CHAPTER 20
MY HAND !!

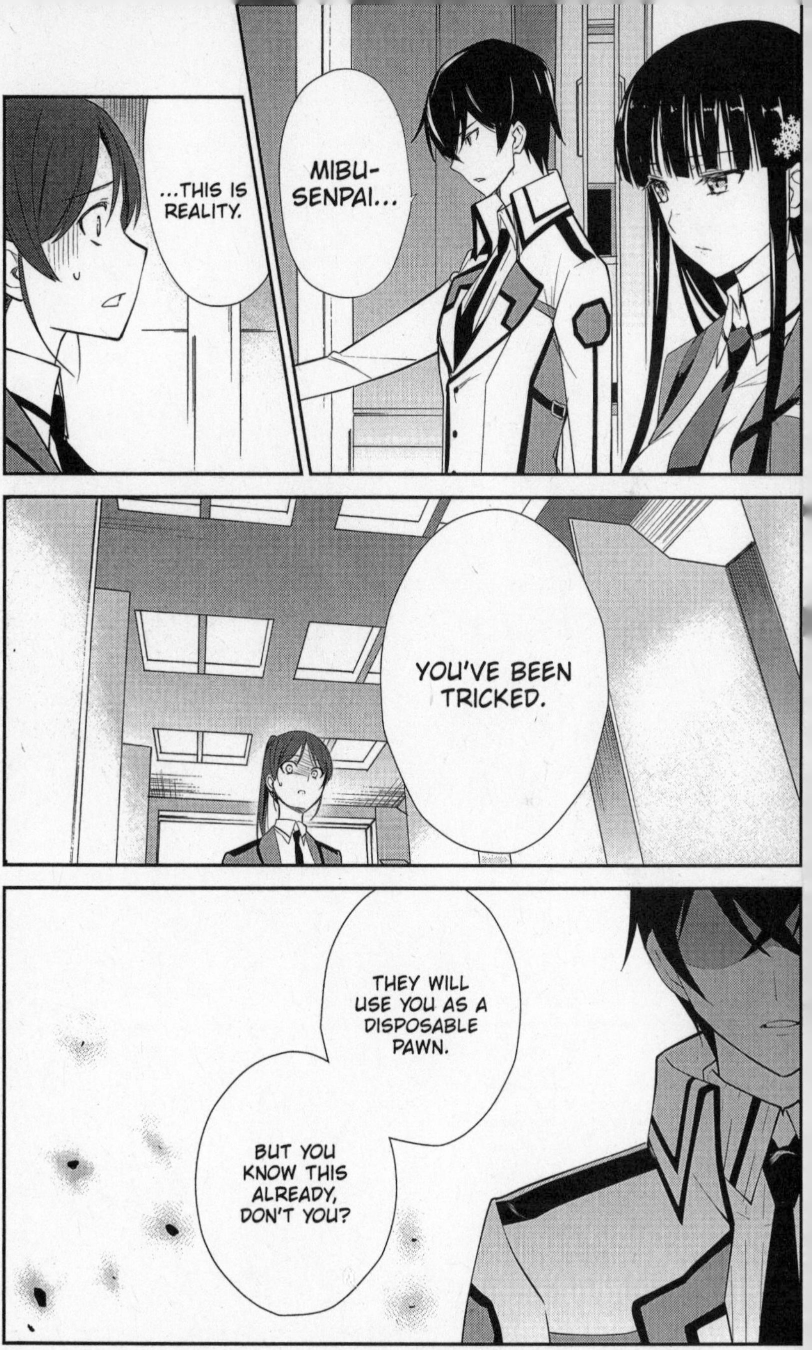
MIBU-SENPAI...
...THIS IS REALITY.
YOU'VE BEEN TRICKED.
THEY WILL USE YOU AS A DISPOSABLE PAWN.
BUT YOU KNOW THIS ALREADY, DON'T YOU?

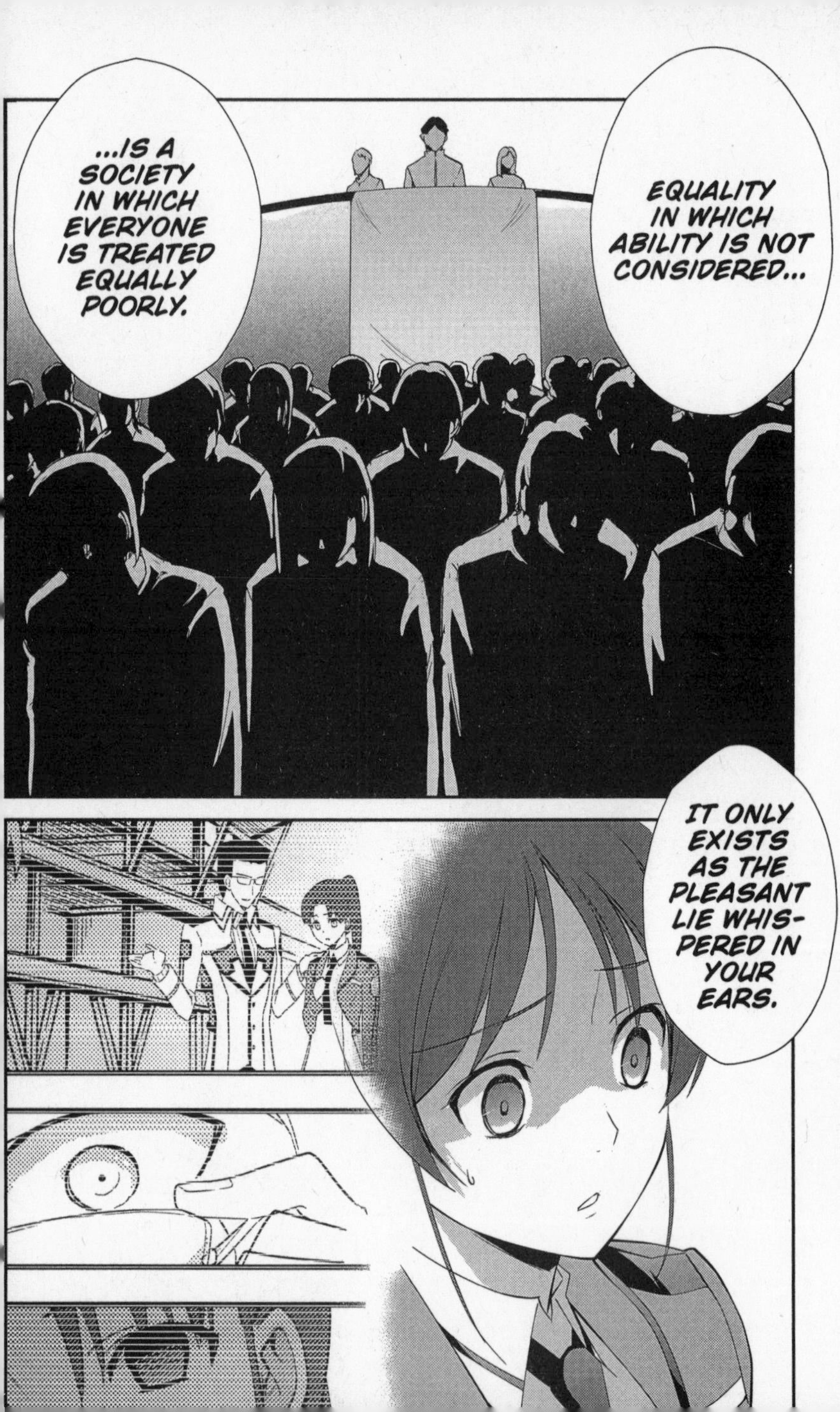
EQUALITY IN WHICH ABILITY IS NOT CONSIDERED...
...IS A SOCIETY IN WHICH EVERYONE IS TREATED EQUALLY POORLY.
IT ONLY EXISTS AS THE PLEASANT LIE WHIS-PERED IN YOUR EARS.

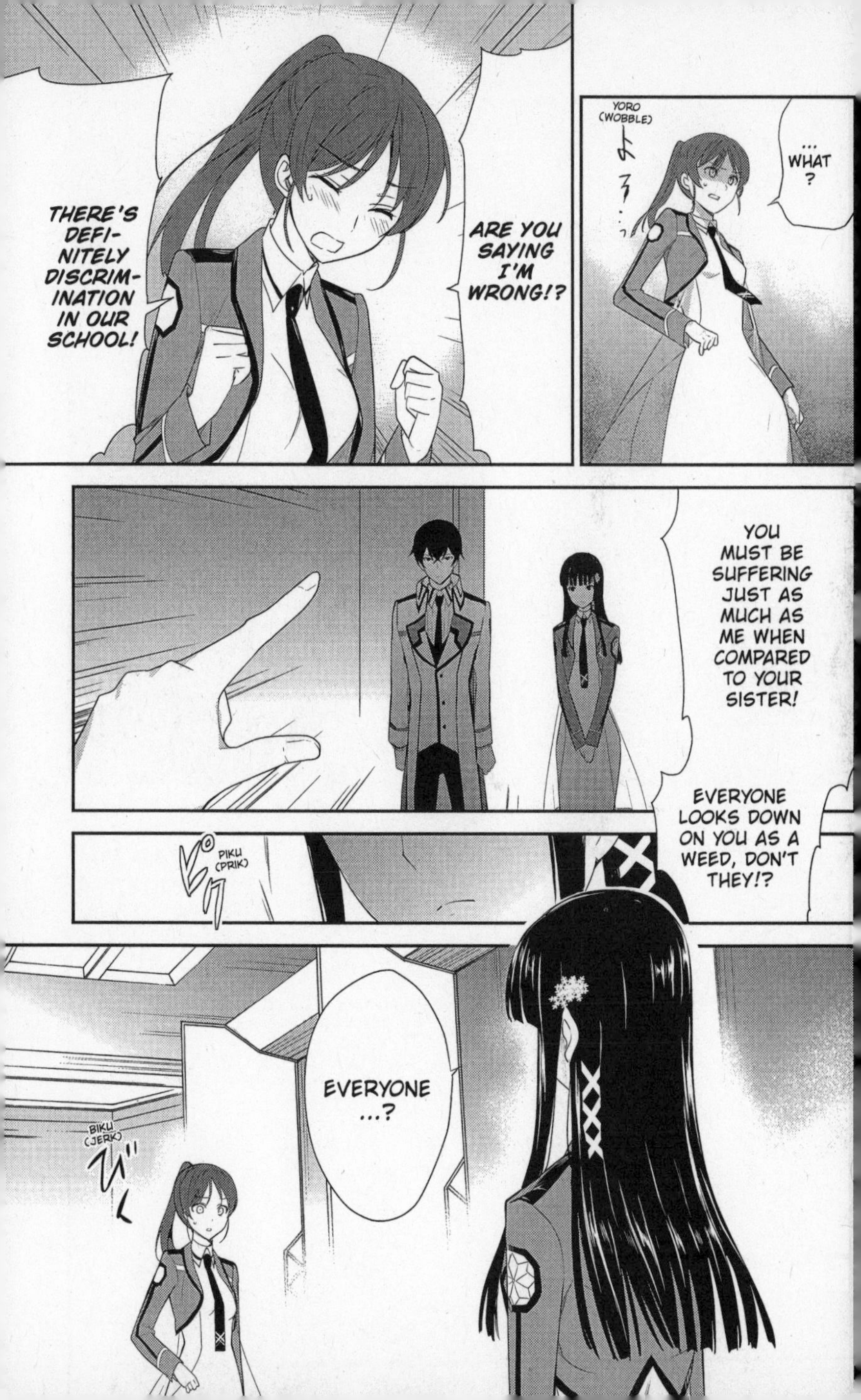
YORO (WOBBLE)
よろ…
... WHAT?
ARE YOU SAYING I'M WRONG!?
THERE'S DEFINITELY DISCRIMINATION IN OUR SCHOOL!
YOU MUST BE SUFFERING JUST AS MUCH AS ME WHEN COMPARED TO YOUR SISTER!
EVERYONE LOOKS DOWN ON YOU AS A WEED, DON'T THEY!?
PIKU (PRIK)
ピク
EVERYONE ...?
BIKU (JERK)
びく

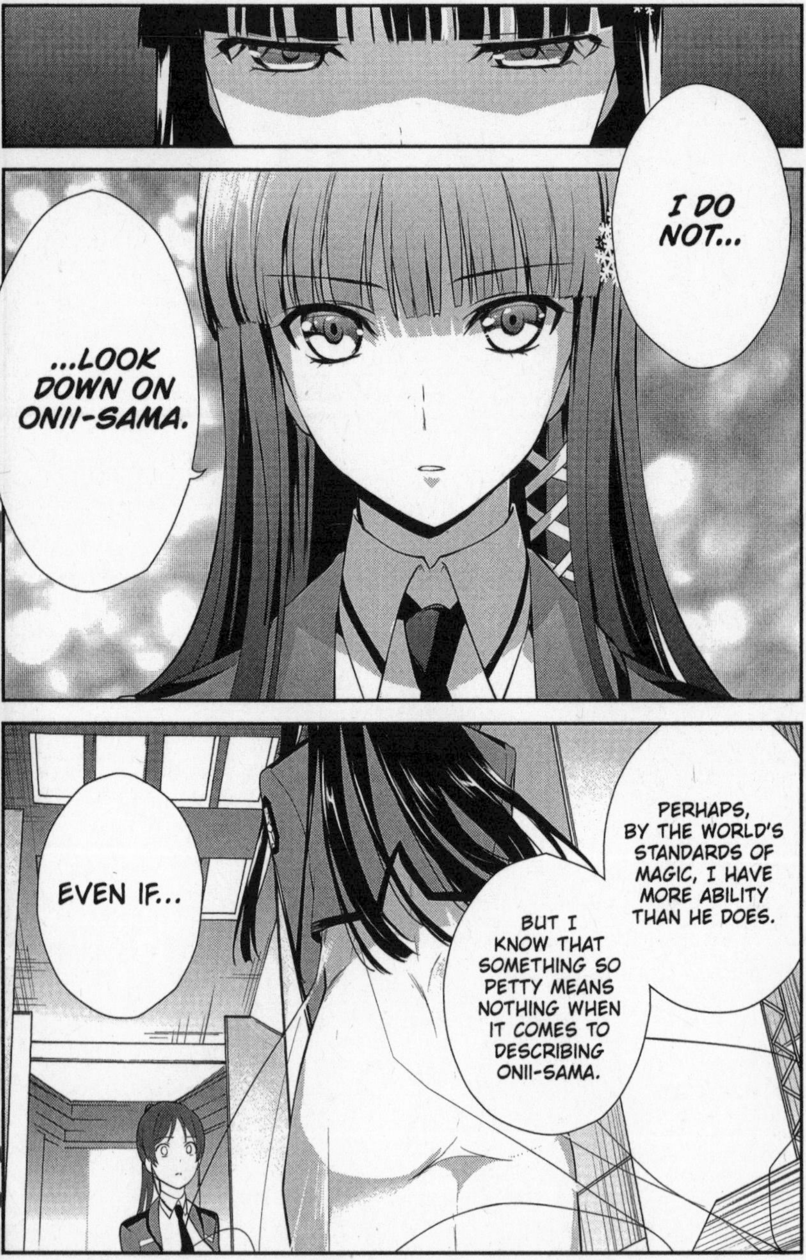
I DO NOT...
...LOOK DOWN ON ONII-SAMA.
PERHAPS, BY THE WORLD'S STANDARDS OF MAGIC, I HAVE MORE ABILITY THAN HE DOES.
EVEN IF...
BUT I KNOW THAT SOMETHING SO PETTY MEANS NOTHING WHEN IT COMES TO DESCRIBING ONII-SAMA.

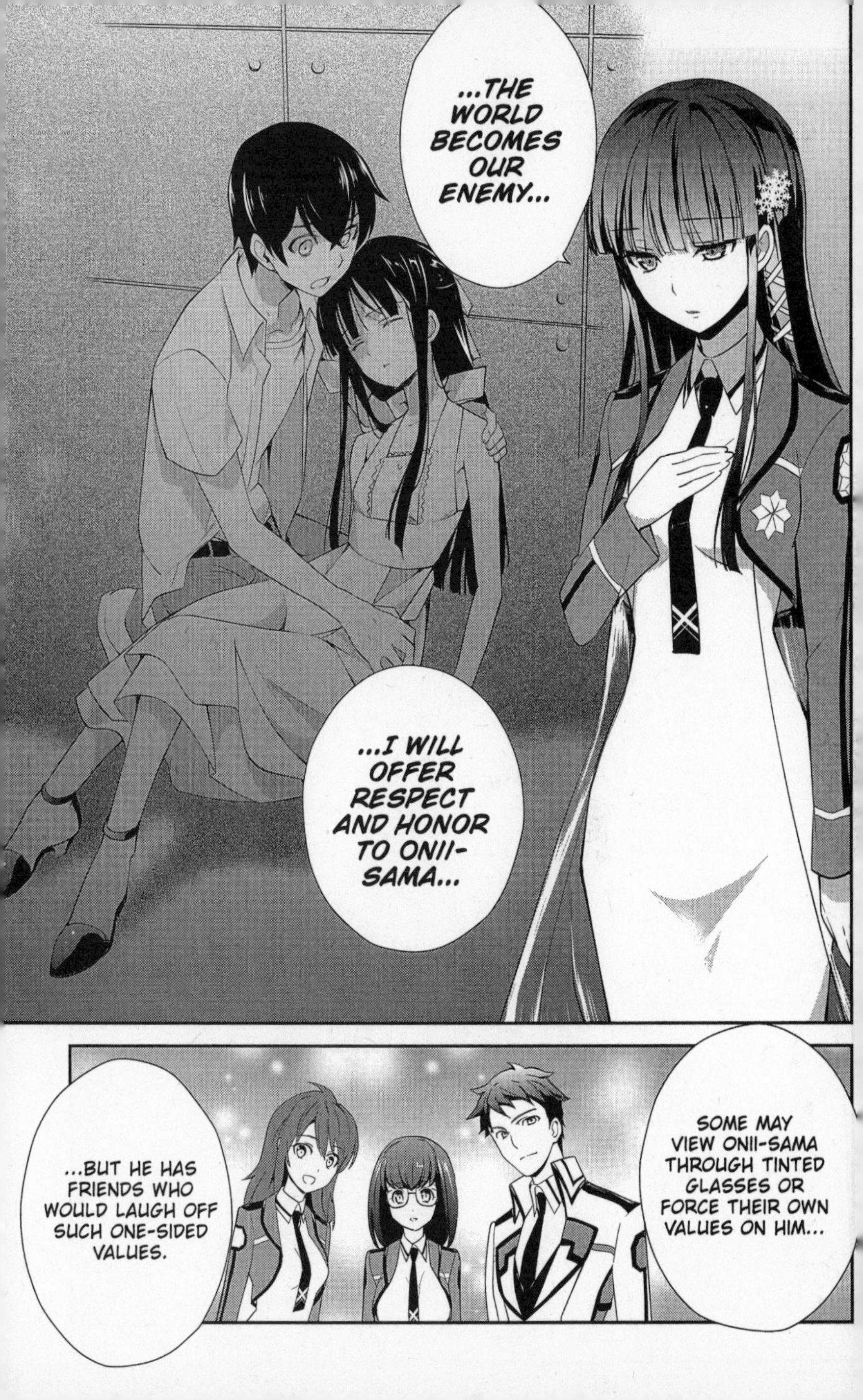
...THE WORLD BECOMES OUR ENEMY...
...I WILL OFFER RESPECT AND HONOR TO ONII-SAMA...
SOME MAY VIEW ONII-SAMA THROUGH TINTED GLASSES OR FORCE THEIR OWN VALUES ON HIM...
...BUT HE HAS FRIENDS WHO WOULD LAUGH OFF SUCH ONE-SIDED VALUES.

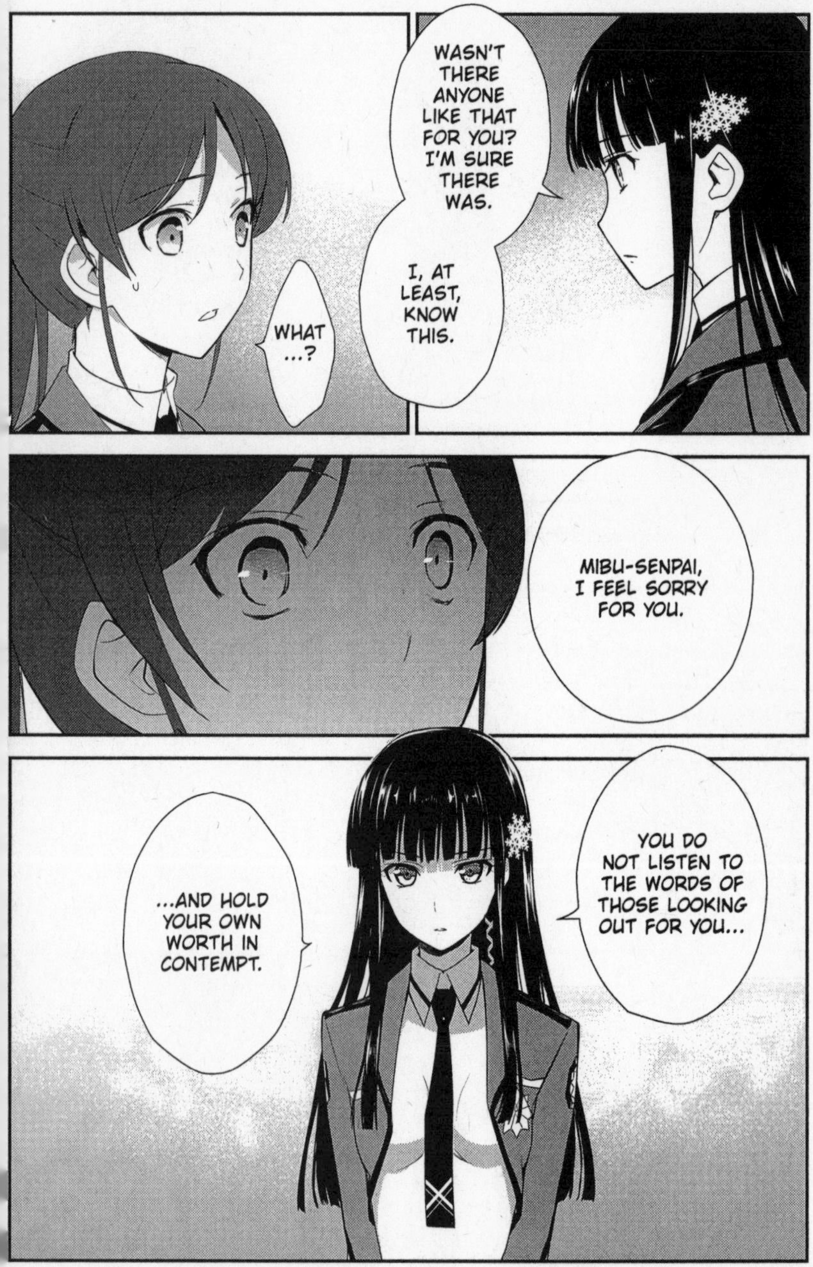
WASN'T THERE ANYONE LIKE THAT FOR YOU? I'M SURE THERE WAS.
I, AT LEAST, KNOW THIS.
WHAT ...?
MIBU-SENPAI, I FEEL SORRY FOR YOU.
YOU DO NOT LISTEN TO THE WORDS OF THOSE LOOKING OUT FOR YOU...
...AND HOLD YOUR OWN WORTH IN CONTEMPT.

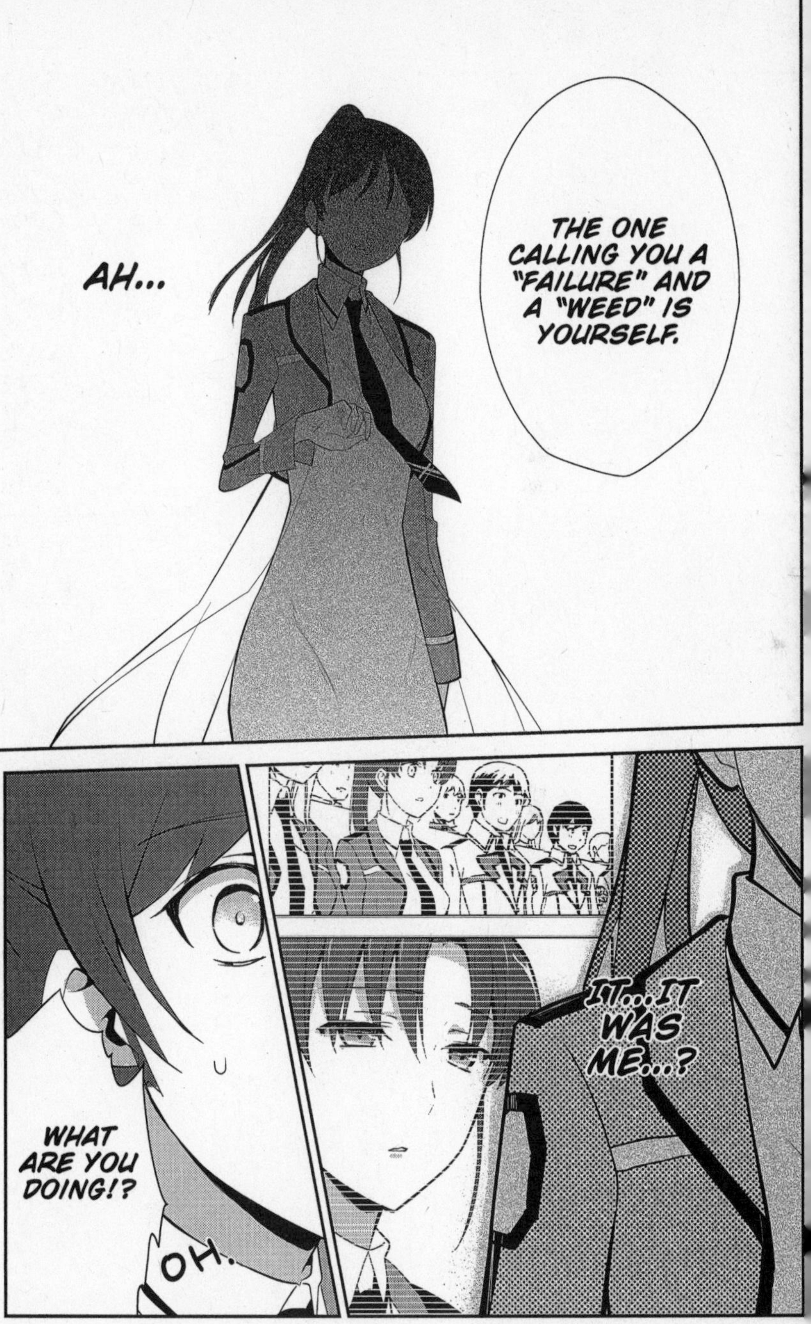
THE ONE CALLING YOU A "FAILURE" AND A "WEED" IS YOURSELF.
AH...
IT...IT WAS ME...?
WHAT ARE YOU DOING!?
OH.

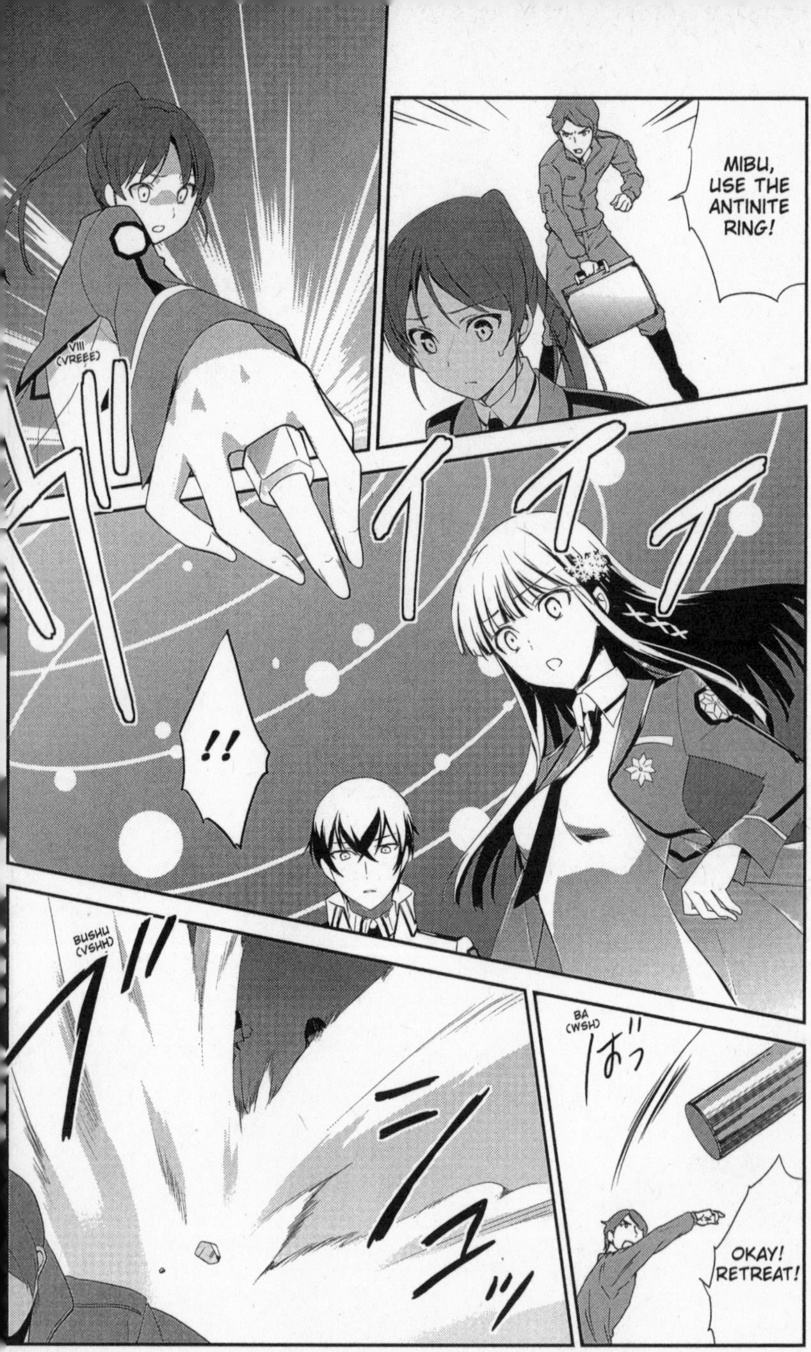
MIBU, USE THE ANTINITE RING!
VIII (VREEE)
!!
BA (WSH)
OKAY! RETREAT!
BUSHU (VSHH)

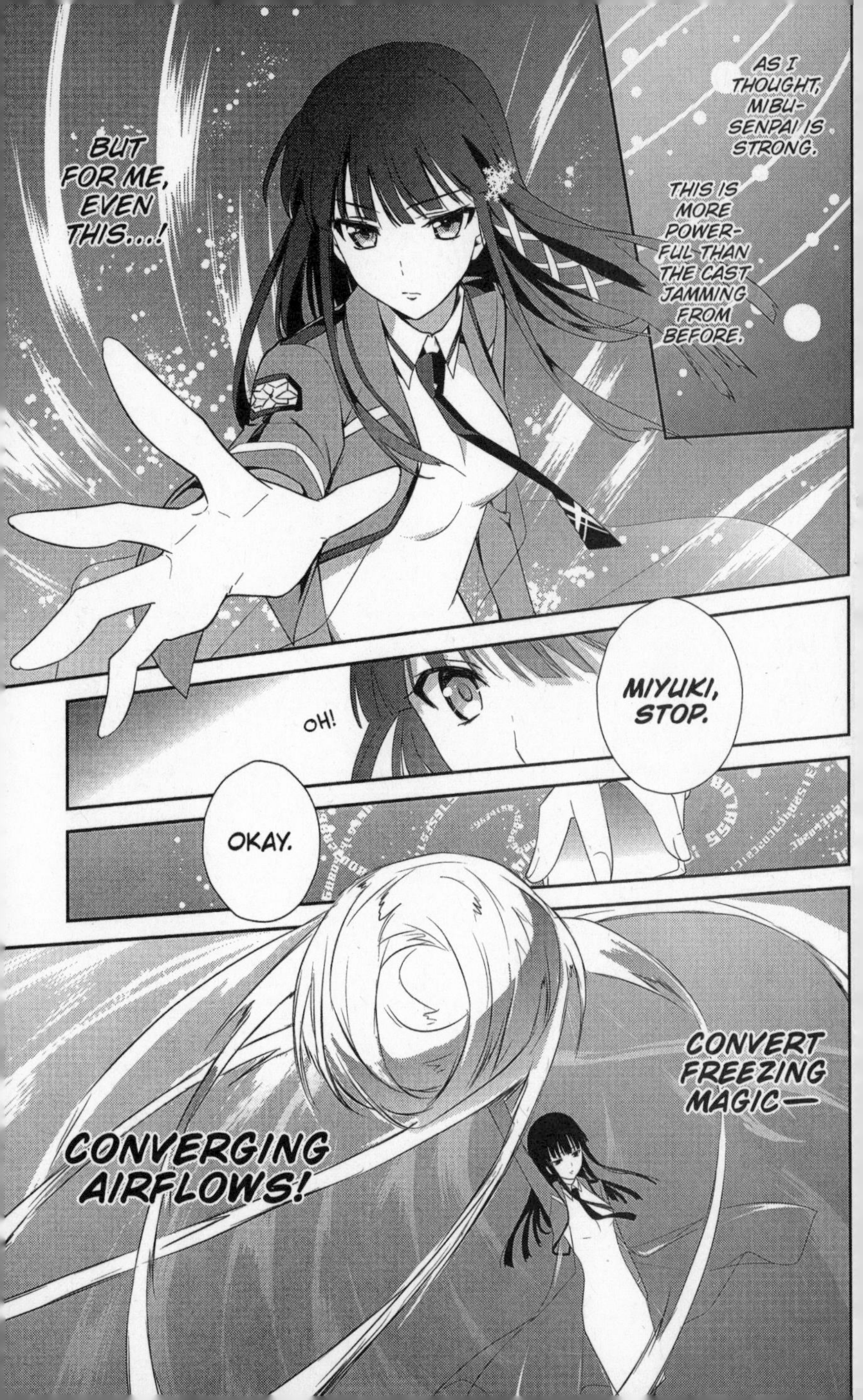
AS I THOUGHT, MIBU-SENPAI IS STRONG.
THIS IS MORE POWER-FUL THAN THE CAST JAMMING FROM BEFORE.
BUT FOR ME, EVEN THIS...!
MIYUKI, STOP.
OH!
OKAY.
CONVERT FREEZING MAGIC—
CONVERGING AIRFLOWS!

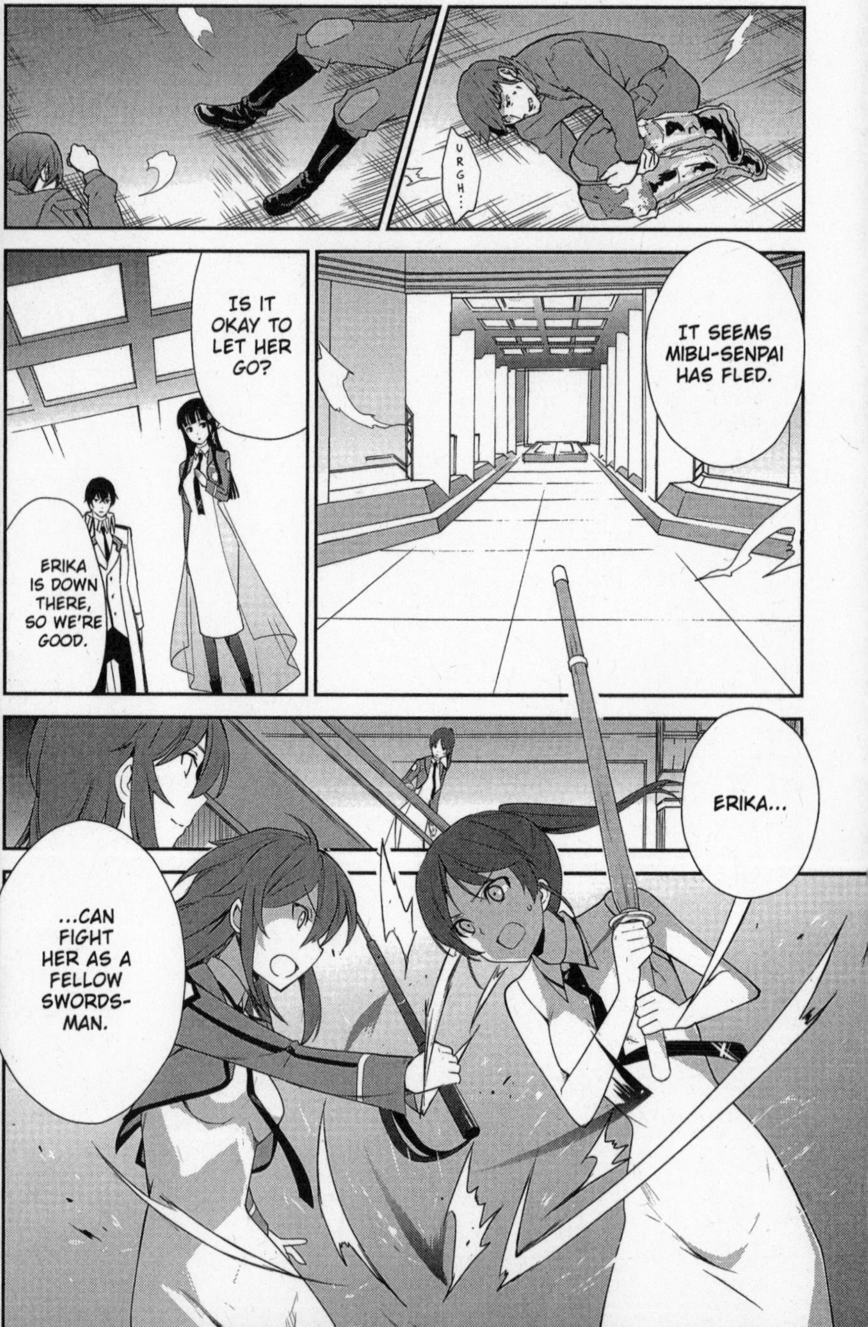
URGH...
IT SEEMS MIBU-SENPAI HAS FLED.
IS IT OKAY TO LET HER GO?
ERIKA IS DOWN THERE, SO WE'RE GOOD.
ERIKA...
...CAN FIGHT HER AS A FELLOW SWORDS-MAN.

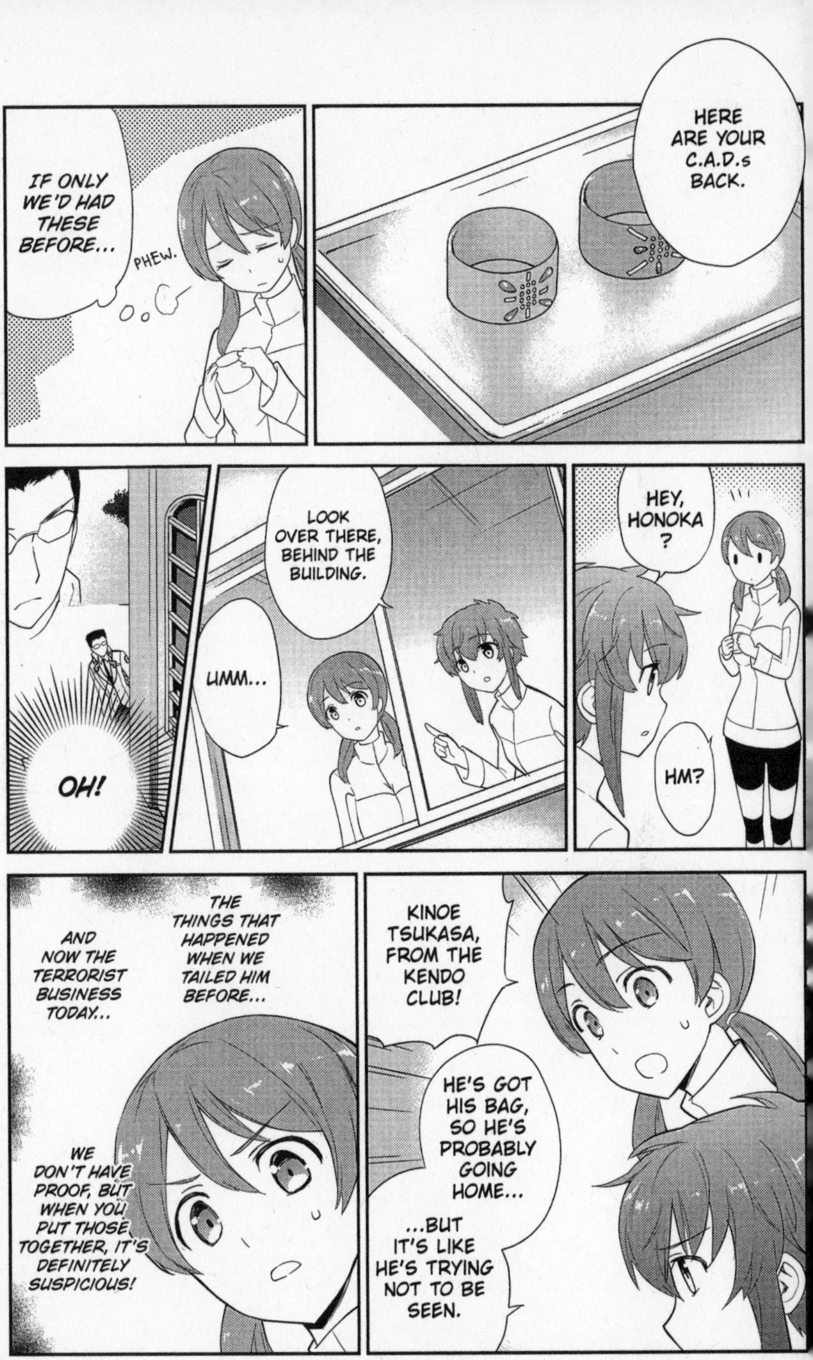
HERE ARE YOUR C.A.D.s BACK.
IF ONLY WE'D HAD THESE BEFORE...
PHEW.
HEY, HONOKA?
HM?
LOOK OVER THERE, BEHIND THE BUILDING.
UMM...
OH!
KINOE TSUKASA, FROM THE KENDO CLUB!
HE'S GOT HIS BAG, SO HE'S PROBABLY GOING HOME...
...BUT IT'S LIKE HE'S TRYING NOT TO BE SEEN.
THE THINGS THAT HAPPENED WHEN WE TAILED HIM BEFORE...
AND NOW THE TERRORIST BUSINESS TODAY...
WE DON'T HAVE PROOF, BUT WHEN YOU PUT THOSE TOGETHER, IT'S DEFINITELY SUSPICIOUS!

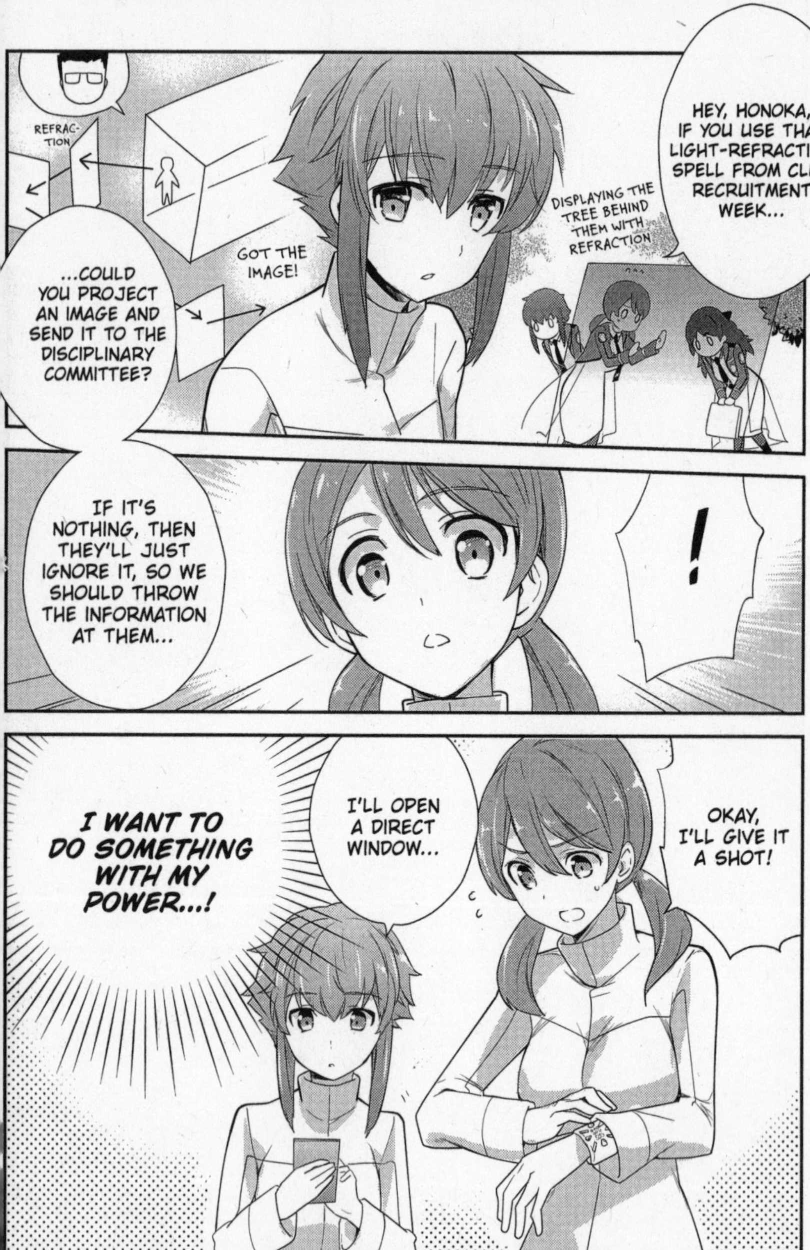
HEY, HONOKA, IF YOU USE THAT LIGHT-REFRACTING SPELL FROM CLUB RECRUITMENT WEEK...
DISPLAYING THE TREE BEHIND THEM WITH REFRACTION
GOT THE IMAGE!
REFRAC-TION
...COULD YOU PROJECT AN IMAGE AND SEND IT TO THE DISCIPLINARY COMMITTEE?
!
IF IT'S NOTHING, THEN THEY'LL JUST IGNORE IT, SO WE SHOULD THROW THE INFORMATION AT THEM...
OKAY, I'LL GIVE IT A SHOT!
I'LL OPEN A DIRECT WINDOW...
I WANT TO DO SOMETHING WITH MY POWER...!

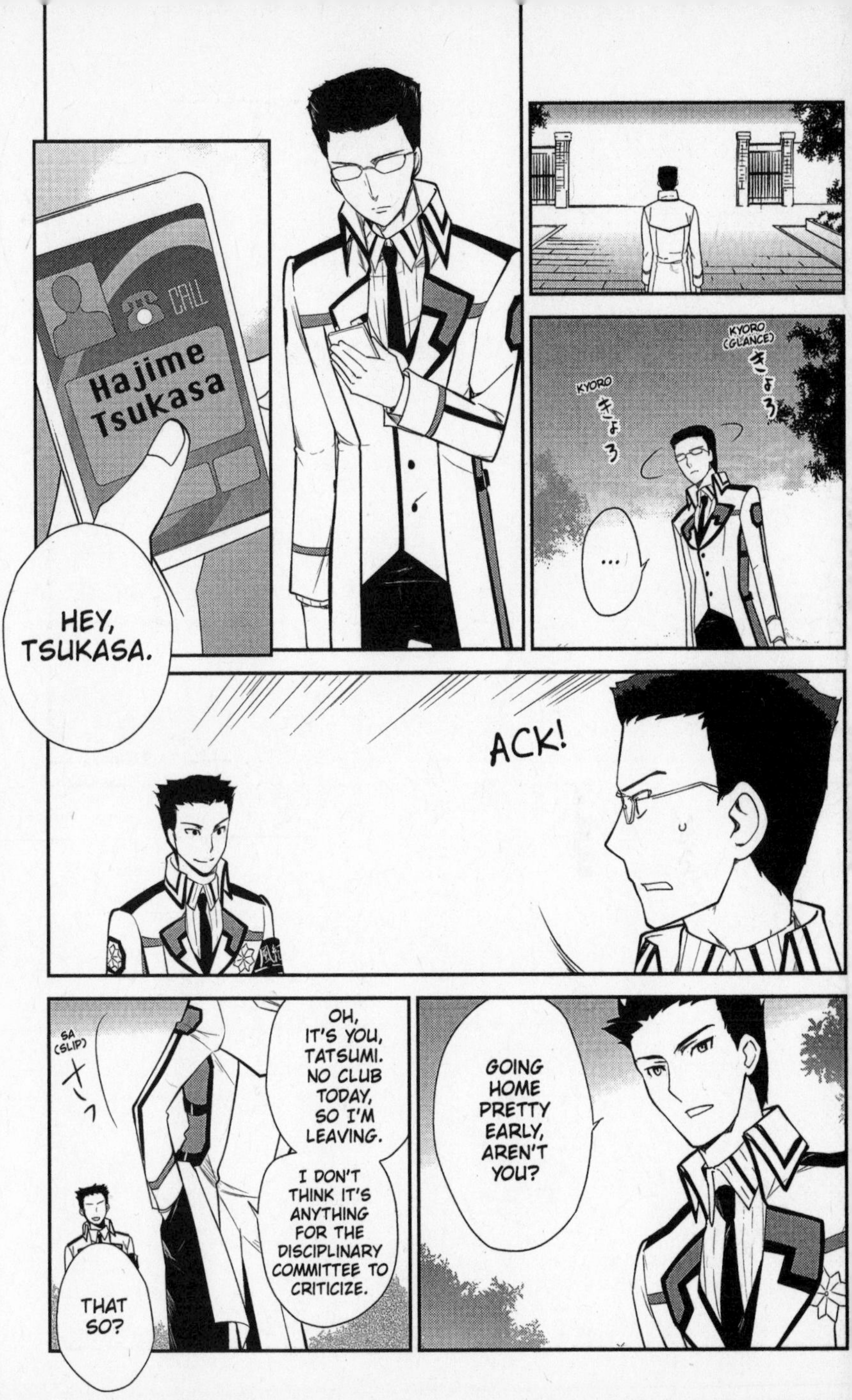
KYORO (GLANCE) きょろ
KYORO きょろ
...
CALL
Hajime Tsukasa
HEY, TSUKASA.
ACK!
GOING HOME PRETTY EARLY, AREN'T YOU?
OH, IT'S YOU, TATSUMI. NO CLUB TODAY, SO I'M LEAVING.
SA (SLIP) さっ
I DON'T THINK IT'S ANYTHING FOR THE DISCIPLINARY COMMITTEE TO CRITICIZE.
THAT SO?

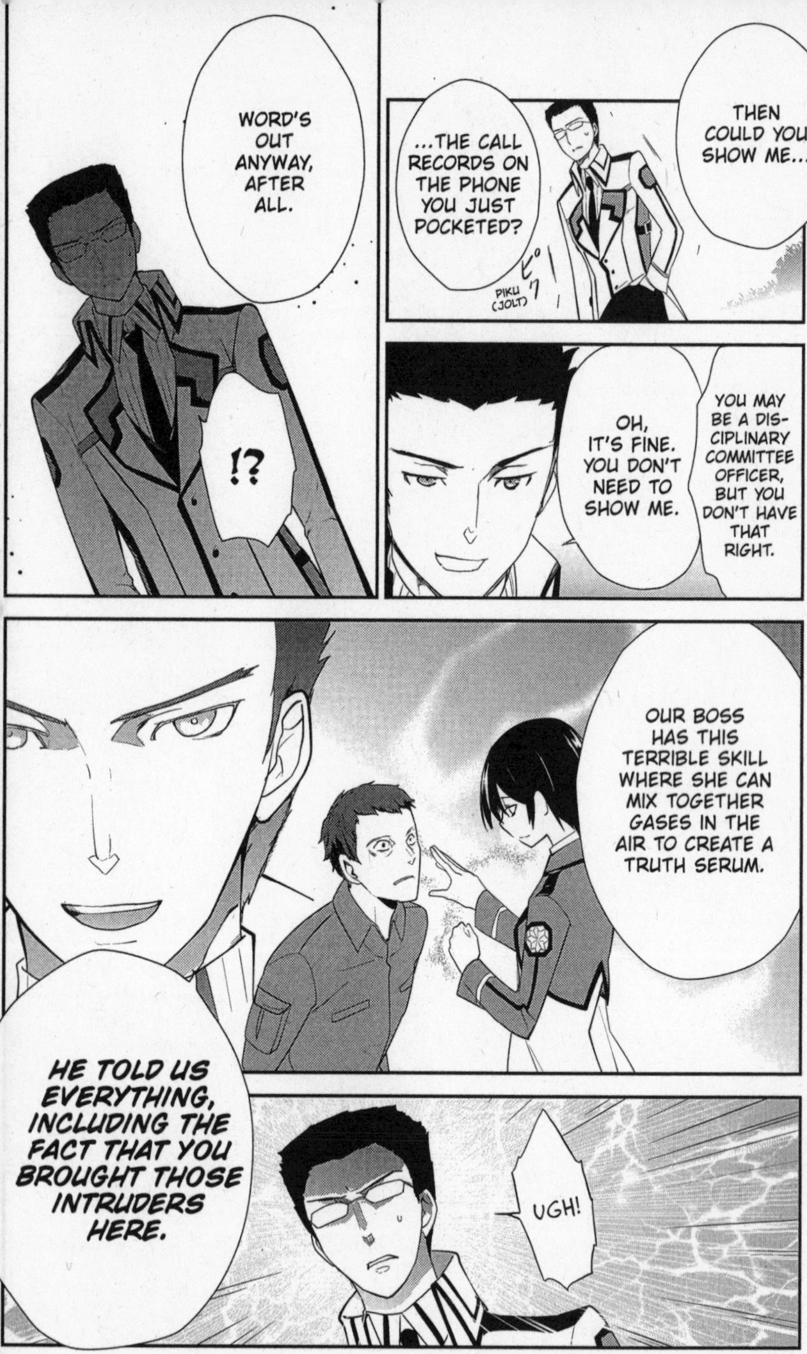
THEN COULD YOU SHOW ME...
...THE CALL RECORDS ON THE PHONE YOU JUST POCKETED?
ピク
PIKU (JOLT)
YOU MAY BE A DIS-CIPLINARY COMMITTEE OFFICER, BUT YOU DON'T HAVE THAT RIGHT.
OH, IT'S FINE. YOU DON'T NEED TO SHOW ME.
WORD'S OUT ANYWAY, AFTER ALL.
!?
OUR BOSS HAS THIS TERRIBLE SKILL WHERE SHE CAN MIX TOGETHER GASES IN THE AIR TO CREATE A TRUTH SERUM.
HE TOLD US EVERYTHING, INCLUDING THE FACT THAT YOU BROUGHT THOSE INTRUDERS HERE.
UGH!

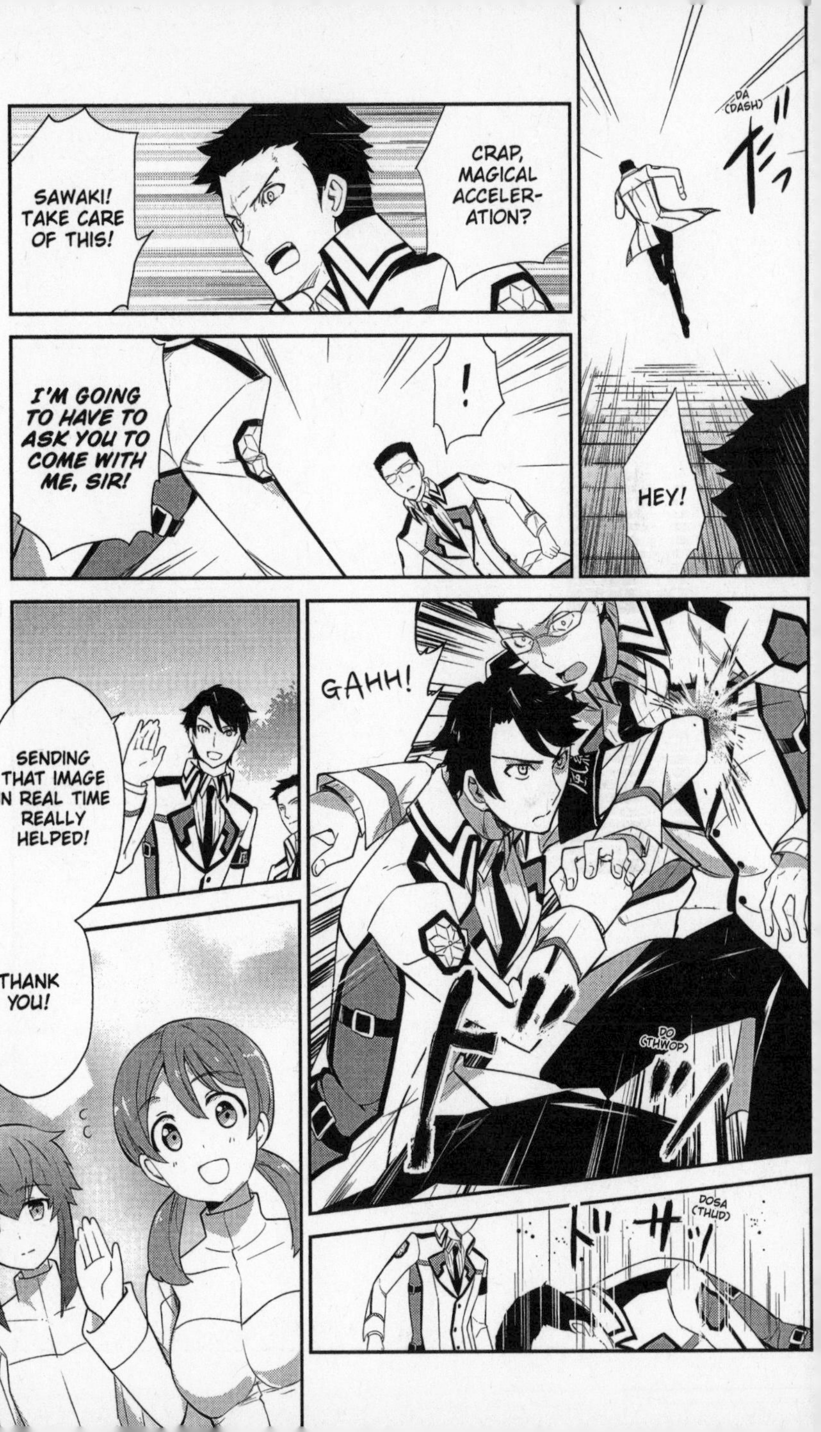
DA (DASH)
HEY!
CRAP, MAGICAL ACCELER-ATION?
SAWAKI! TAKE CARE OF THIS!
!
I'M GOING TO HAVE TO ASK YOU TO COME WITH ME, SIR!
GAHH!
DO (THWOP)
DOSA (THUD)
SENDING THAT IMAGE IN REAL TIME REALLY HELPED!
THANK YOU!

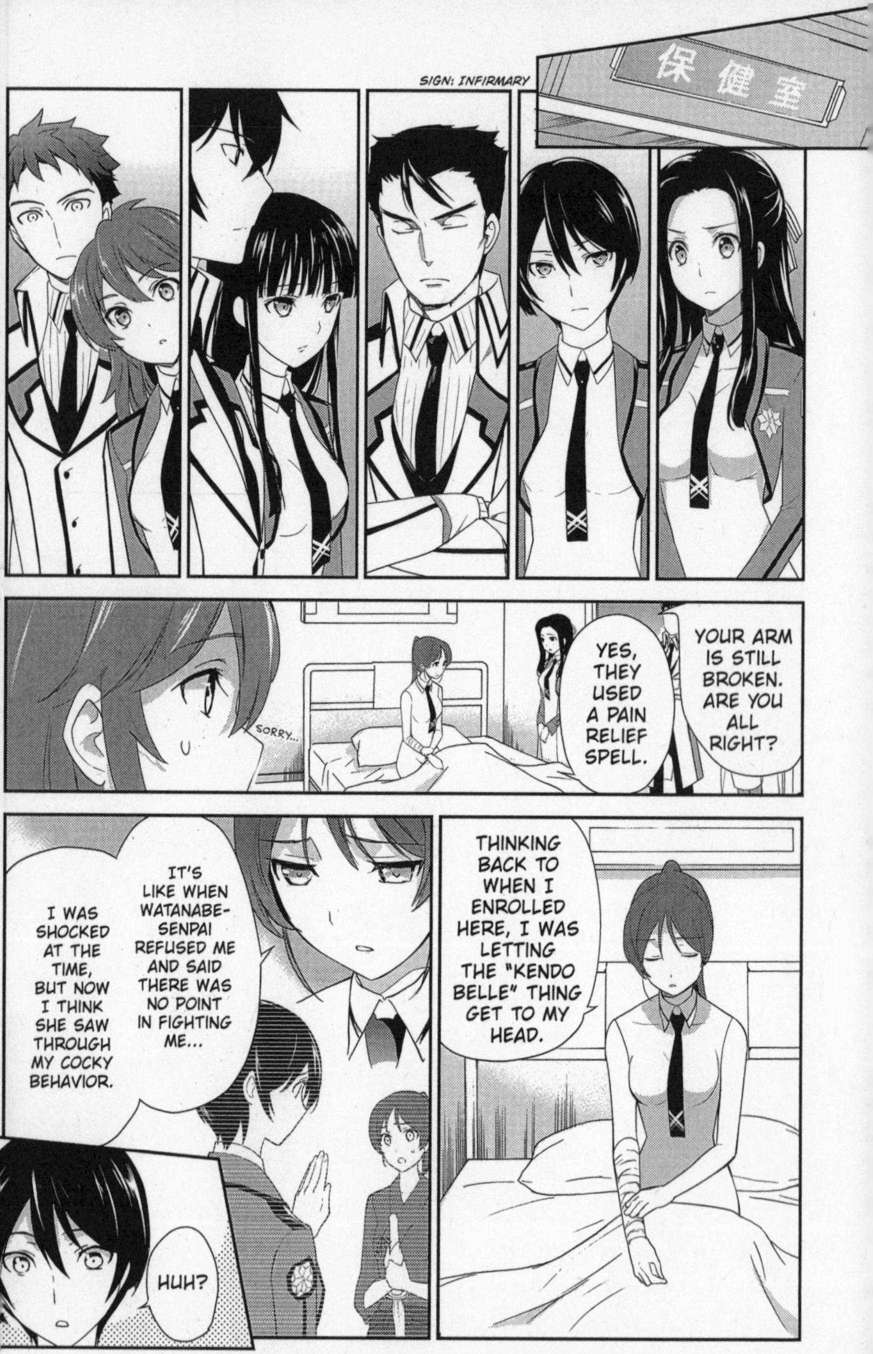
SIGN: INFIRMARY
保健室
YOUR ARM IS STILL BROKEN. ARE YOU ALL RIGHT?
YES, THEY USED A PAIN RELIEF SPELL.
SORRY...
THINKING BACK TO WHEN I ENROLLED HERE, I WAS LETTING THE "KENDO BELLE" THING GET TO MY HEAD.
IT'S LIKE WHEN WATANABE-SENPAI REFUSED ME AND SAID THERE WAS NO POINT IN FIGHTING ME...
I WAS SHOCKED AT THE TIME, BUT NOW I THINK SHE SAW THROUGH MY COCKY BEHAVIOR.
HUH?

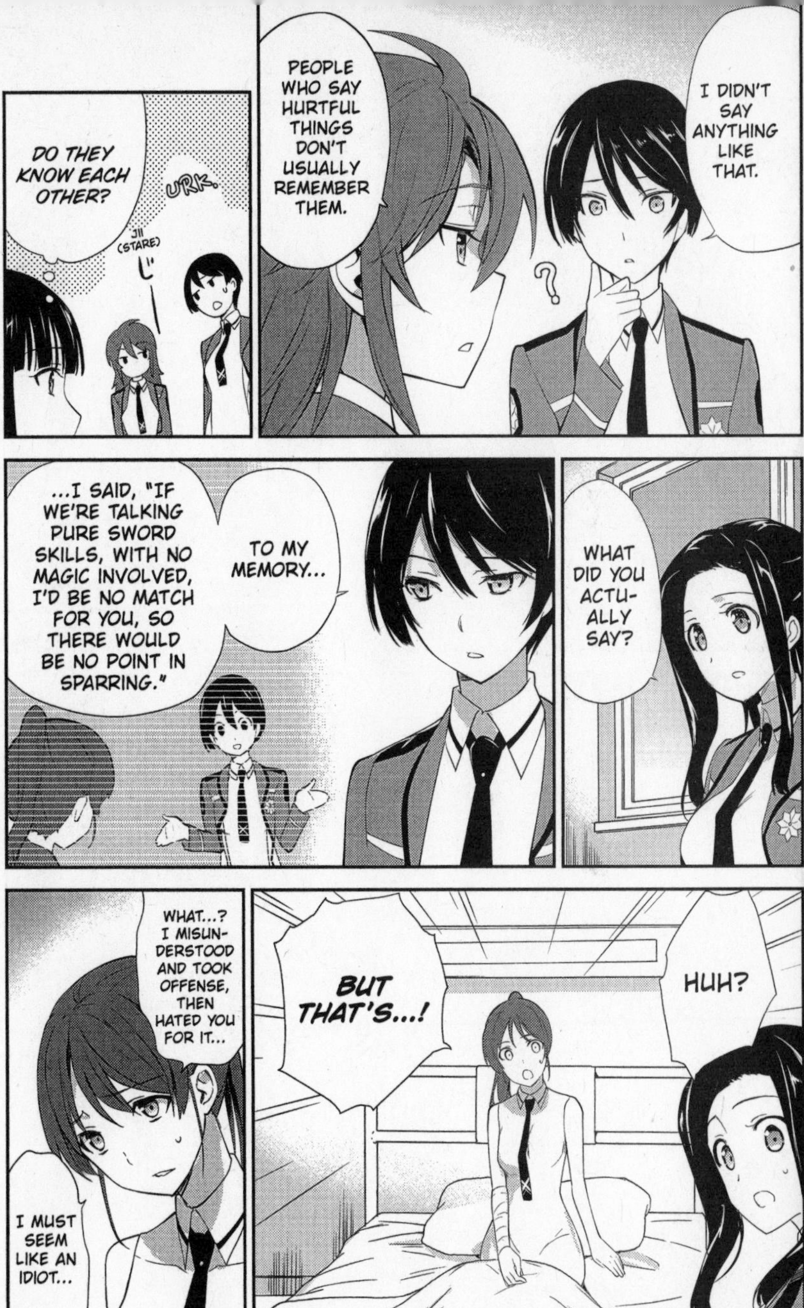
I DIDN'T SAY ANYTHING LIKE THAT.
PEOPLE WHO SAY HURTFUL THINGS DON'T USUALLY REMEMBER THEM.
DO THEY KNOW EACH OTHER?
URK.
JII (STARE)
じー
WHAT DID YOU ACTU-ALLY SAY?
TO MY MEMORY...
...I SAID, "IF WE'RE TALKING PURE SWORD SKILLS, WITH NO MAGIC INVOLVED, I'D BE NO MATCH FOR YOU, SO THERE WOULD BE NO POINT IN SPARRING."
HUH?
BUT THAT'S...!
WHAT...? I MISUN-DERSTOOD AND TOOK OFFENSE, THEN HATED YOU FOR IT...
I MUST SEEM LIKE AN IDIOT...

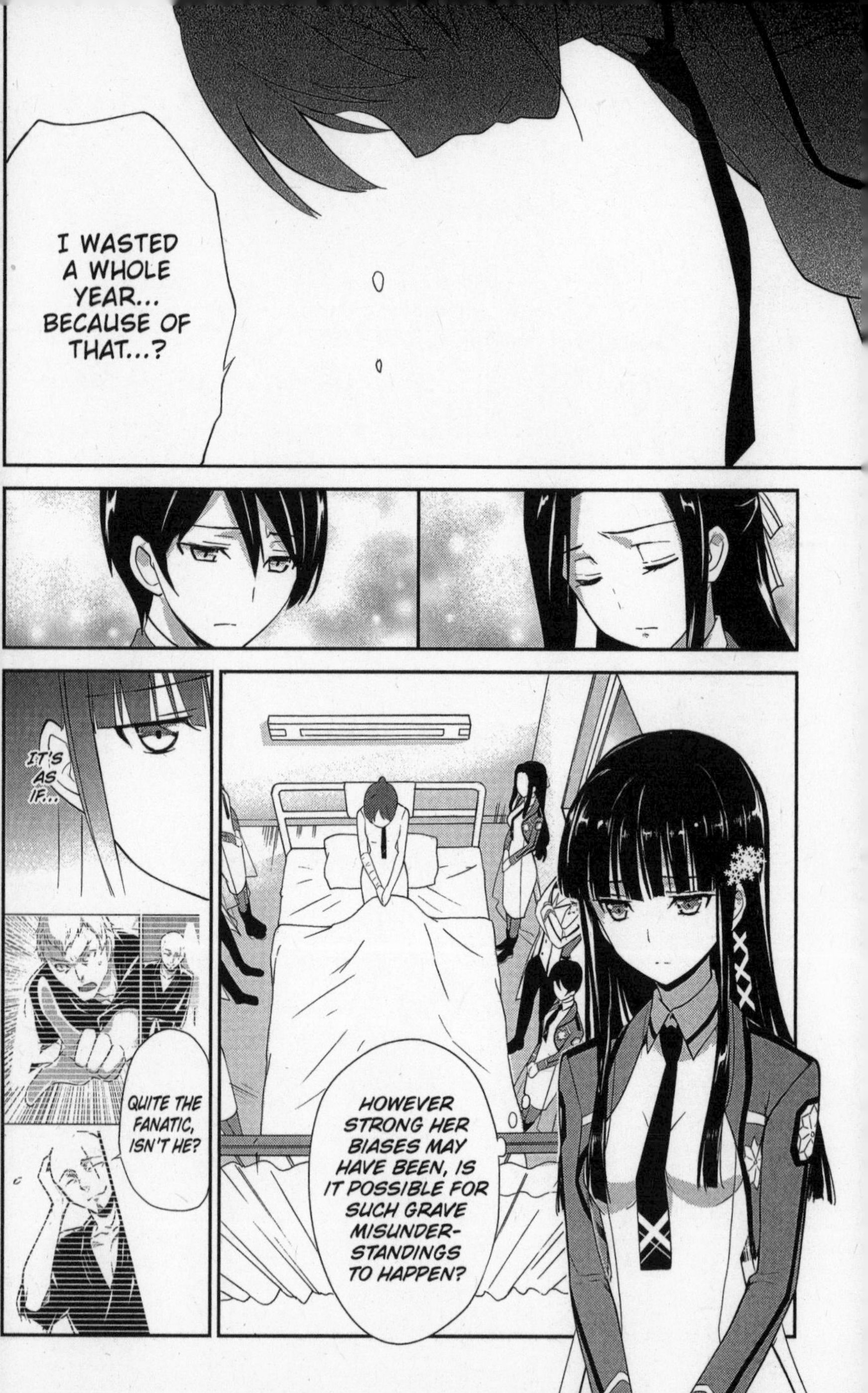
I WASTED A WHOLE YEAR... BECAUSE OF THAT...?
HOWEVER STRONG HER BIASES MAY HAVE BEEN, IS IT POSSIBLE FOR SUCH GRAVE MISUNDER-STANDINGS TO HAPPEN?
IT'S AS IF...
QUITE THE FANATIC, ISN'T HE?

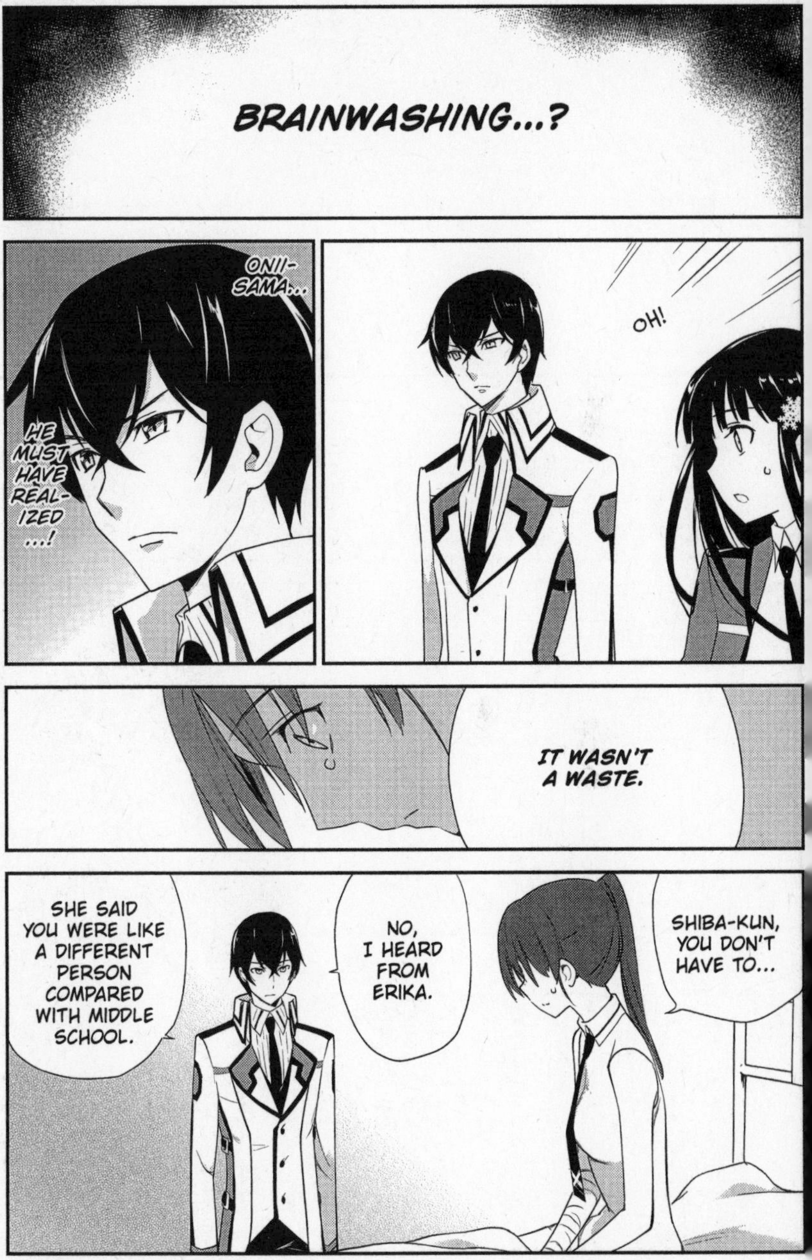
BRAINWASHING...?
OH!
ONII-SAMA...
HE MUST HAVE REALIZED ...!
IT WASN'T A WASTE.
SHIBA-KUN, YOU DON'T HAVE TO...
NO, I HEARD FROM ERIKA.
SHE SAID YOU WERE LIKE A DIFFERENT PERSON COMPARED WITH MIDDLE SCHOOL.

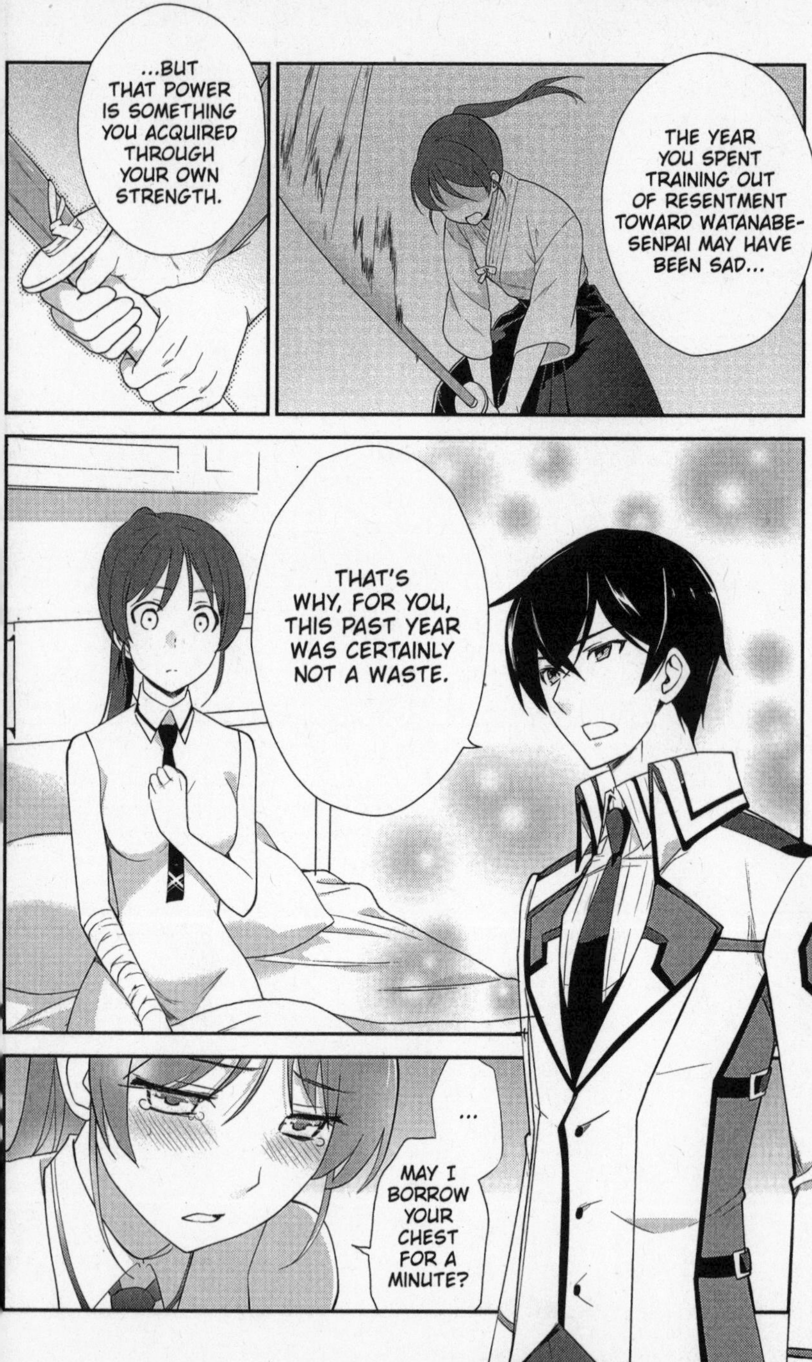
THE YEAR YOU SPENT TRAINING OUT OF RESENTMENT TOWARD WATANABE-SENPAI MAY HAVE BEEN SAD...
...BUT THAT POWER IS SOMETHING YOU ACQUIRED THROUGH YOUR OWN STRENGTH.
THAT'S WHY, FOR YOU, THIS PAST YEAR WAS CERTAINLY NOT A WASTE.
...
MAY I BORROW YOUR CHEST FOR A MINUTE?

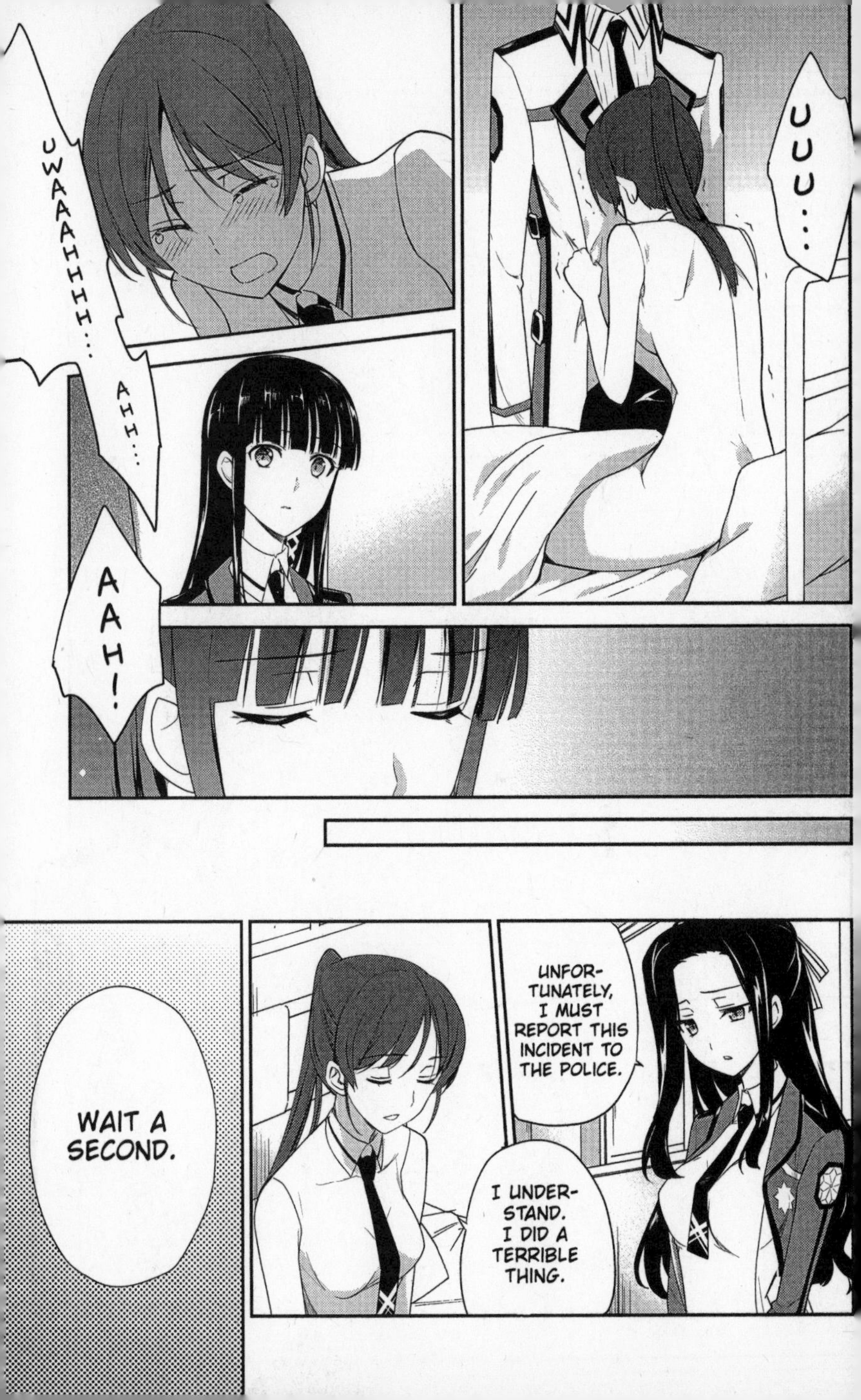
UUU...
UWAAAHHHH...
AHH...
AAH!
UNFORTUNATELY, I MUST REPORT THIS INCIDENT TO THE POLICE.
I UNDERSTAND. I DID A TERRIBLE THING.
WAIT A SECOND.

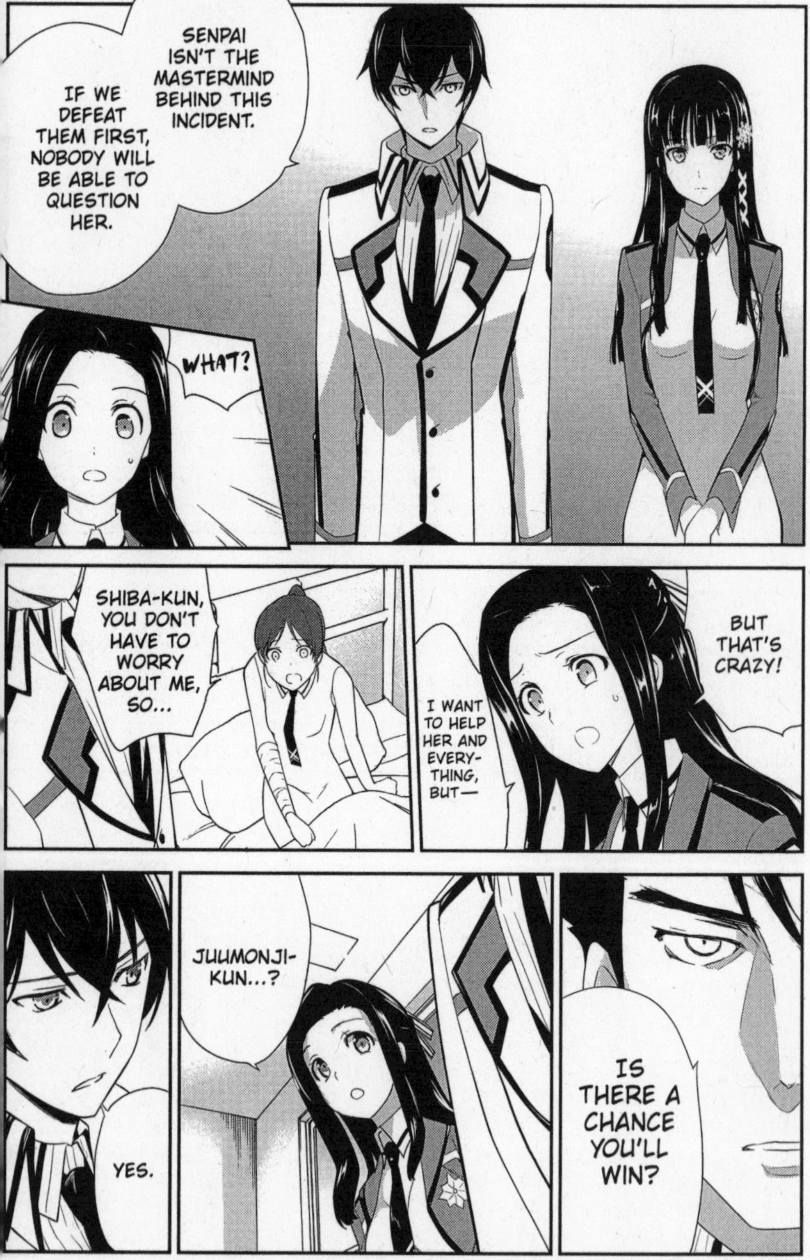
SENPAI ISN'T THE MASTERMIND BEHIND THIS INCIDENT.
IF WE DEFEAT THEM FIRST, NOBODY WILL BE ABLE TO QUESTION HER.
WHAT?
BUT THAT'S CRAZY!
I WANT TO HELP HER AND EVERYTHING, BUT—
SHIBA-KUN, YOU DON'T HAVE TO WORRY ABOUT ME, SO...
IS THERE A CHANCE YOU'LL WIN?
JUUMONJI-KUN...?
YES.

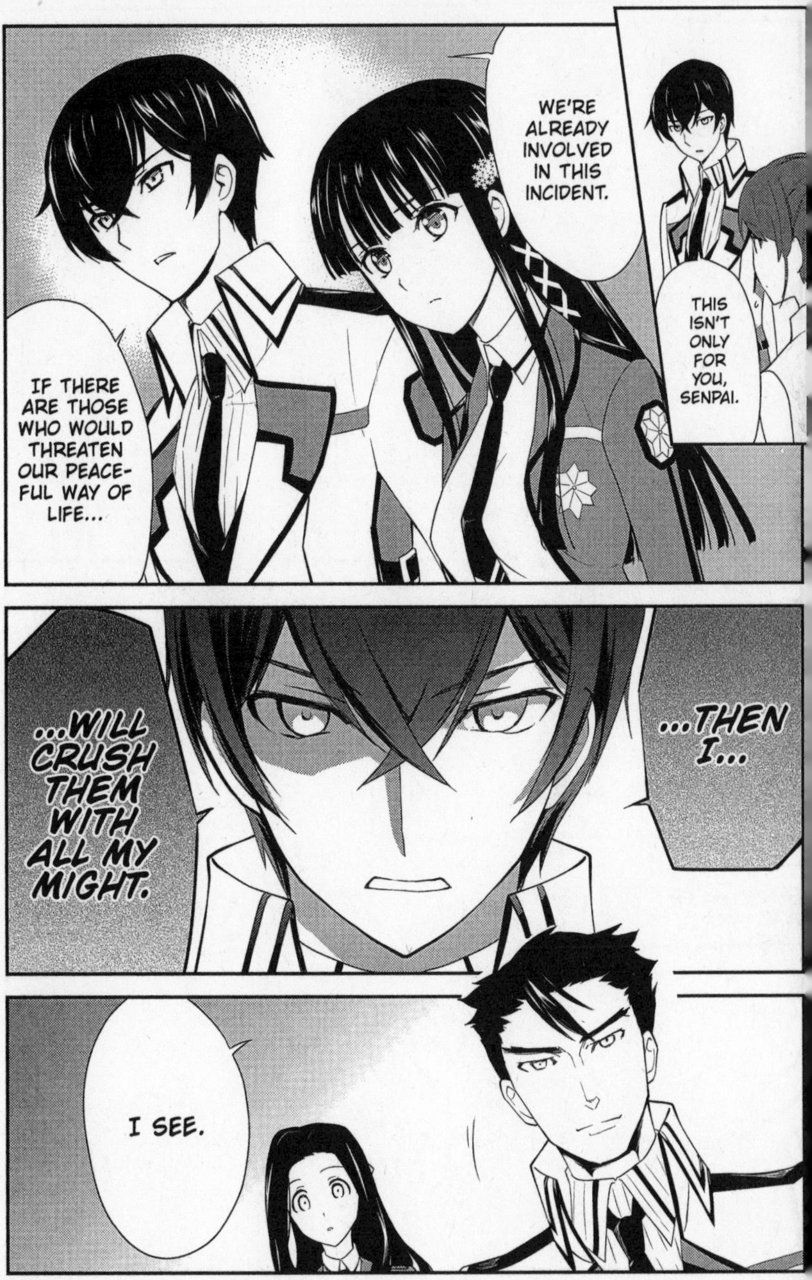
THIS ISN'T ONLY FOR YOU, SENPAI.
WE'RE ALREADY INVOLVED IN THIS INCIDENT.
IF THERE ARE THOSE WHO WOULD THREATEN OUR PEACE-FUL WAY OF LIFE...
...THEN I...
...WILL CRUSH THEM WITH ALL MY MIGHT.
I SEE.

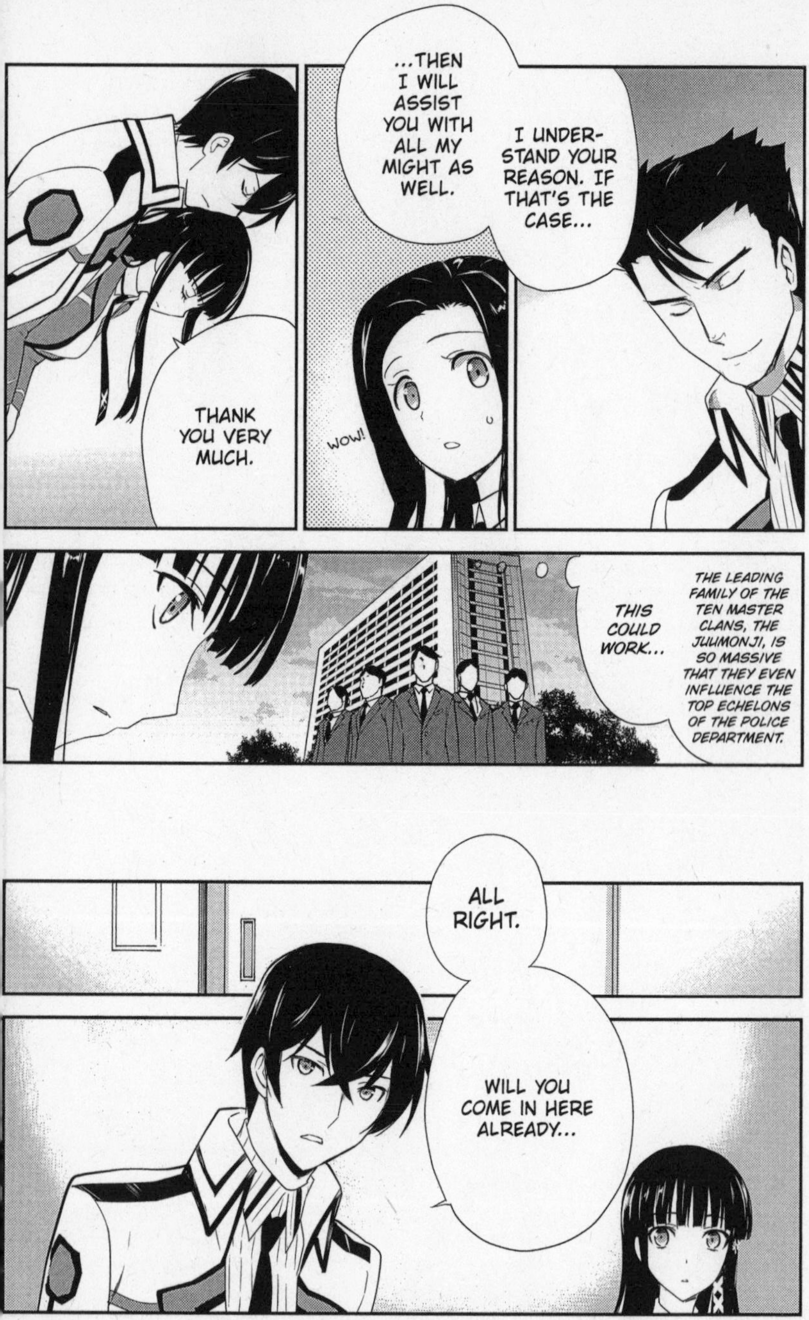
I UNDER-STAND YOUR REASON. IF THAT'S THE CASE...
...THEN I WILL ASSIST YOU WITH ALL MY MIGHT AS WELL.
WOW!
THANK YOU VERY MUCH.
THE LEADING FAMILY OF THE TEN MASTER CLANS, THE JUUMONJI, IS SO MASSIVE THAT THEY EVEN INFLUENCE THE TOP ECHELONS OF THE POLICE DEPARTMENT.
THIS COULD WORK...
ALL RIGHT.
WILL YOU COME IN HERE ALREADY...

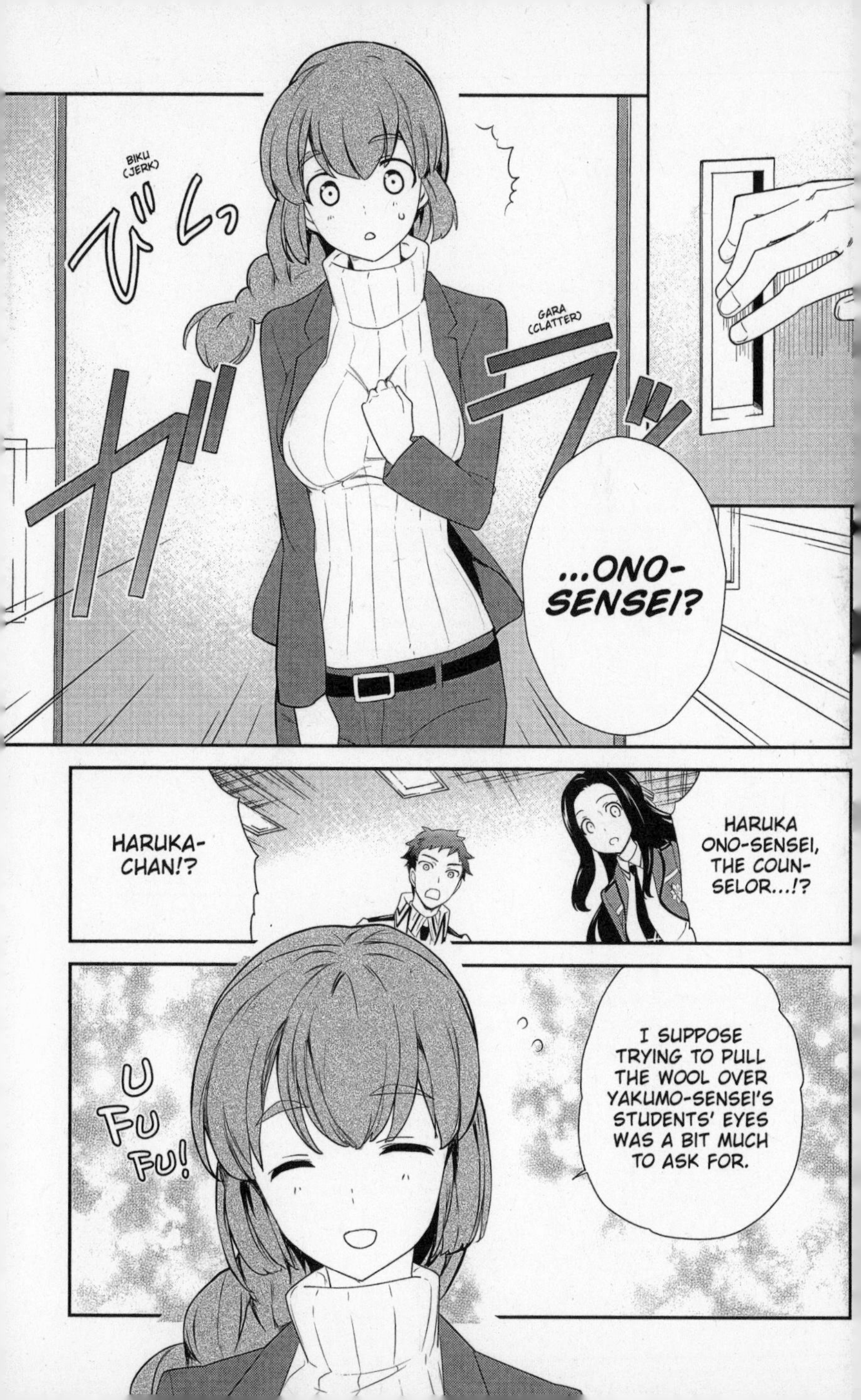
GARA (CLATTER)
BIKU (JERK)
...ONO-SENSEI?
HARUKA ONO-SENSEI, THE COUNSELOR...!?
HARUKA-CHAN!?
I SUPPOSE TRYING TO PULL THE WOOL OVER YAKUMO-SENSEI'S STUDENTS' EYES WAS A BIT MUCH TO ASK FOR.
U FU FU!

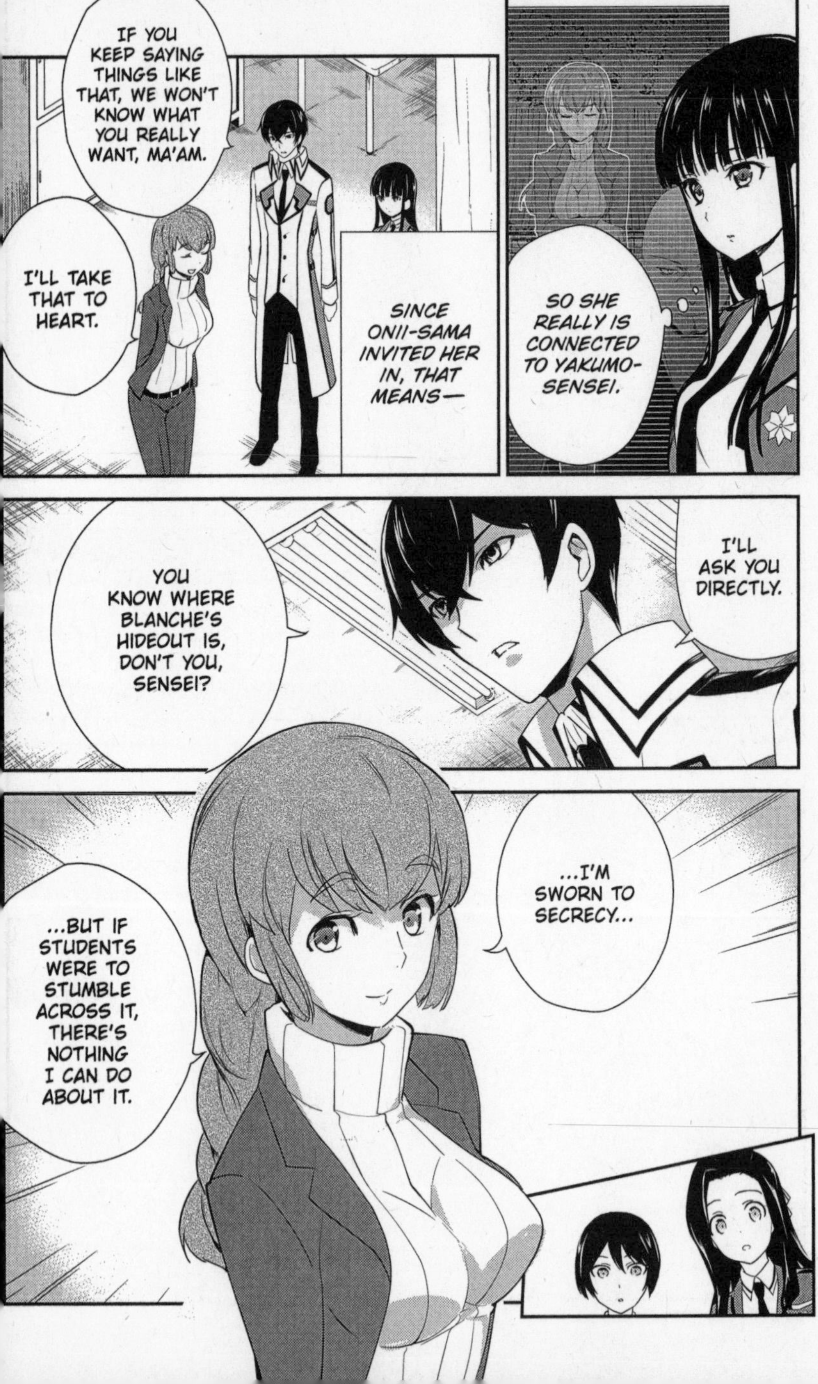
SO SHE REALLY IS CONNECTED TO YAKUMO-SENSEI.
IF YOU KEEP SAYING THINGS LIKE THAT, WE WON'T KNOW WHAT YOU REALLY WANT, MA'AM.
I'LL TAKE THAT TO HEART.
SINCE ONII-SAMA INVITED HER IN, THAT MEANS—
I'LL ASK YOU DIRECTLY.
YOU KNOW WHERE BLANCHE'S HIDEOUT IS, DON'T YOU, SENSEI?
...I'M SWORN TO SECRECY...
...BUT IF STUDENTS WERE TO STUMBLE ACROSS IT, THERE'S NOTHING I CAN DO ABOUT IT.

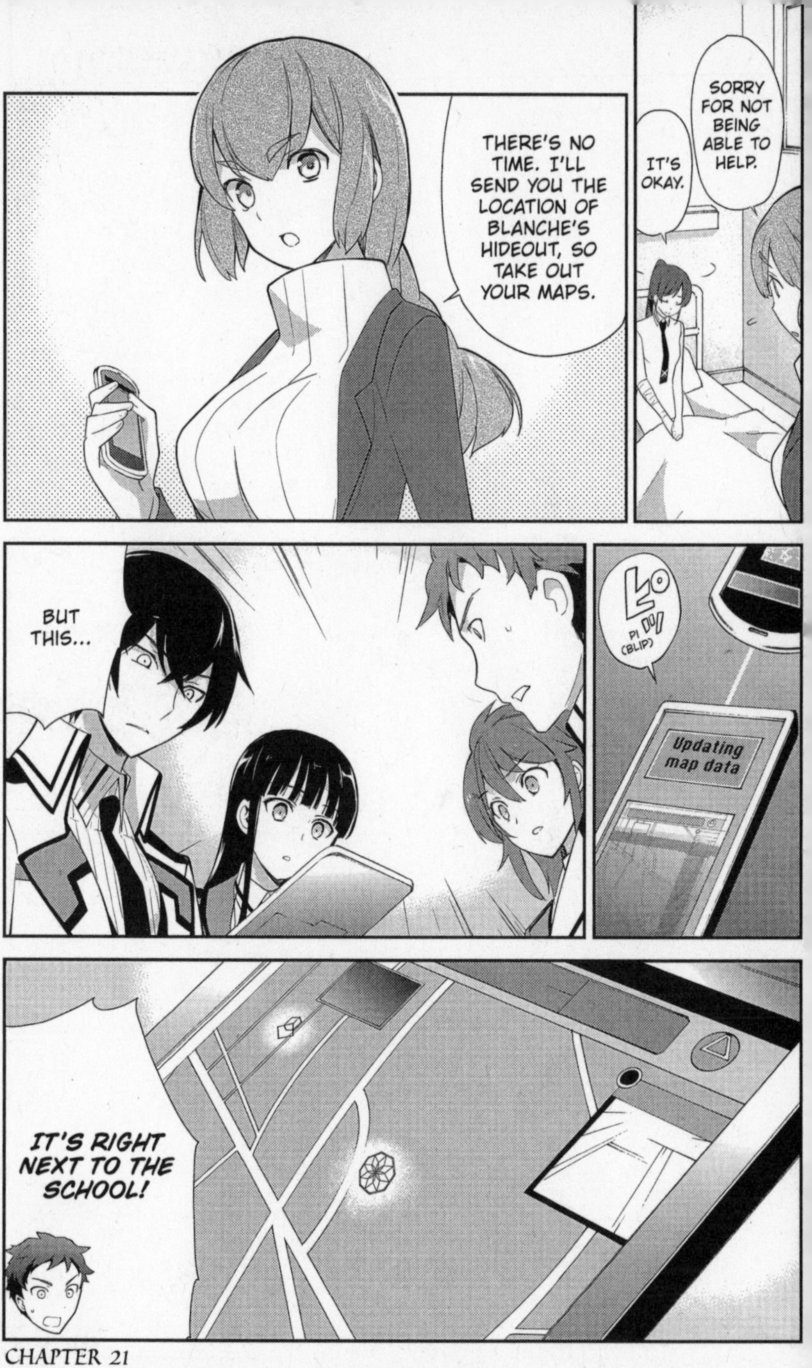
SORRY FOR NOT BEING ABLE TO HELP.
IT'S OKAY.
THERE'S NO TIME. I'LL SEND YOU THE LOCATION OF BLANCHE'S HIDEOUT, SO TAKE OUT YOUR MAPS.
PI (BLIP)
Updating map data
BUT THIS...
IT'S RIGHT NEXT TO THE SCHOOL!

CHAPTER 21

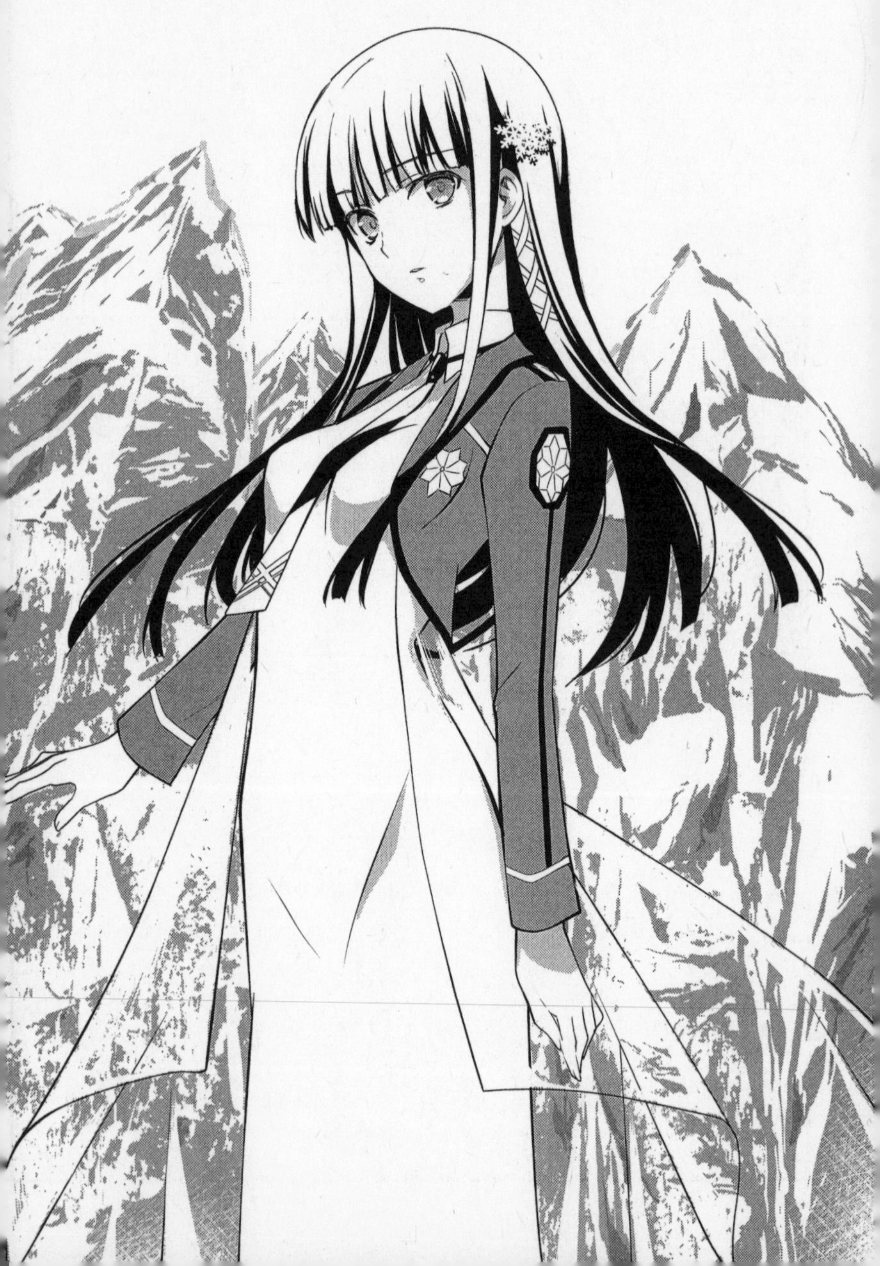

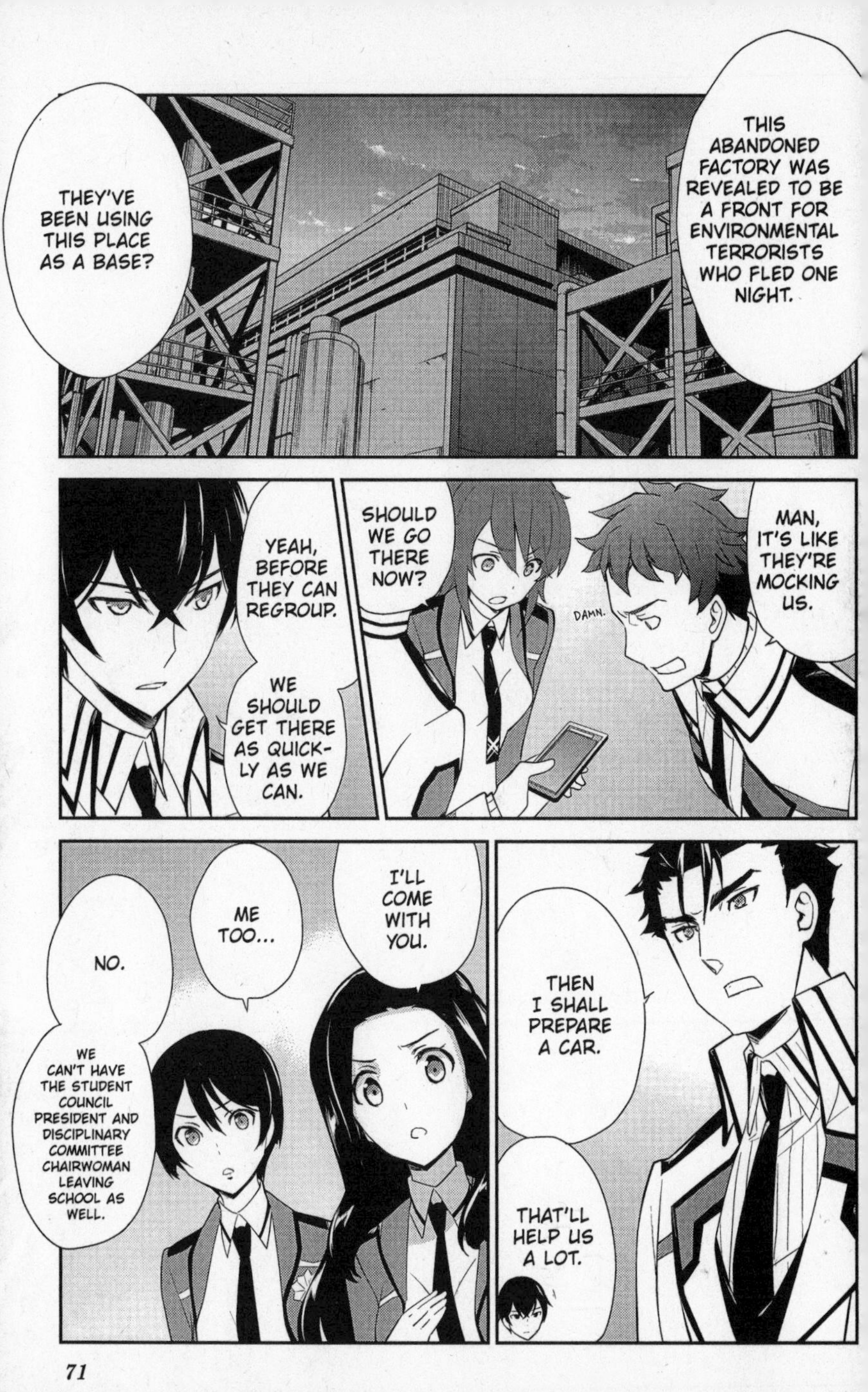
THIS ABANDONED FACTORY WAS REVEALED TO BE A FRONT FOR ENVIRONMENTAL TERRORISTS WHO FLED ONE NIGHT.
THEY'VE BEEN USING THIS PLACE AS A BASE?
MAN, IT'S LIKE THEY'RE MOCKING US.
DAMN.
SHOULD WE GO THERE NOW?
YEAH, BEFORE THEY CAN REGROUP.
WE SHOULD GET THERE AS QUICKLY AS WE CAN.
THEN I SHALL PREPARE A CAR.
THAT'LL HELP US A LOT.
I'LL COME WITH YOU.
ME TOO...
NO.
WE CAN'T HAVE THE STUDENT COUNCIL PRESIDENT AND DISCIPLINARY COMMITTEE CHAIRWOMAN LEAVING SCHOOL AS WELL.

OH WELL.

... ROGER.

SORRY, BUT YOU'LL HAVE TO LEAVE THIS ONE TO US.

OKAY.

WE'LL MAKE OUR ASSAULT WITH THESE MEMBERS.

BA (BOW)

AS WELL AS...

THIS IS KIRIHARA. HE HAS HIS OWN REASONS FOR JOINING.

THAT PER- SON...

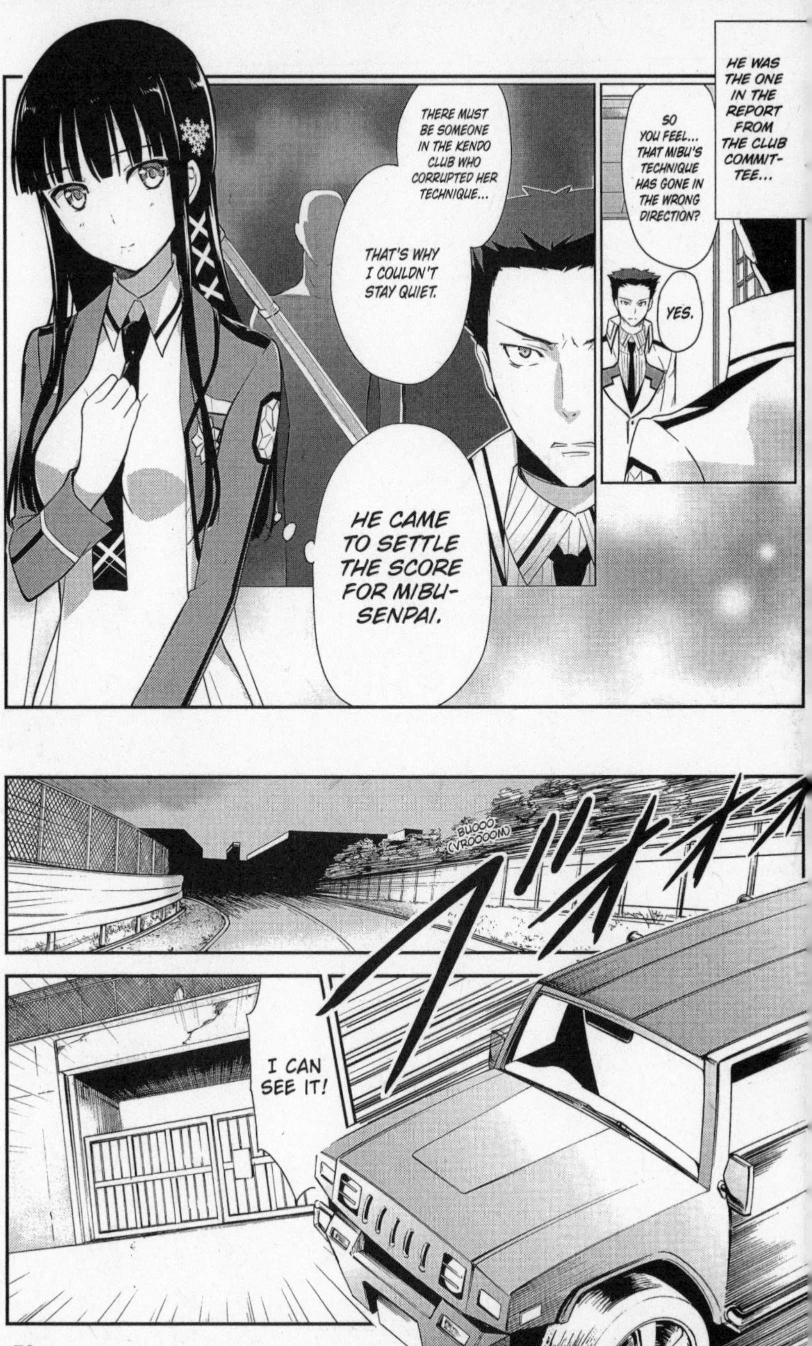
HE WAS THE ONE IN THE REPORT FROM THE CLUB COMMIT-TEE...
SO YOU FEEL... THAT MIBU'S TECHNIQUE HAS GONE IN THE WRONG DIRECTION?
YES.
THERE MUST BE SOMEONE IN THE KENDO CLUB WHO CORRUPTED HER TECHNIQUE...
THAT'S WHY I COULDN'T STAY QUIET.
HE CAME TO SETTLE THE SCORE FOR MIBU-SENPAI.
BUOOO (VROOOOM)
I CAN SEE IT!

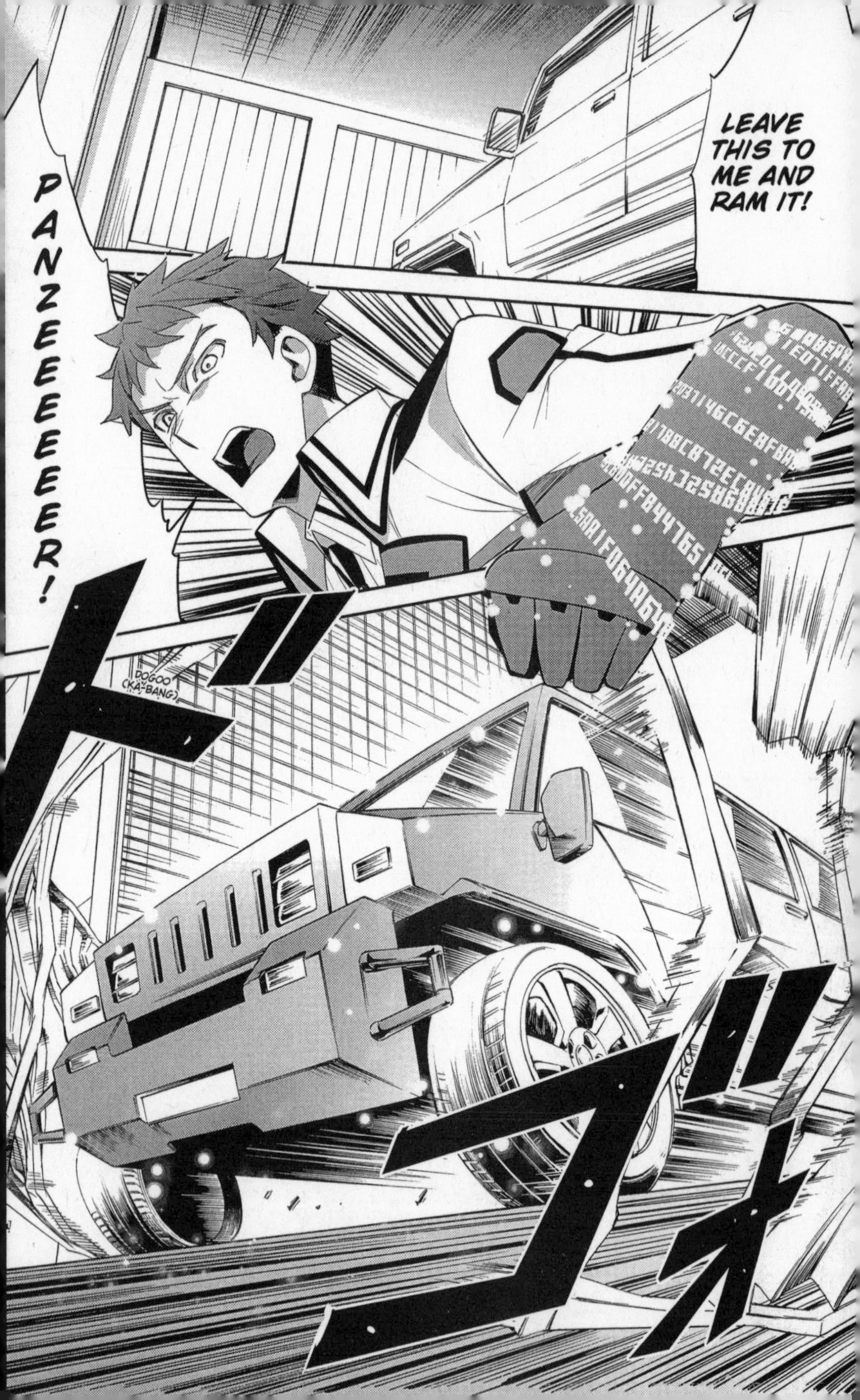
LEAVE THIS TO ME AND RAM IT!
PANZEEEEEEER!
DOGOO (KA-BANG)

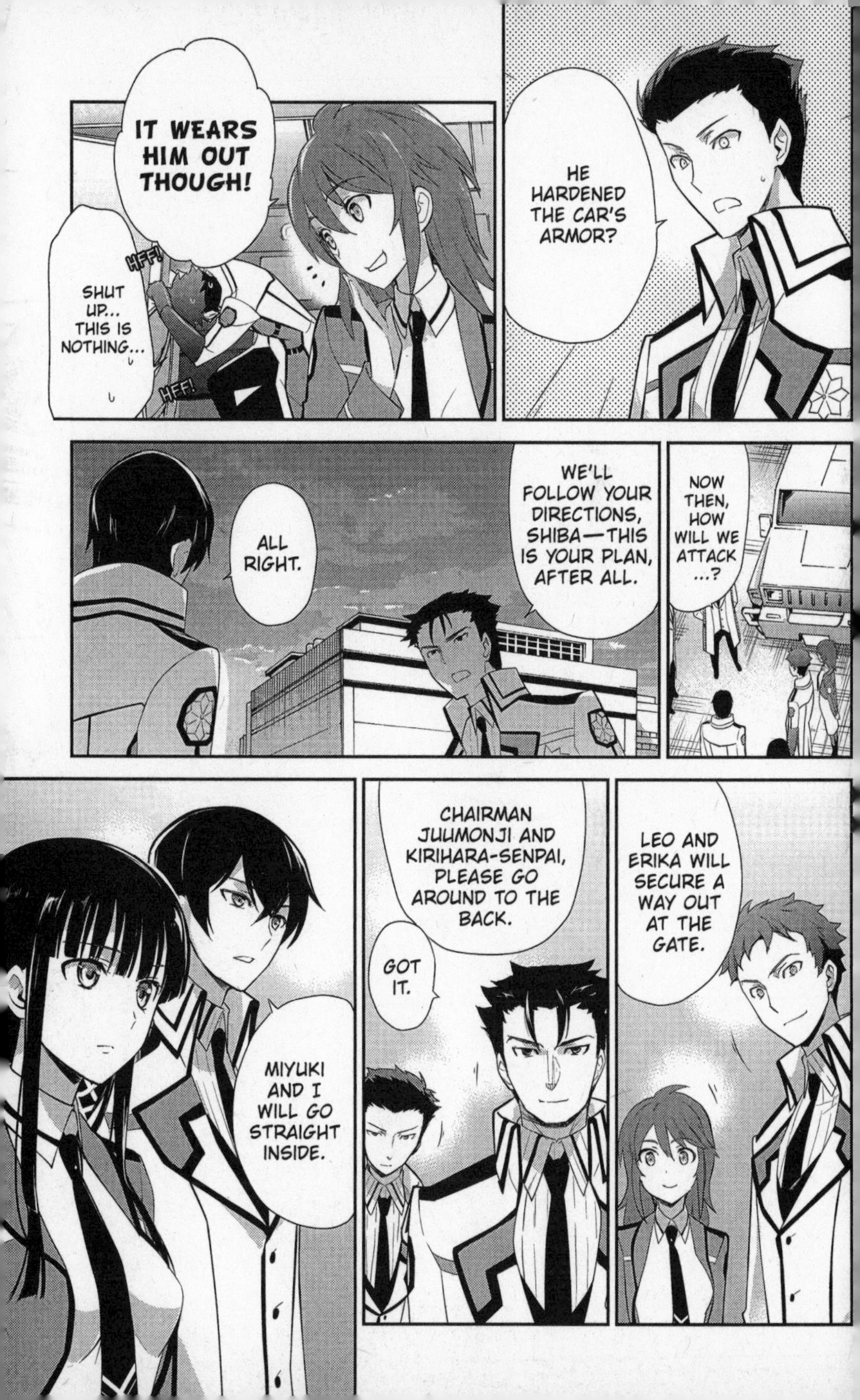
HE HARDENED THE CAR'S ARMOR?
IT WEARS HIM OUT THOUGH!
HFF!
SHUT UP... THIS IS NOTHING...
HFF!
NOW THEN, HOW WILL WE ATTACK ...?
WE'LL FOLLOW YOUR DIRECTIONS, SHIBA—THIS IS YOUR PLAN, AFTER ALL.
ALL RIGHT.
LEO AND ERIKA WILL SECURE A WAY OUT AT THE GATE.
CHAIRMAN JUUMONJI AND KIRIHARA-SENPAI, PLEASE GO AROUND TO THE BACK.
GOT IT.
MIYUKI AND I WILL GO STRAIGHT INSIDE.

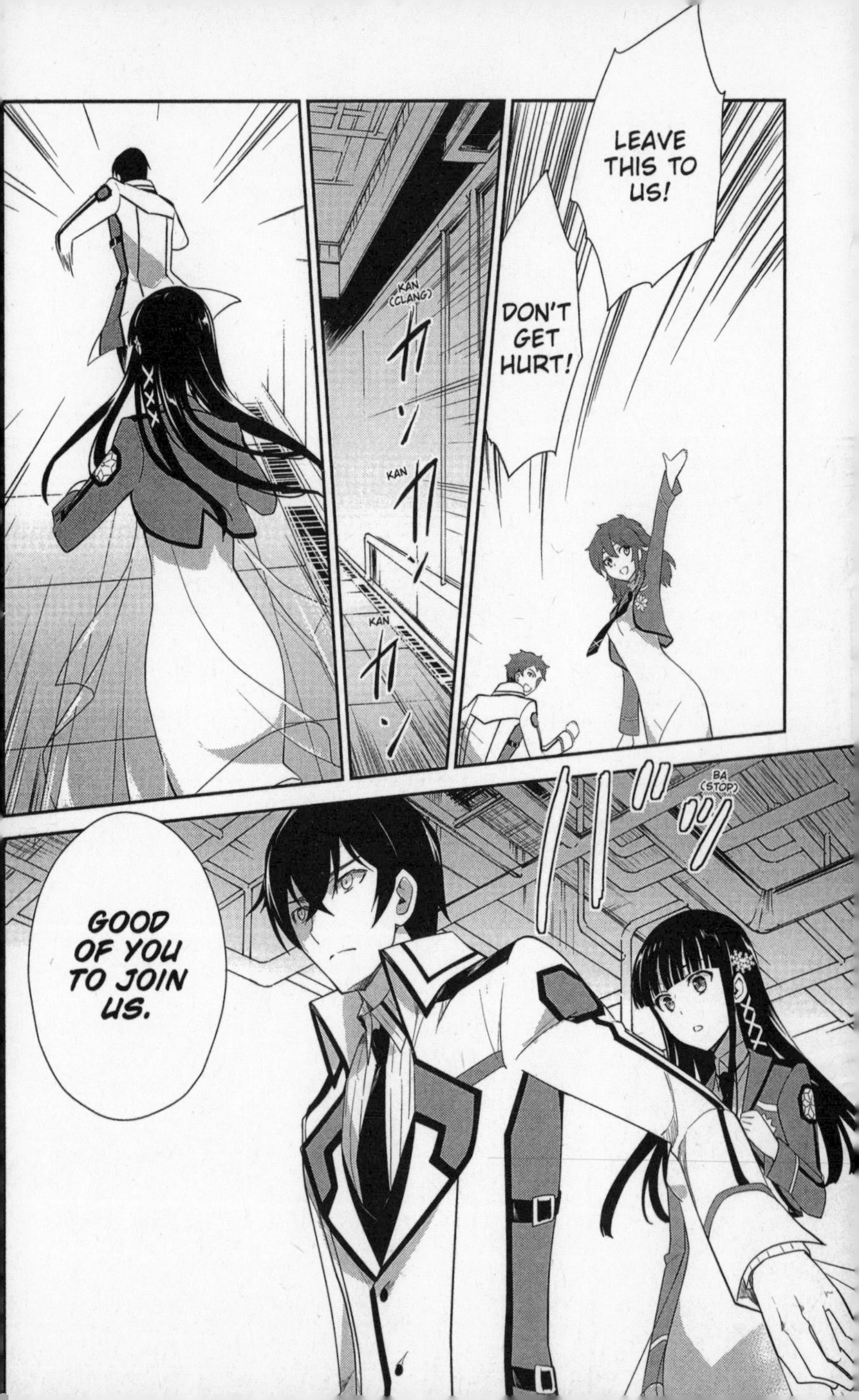
LEAVE THIS TO US!
DON'T GET HURT!
KAN (CLANG)
KAN
KAN
BA (STOP)
GOOD OF YOU TO JOIN US.

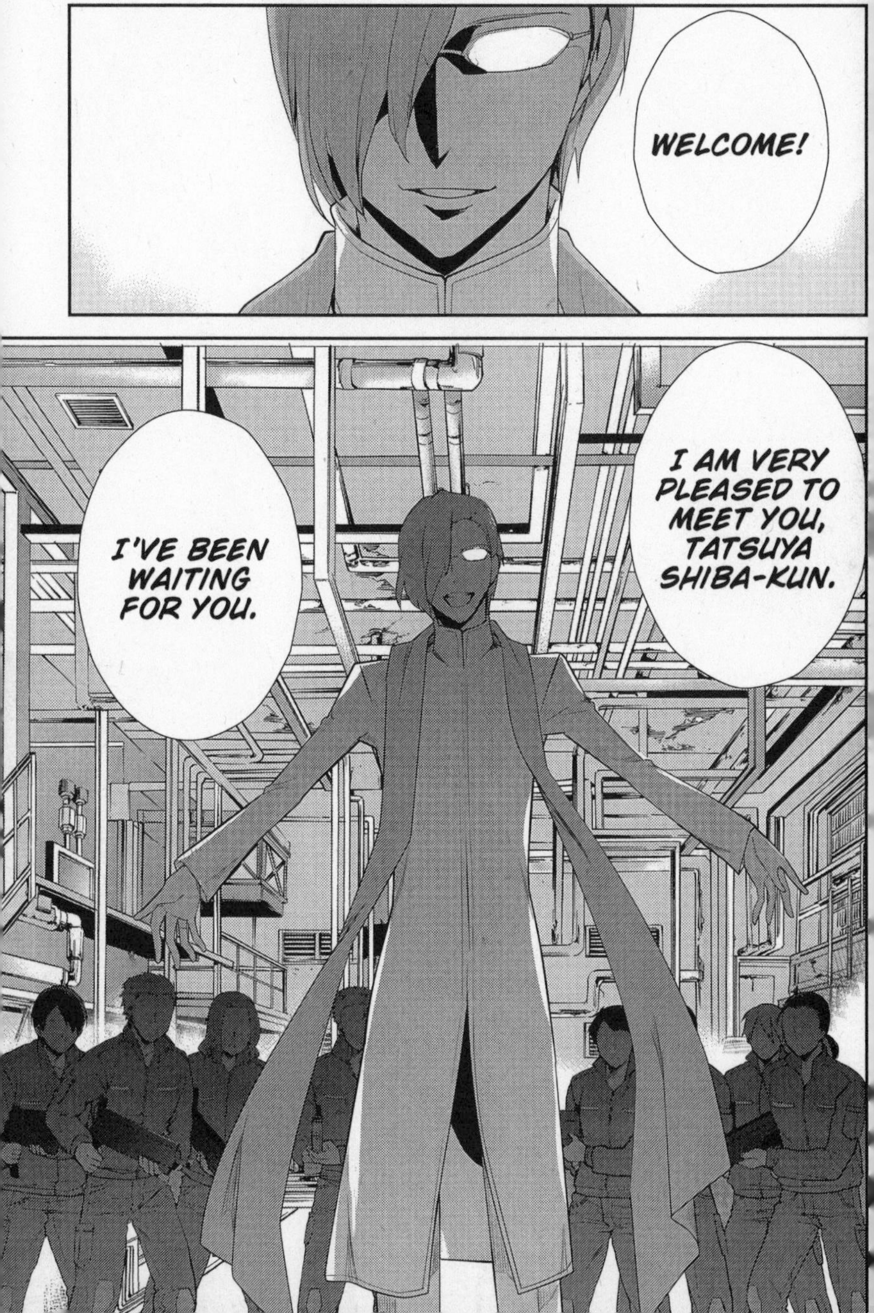
WELCOME!
I AM VERY PLEASED TO MEET YOU, TATSUYA SHIBA-KUN.
I'VE BEEN WAITING FOR YOU.

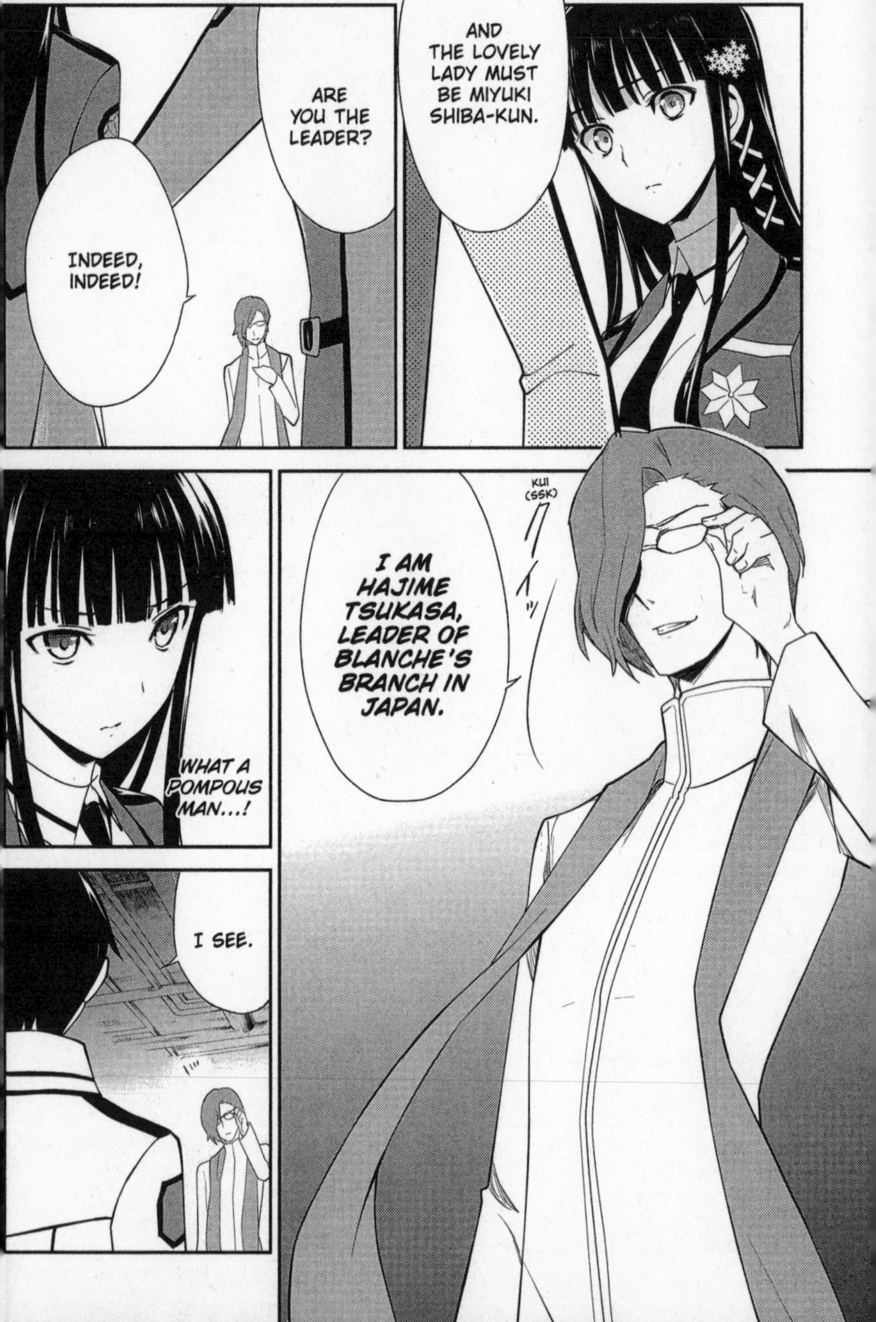
AND THE LOVELY LADY MUST BE MIYUKI SHIBA-KUN.
ARE YOU THE LEADER?
INDEED, INDEED!
KUI (SSK)
I AM HAJIME TSUKASA, LEADER OF BLANCHE'S BRANCH IN JAPAN.
WHAT A POMPOUS MAN...!
I SEE.

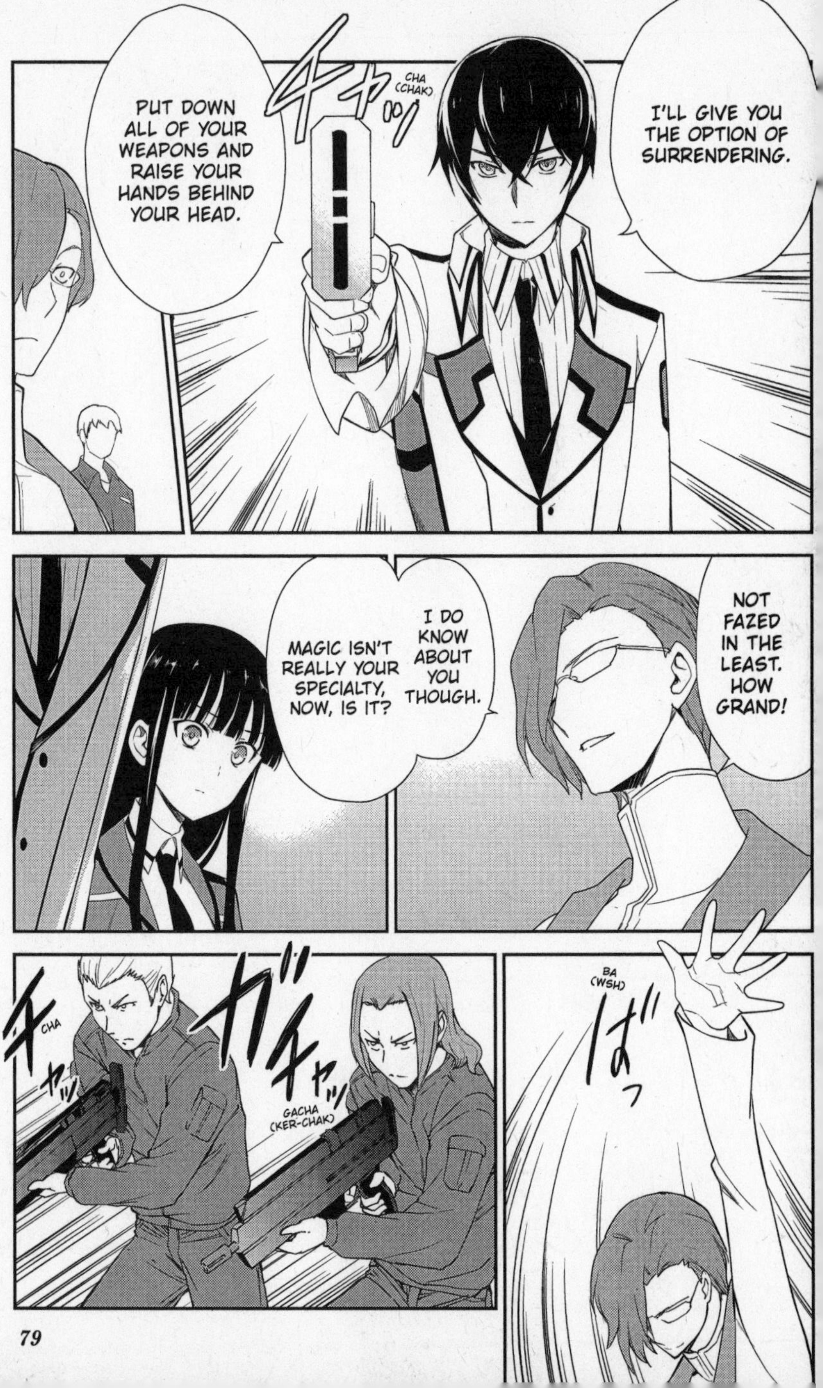
I'LL GIVE YOU THE OPTION OF SURRENDERING.
CHA (CHAK)
PUT DOWN ALL OF YOUR WEAPONS AND RAISE YOUR HANDS BEHIND YOUR HEAD.
NOT FAZED IN THE LEAST. HOW GRAND!
I DO KNOW ABOUT YOU THOUGH.
MAGIC ISN'T REALLY YOUR SPECIALTY, NOW, IS IT?
BA (WSH)
GACHA (KER-CHAK)
CHA

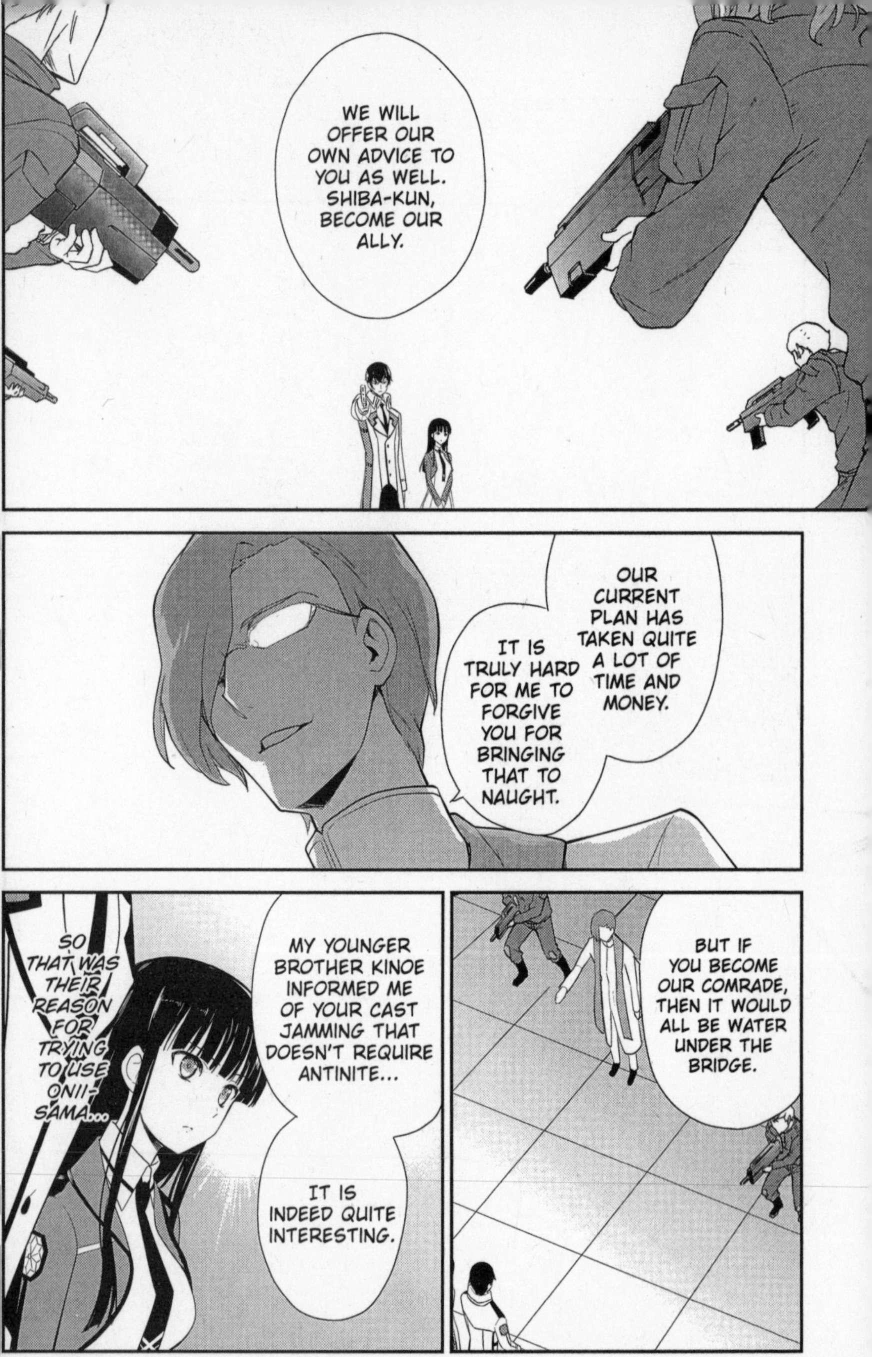
WE WILL OFFER OUR OWN ADVICE TO YOU AS WELL. SHIBA-KUN, BECOME OUR ALLY.
OUR CURRENT PLAN HAS TAKEN QUITE A LOT OF TIME AND MONEY.
IT IS TRULY HARD FOR ME TO FORGIVE YOU FOR BRINGING THAT TO NAUGHT.
BUT IF YOU BECOME OUR COMRADE, THEN IT WOULD ALL BE WATER UNDER THE BRIDGE.
MY YOUNGER BROTHER KINOE INFORMED ME OF YOUR CAST JAMMING THAT DOESN'T REQUIRE ANTINITE...
SO THAT WAS THEIR REASON FOR TRYING TO USE ONII-SAMA...
IT IS INDEED QUITE INTERESTING.

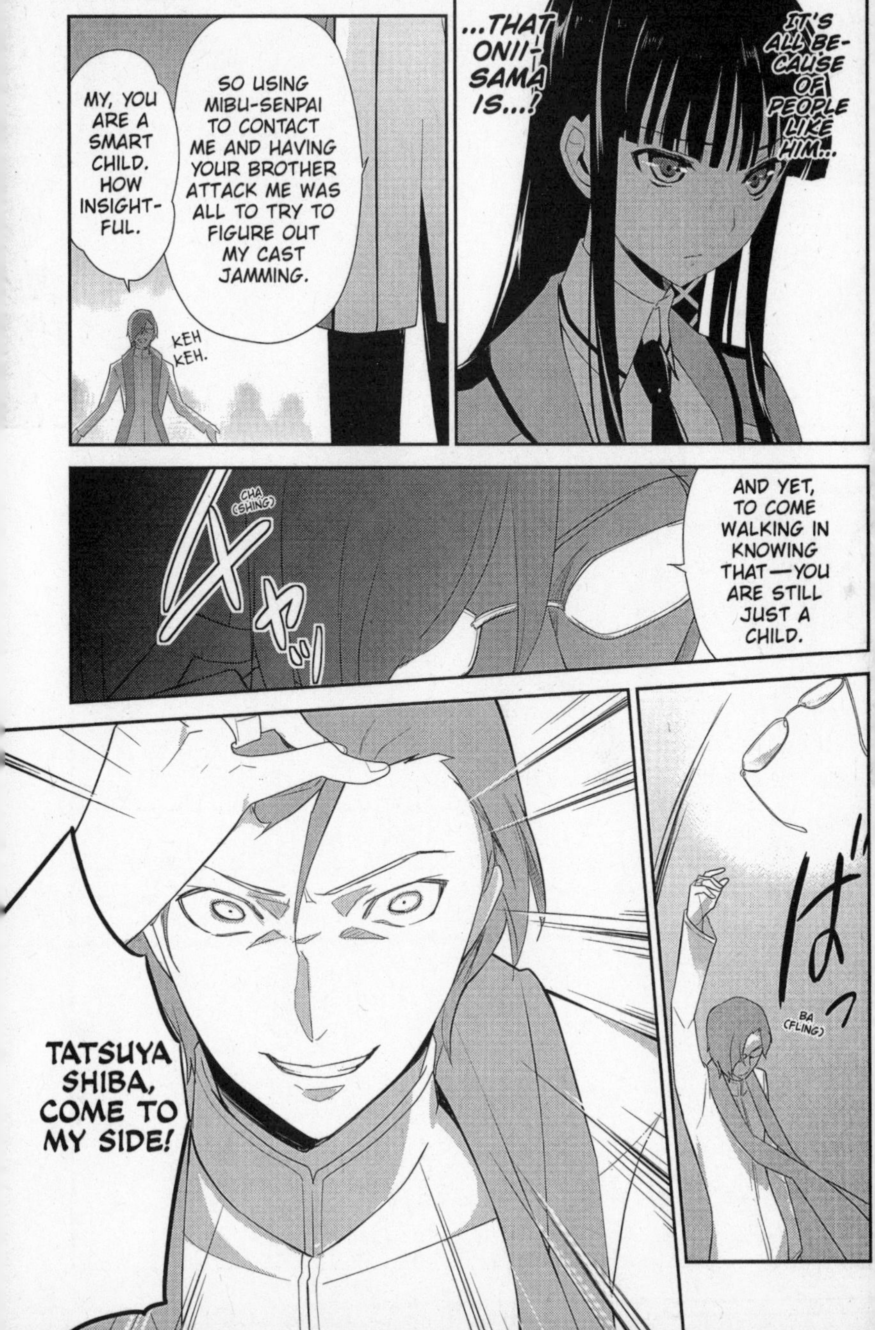
IT'S ALL BE-CAUSE OF PEOPLE LIKE HIM...
...THAT ONII-SAMA IS...!
SO USING MIBU-SENPAI TO CONTACT ME AND HAVING YOUR BROTHER ATTACK ME WAS ALL TO TRY TO FIGURE OUT MY CAST JAMMING.
MY, YOU ARE A SMART CHILD. HOW INSIGHT-FUL.
KEH KEH.
AND YET, TO COME WALKING IN KNOWING THAT—YOU ARE STILL JUST A CHILD.
CHA (SHING)
BA (FLING)
TATSUYA SHIBA, COME TO MY SIDE!

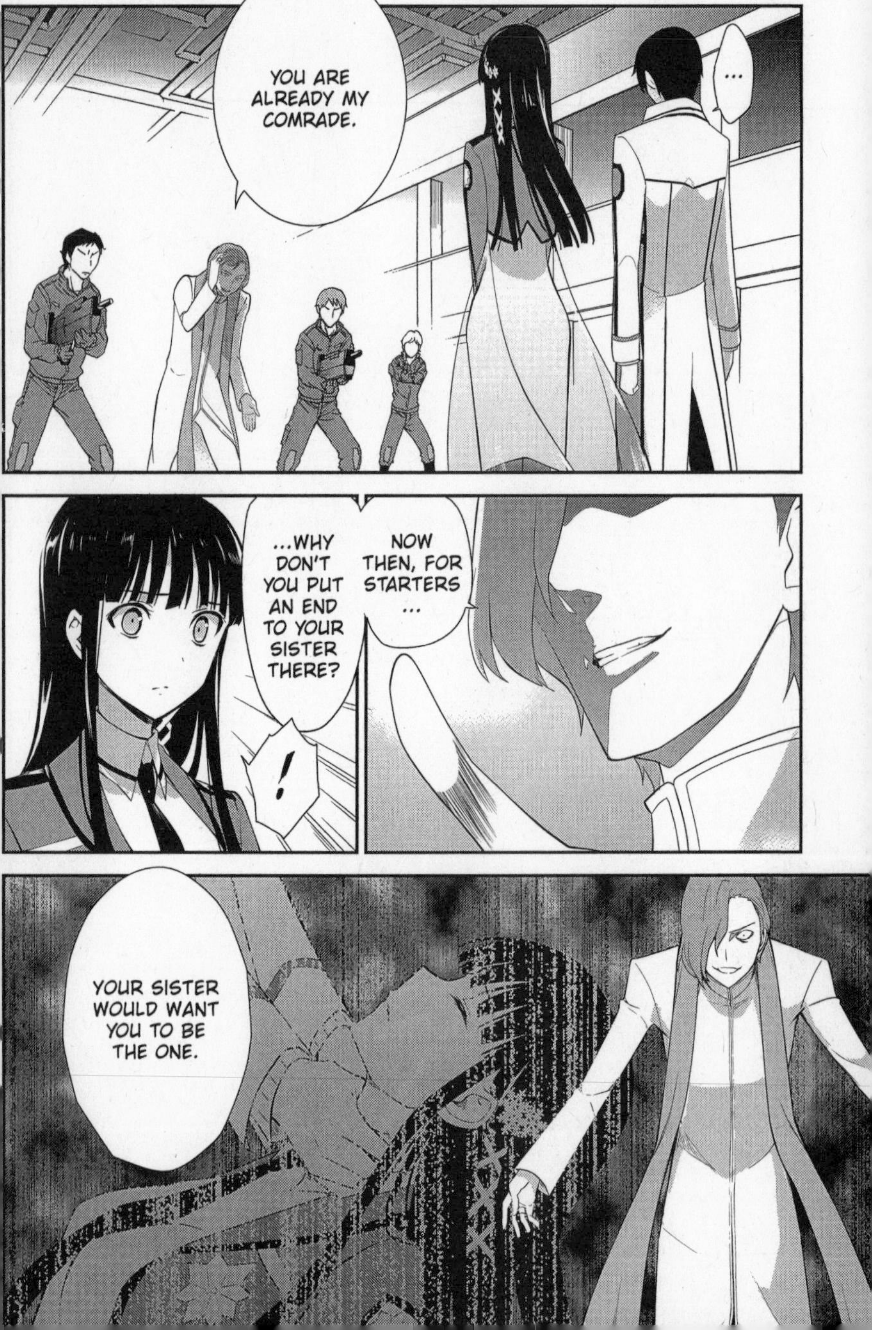
...
YOU ARE ALREADY MY COMRADE.
NOW THEN, FOR STARTERS ...
...WHY DON'T YOU PUT AN END TO YOUR SISTER THERE?
!
YOUR SISTER WOULD WANT YOU TO BE THE ONE.

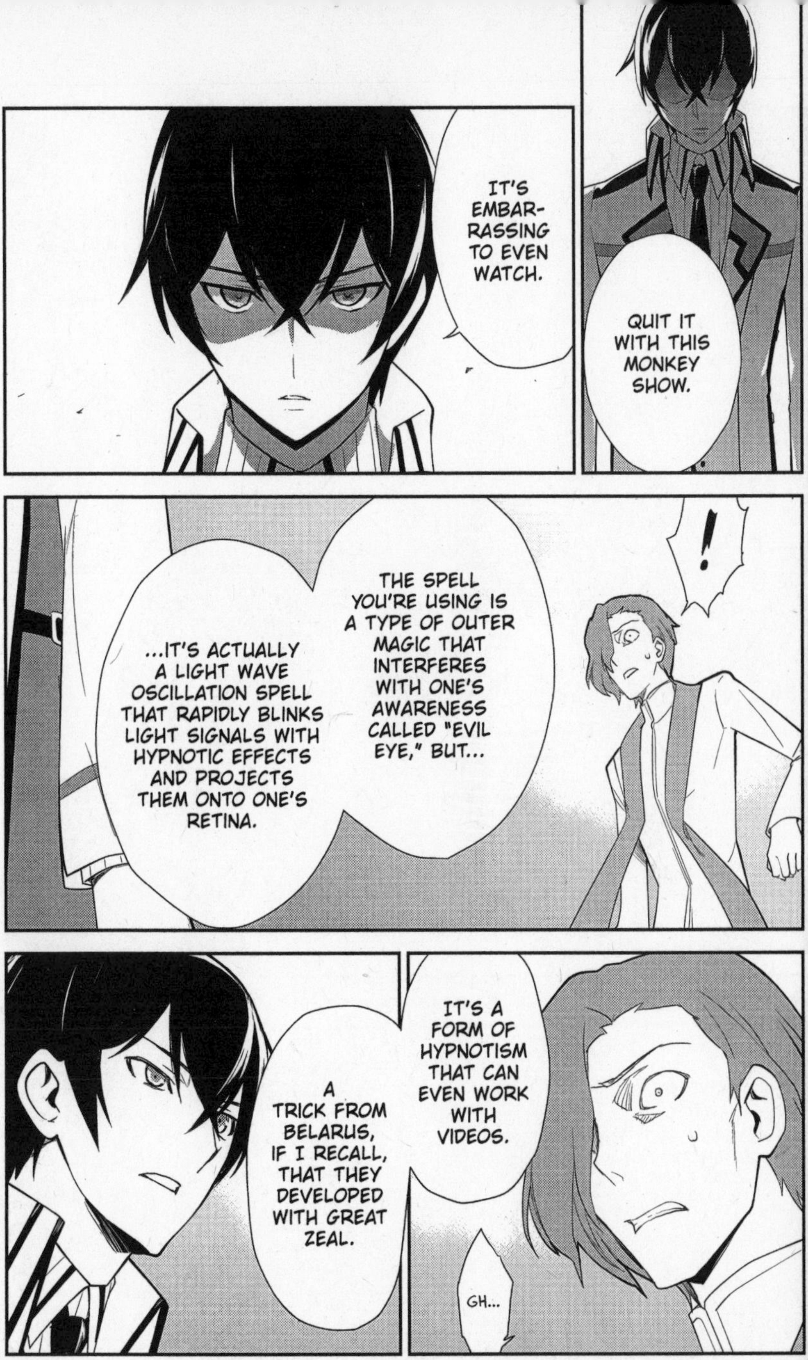
QUIT IT WITH THIS MONKEY SHOW.
IT'S EMBAR-RASSING TO EVEN WATCH.
!
THE SPELL YOU'RE USING IS A TYPE OF OUTER MAGIC THAT INTERFERES WITH ONE'S AWARENESS CALLED "EVIL EYE," BUT...
...IT'S ACTUALLY A LIGHT WAVE OSCILLATION SPELL THAT RAPIDLY BLINKS LIGHT SIGNALS WITH HYPNOTIC EFFECTS AND PROJECTS THEM ONTO ONE'S RETINA.
IT'S A FORM OF HYPNOTISM THAT CAN EVEN WORK WITH VIDEOS.
GH...
A TRICK FROM BELARUS, IF I RECALL, THAT THEY DEVELOPED WITH GREAT ZEAL.

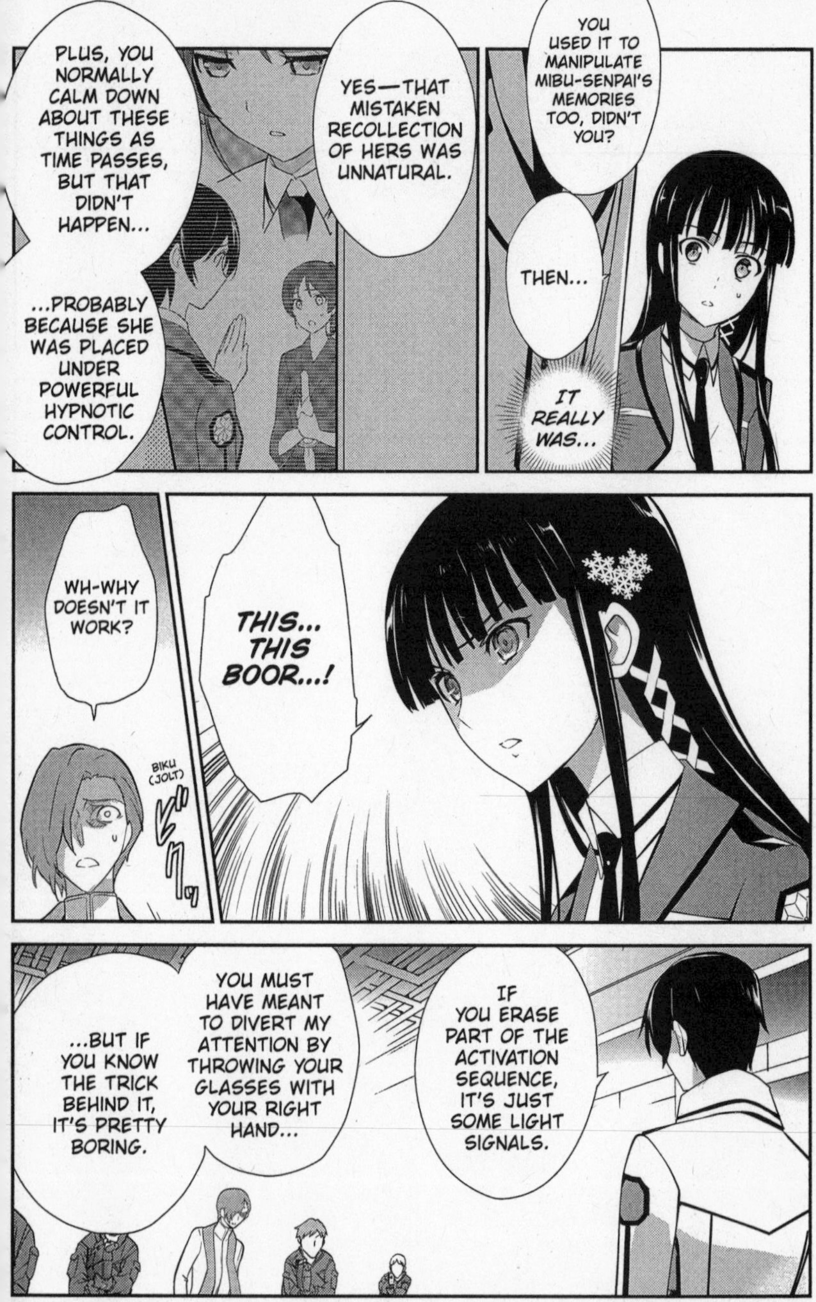
YOU USED IT TO MANIPULATE MIBU-SENPAI'S MEMORIES TOO, DIDN'T YOU?
THEN...
IT REALLY WAS...
YES—THAT MISTAKEN RECOLLECTION OF HERS WAS UNNATURAL.
PLUS, YOU NORMALLY CALM DOWN ABOUT THESE THINGS AS TIME PASSES, BUT THAT DIDN'T HAPPEN...
...PROBABLY BECAUSE SHE WAS PLACED UNDER POWERFUL HYPNOTIC CONTROL.
THIS... THIS BOOR...!
WH-WHY DOESN'T IT WORK?
BIKU (JOLT)
IF YOU ERASE PART OF THE ACTIVATION SEQUENCE, IT'S JUST SOME LIGHT SIGNALS.
YOU MUST HAVE MEANT TO DIVERT MY ATTENTION BY THROWING YOUR GLASSES WITH YOUR RIGHT HAND...
...BUT IF YOU KNOW THE TRICK BEHIND IT, IT'S PRETTY BORING.

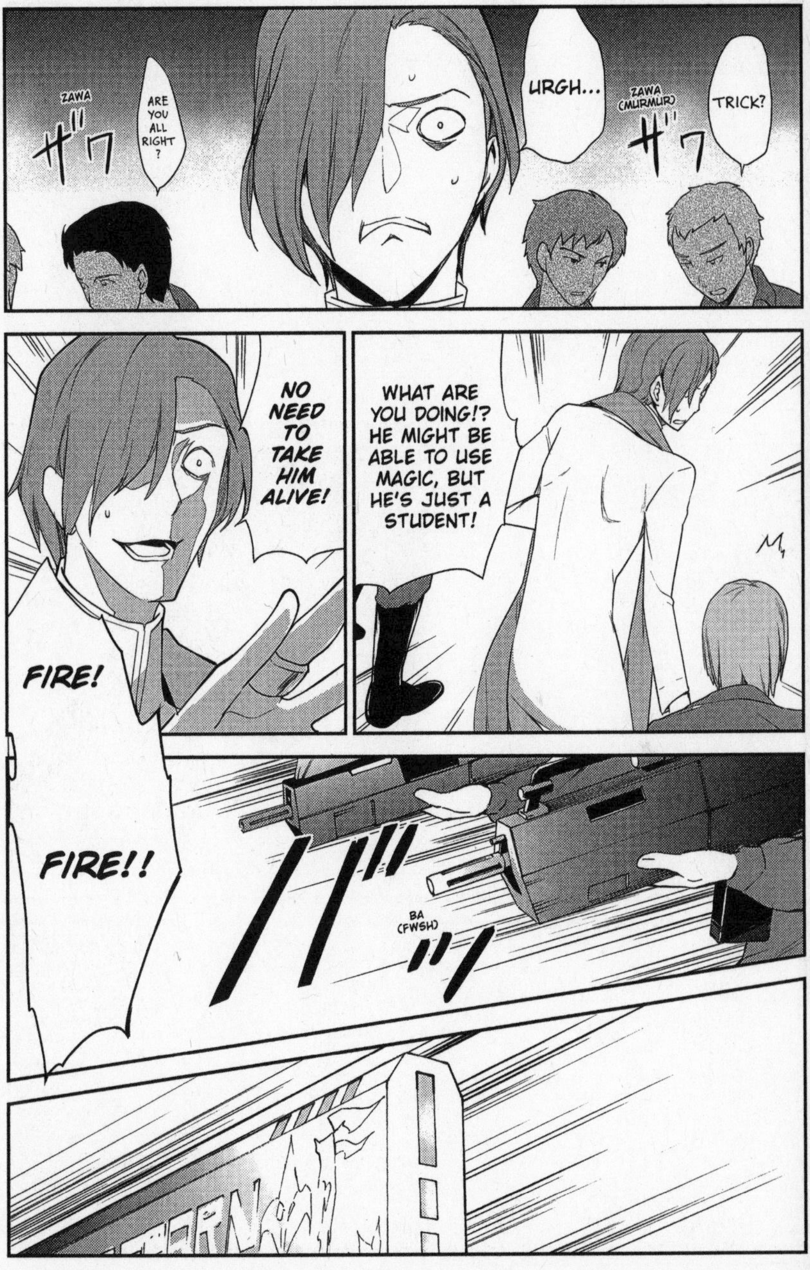
TRICK?
ZAWA (MURMUR)
ザワ
URGH...
ARE YOU ALL RIGHT?
ZAWA
ザワ
WHAT ARE YOU DOING!? HE MIGHT BE ABLE TO USE MAGIC, BUT HE'S JUST A STUDENT!
NO NEED TO TAKE HIM ALIVE!
FIRE!
FIRE!!
BA (FWSH)
バッ

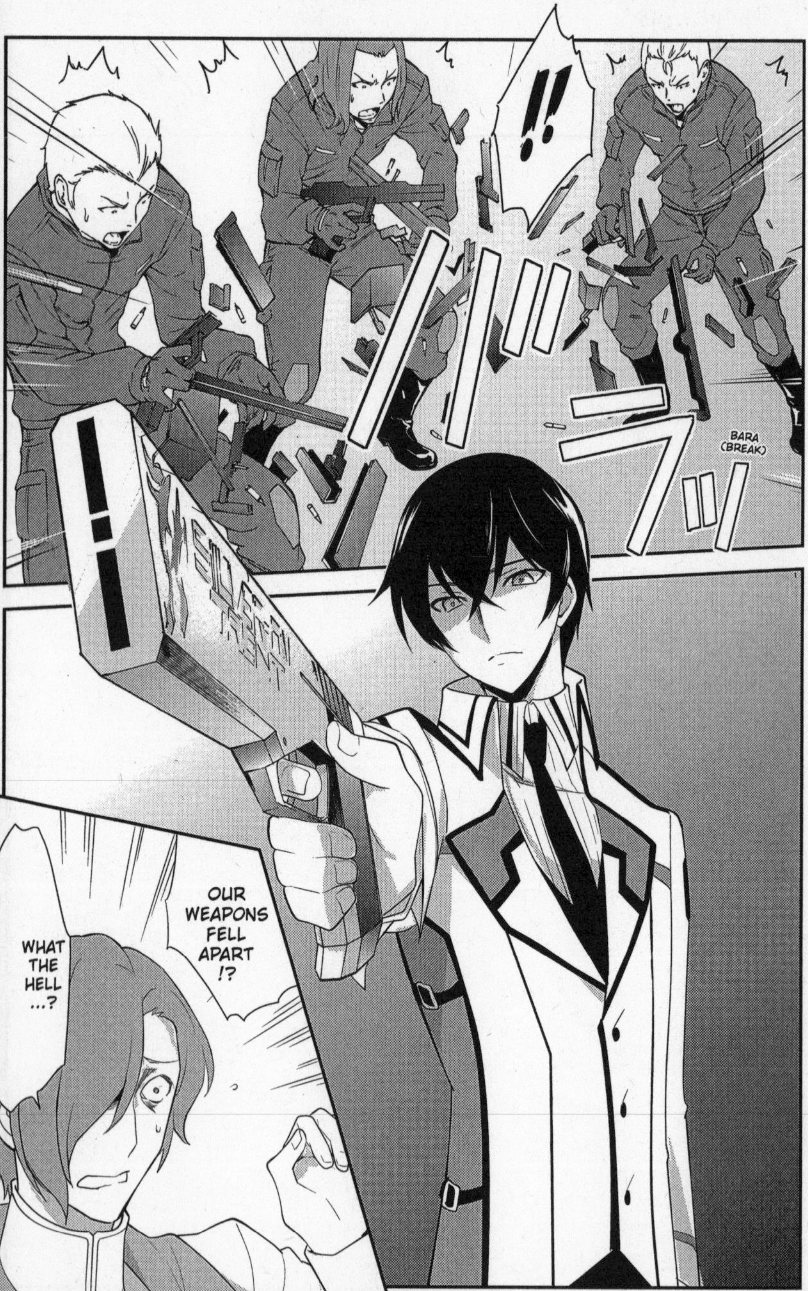
!!
バラッ
BARA (BREAK)
OUR WEAPONS FELL APART !?
WHAT THE HELL ...?

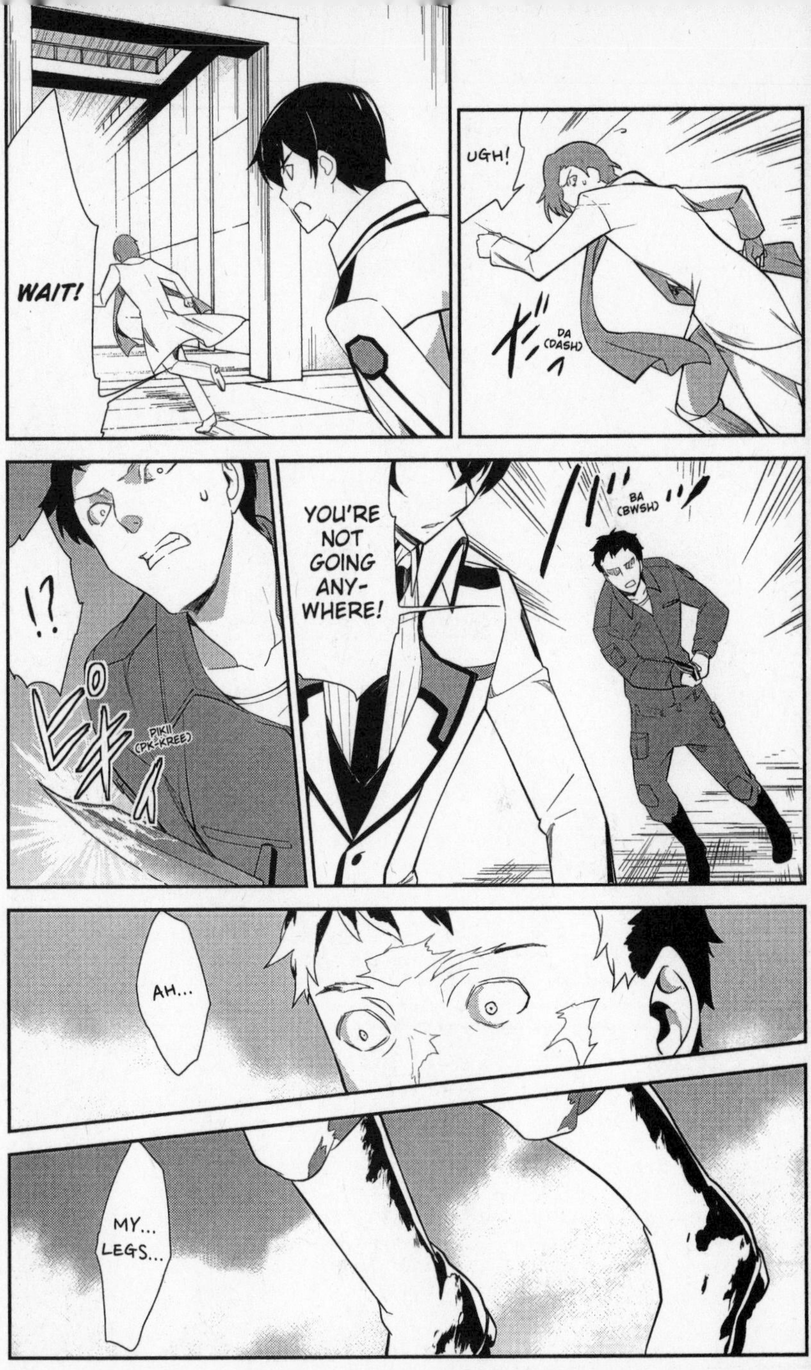
UGH!
DA (DASH)
WAIT!
BA (BWSH)
YOU'RE NOT GOING ANY-WHERE!
!?
PIKII (PK-KREE)
AH...
MY... LEGS...

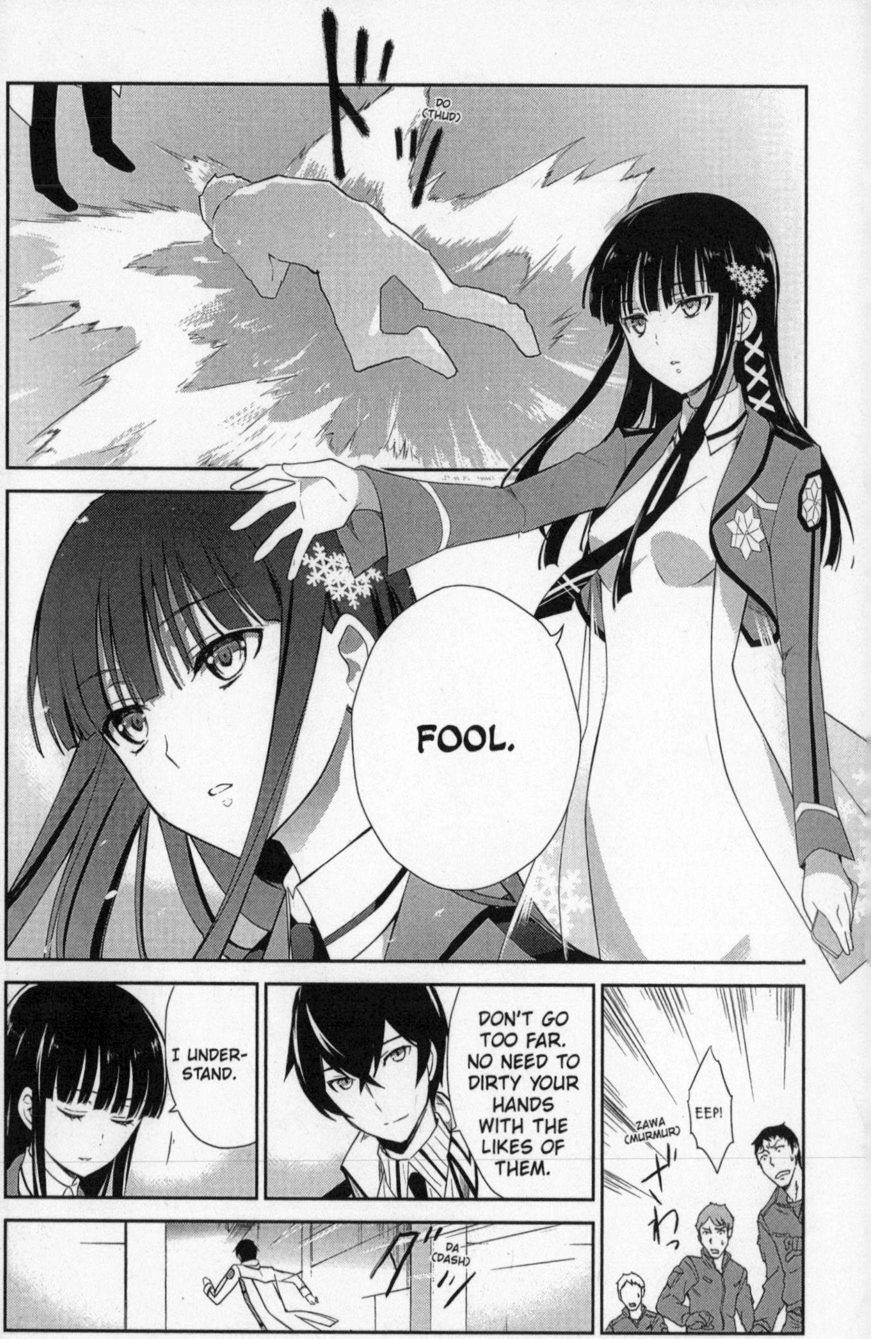
DO (THUD)
FOOL.
EEP!
ZAWA (MURMUR)
DON'T GO TOO FAR. NO NEED TO DIRTY YOUR HANDS WITH THE LIKES OF THEM.
I UNDER-STAND.
DA (DASH)

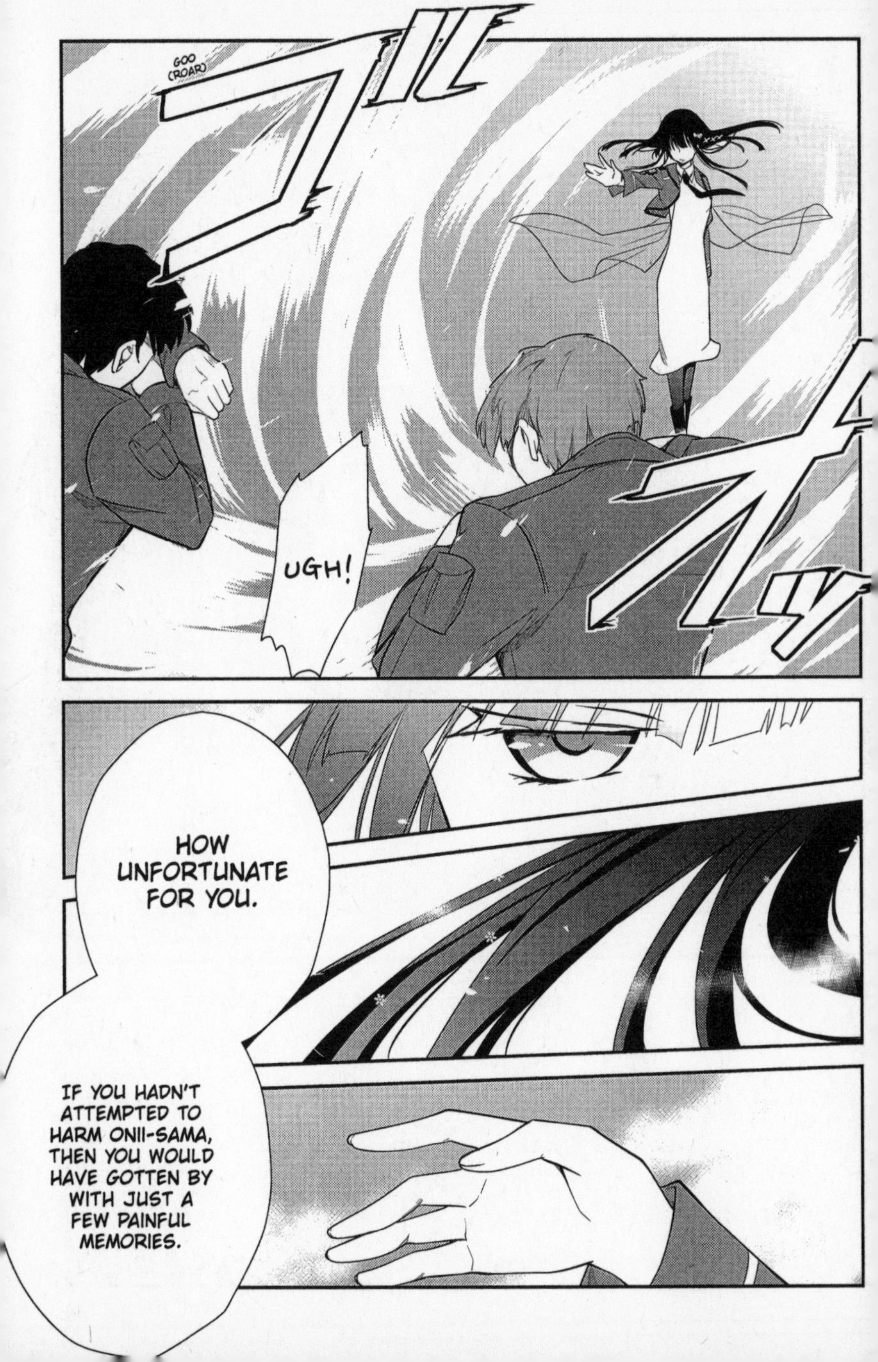
GOO (ROAR)
UGH!
HOW UNFORTUNATE FOR YOU.
IF YOU HADN'T ATTEMPTED TO HARM ONII-SAMA, THEN YOU WOULD HAVE GOTTEN BY WITH JUST A FEW PAINFUL MEMORIES.

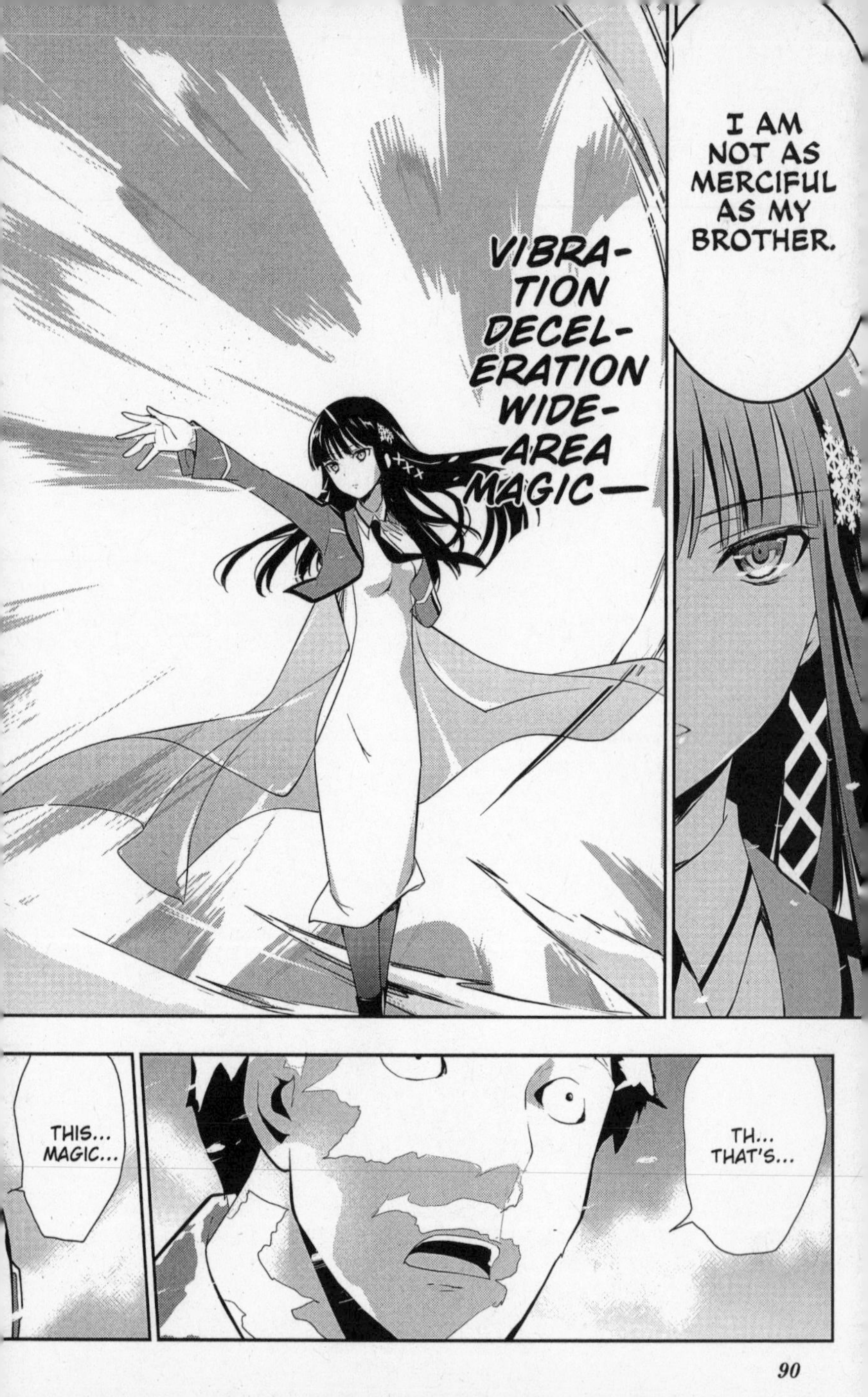
I AM NOT AS MERCIFUL AS MY BROTHER.
VIBRATION DECELERATION WIDE-AREA MAGIC—
TH... THAT'S...
THIS... MAGIC...

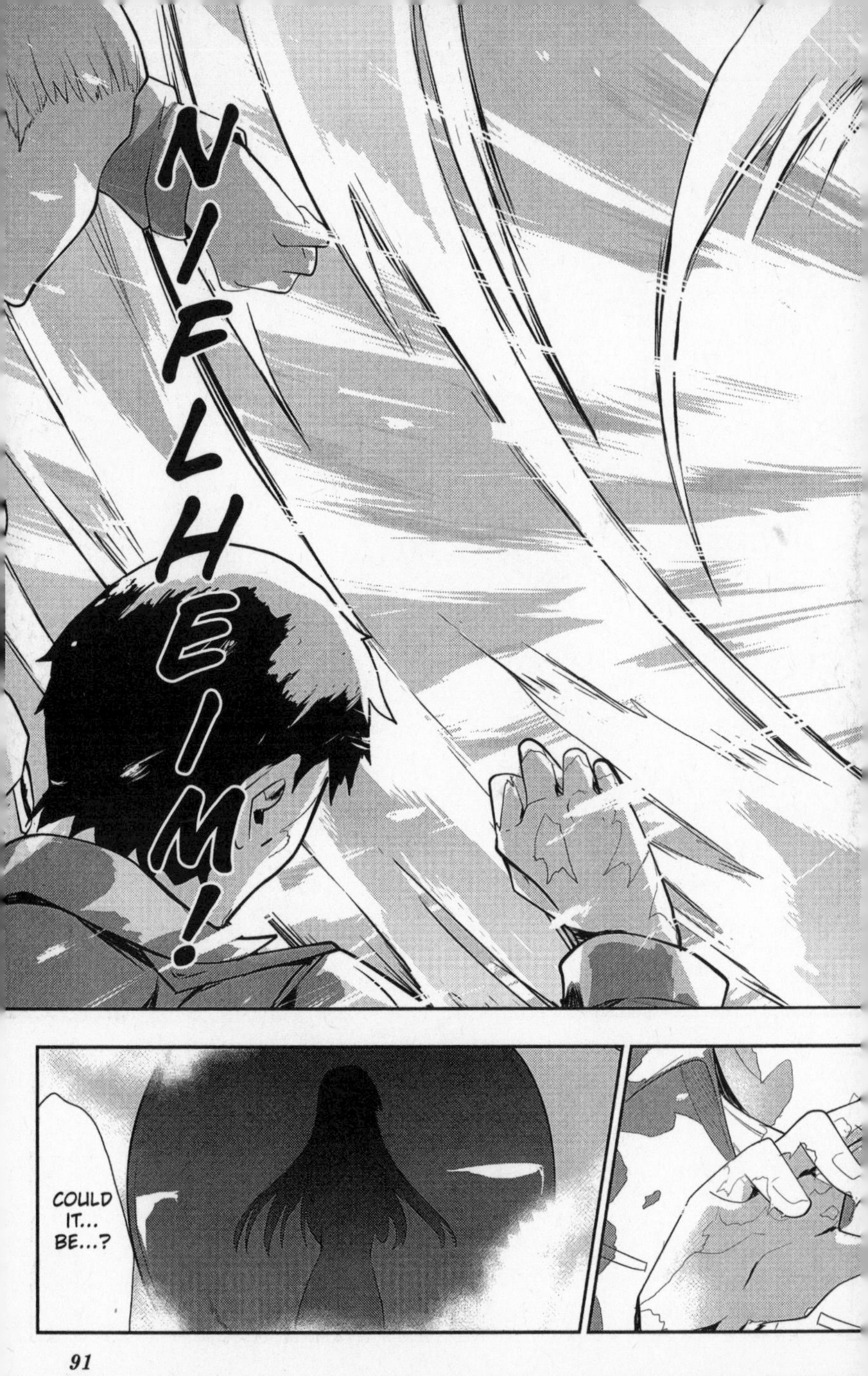
NIFLHEIM!
COULD IT... BE...?

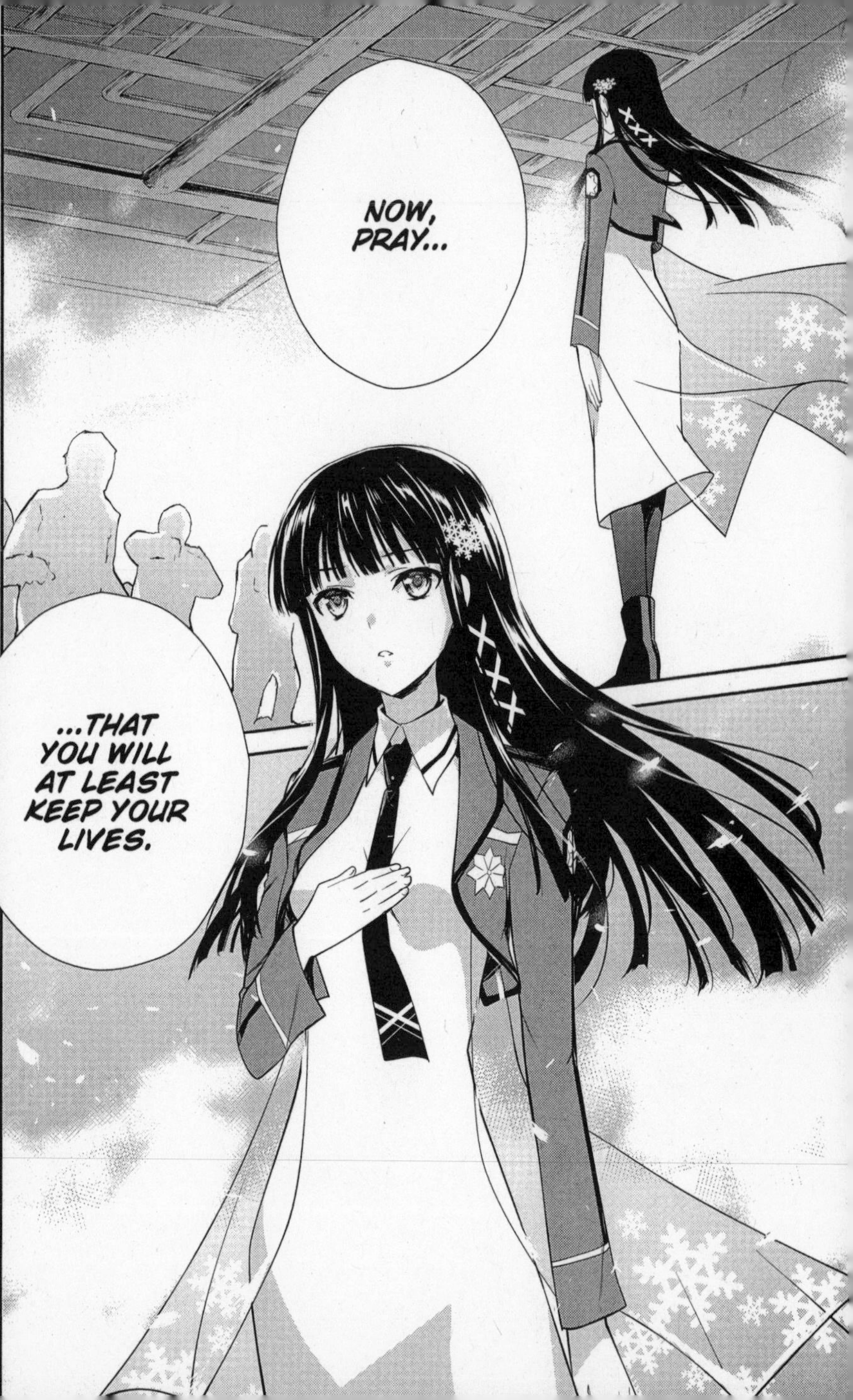
NOW, PRAY...
...THAT YOU WILL AT LEAST KEEP YOUR LIVES.

THE HONOR STUDENT AT MAGIC HIGH SCHOOL

CHAPTER 22

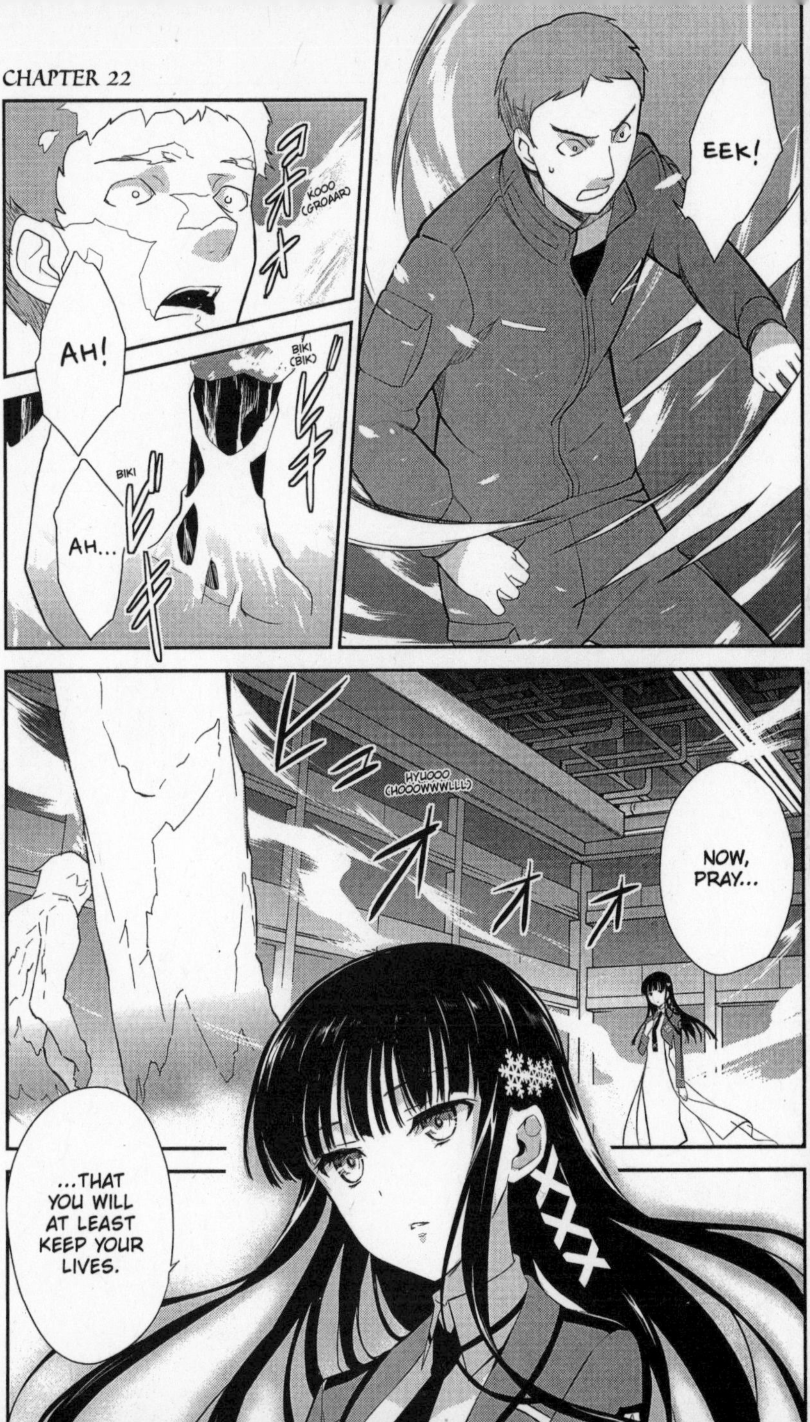
EEK!
KOOO (GROAAR)
AH!
BIKI (BIK)
BIKI
AH...
HYUOOO (HOOOWWWLLL)
NOW, PRAY...
...THAT YOU WILL AT LEAST KEEP YOUR LIVES.

CHAPTER 22

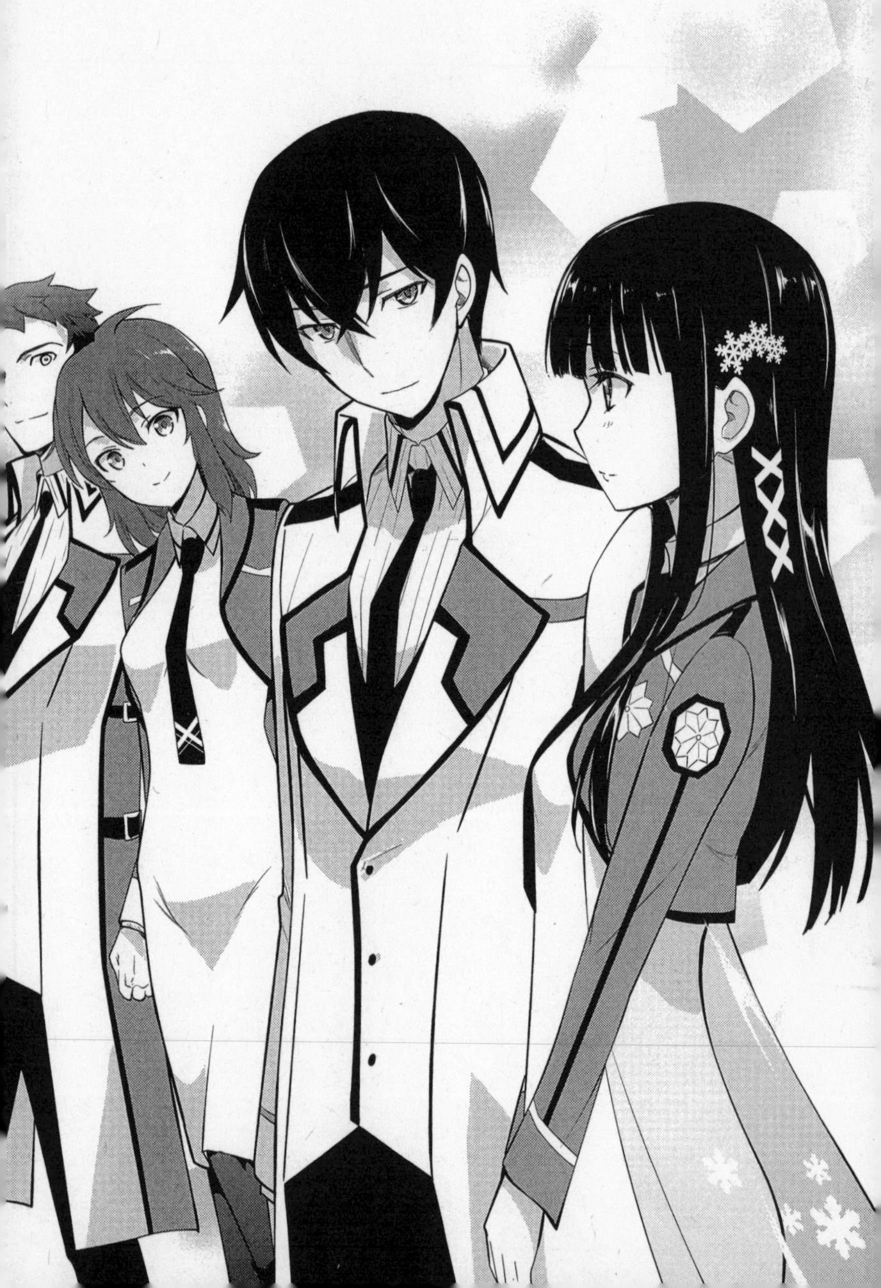

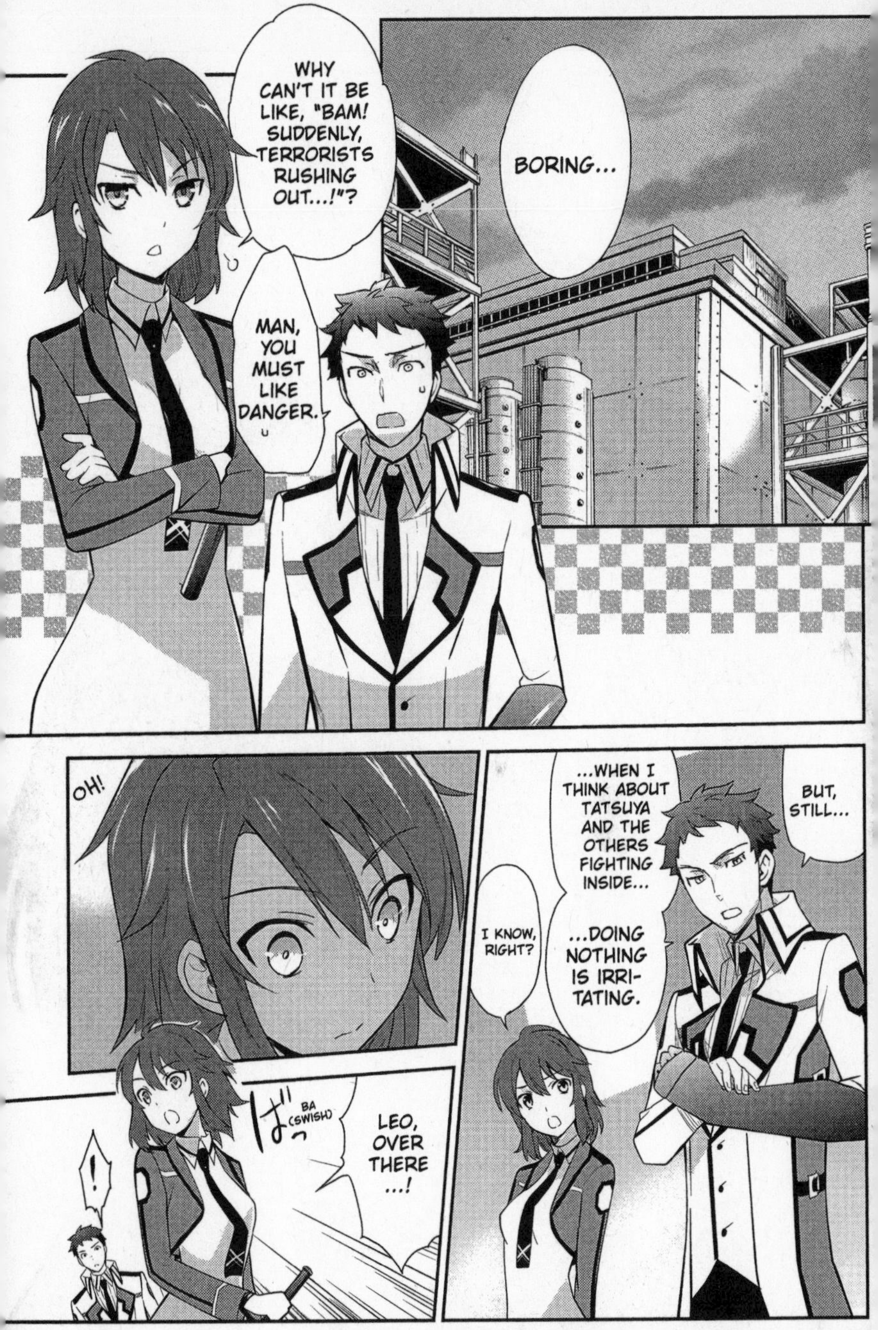
BORING...
WHY CAN'T IT BE LIKE, "BAM! SUDDENLY, TERRORISTS RUSHING OUT...!"?
MAN, YOU MUST LIKE DANGER.
BUT, STILL...
...WHEN I THINK ABOUT TATSUYA AND THE OTHERS FIGHTING INSIDE...
...DOING NOTHING IS IRRITATING.
I KNOW, RIGHT?
OH!
LEO, OVER THERE...!
ば
BA (SWISH)
!

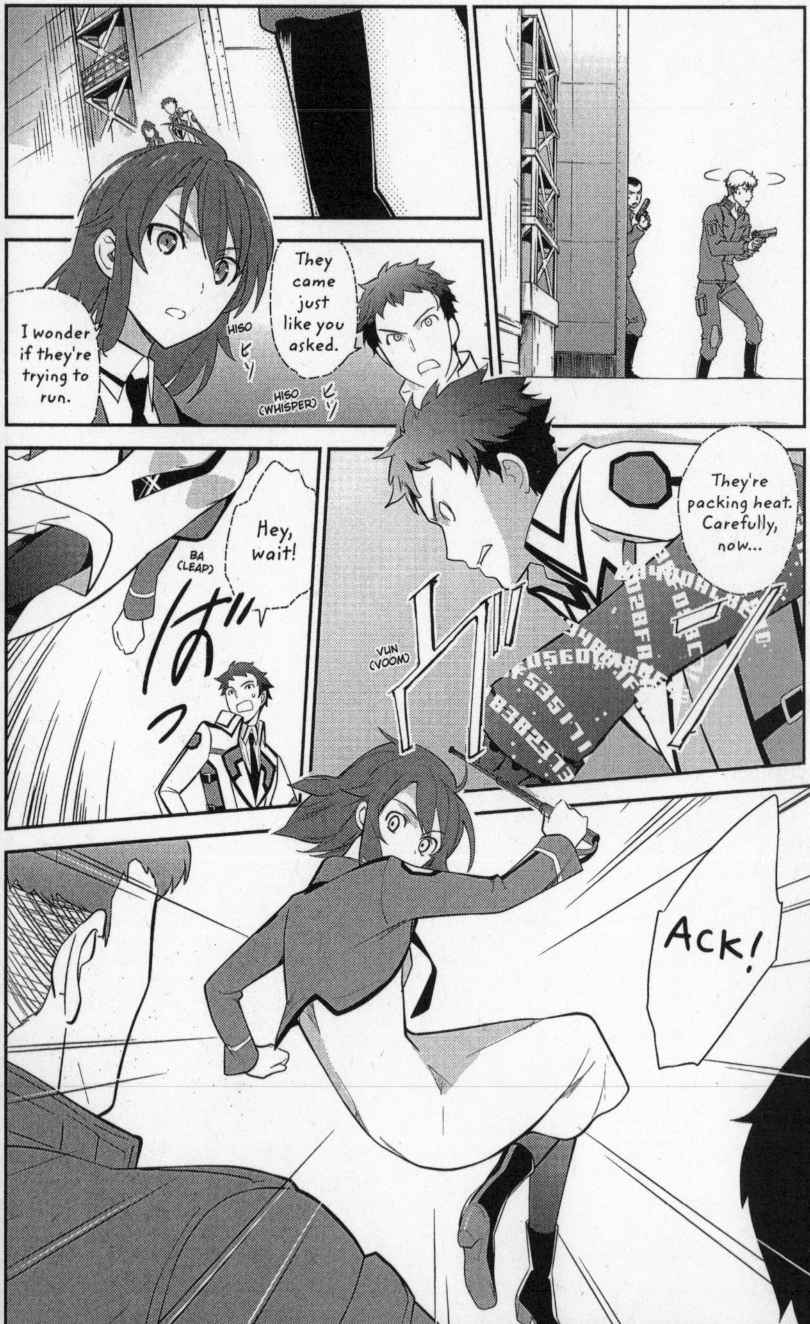
They came just like you asked.
HISO
HISO (WHISPER)
I wonder if they're trying to run.
They're packing heat. Carefully, now...
VUN (VOOM)
Hey, wait!
BA (LEAP)
Ack!

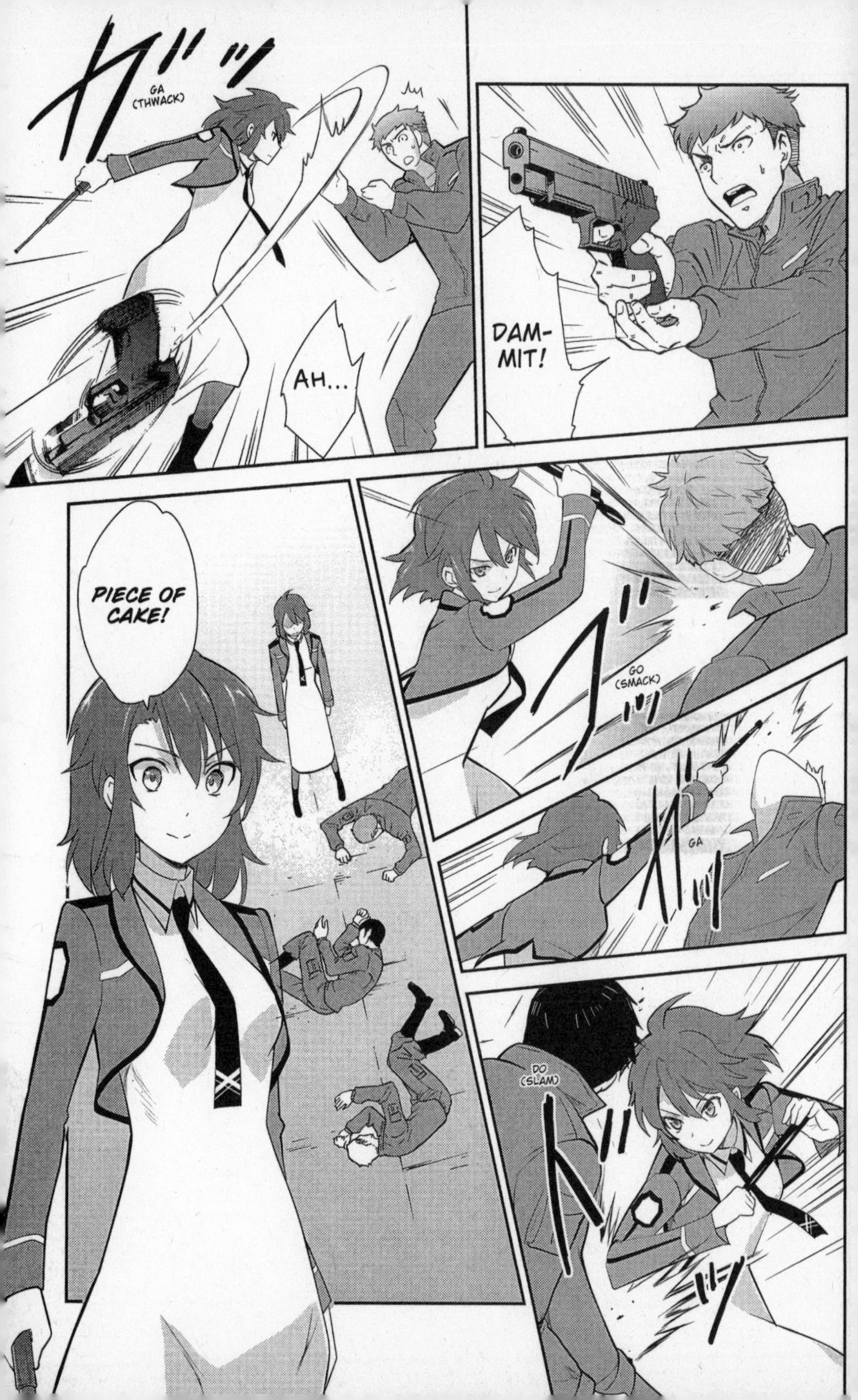
DAM-
MIT!
GA
(THWACK)
AH...
GO
(SMACK)
GA
DO
(SLAM)
PIECE OF
CAKE!

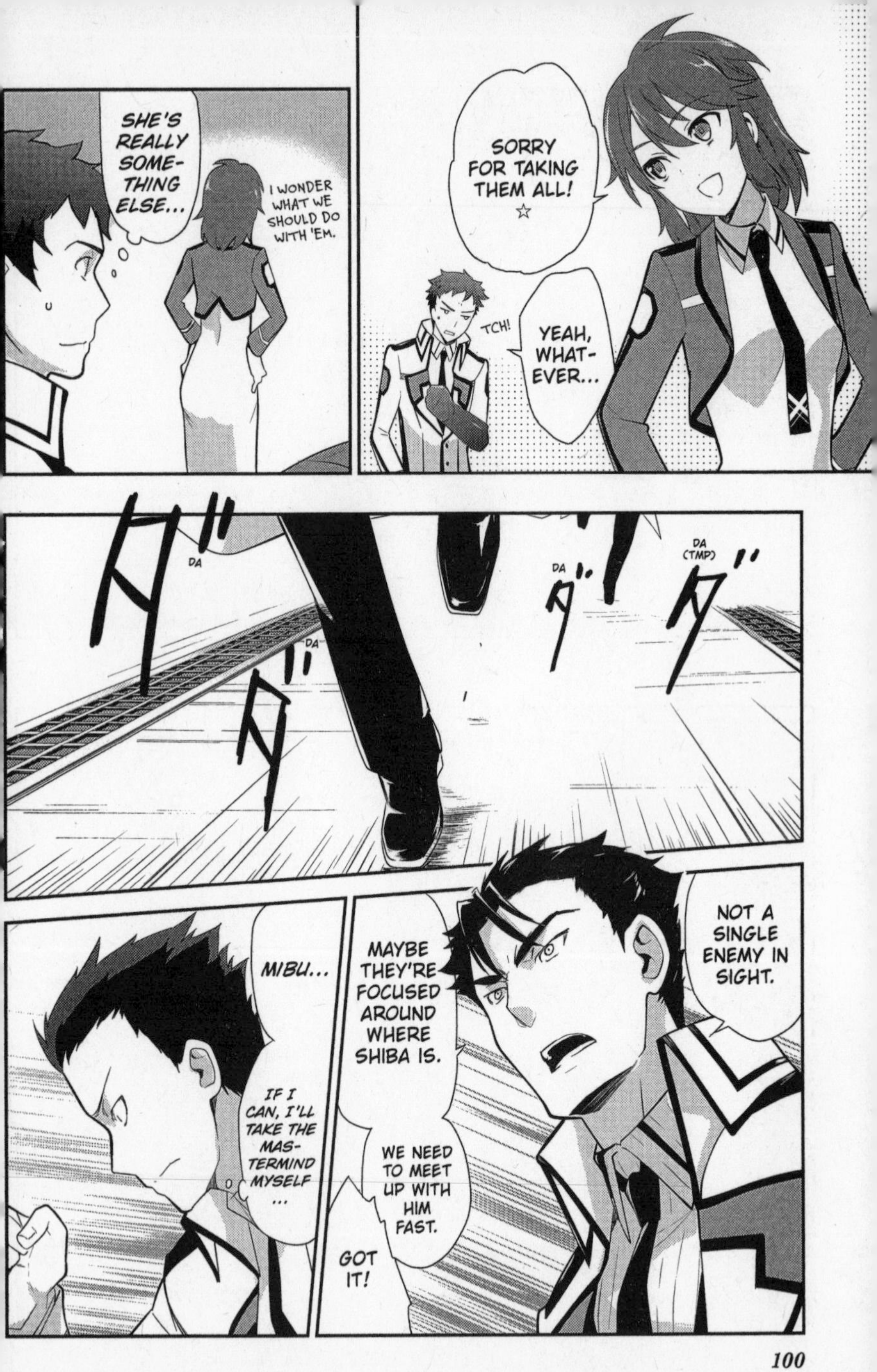
SORRY FOR TAKING THEM ALL! ☆
TCH!
YEAH, WHATEVER...
SHE'S REALLY SOMETHING ELSE...
I WONDER WHAT WE SHOULD DO WITH 'EM.
DA (TMP)
DA
DA
DA
NOT A SINGLE ENEMY IN SIGHT.
MAYBE THEY'RE FOCUSED AROUND WHERE SHIBA IS.
WE NEED TO MEET UP WITH HIM FAST.
GOT IT!
MIBU...
IF I CAN, I'LL TAKE THE MASTERMIND MYSELF...

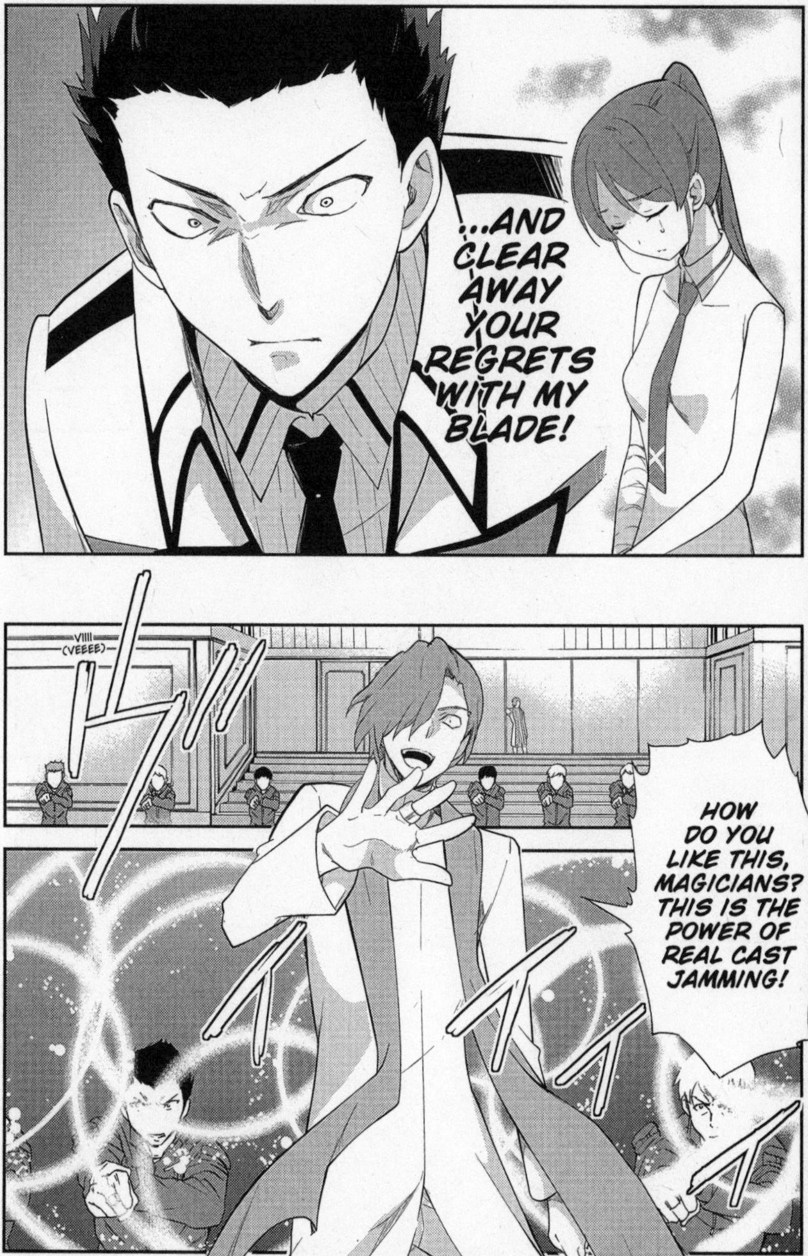
...AND CLEAR AWAY YOUR REGRETS WITH MY BLADE!
VIIII (VEEEE)
HOW DO YOU LIKE THIS, MAGICIANS? THIS IS THE POWER OF REAL CAST JAMMING!

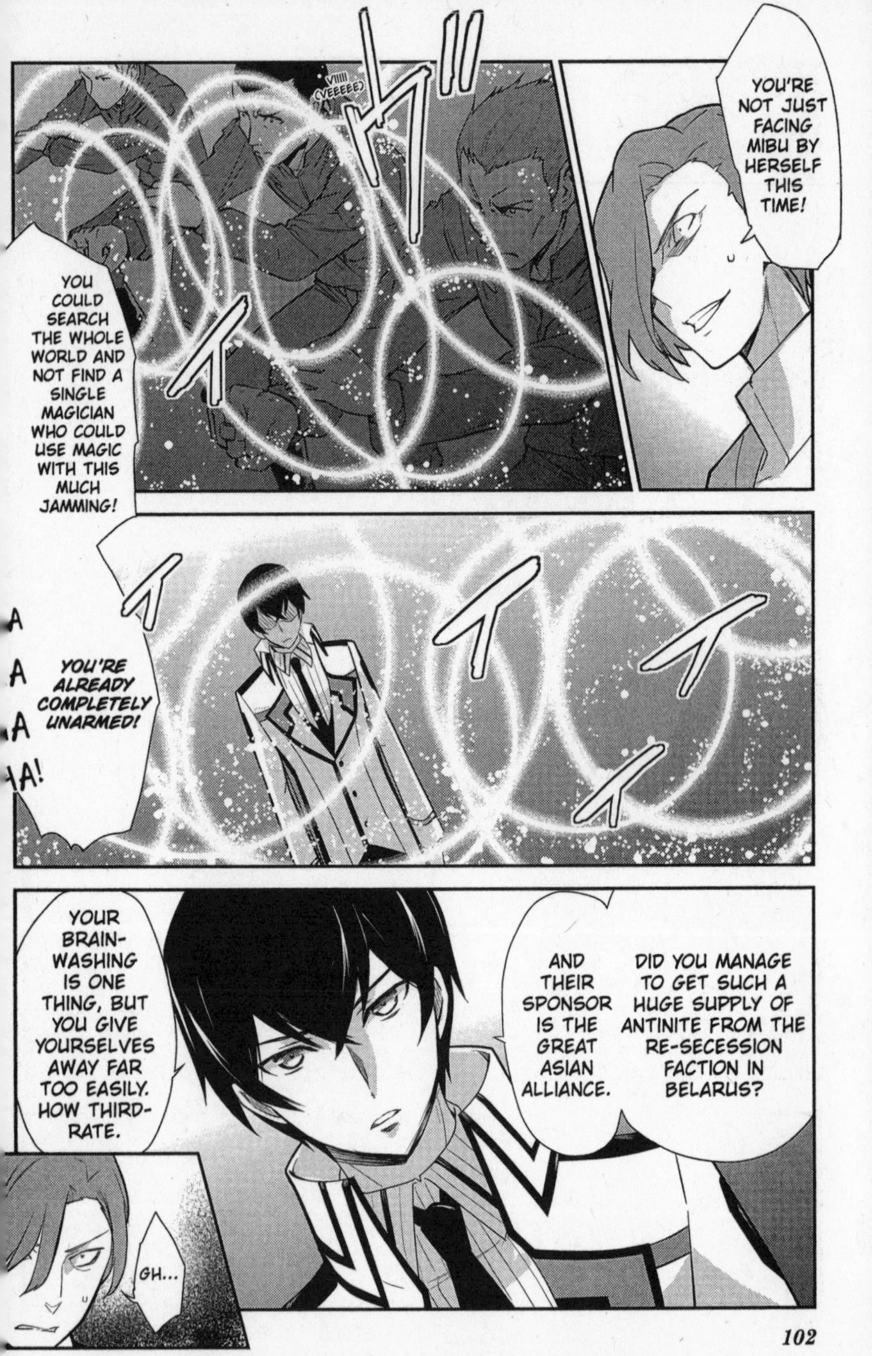
YOU'RE NOT JUST FACING MIBU BY HERSELF THIS TIME!
VIIII (VEEEEE)
YOU COULD SEARCH THE WHOLE WORLD AND NOT FIND A SINGLE MAGICIAN WHO COULD USE MAGIC WITH THIS MUCH JAMMING!
YOU'RE ALREADY COMPLETELY UNARMED!
A A A HA!
DID YOU MANAGE TO GET SUCH A HUGE SUPPLY OF ANTINITE FROM THE RE-SECESSION FACTION IN BELARUS?
AND THEIR SPONSOR IS THE GREAT ASIAN ALLIANCE.
YOUR BRAIN-WASHING IS ONE THING, BUT YOU GIVE YOURSELVES AWAY FAR TOO EASILY. HOW THIRD-RATE.
GH...

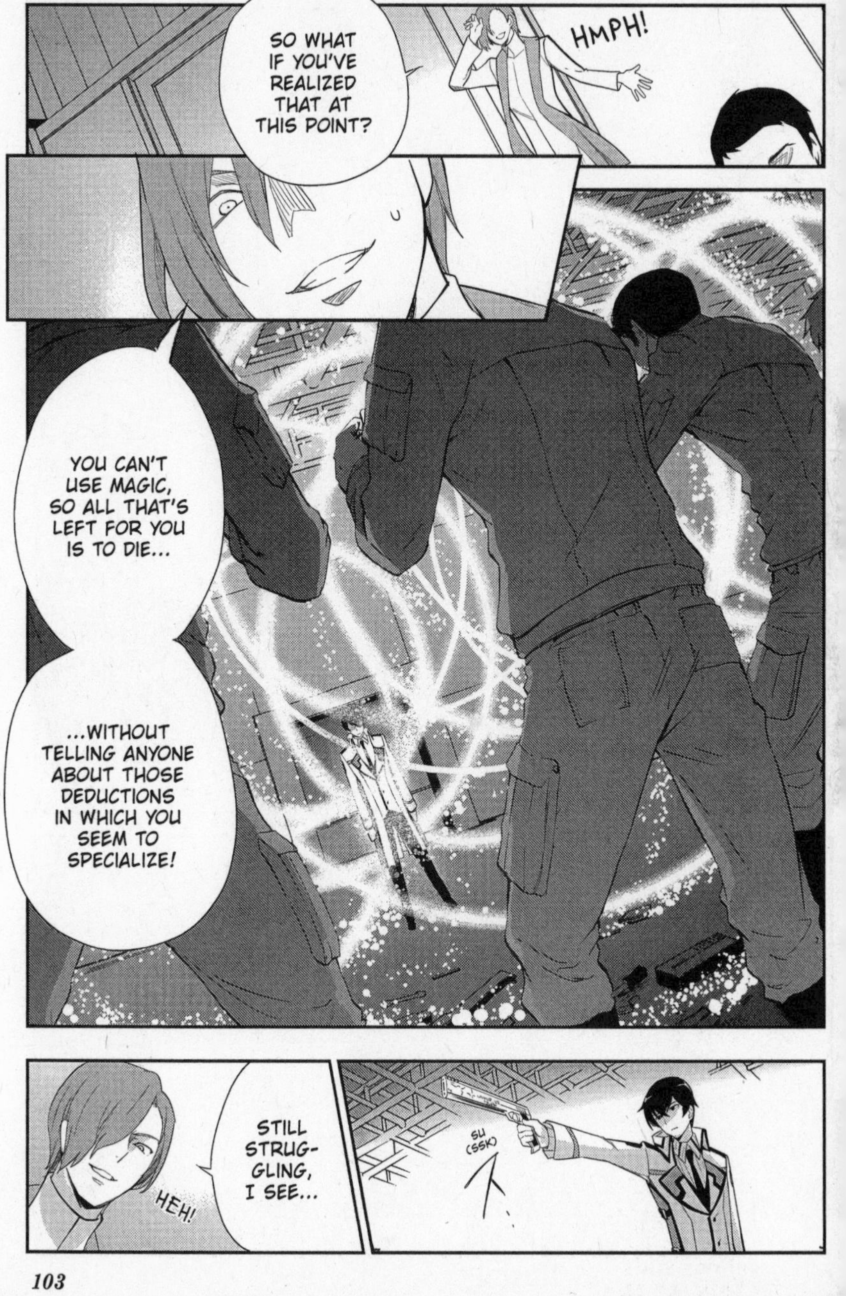
SO WHAT IF YOU'VE REALIZED THAT AT THIS POINT?
HMPH!
YOU CAN'T USE MAGIC, SO ALL THAT'S LEFT FOR YOU IS TO DIE...
...WITHOUT TELLING ANYONE ABOUT THOSE DEDUCTIONS IN WHICH YOU SEEM TO SPECIALIZE!
HEH!
STILL STRUG-GLING, I SEE...
SU (SSK)

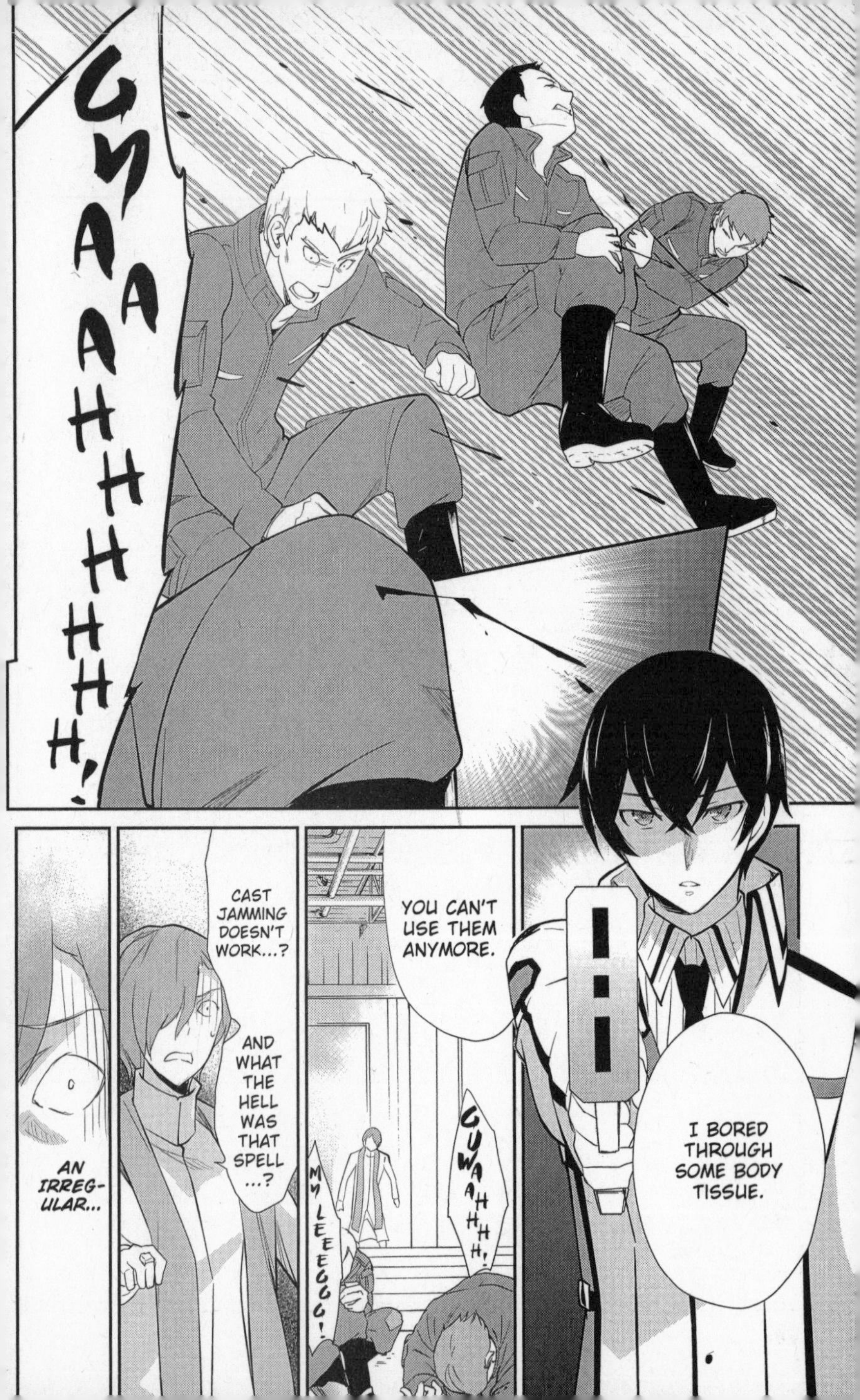
GYAAAAHHHHHHHH!
I BORED THROUGH SOME BODY TISSUE.
YOU CAN'T USE THEM ANYMORE.
GUWAAHHHH!
MY LEEEGGG!
CAST JAMMING DOESN'T WORK...?
AND WHAT THE HELL WAS THAT SPELL...?
AN IRREGULAR...

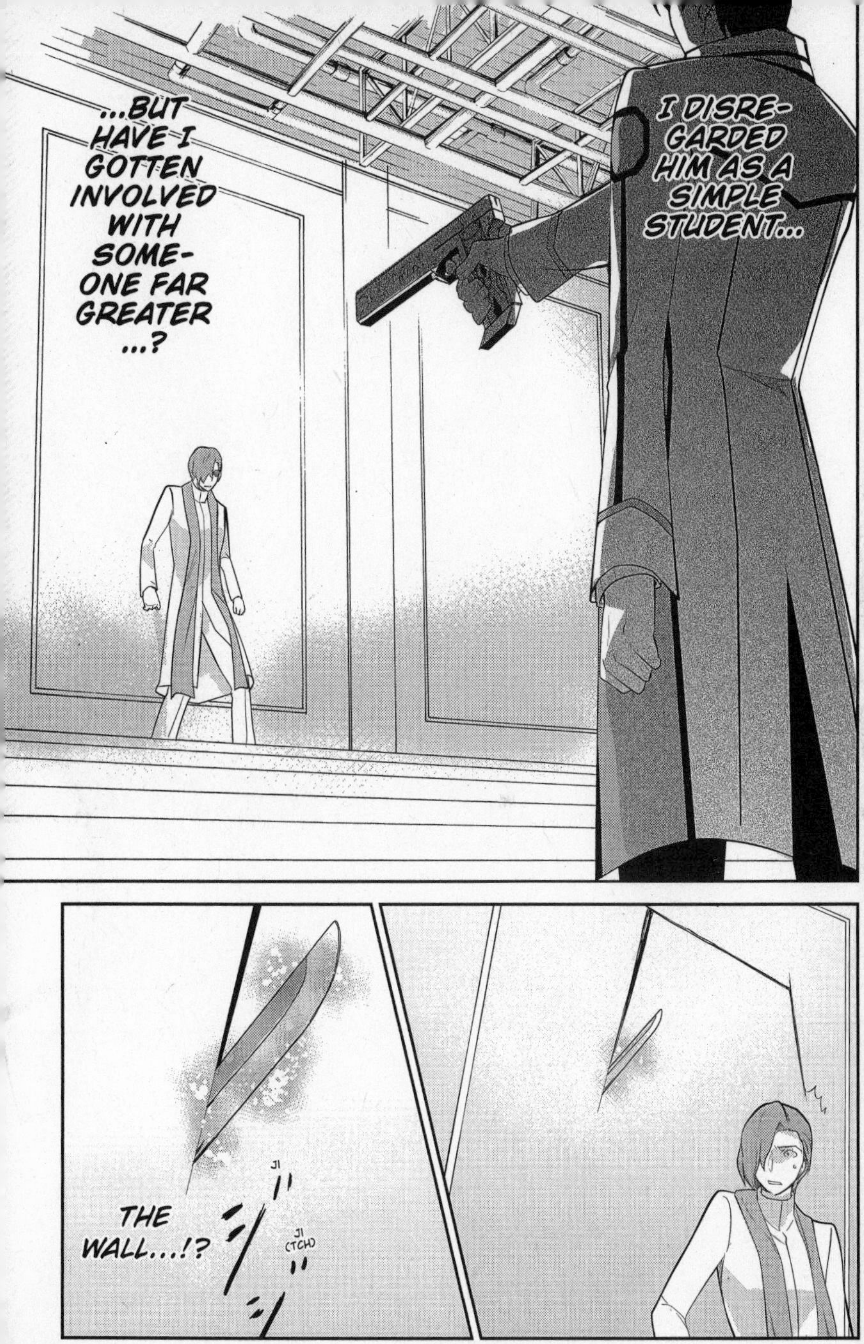
I DISREGARDED HIM AS A SIMPLE STUDENT...
...BUT HAVE I GOTTEN INVOLVED WITH SOMEONE FAR GREATER ...?
JI
THE WALL...!?
JI (TCH)

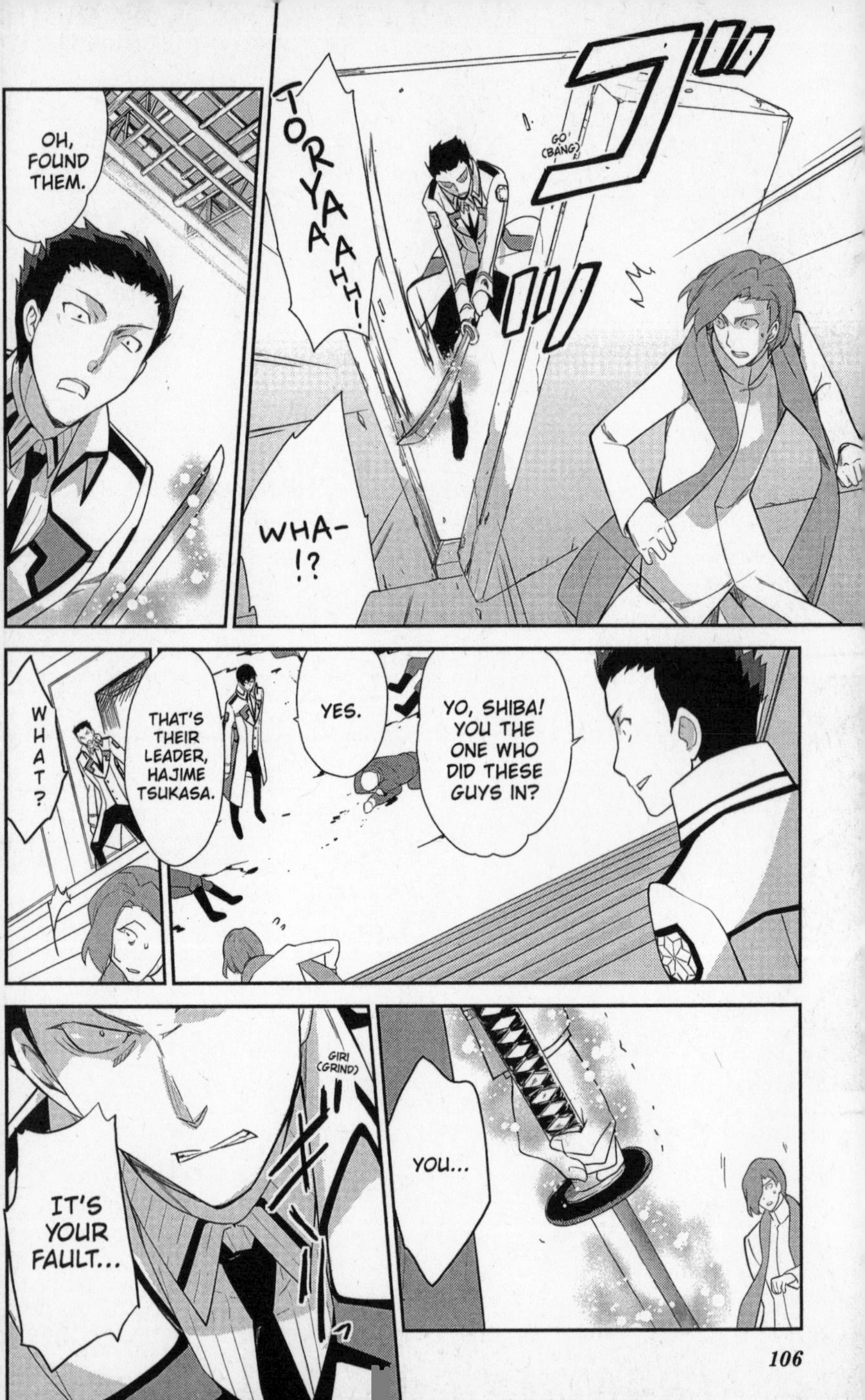
GO (BANG)
TORYAAHH!
WHA-!?
OH, FOUND THEM.
YO, SHIBA! YOU THE ONE WHO DID THESE GUYS IN?
YES.
THAT'S THEIR LEADER, HAJIME TSUKASA.
WHAT?
YOU...
GIRI (GRIND)
IT'S YOUR FAULT...

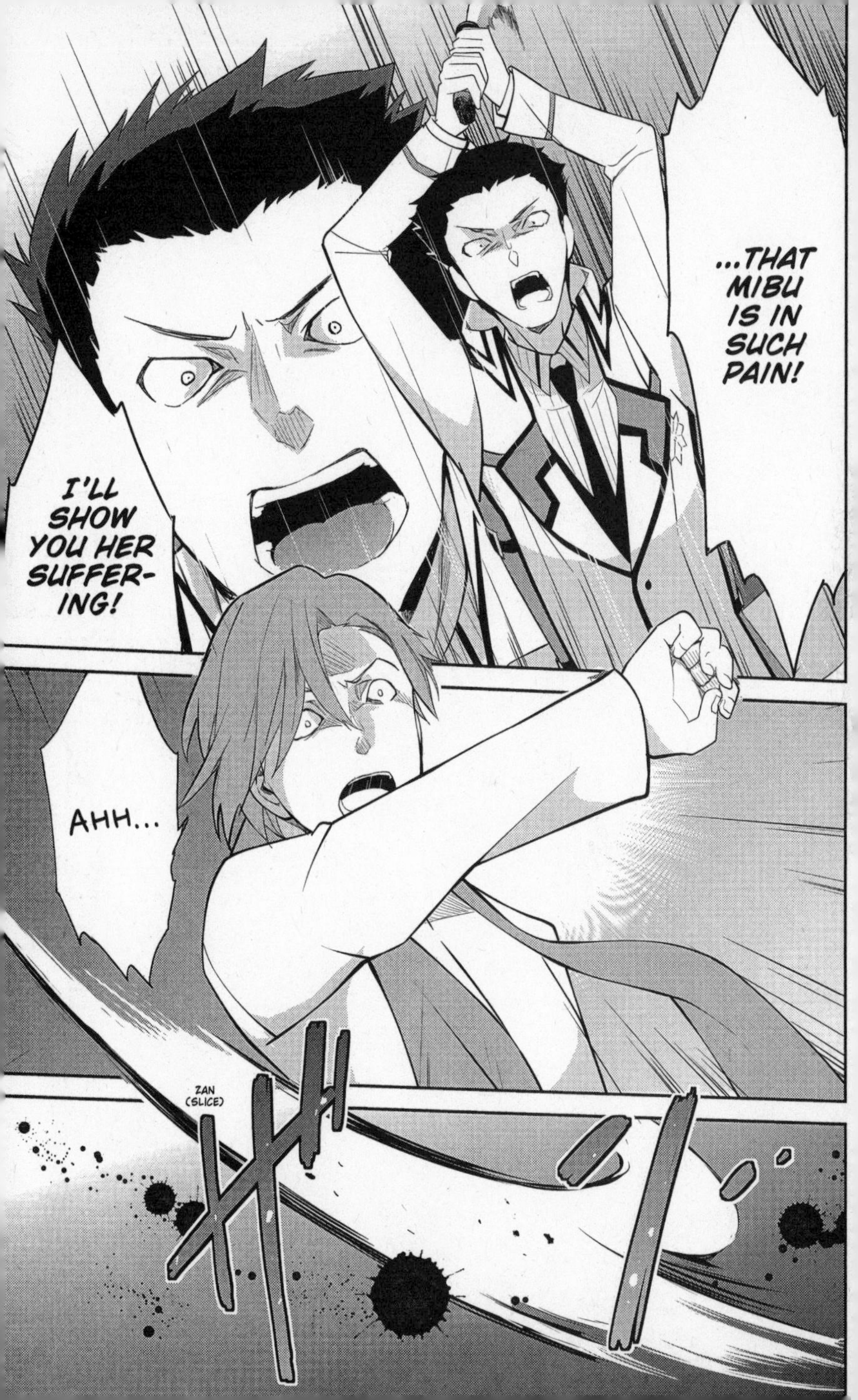
...THAT MIBU IS IN SUCH PAIN!
I'LL SHOW YOU HER SUFFER-ING!
AHH...
ZAN (SLICE)

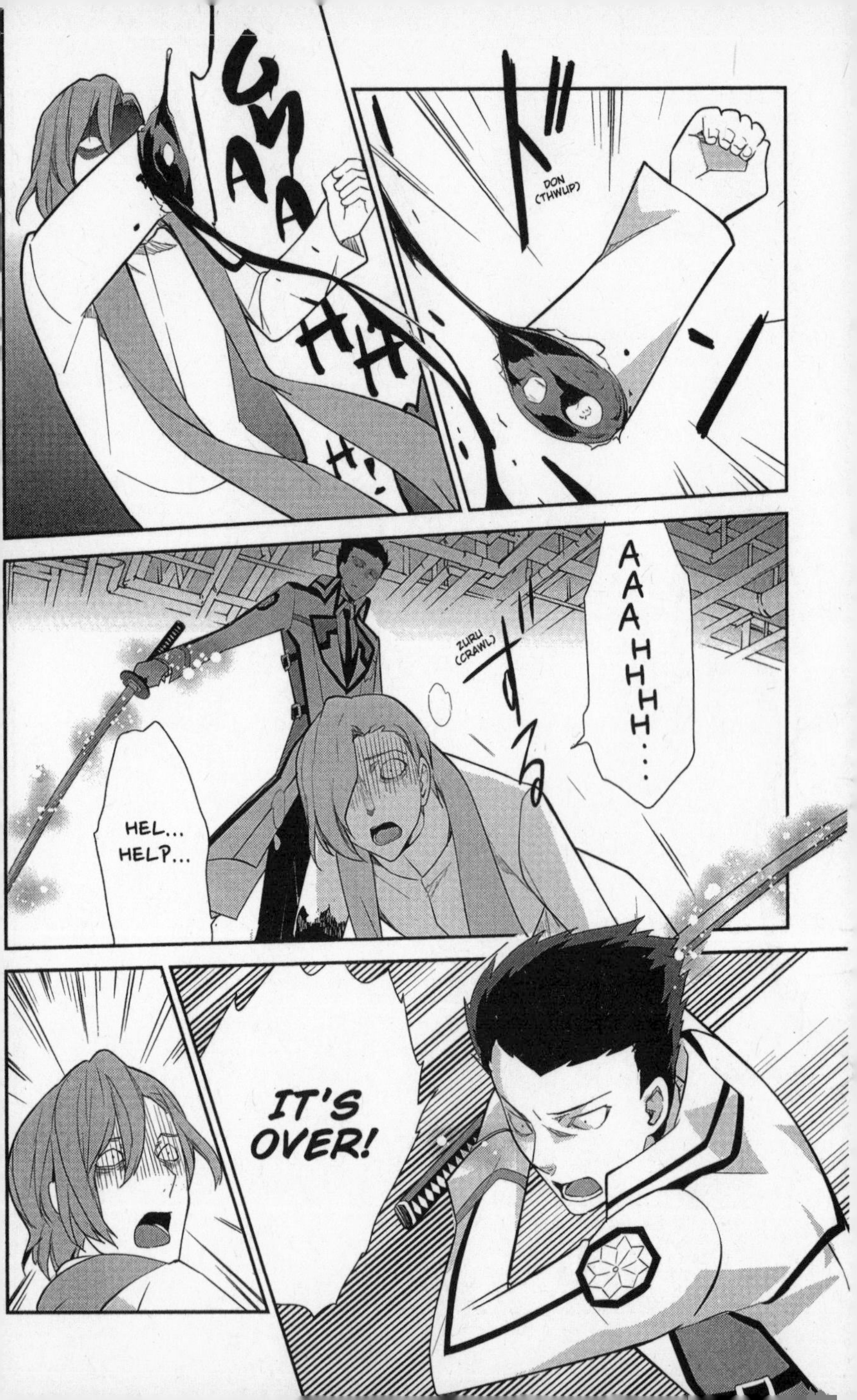
DON (THWUP)
UWAAAHHH!
AAAHHHH...
ZURU (CRAWL)
HEL... HELP...
IT'S OVER!

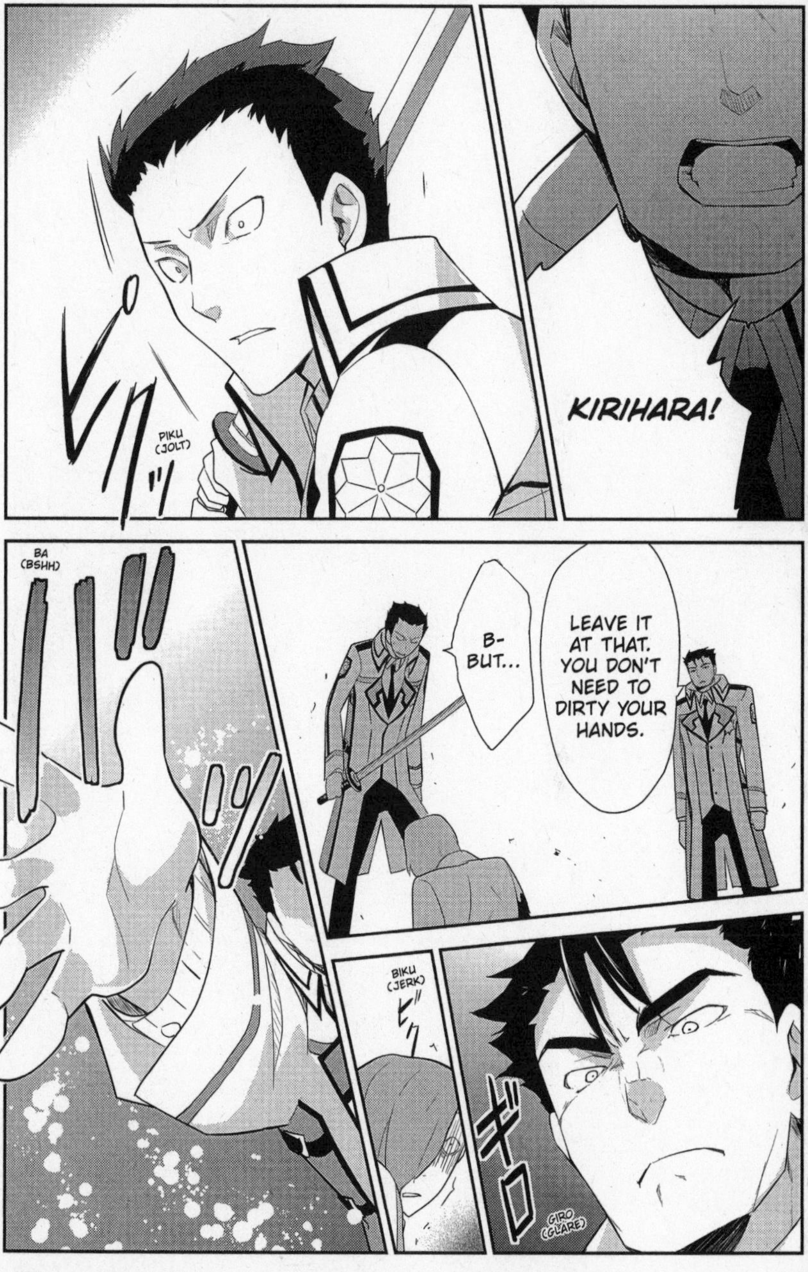
KIRIHARA!
PIKU (JOLT)
LEAVE IT AT THAT. YOU DON'T NEED TO DIRTY YOUR HANDS.
B-BUT...
GIRO (GLARE)
BIKU (JERK)
BA (BSHH)

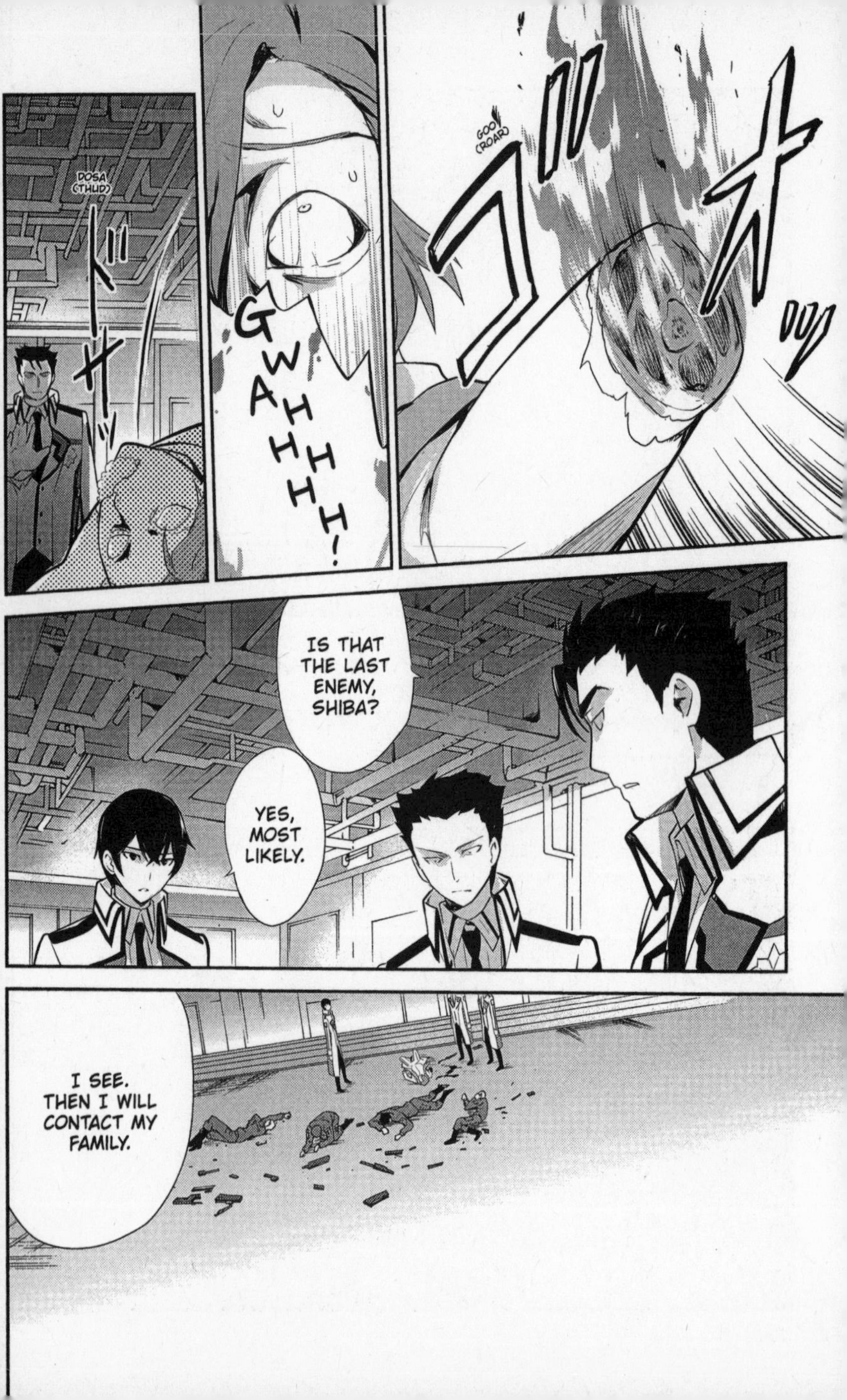
GOO (ROAR)
GWAHHHHH!
DOSA (THUD)
IS THAT THE LAST ENEMY, SHIBA?
YES, MOST LIKELY.
I SEE. THEN I WILL CONTACT MY FAMILY.

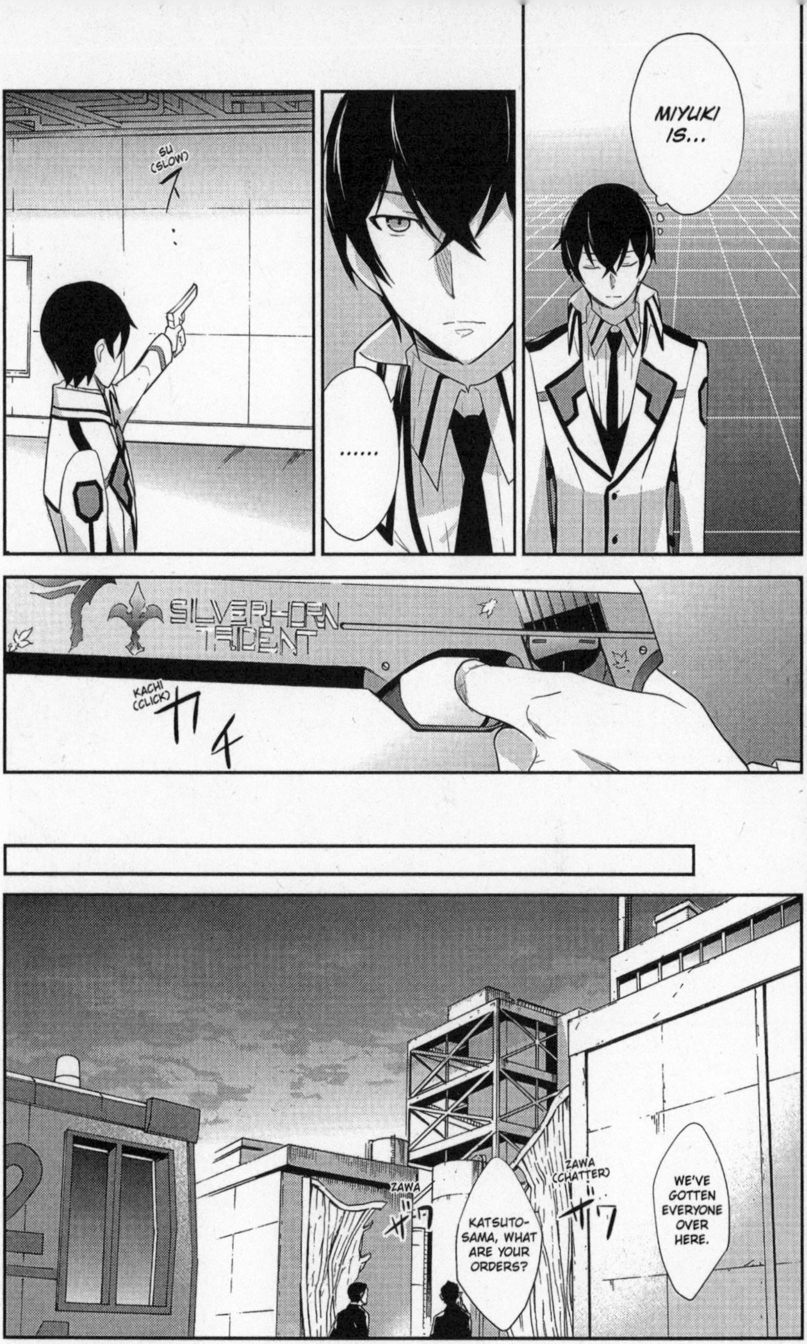
MIYUKI IS...
......
SU (SLOW)
KACHI (CLICK)
SILVERHORN TRIDENT
WE'VE GOTTEN EVERYONE OVER HERE.
ZAWA (CHATTER)
KATSUTO-SAMA, WHAT ARE YOUR ORDERS?
ZAWA

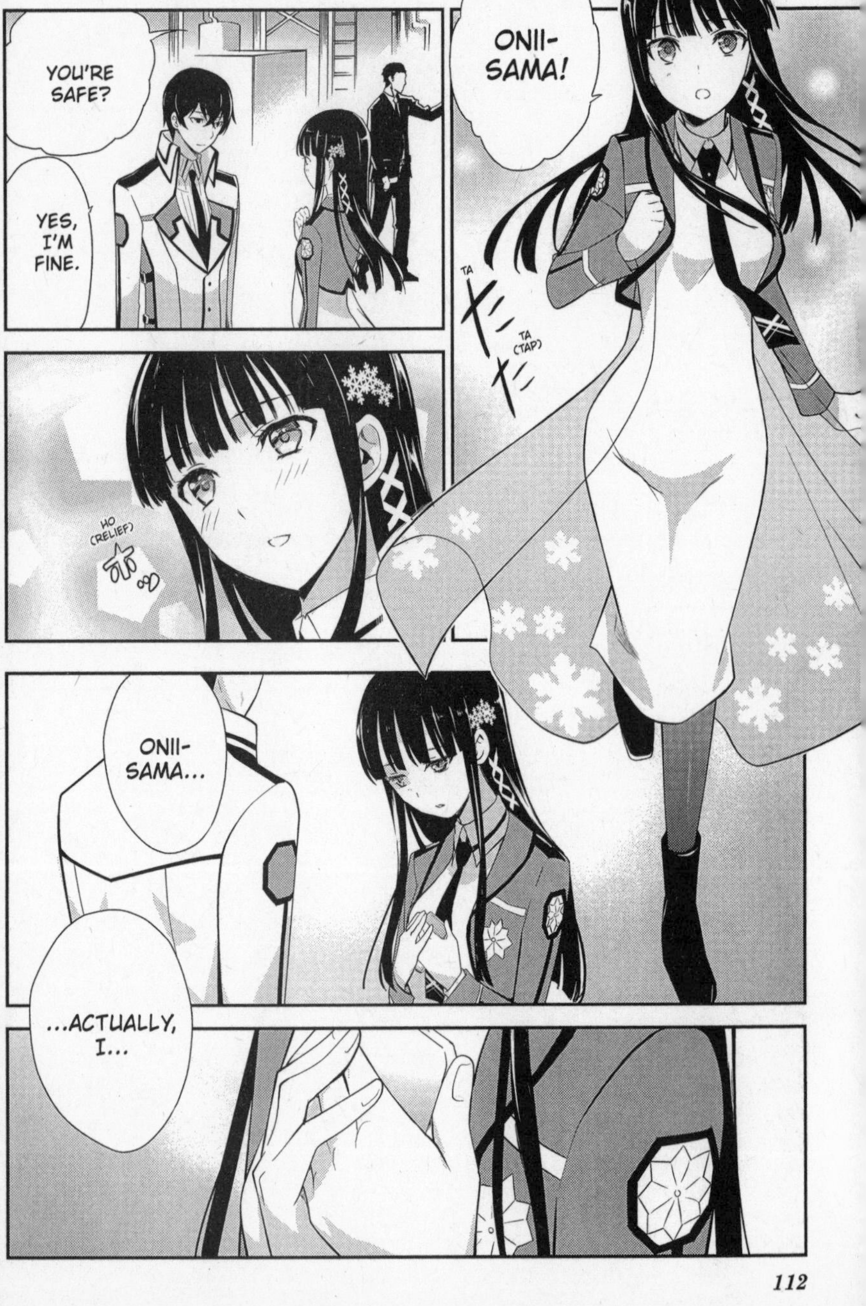
ONII-SAMA!
TA
TA (TAP)
YOU'RE SAFE?
YES, I'M FINE.
HO (RELIEF)
ONII-SAMA...
...ACTUALLY, I...

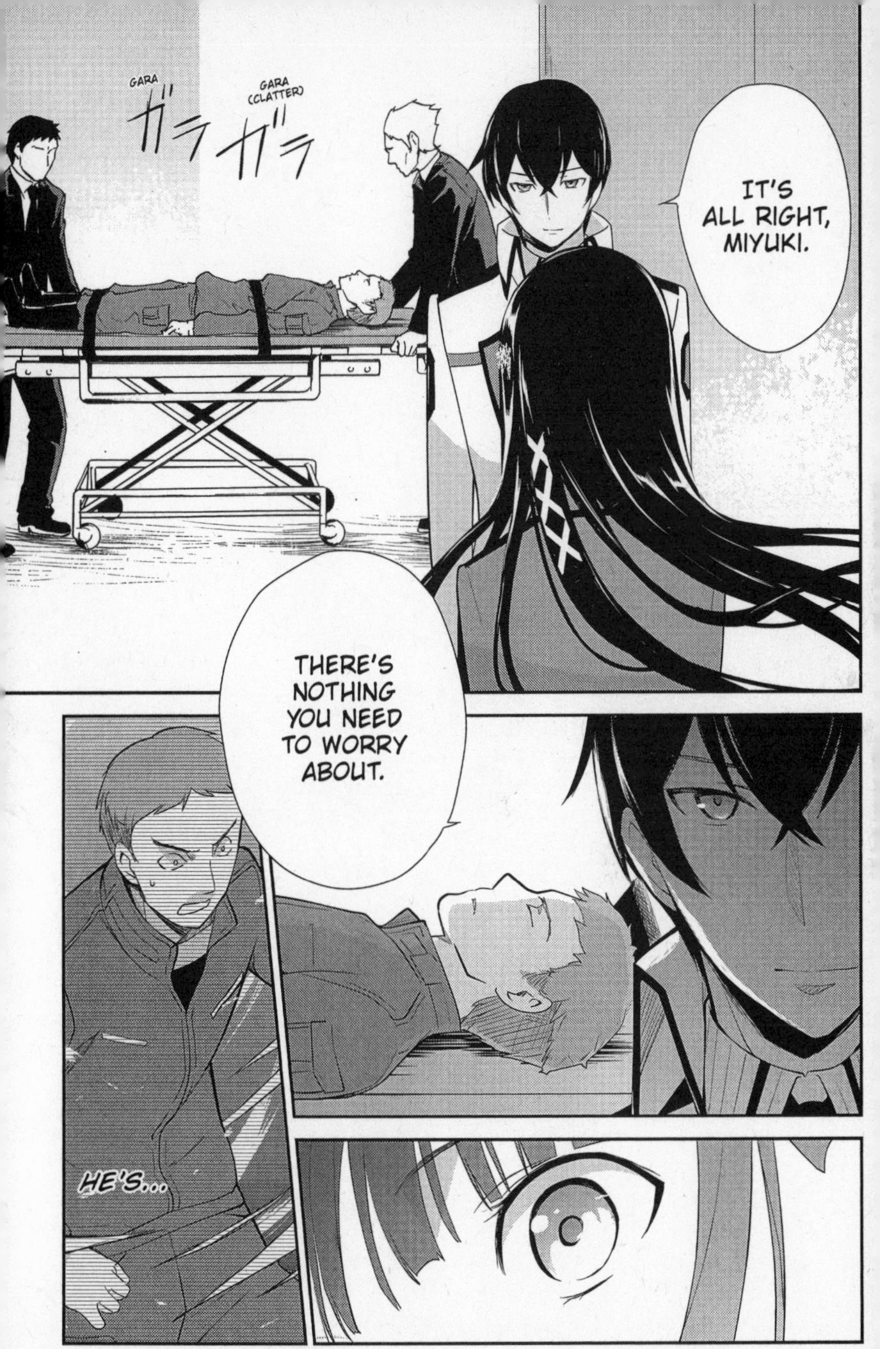
IT'S ALL RIGHT, MIYUKI.
ガラガラ
GARA GARA (CLATTER)
THERE'S NOTHING YOU NEED TO WORRY ABOUT.
HE'S...

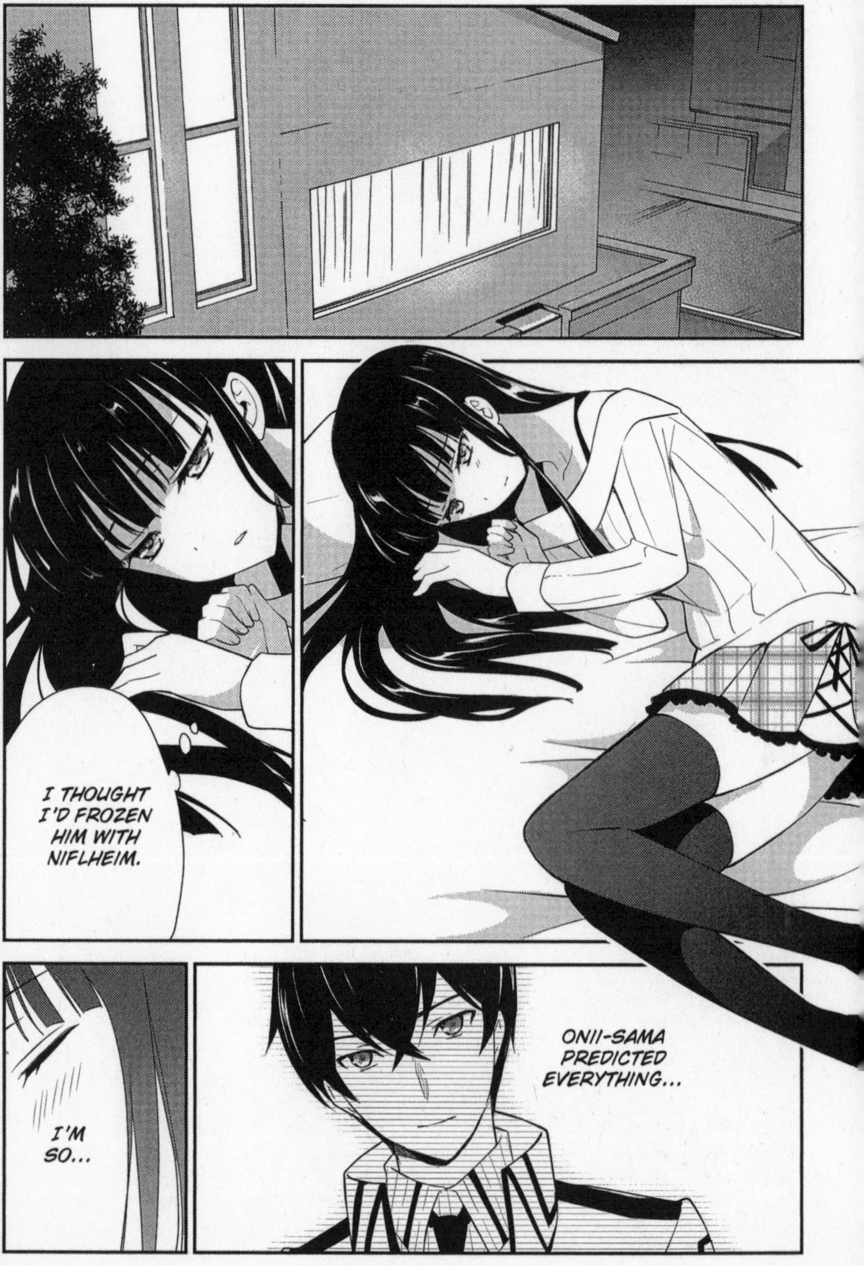
I THOUGHT I'D FROZEN HIM WITH NIFLHEIM.
ONII-SAMA PREDICTED EVERYTHING...
I'M SO...

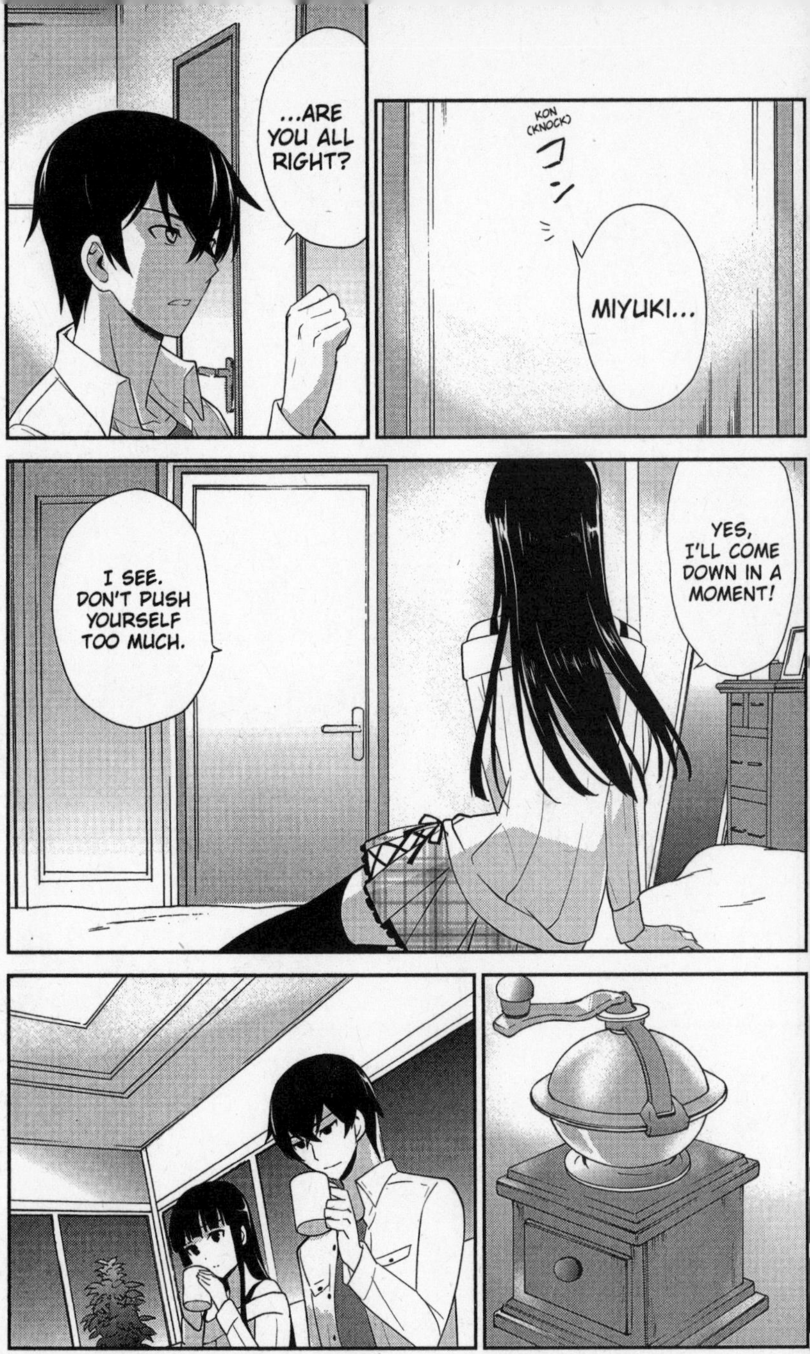
KON (KNOCK)
MIYUKI...
...ARE YOU ALL RIGHT?
YES, I'LL COME DOWN IN A MOMENT!
I SEE. DON'T PUSH YOURSELF TOO MUCH.

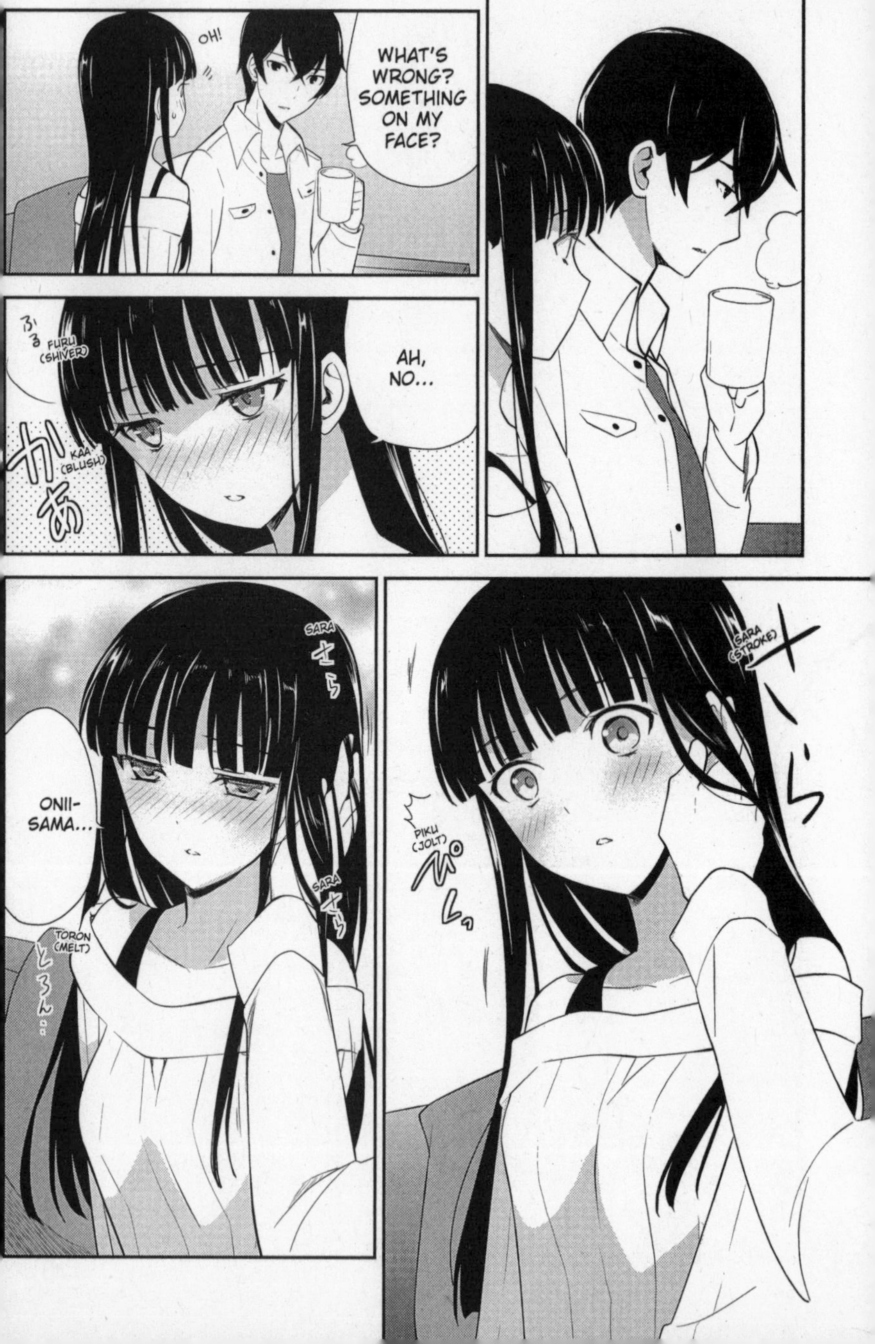
OH!
WHAT'S WRONG? SOMETHING ON MY FACE?
AH, NO...
ふる FURU (SHIVER)
かぁ KAA (BLUSH)
さら SARA (STROKE)
ぴくっ PIKU (JOLT)
さら SARA
ONII-SAMA...
さら SARA
とろん.. TORON (MELT)

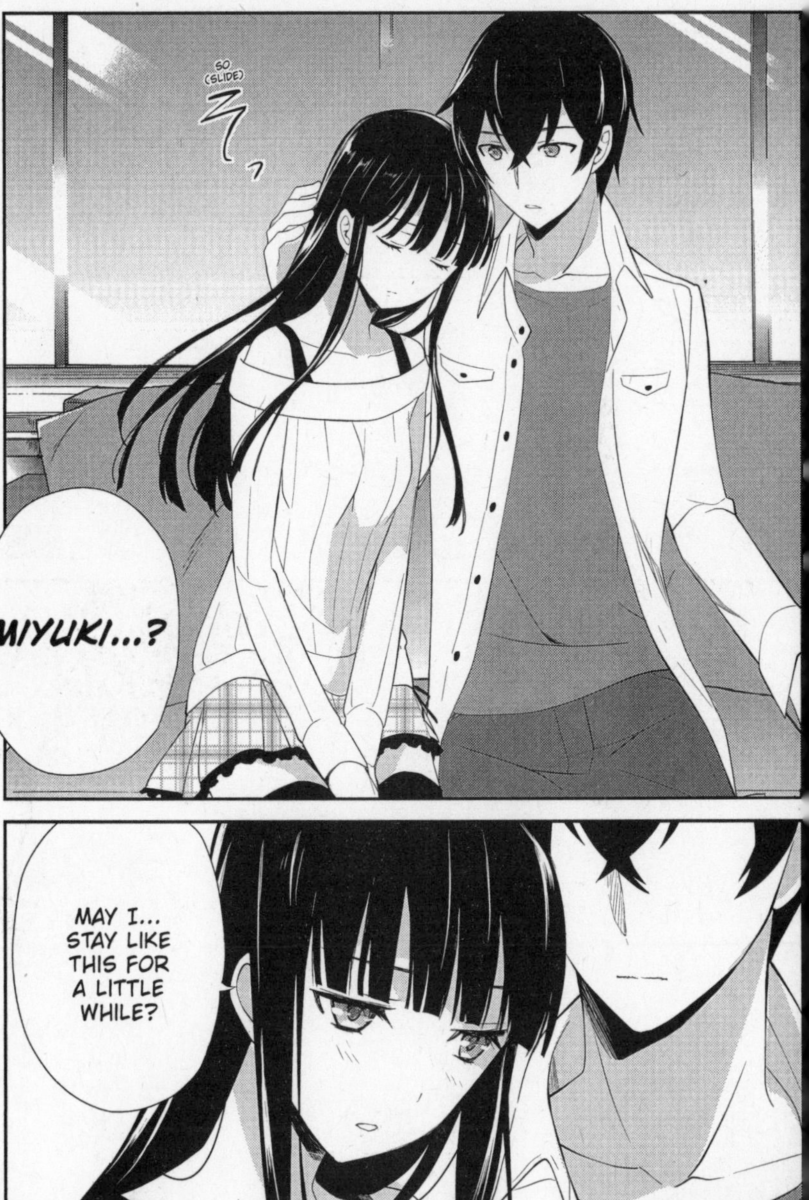
SO (SLIDE)
MIYUKI...?
MAY I... STAY LIKE THIS FOR A LITTLE WHILE?

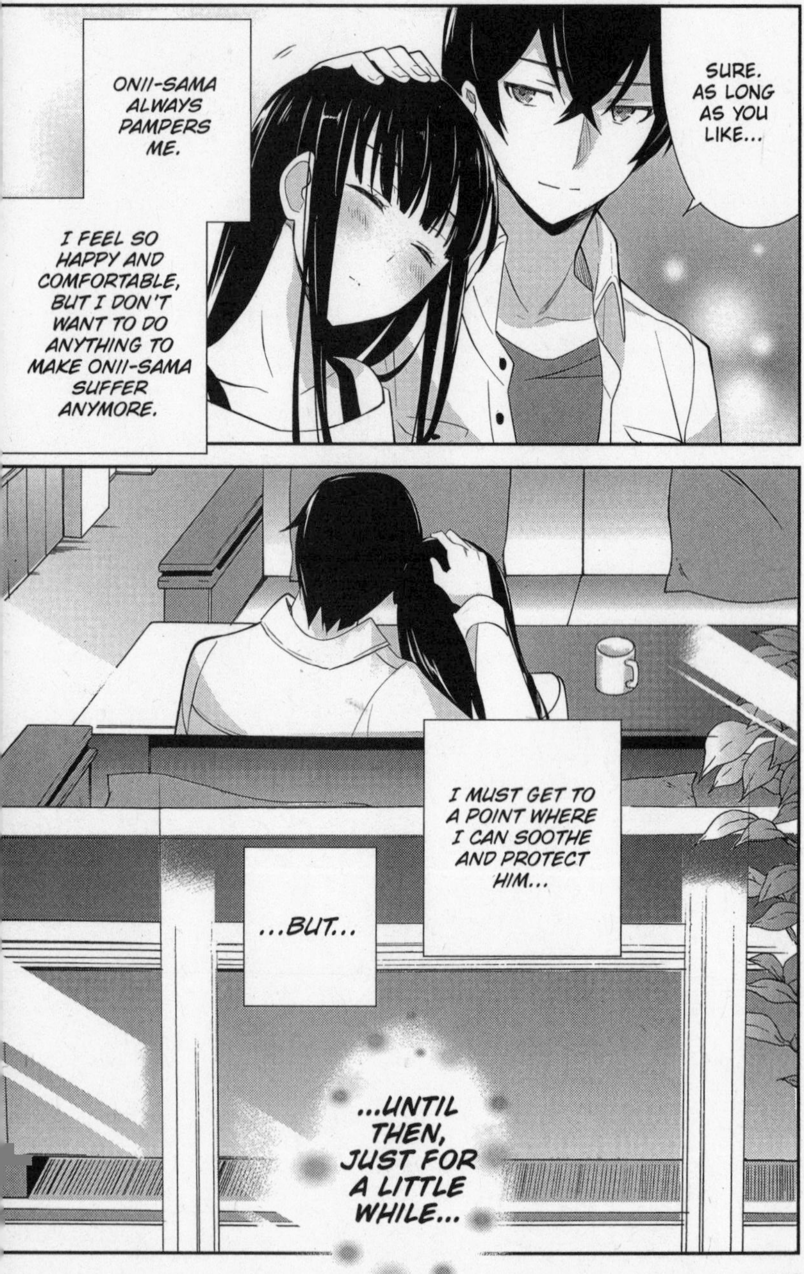
SURE. AS LONG AS YOU LIKE...
ONII-SAMA ALWAYS PAMPERS ME.
I FEEL SO HAPPY AND COMFORTABLE, BUT I DON'T WANT TO DO ANYTHING TO MAKE ONII-SAMA SUFFER ANYMORE.
I MUST GET TO A POINT WHERE I CAN SOOTHE AND PROTECT HIM...
...BUT...
...UNTIL THEN, JUST FOR A LITTLE WHILE...

THE
HONOR
STUDENT
AT
Magic High
School

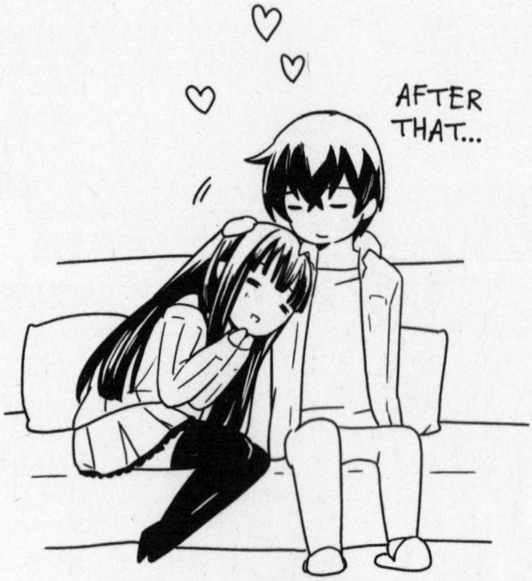
AFTER THAT...

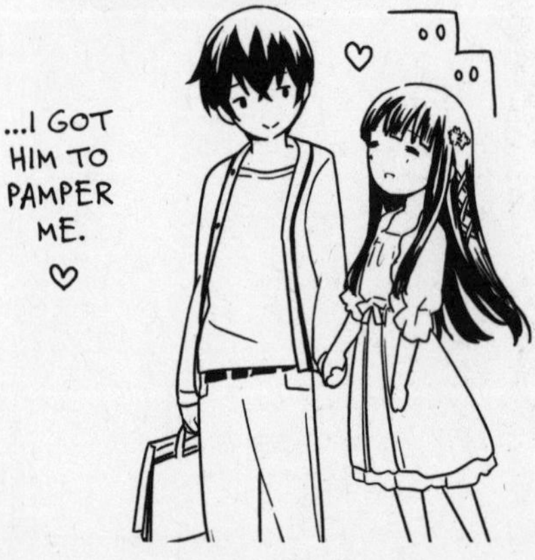
...I GOT HIM TO PAMPER ME.

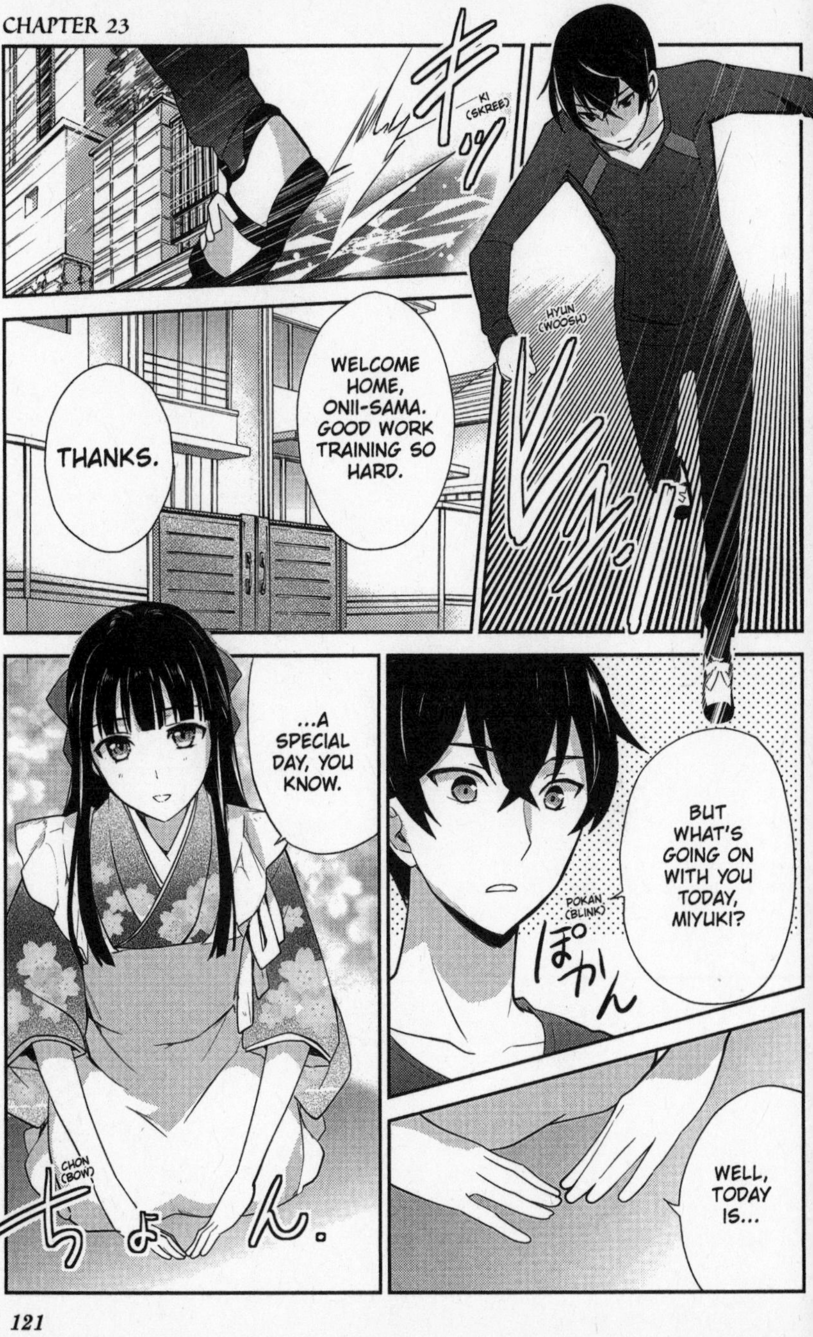
キッ
KI (SKREE)
ヒュン。
HYUN (WOOSH)
WELCOME HOME, ONII-SAMA. GOOD WORK TRAINING SO HARD.
THANKS.
BUT WHAT'S GOING ON WITH YOU TODAY, MIYUKI?
ぽかん
POKAN (BLINK)
WELL, TODAY IS...
...A SPECIAL DAY, YOU KNOW.
ちょん。
CHON (BOW)

CHAPTER 23

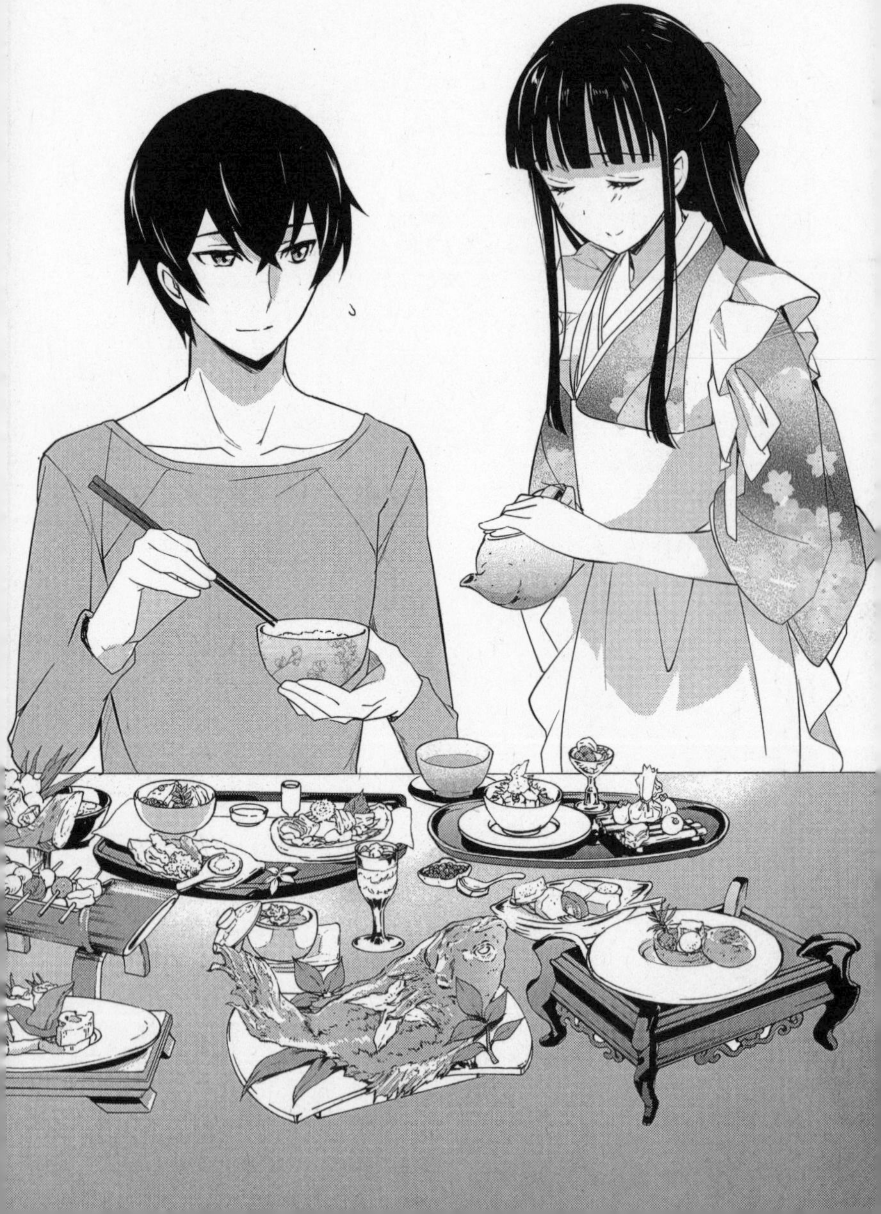

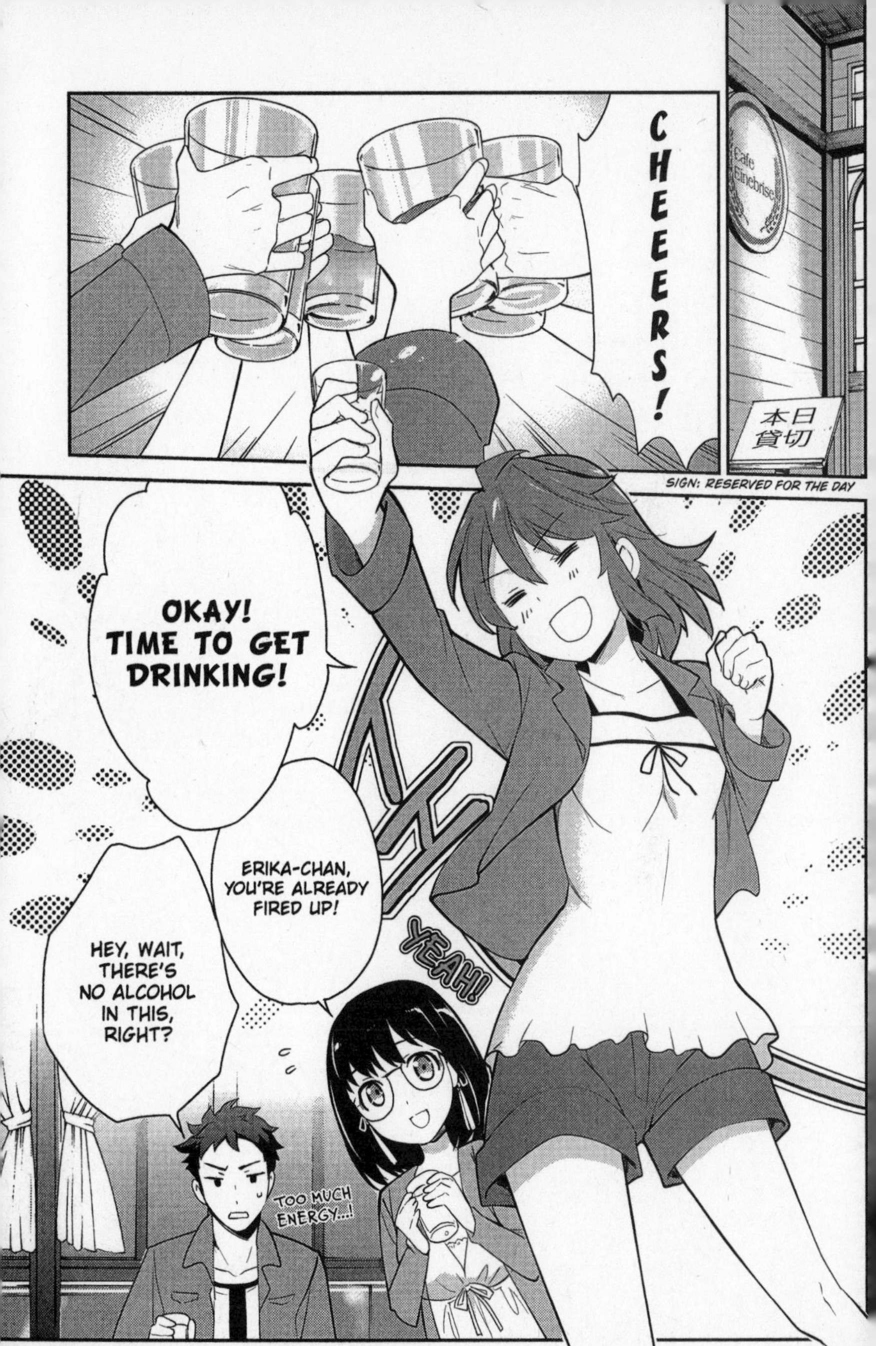
本日
貸切
SIGN: RESERVED FOR THE DAY
CHEEERS!
OKAY! TIME TO GET DRINKING!
YEAH!
ERIKA-CHAN, YOU'RE ALREADY FIRED UP!
HEY, WAIT, THERE'S NO ALCOHOL IN THIS, RIGHT?
TOO MUCH ENERGY...!

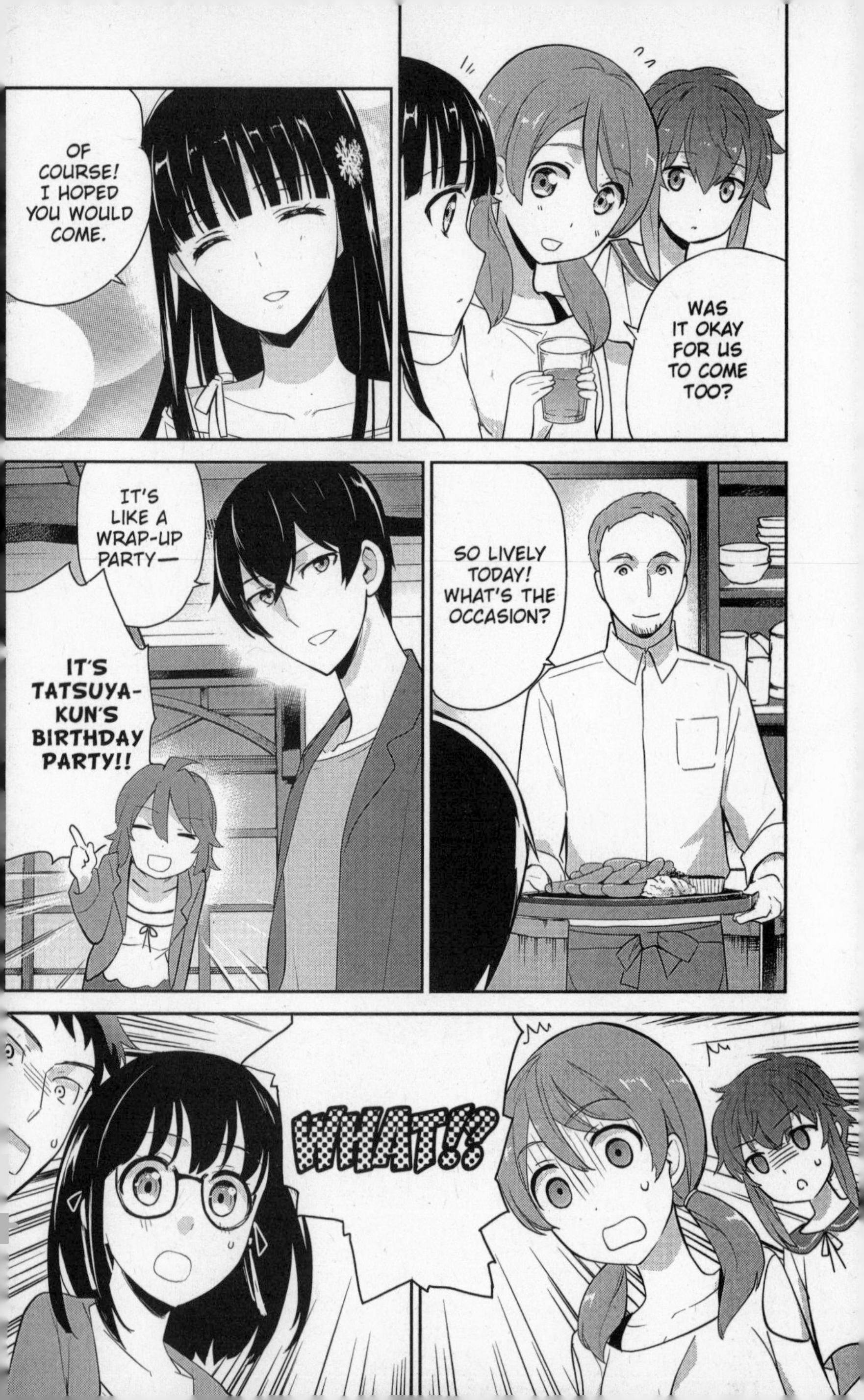
WAS IT OKAY FOR US TO COME TOO?
OF COURSE! I HOPED YOU WOULD COME.
SO LIVELY TODAY! WHAT'S THE OCCASION?
IT'S LIKE A WRAP-UP PARTY—
IT'S TATSUYA-KUN'S BIRTHDAY PARTY!!
WHAT!?

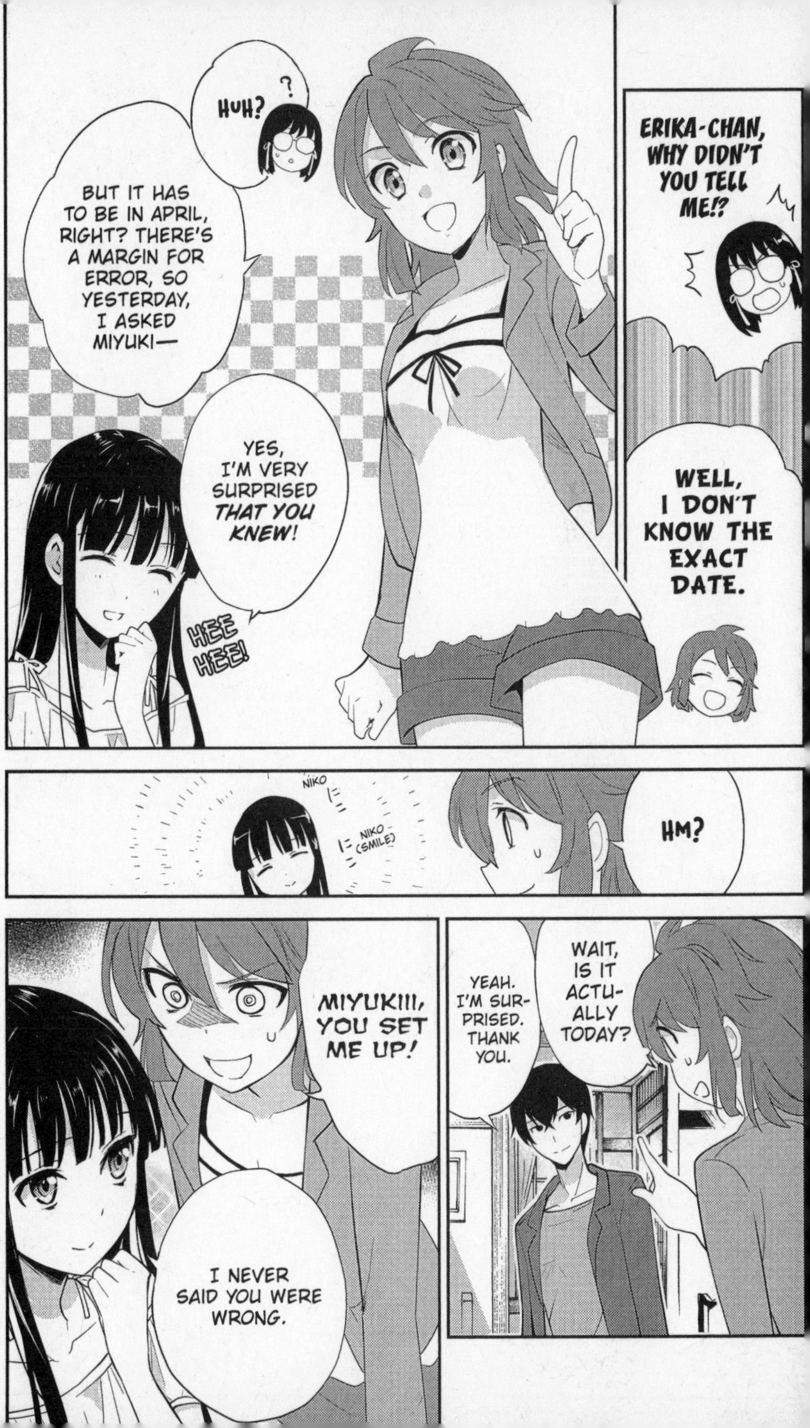
ERIKA-CHAN, WHY DIDN'T YOU TELL ME!?
WELL, I DON'T KNOW THE EXACT DATE.
?
HUH?
BUT IT HAS TO BE IN APRIL, RIGHT? THERE'S A MARGIN FOR ERROR, SO YESTERDAY, I ASKED MIYUKI—
YES, I'M VERY SURPRISED *THAT YOU KNEW!*
HEE HEE!
HM?
NIKO
NIKO (SMILE)
WAIT, IS IT ACTUALLY TODAY?
YEAH. I'M SURPRISED. THANK YOU.
MIYUKIII, YOU SET ME UP!
I NEVER SAID YOU WERE WRONG.

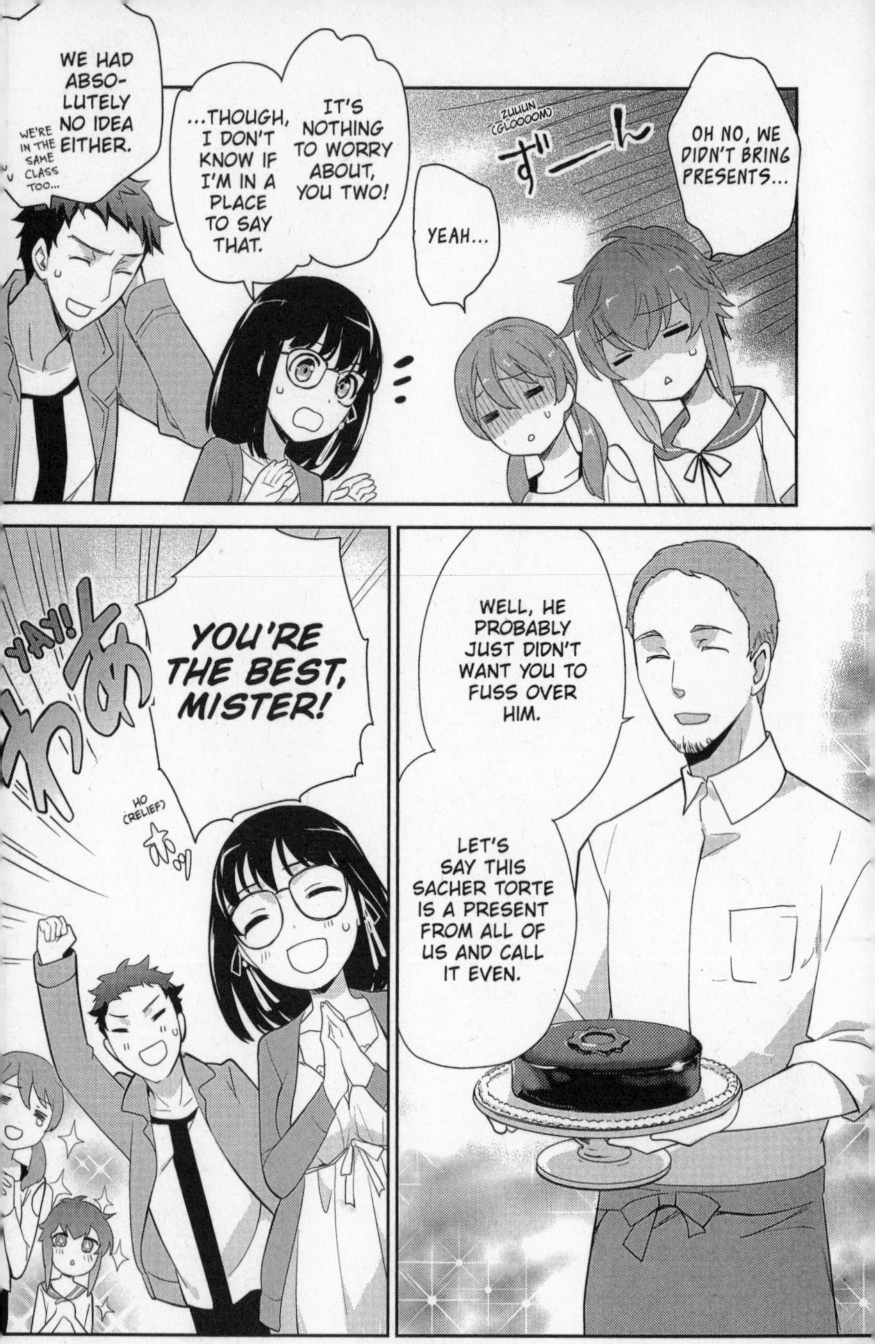

OH NO, WE DIDN'T BRING PRESENTS...
ZUUUN (GLOOOOM)
ずーん
YEAH...
IT'S NOTHING TO WORRY ABOUT, YOU TWO!
...THOUGH, I DON'T KNOW IF I'M IN A PLACE TO SAY THAT.
WE HAD ABSOLUTELY NO IDEA EITHER.
WE'RE IN THE SAME CLASS TOO...
WELL, HE PROBABLY JUST DIDN'T WANT YOU TO FUSS OVER HIM.
LET'S SAY THIS SACHER TORTE IS A PRESENT FROM ALL OF US AND CALL IT EVEN.
YAY!
YOU'RE THE BEST, MISTER!
HO (RELIEF)
ほっ

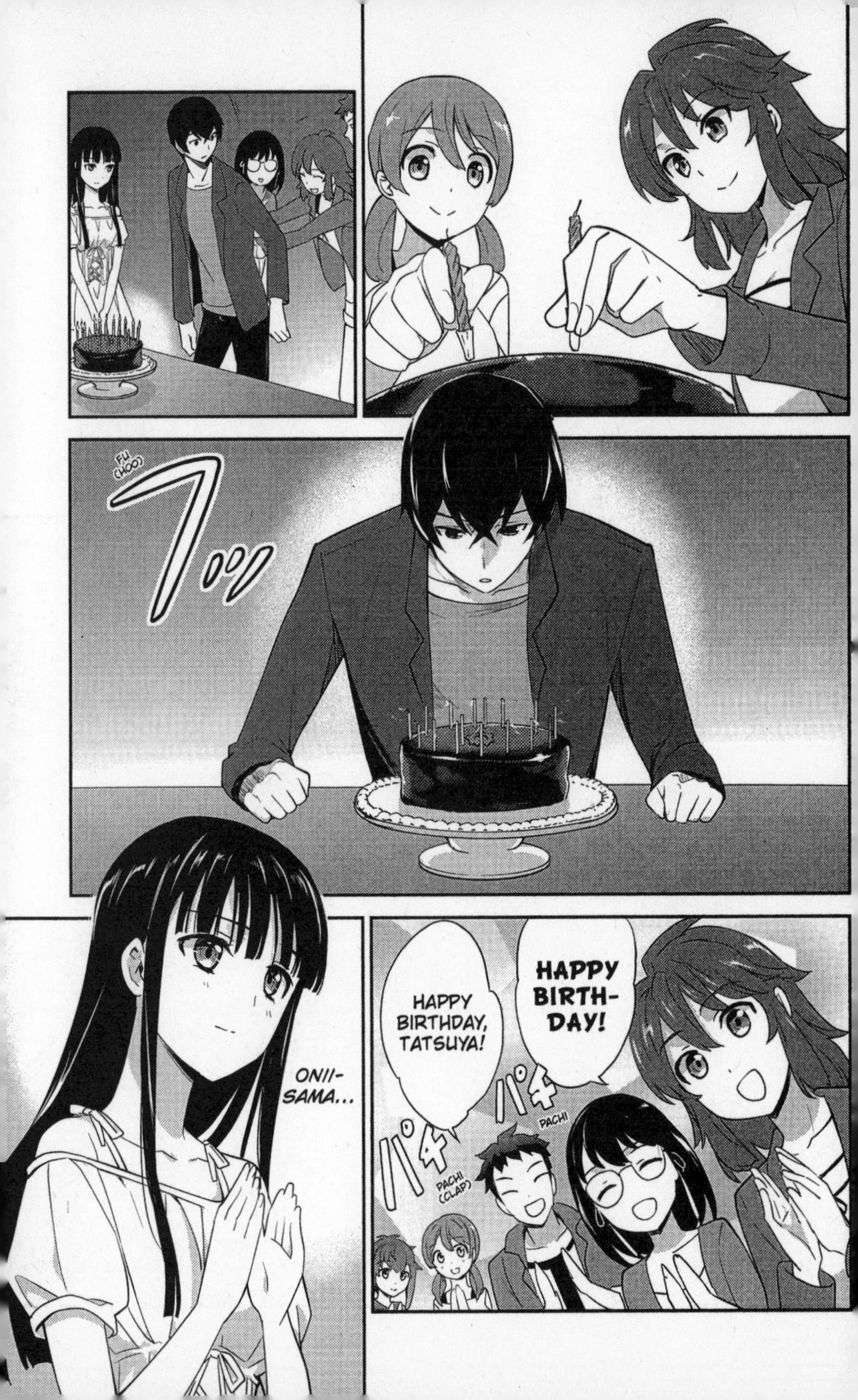
FU (HOO)
フッ
HAPPY BIRTH-DAY!
HAPPY BIRTHDAY, TATSUYA!
パチ
PACHI
パチ
PACHI (CLAP)
ONII-SAMA...

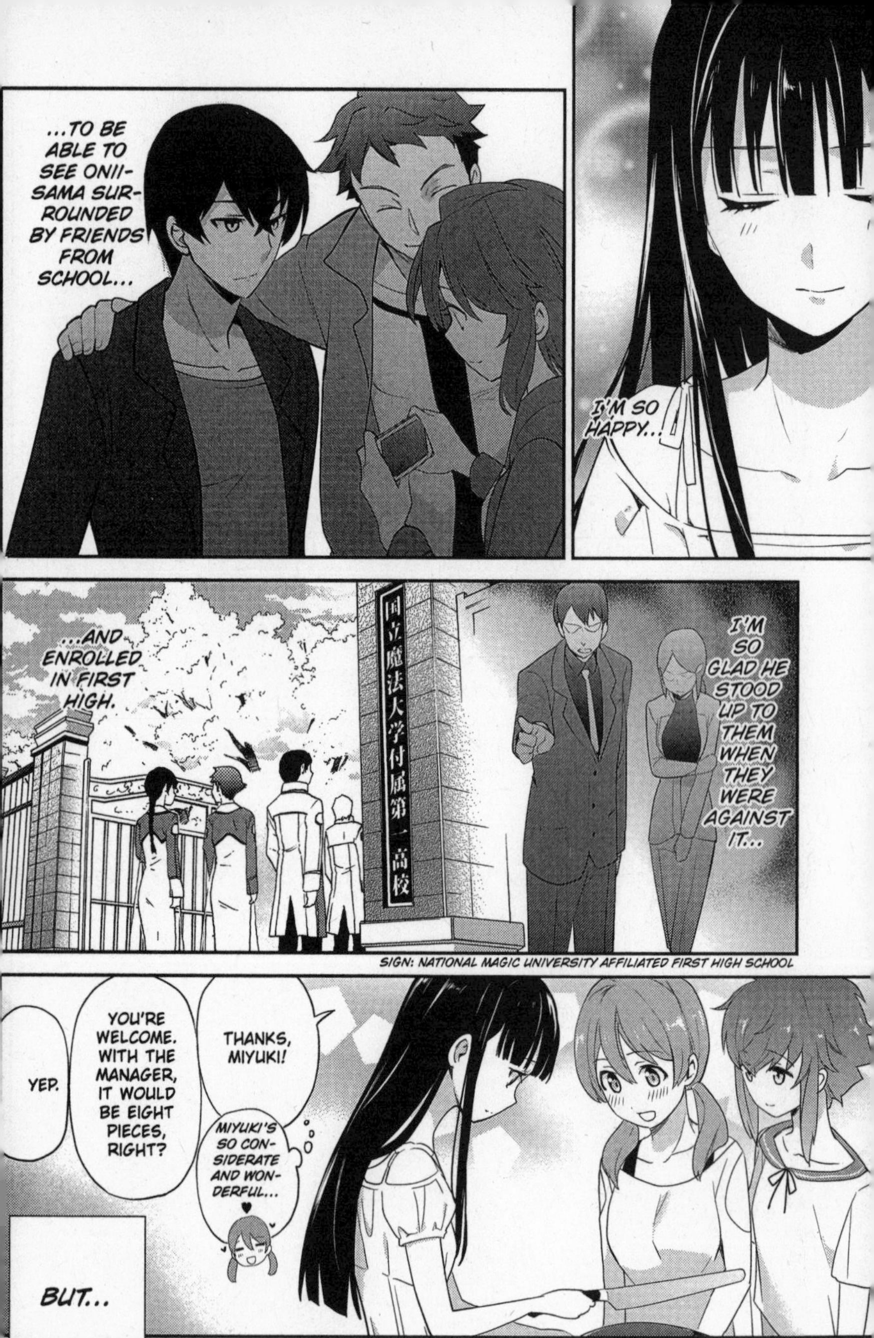
I'M SO HAPPY...
...TO BE ABLE TO SEE ONII-SAMA SURROUNDED BY FRIENDS FROM SCHOOL...
I'M SO GLAD HE STOOD UP TO THEM WHEN THEY WERE AGAINST IT...
...AND ENROLLED IN FIRST HIGH.
国立魔法大学付属第一高校
SIGN: NATIONAL MAGIC UNIVERSITY AFFILIATED FIRST HIGH SCHOOL
THANKS, MIYUKI!
MIYUKI'S SO CONSIDERATE AND WONDERFUL...
YOU'RE WELCOME. WITH THE MANAGER, IT WOULD BE EIGHT PIECES, RIGHT?
YEP.
BUT...

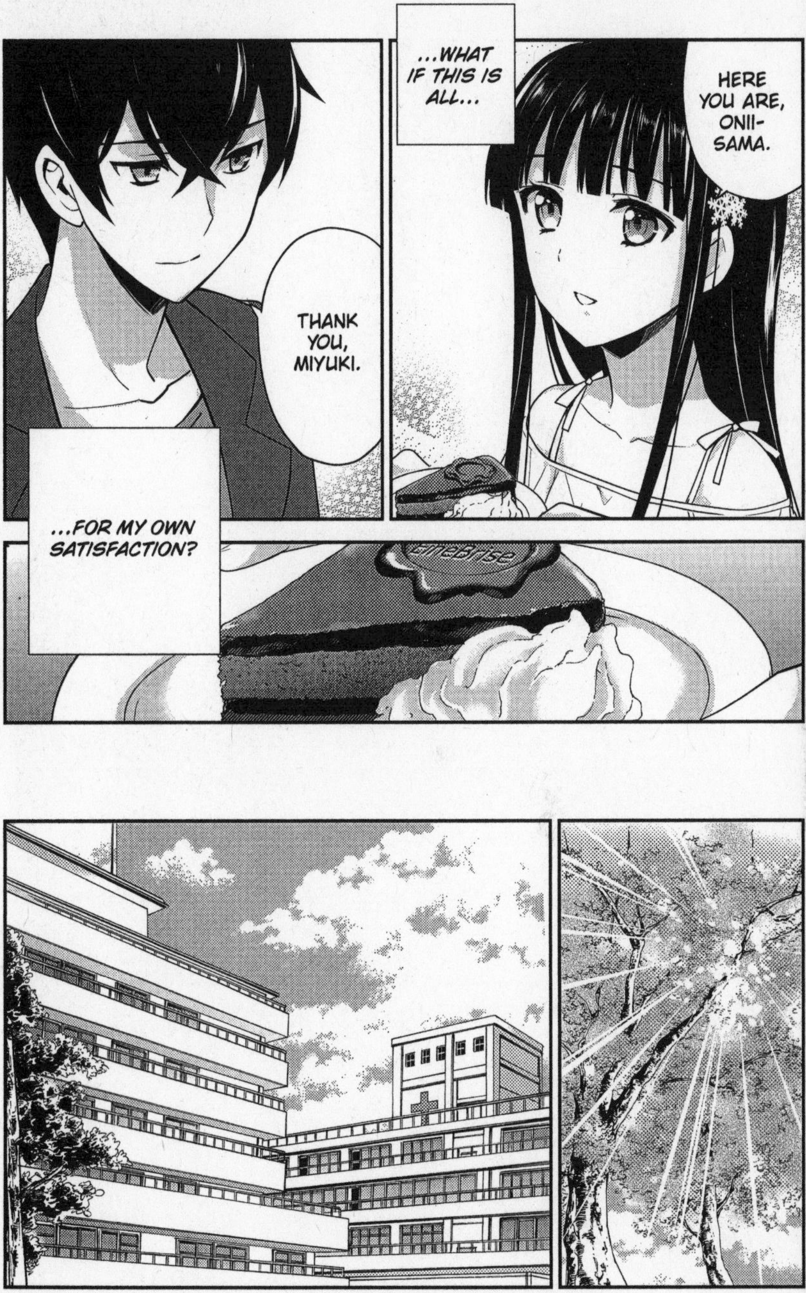
HERE YOU ARE, ONII-SAMA.
...WHAT IF THIS IS ALL...
THANK YOU, MIYUKI.
...FOR MY OWN SATISFACTION?

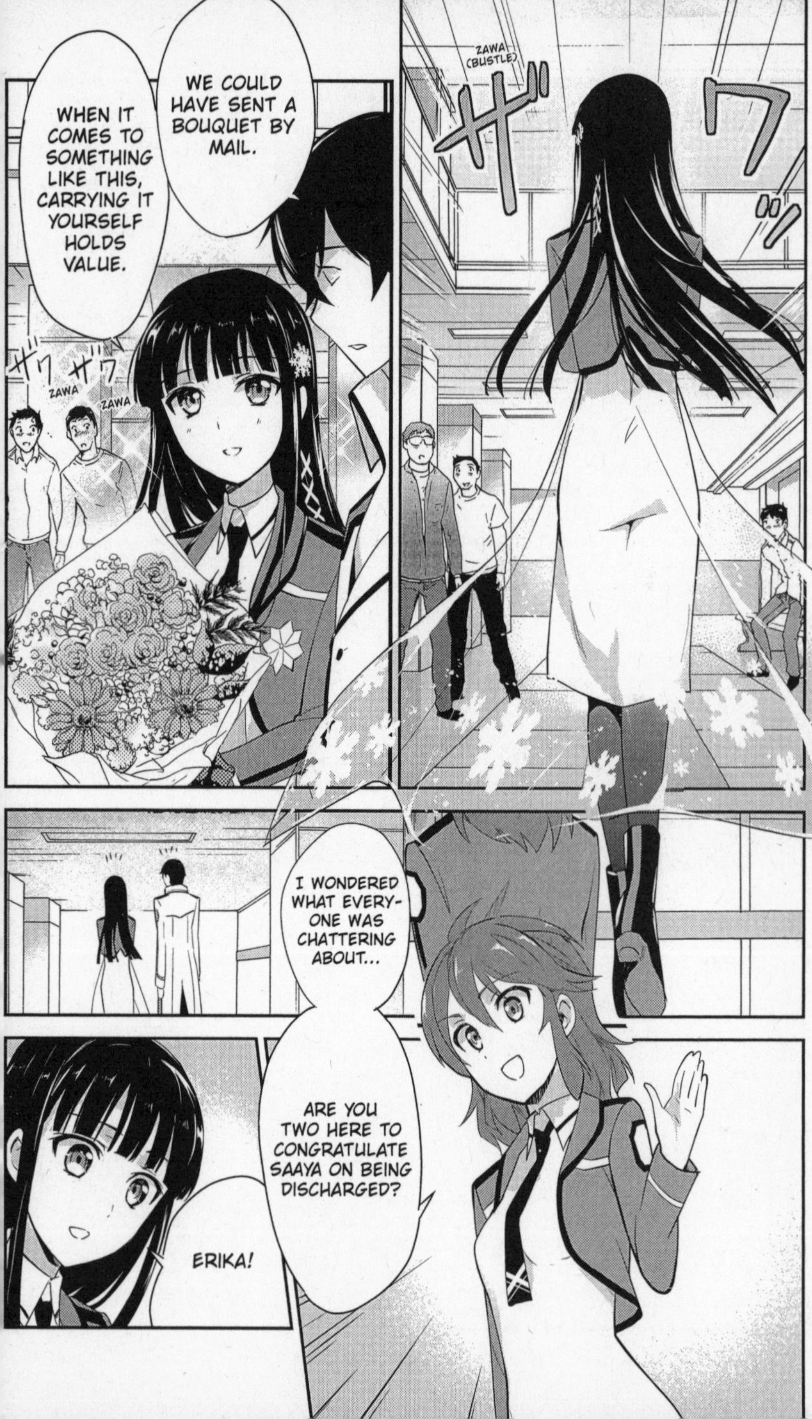
ザワッ
ZAWA (BUSTLE)
WE COULD HAVE SENT A BOUQUET BY MAIL.
WHEN IT COMES TO SOMETHING LIKE THIS, CARRYING IT YOURSELF HOLDS VALUE.
ザワ ザワ
ZAWA ZAWA
I WONDERED WHAT EVERY-ONE WAS CHATTERING ABOUT...
ARE YOU TWO HERE TO CONGRATULATE SAAYA ON BEING DISCHARGED?
ERIKA!

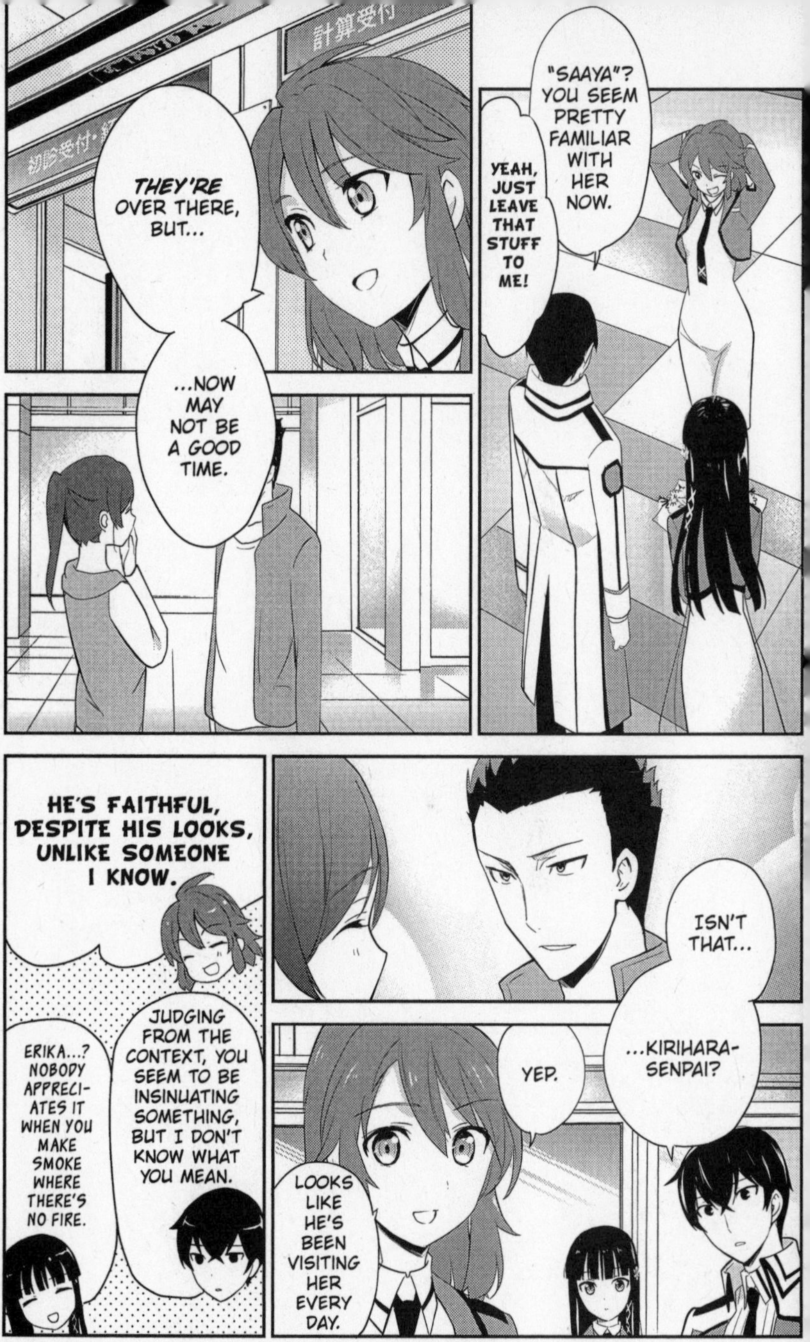
"SAAYA"? YOU SEEM PRETTY FAMILIAR WITH HER NOW.
YEAH, JUST LEAVE THAT STUFF TO ME!
THEY'RE OVER THERE, BUT...
...NOW MAY NOT BE A GOOD TIME.
ISN'T THAT...
...KIRIHARA-SENPAI?
YEP.
LOOKS LIKE HE'S BEEN VISITING HER EVERY DAY.
HE'S FAITHFUL, DESPITE HIS LOOKS, UNLIKE SOMEONE I KNOW.
JUDGING FROM THE CONTEXT, YOU SEEM TO BE INSINUATING SOMETHING, BUT I DON'T KNOW WHAT YOU MEAN.
ERIKA...? NOBODY APPRECIATES IT WHEN YOU MAKE SMOKE WHERE THERE'S NO FIRE.

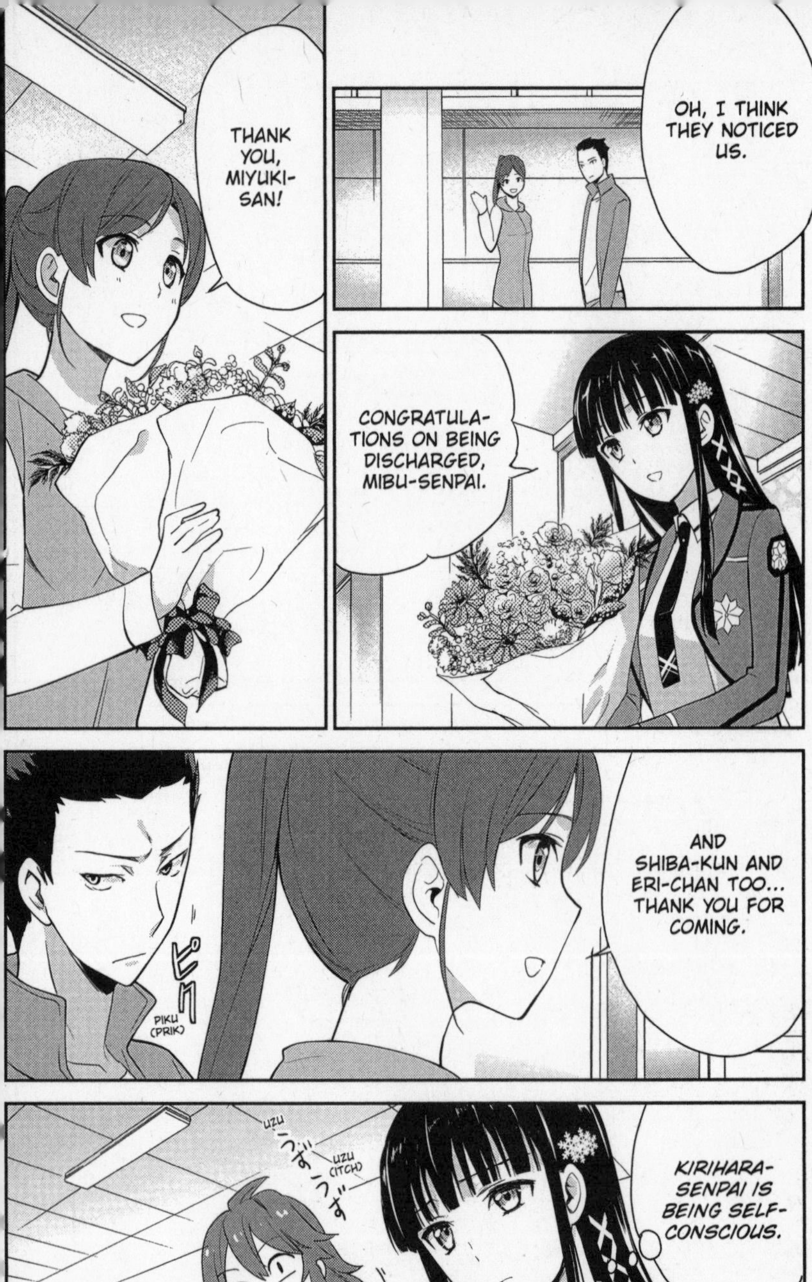
OH, I THINK THEY NOTICED US.
CONGRATULATIONS ON BEING DISCHARGED, MIBU-SENPAI.
THANK YOU, MIYUKI-SAN!
AND SHIBA-KUN AND ERI-CHAN TOO... THANK YOU FOR COMING.
PIKU (PRIK)
KIRIHARA-SENPAI IS BEING SELF-CONSCIOUS.
UZU UZU (ITCH)

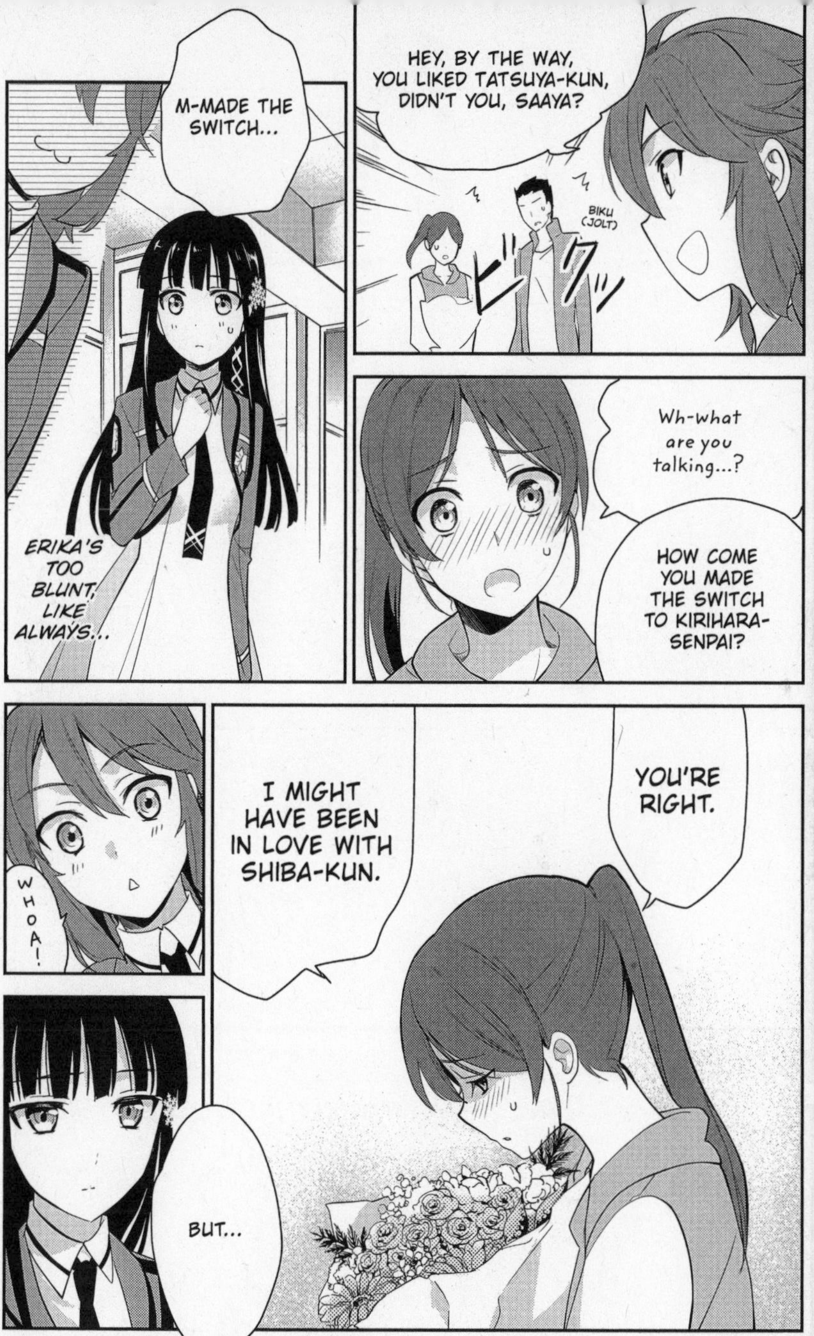
HEY, BY THE WAY, YOU LIKED TATSUYA-KUN, DIDN'T YOU, SAAYA?
BIKU (JOLT)
Wh-what are you talking...?
HOW COME YOU MADE THE SWITCH TO KIRIHARA-SENPAI?
M-MADE THE SWITCH...
ERIKA'S TOO BLUNT, LIKE ALWAYS...
YOU'RE RIGHT.
I MIGHT HAVE BEEN IN LOVE WITH SHIBA-KUN.
WHOA!
BUT...

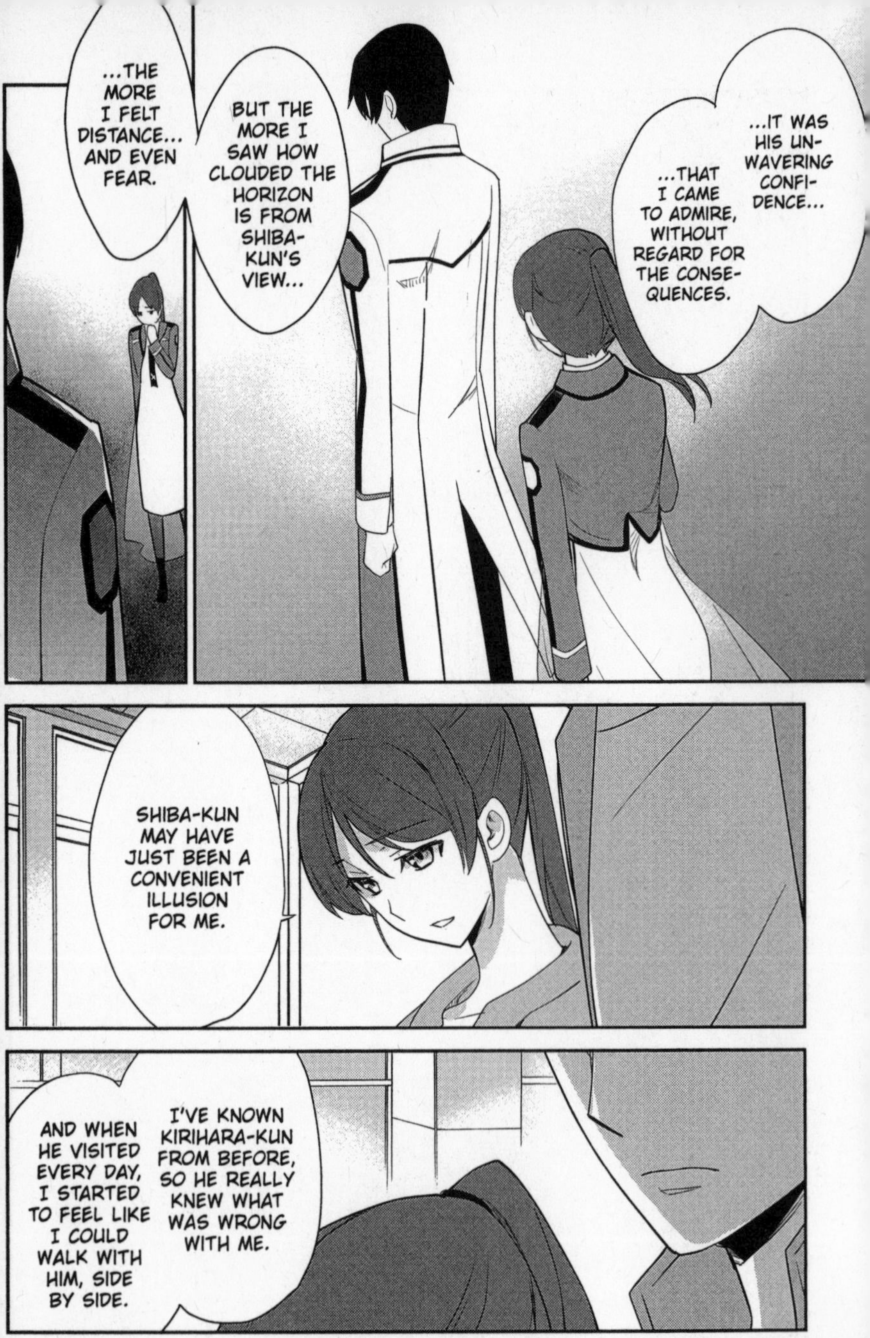
...IT WAS HIS UN-WAVERING CONFI-DENCE...
...THAT I CAME TO ADMIRE, WITHOUT REGARD FOR THE CONSE-QUENCES.
BUT THE MORE I SAW HOW CLOUDED THE HORIZON IS FROM SHIBA-KUN'S VIEW...
...THE MORE I FELT DISTANCE... AND EVEN FEAR.
SHIBA-KUN MAY HAVE JUST BEEN A CONVENIENT ILLUSION FOR ME.
I'VE KNOWN KIRIHARA-KUN FROM BEFORE, SO HE REALLY KNEW WHAT WAS WRONG WITH ME.
AND WHEN HE VISITED EVERY DAY, I STARTED TO FEEL LIKE I COULD WALK WITH HIM, SIDE BY SIDE.

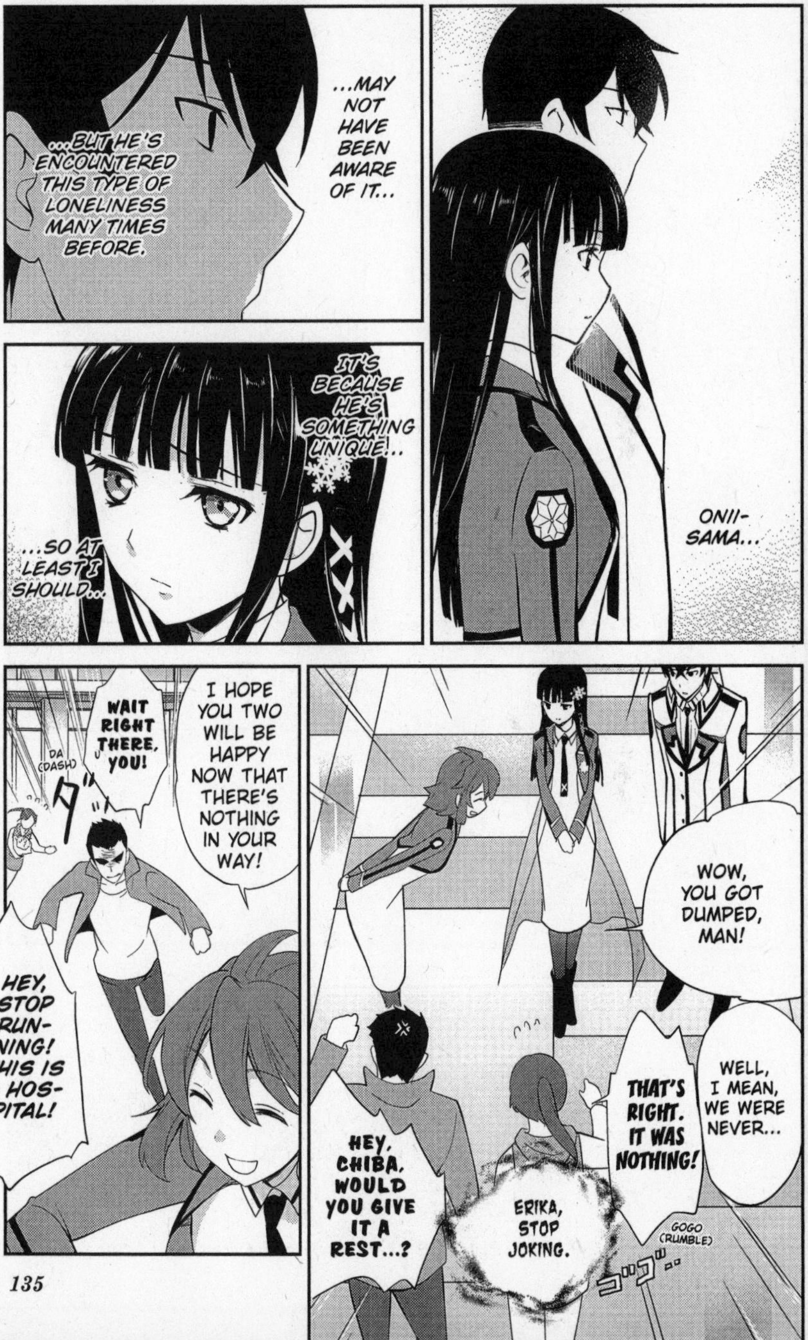
ONII-SAMA...
...MAY NOT HAVE BEEN AWARE OF IT...
...BUT HE'S ENCOUNTERED THIS TYPE OF LONELINESS MANY TIMES BEFORE.
IT'S BECAUSE HE'S SOMETHING UNIQUE...
...SO AT LEAST I SHOULD...
WOW, YOU GOT DUMPED, MAN!
WELL, I MEAN, WE WERE NEVER...
THAT'S RIGHT. IT WAS NOTHING!
GOGO (RUMBLE)
ERIKA, STOP JOKING.
HEY, CHIBA, WOULD YOU GIVE IT A REST...?
I HOPE YOU TWO WILL BE HAPPY NOW THAT THERE'S NOTHING IN YOUR WAY!
WAIT RIGHT THERE, YOU!
DA (DASH)
HEY, STOP RUN-NING! THIS IS A HOS-PITAL!

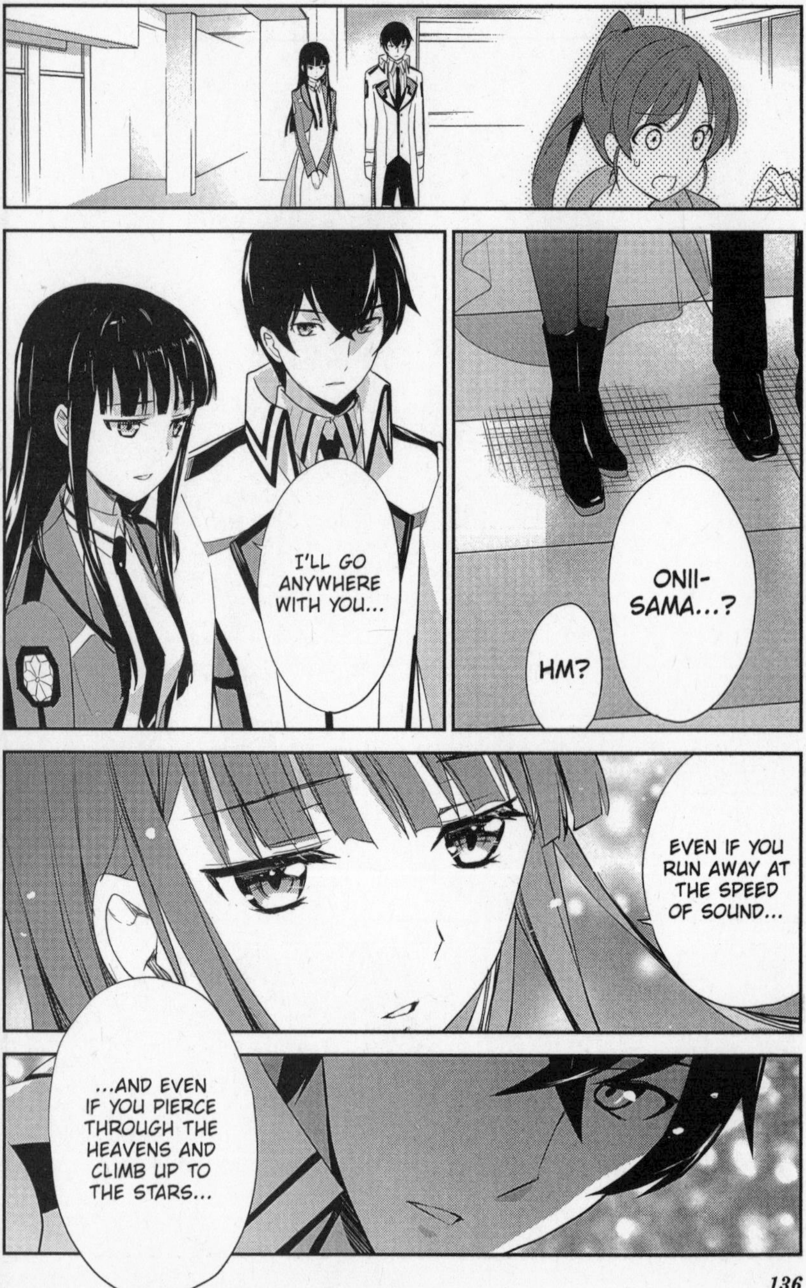
ONII-SAMA...?
HM?
I'LL GO ANYWHERE WITH YOU...
EVEN IF YOU RUN AWAY AT THE SPEED OF SOUND...
...AND EVEN IF YOU PIERCE THROUGH THE HEAVENS AND CLIMB UP TO THE STARS...

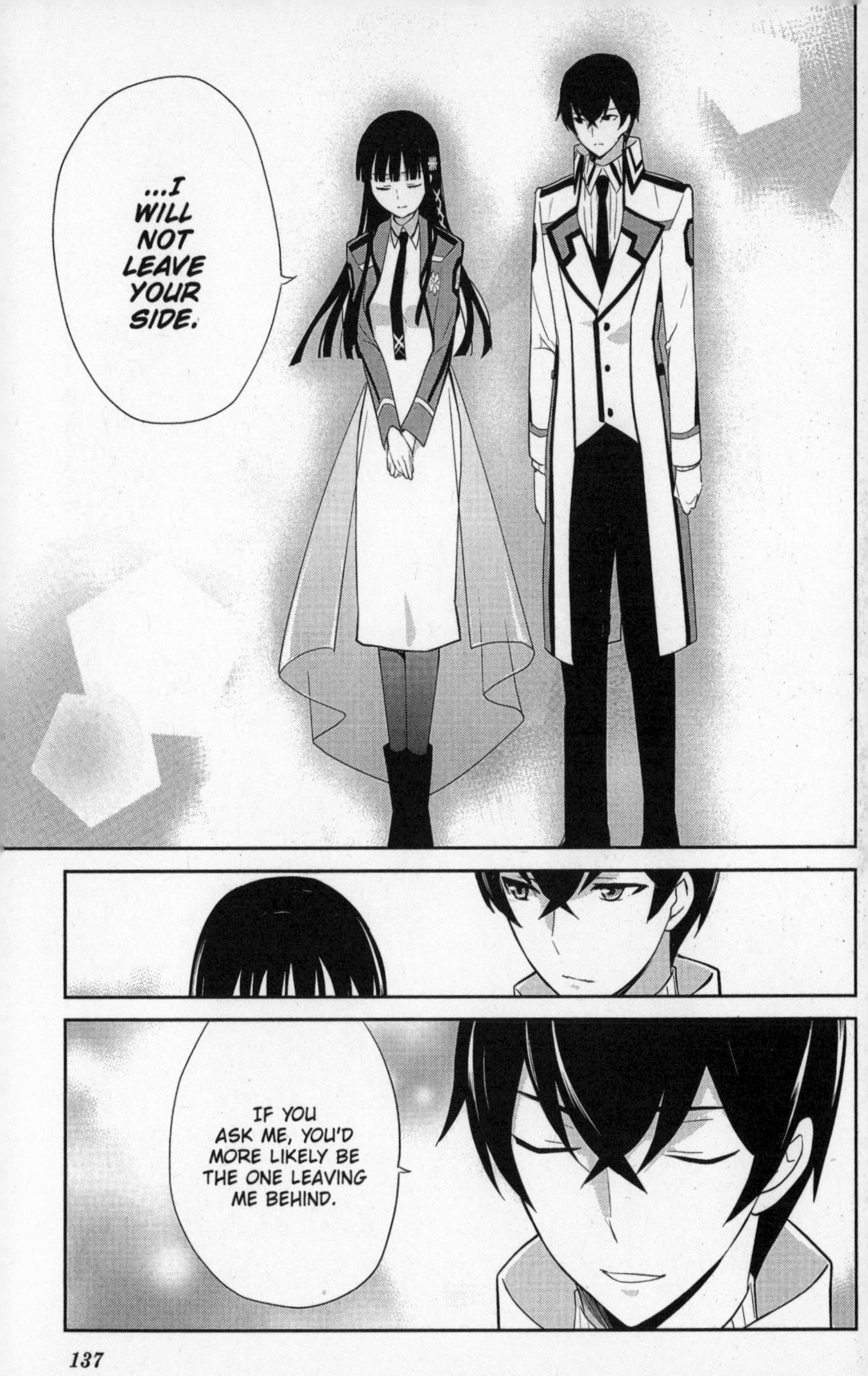
...I WILL NOT LEAVE YOUR SIDE.
IF YOU ASK ME, YOU'D MORE LIKELY BE THE ONE LEAVING ME BEHIND.

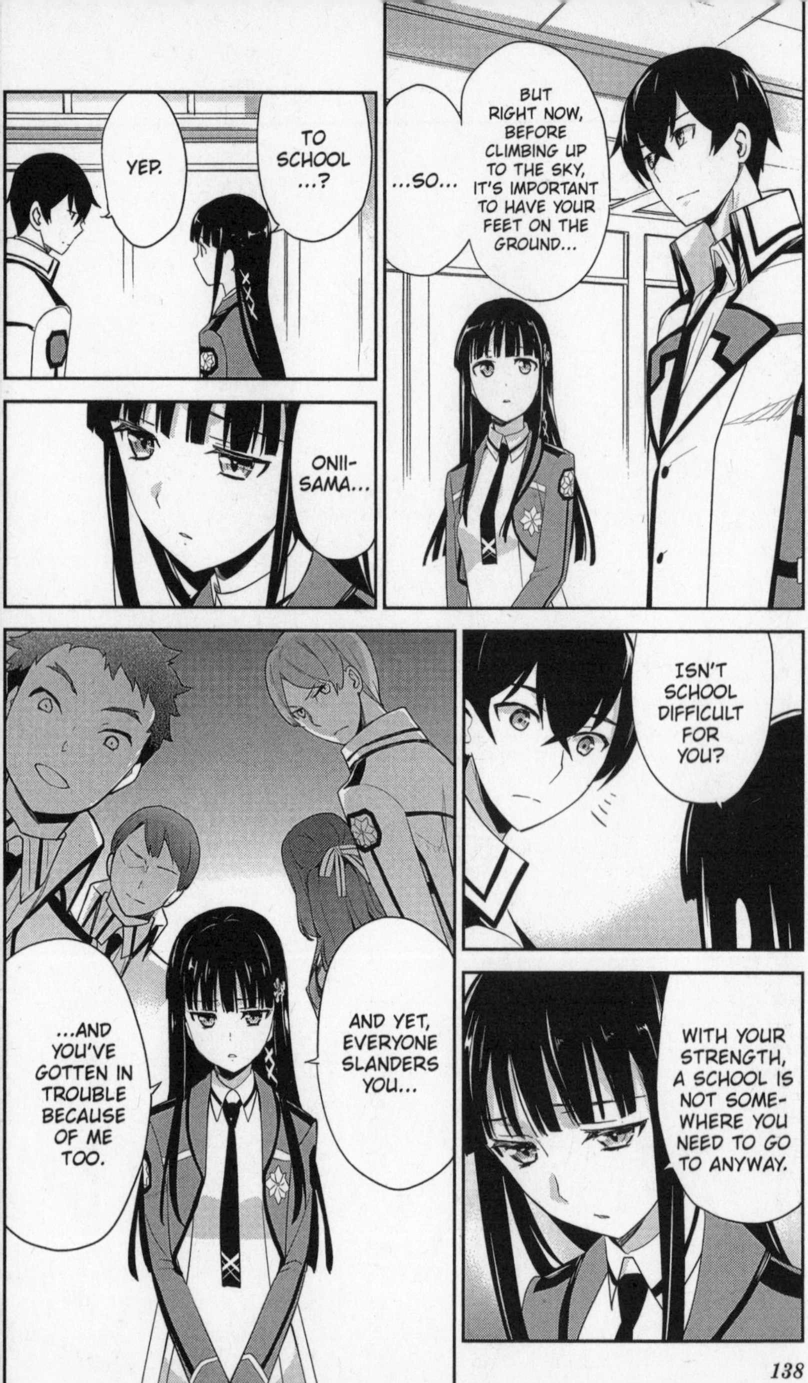
BUT RIGHT NOW, BEFORE CLIMBING UP TO THE SKY, IT'S IMPORTANT TO HAVE YOUR FEET ON THE GROUND...
...SO...
TO SCHOOL ...?
YEP.
ONII-SAMA...
ISN'T SCHOOL DIFFICULT FOR YOU?
WITH YOUR STRENGTH, A SCHOOL IS NOT SOME-WHERE YOU NEED TO GO TO ANYWAY.
AND YET, EVERYONE SLANDERS YOU...
...AND YOU'VE GOTTEN IN TROUBLE BECAUSE OF ME TOO.

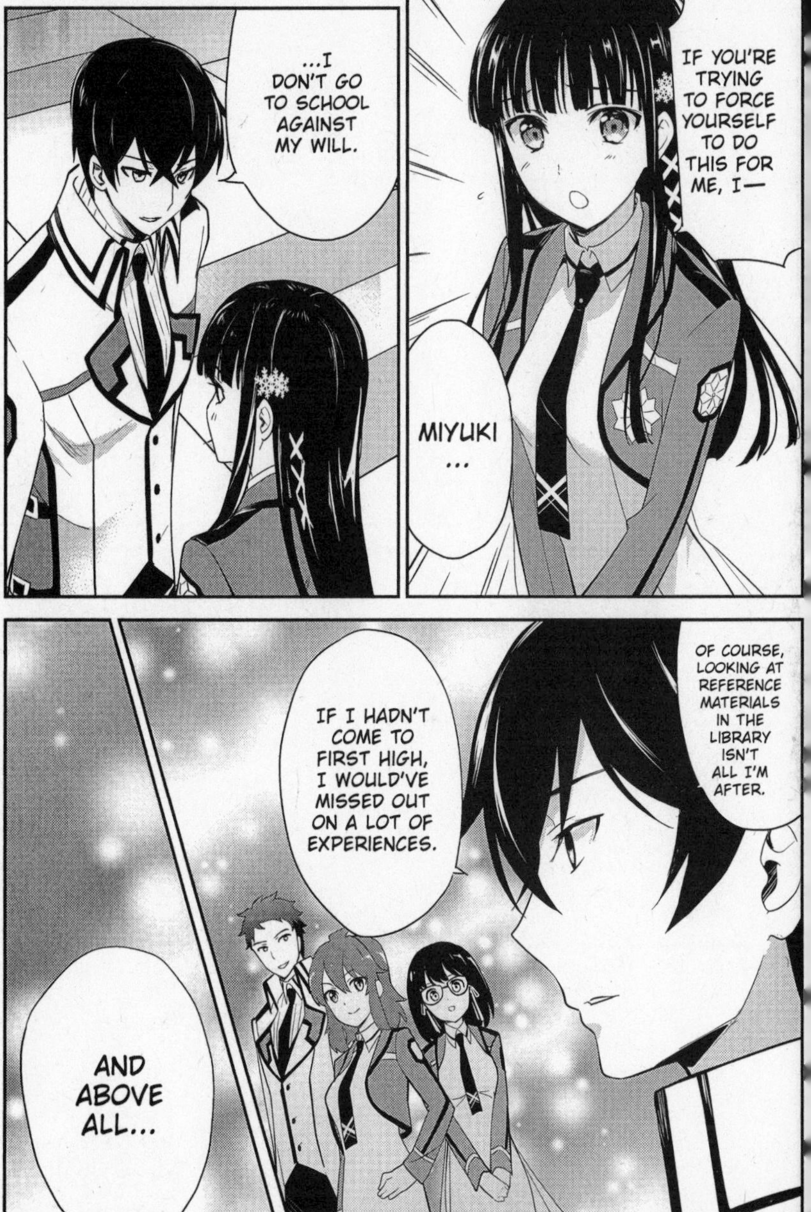
IF YOU'RE TRYING TO FORCE YOURSELF TO DO THIS FOR ME, I—
MIYUKI...
...I DON'T GO TO SCHOOL AGAINST MY WILL.
OF COURSE, LOOKING AT REFERENCE MATERIALS IN THE LIBRARY ISN'T ALL I'M AFTER.
IF I HADN'T COME TO FIRST HIGH, I WOULD'VE MISSED OUT ON A LOT OF EXPERIENCES.
AND ABOVE ALL...

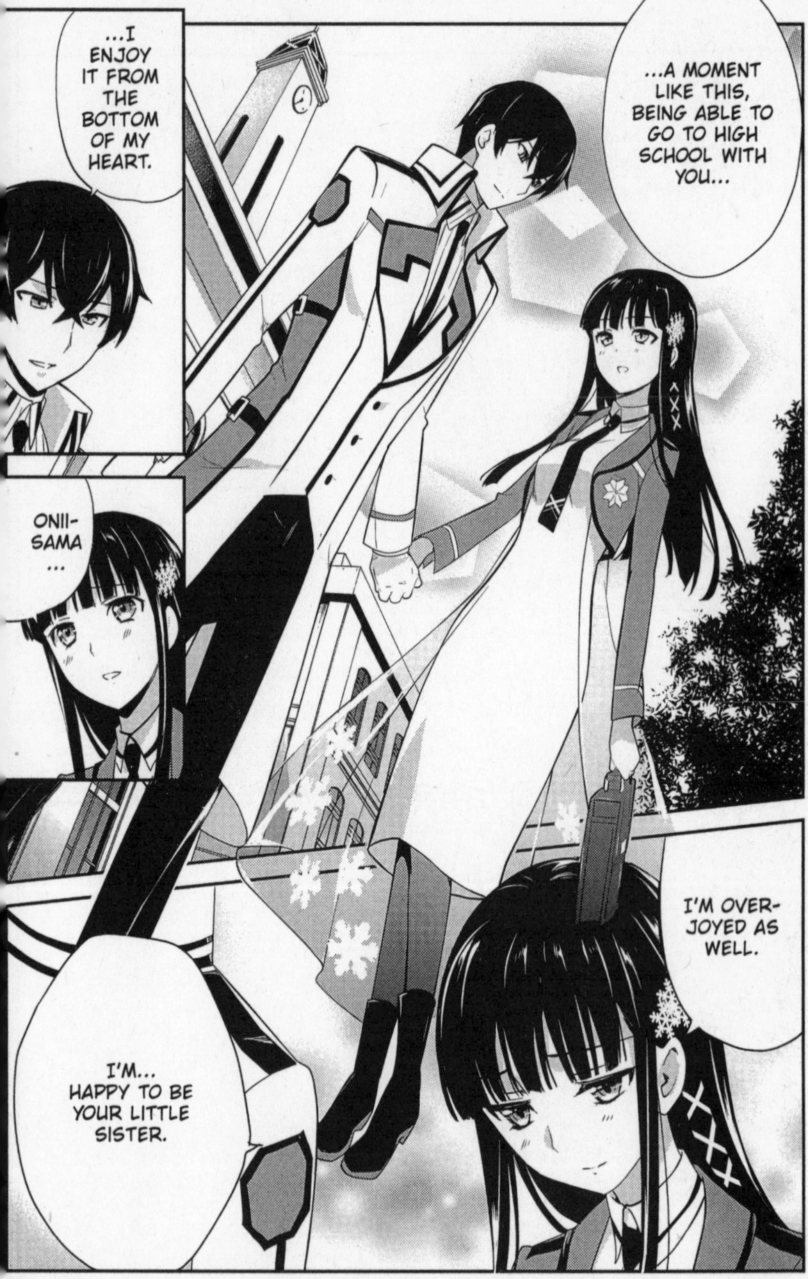
...A MOMENT LIKE THIS, BEING ABLE TO GO TO HIGH SCHOOL WITH YOU...
...I ENJOY IT FROM THE BOTTOM OF MY HEART.
ONII-SAMA ...
I'M OVER-JOYED AS WELL.
I'M... HAPPY TO BE YOUR LITTLE SISTER.

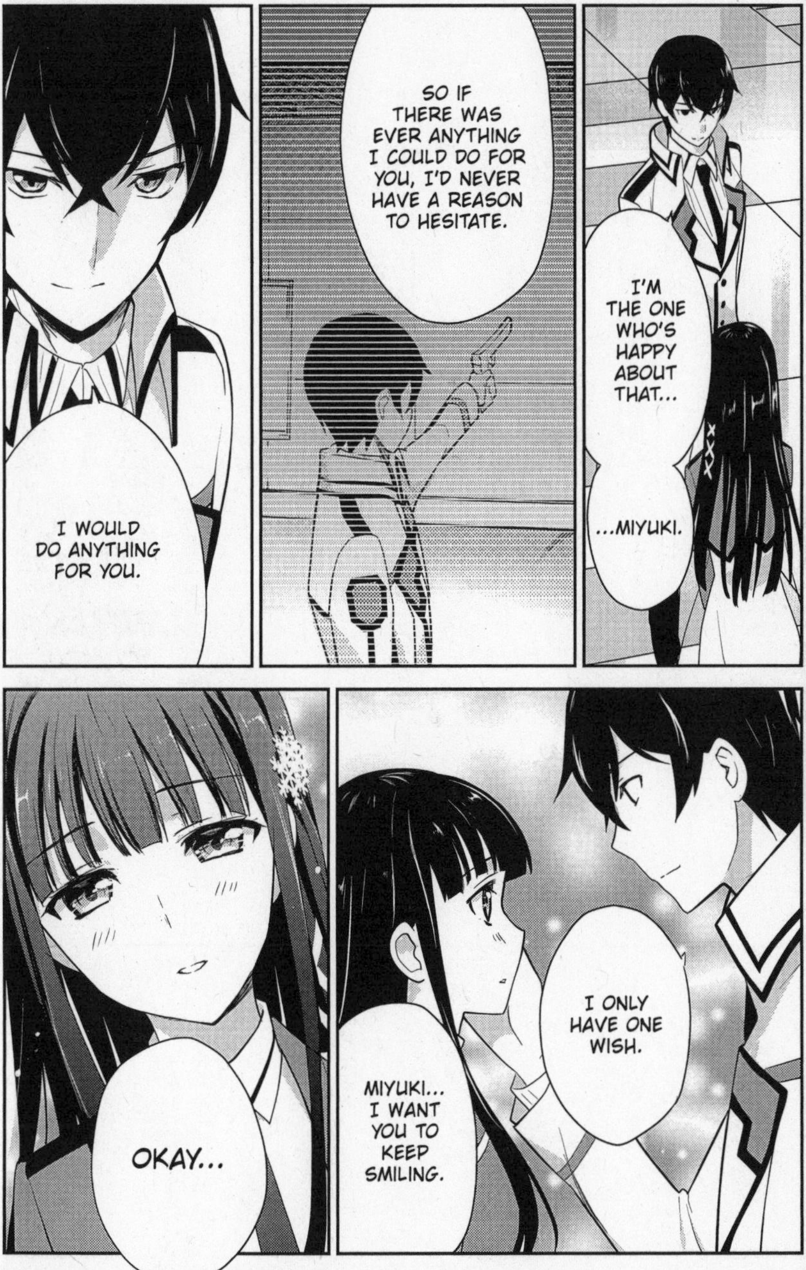
I'M THE ONE WHO'S HAPPY ABOUT THAT...
...MIYUKI.
SO IF THERE WAS EVER ANYTHING I COULD DO FOR YOU, I'D NEVER HAVE A REASON TO HESITATE.
I WOULD DO ANYTHING FOR YOU.
I ONLY HAVE ONE WISH.
MIYUKI... I WANT YOU TO KEEP SMILING.
OKAY...

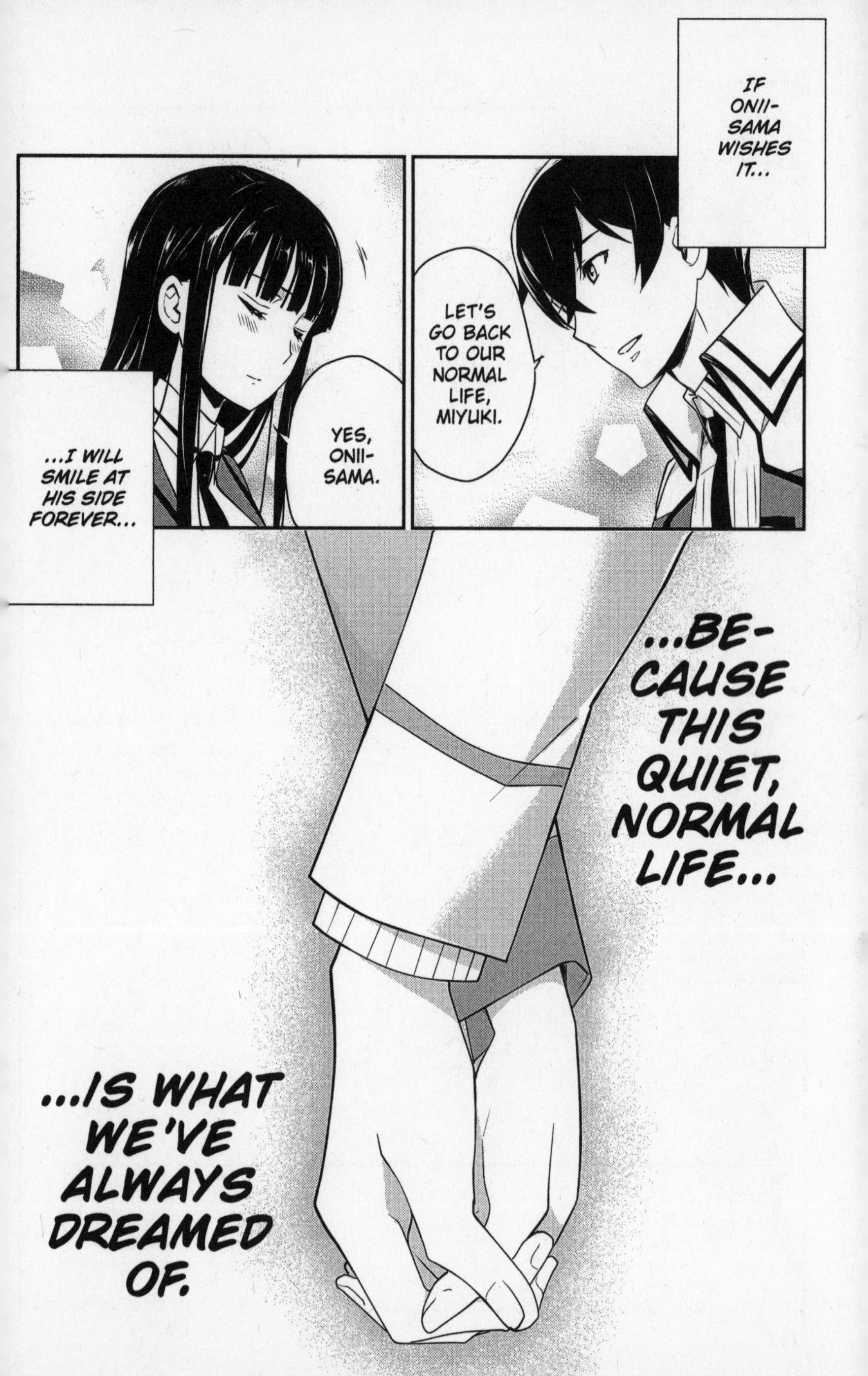
IF ONII-SAMA WISHES IT...
LET'S GO BACK TO OUR NORMAL LIFE, MIYUKI.
YES, ONII-SAMA.
...I WILL SMILE AT HIS SIDE FOREVER...
...BE-CAUSE THIS QUIET, NORMAL LIFE...
...IS WHAT WE'VE ALWAYS DREAMED OF.

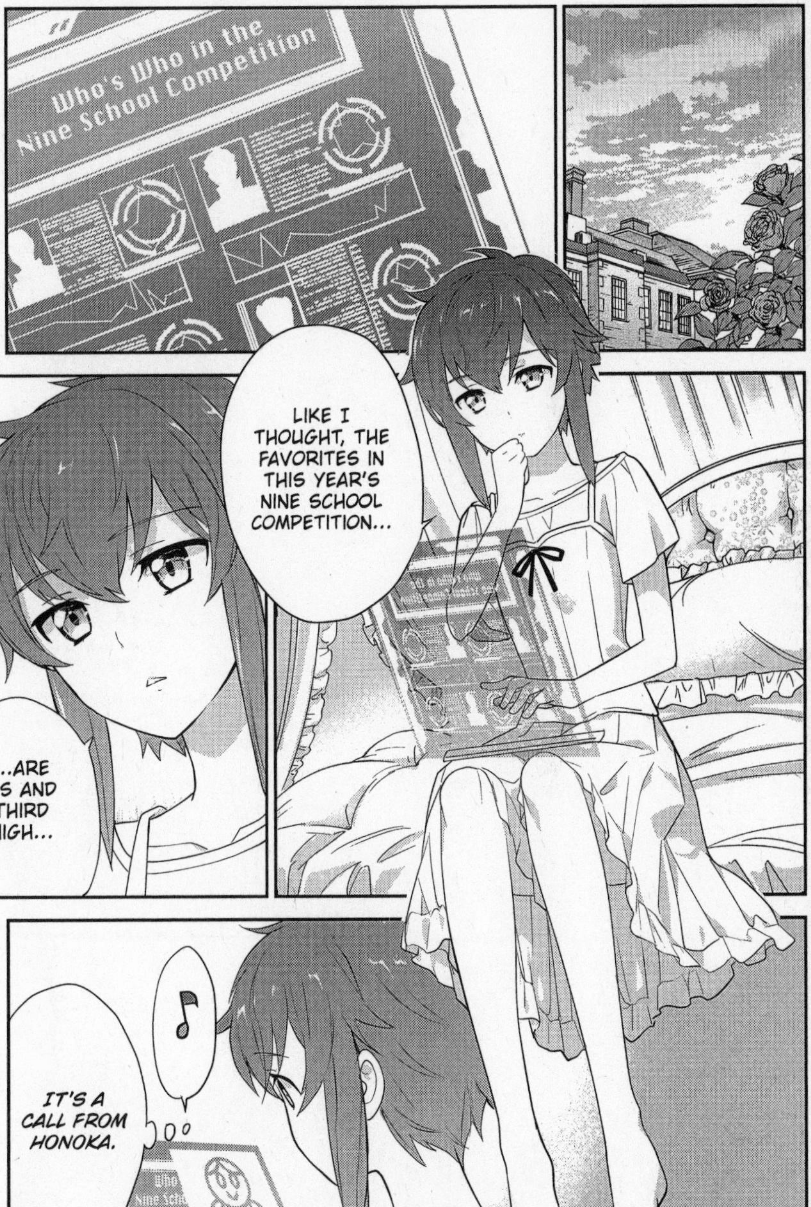
Who's Who in the Nine School Competition
LIKE I THOUGHT, THE FAVORITES IN THIS YEAR'S NINE SCHOOL COMPETITION...
...ARE US AND THIRD HIGH...
♪
IT'S A CALL FROM HONOKA.

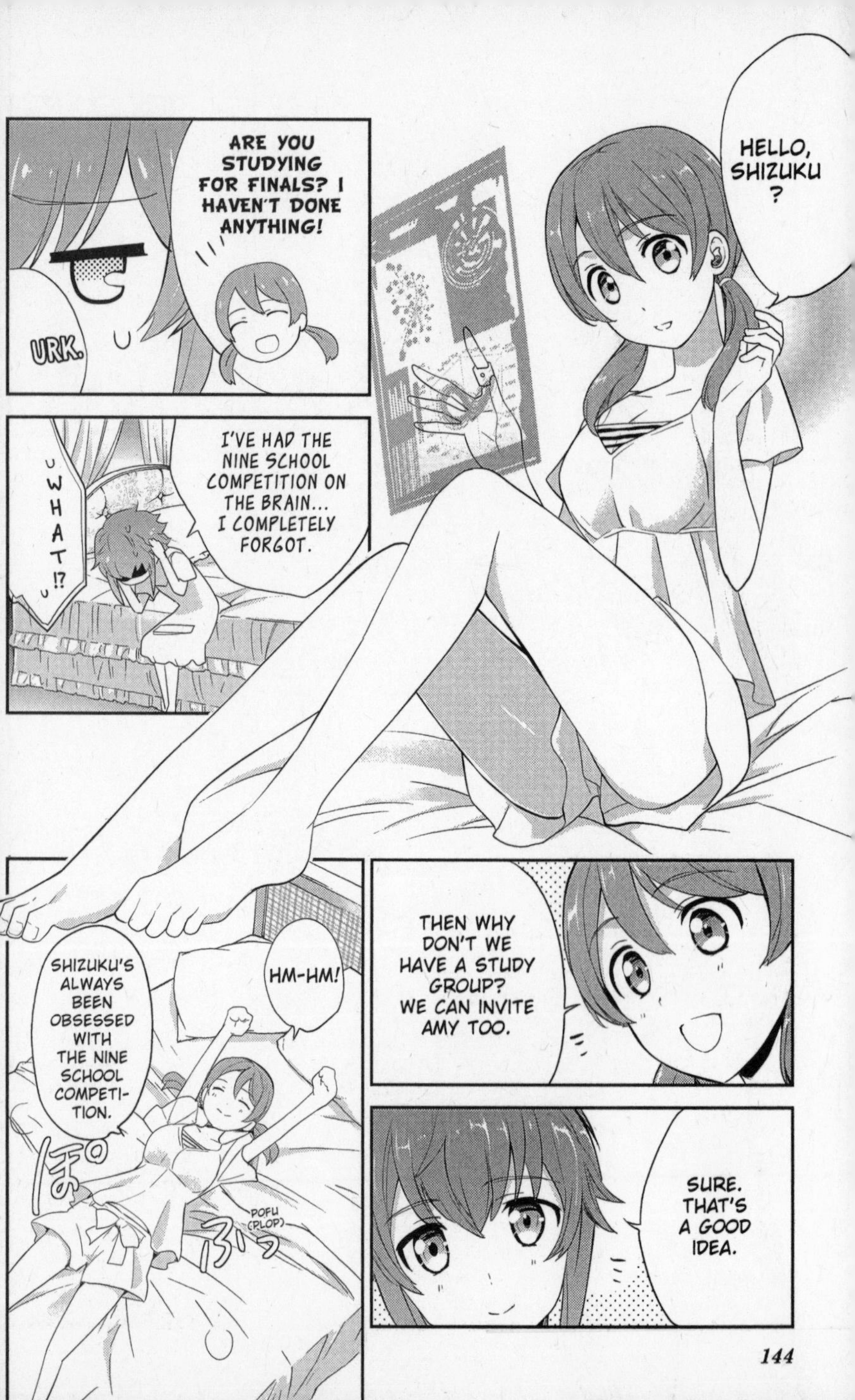
HELLO, SHIZUKU?
ARE YOU STUDYING FOR FINALS? I HAVEN'T DONE ANYTHING!
URK.
I'VE HAD THE NINE SCHOOL COMPETITION ON THE BRAIN... I COMPLETELY FORGOT.
WHAT!?
THEN WHY DON'T WE HAVE A STUDY GROUP? WE CAN INVITE AMY TOO.
SURE. THAT'S A GOOD IDEA.
HM-HM!
SHIZUKU'S ALWAYS BEEN OBSESSED WITH THE NINE SCHOOL COMPETI-TION.
ぽふっ
POFU (PLOP)

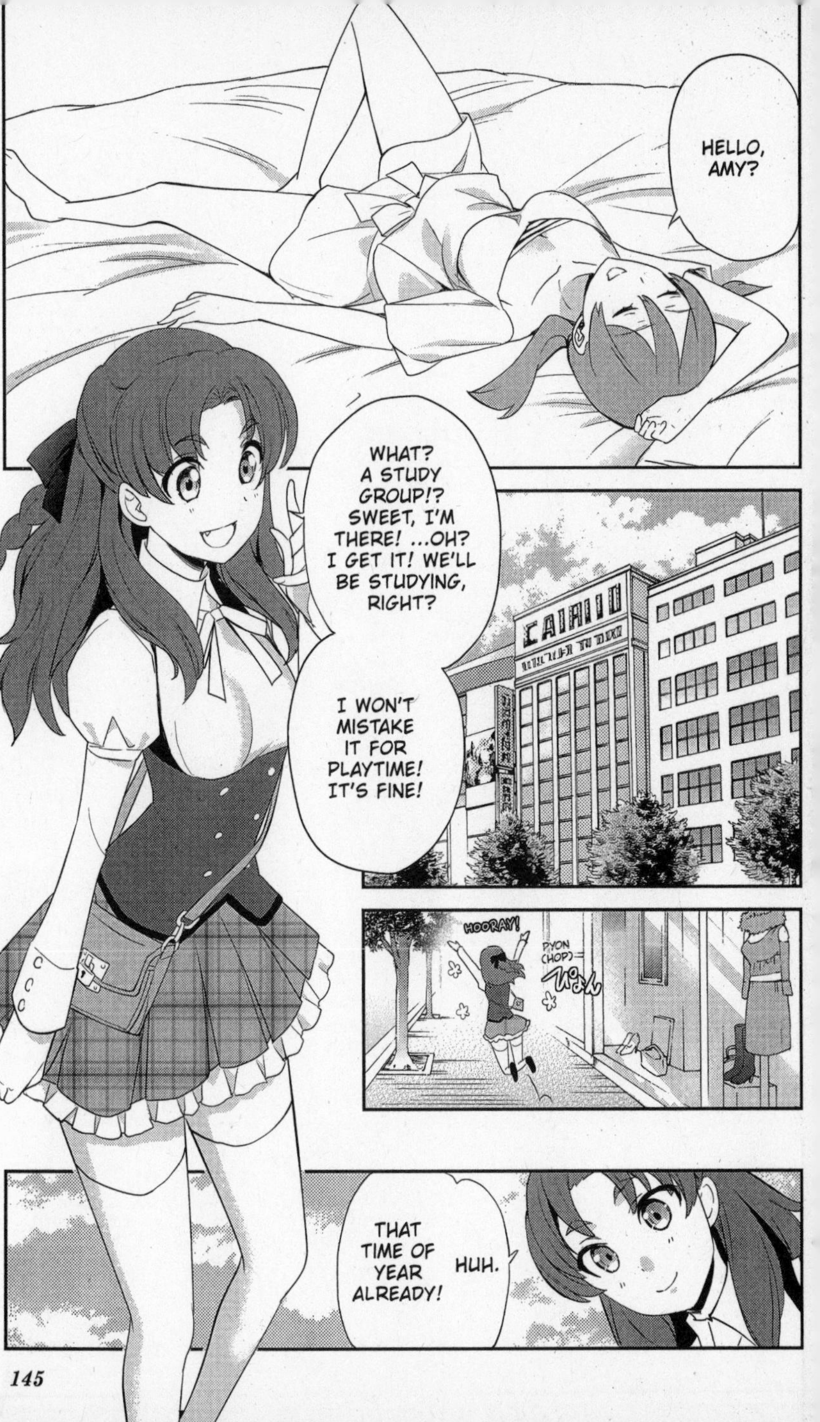
HELLO, AMY?
WHAT? A STUDY GROUP!? SWEET, I'M THERE! ...OH? I GET IT! WE'LL BE STUDYING, RIGHT?
I WON'T MISTAKE IT FOR PLAYTIME! IT'S FINE!
HOORAY!
PYON (HOP)
ぴょん
HUH.
THAT TIME OF YEAR ALREADY!

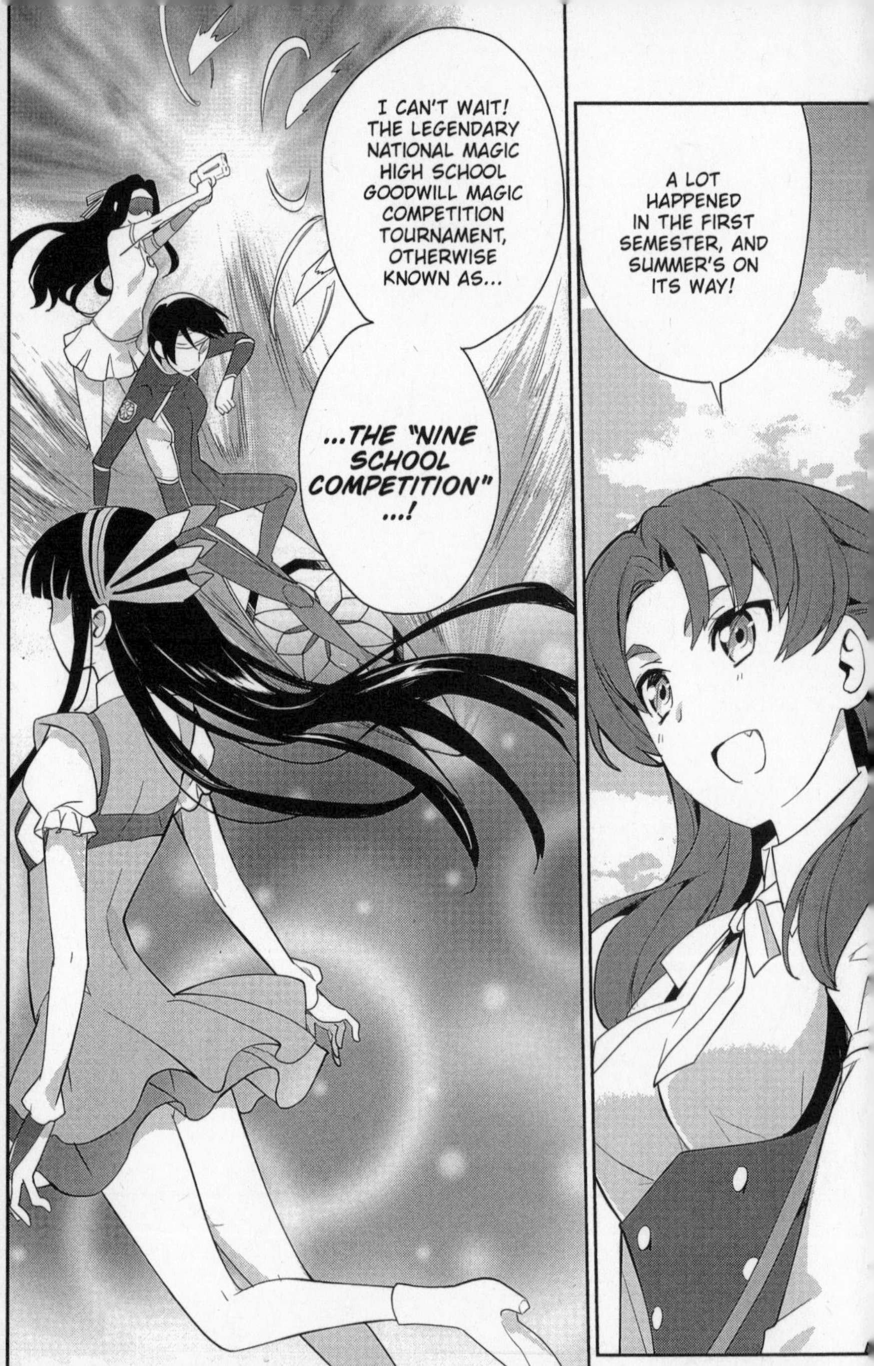
A LOT HAPPENED IN THE FIRST SEMESTER, AND SUMMER'S ON ITS WAY!
I CAN'T WAIT! THE LEGENDARY NATIONAL MAGIC HIGH SCHOOL GOODWILL MAGIC COMPETITION TOURNAMENT, OTHERWISE KNOWN AS...
...THE "NINE SCHOOL COMPETITION" ...!

TO BE CONTINUED IN VOLUME 5

THE HONOR STUDENT AT Magic High School

Activation sequence
The blueprints for magic and the sequences used to construct it. Activation sequence data is stored in a compressed format in C.A.D.s. Design waves are sent from the magician to the device, where they're converted into a signal according to the decompressed data and returned to the magician.

Antinite
A military-grade commodity only produced in lands where ancient alpine civilizations prospered, such as part of the Aztec Empire and the Mayan countries and regions. Extremely valuable due to its limited production quantity and impossible for civilians to acquire.

Blanche
A national anti-magic political organization with the objective of uprooting discrimination in society based on magical ability. They hold protest activities based on the criticism of the fictional concept of the current system giving special political treatment to magicians. Behind the scenes, they engage in terrorism and other illegal activities and are strictly watched by the public safety agencies.

Blooms, Weeds
Terms displaying the gap between Course 1 students and Course 2 students in First High. The left breast of Course 1 student uniforms is emblazoned with an eight-petaled emblem, but it is absent from the Course 2 uniforms.

Cabinets
Small, linear vehicles holding either two or four passengers and controlled by a central station. Used for commuting to work and school as a public transportation replacement for trains.

Cast jamming
A variety of typeless magic that obstructs magic sequences from exerting influence on Eidos. It weakens the process by which magic sequences affect Eidos by scattering large amounts of meaningless psionic waves.

C.A.D. (Casting Assistant Device)
A device that simplifies the activation of magic. Magical programming is recorded inside. The main types are specialized and all-purpose.

Égalité
A branch organization of Blanche. They take in young people who hate politics, so they don't reveal that they're directly related to Blanche.

Eidos (Individual information bodies)
Originally a term from Greek philosophy. In modern magic, Eidos are the bodies of information that accompany phenomena. They record the existence of those phenomena on the world, so they can also be called the footprints that phenomena leave on the world. The definition of "magic" in modern magic refers to the technology that modifies these phenomena by modifying Eidos.

Four Leaves Technology (F.L.T.)
A domestic C.A.D. manufacturer. Originally famous for its magic engineering products, rather than finished C.A.D.s, but with the development of its Silver line of models, its fame skyrocketed as a C.A.D. manufacturer.

Idea (Information body dimension)
Pronounced "ee-dee-ah." Originally a term from Greek philosophy. In modern magic, "Idea" refers to the platform on which Eidos are recorded. Magic's primary form is a technology wherein a magic sequence is output onto this platform, thus rewriting the Eidos recorded within.

Loopcast system
Activation sequences made so that a magician can continually execute a spell as many times as their calculation capacity will permit. Normally, one must re-expand activation sequences from the C.A.D. every time one executes the same spell, but the loopcast system makes it possible by automatically duplicating the activation sequence's final state in the magician's magic calculation region.

Magic Association of Japan
A social group of Japanese magicians based in Kyoto. The Kantou branch location is established within Yokohama Bay Hills Tower.

Magic calculation region
A mental region for the construction of magic sequences. The substance, so to speak, of magical talent. It exists in a magician's unconscious, and even if a magician is normally aware of using his or her magic calculation region, he or she cannot be aware of the processes being conducted within. The magic calculation region can be called a "black box" for the magician himself.

Magic engineer
Refers to engineers who design, develop, and maintain an apparatus that assists, amplifies, and strengthens magic. Their reputation in society is slightly worse than that of magicians. However, magic engineers are indispensable for tuning the C.A.D.s, indispensable tools for magicians, so in the industrial world, they're in higher demand than normal magicians. A first-rate magic engineer's earnings surpass even that of first-rate magicians.

Magic high school
The nickname for the high schools affiliated with the National Magic University. There are nine established throughout the country. Of them, the first through the third have two hundred students per grade and use the Course 1/Course 2 system.

Magic sequence
An information body for the purpose of temporarily altering information attached to phenomena. They are constructed from the Psions possessed by magicians.

Magician
An abbreviation of "magical technician," referring to anyone with the skill to use magic at a practical level.

Nine School Competition
An abbreviation of "National Magic High School Goodwill Magic Competition Tournament." Magic high school students from First through Ninth High, across the country, are gathered to compete with their schools in fierce magic showdowns. There are six events: Speed Shooting, Cloudball, Battle Board, Ice Pillars Break, Mirage Bat, and Monolith Code.

Psions
Non-physical particles belonging to the dimension of psychic phenomena. Psions are elements that record information on consciousness and thought products. Eidos—the theoretical basis for modern magic—as well as activation sequences and magic sequences—supporting its main framework—are all bodies of information constructed from Psions. Also referred to as "thought particles."

Pushions
Non-physical particles belonging to the dimension of psychic phenomena. Their existence has been proven, but their true form and functions have yet to be elucidated. Magicians are generally only able to "feel" the pushions being activated through magic. Also referred to as "spirit particles."

The Ten Master Clans
The strongest group of magicians in Japan. Ten families from a list of twenty-eight are chosen during the Ten Master Clans Selection Conference that happens every four years and are named as the Ten Master Clans. The twenty-eight families are Ichijou, Ichinokura, Isshiki, Futatsugi, Nikaidou, Nihei, Mitsuya, Mikazuki, Yotsuba, Itsuwa, Gotou, Itsumi, Mutsuzuka, Rokkaku, Rokugou, Roppongi, Saegusa, Shippou, Tanabata, Nanase, Yatsushiro, Hassaku, Hachiman, Kudou, Kuki, Kuzumi, Juumonji, and Tooyama.

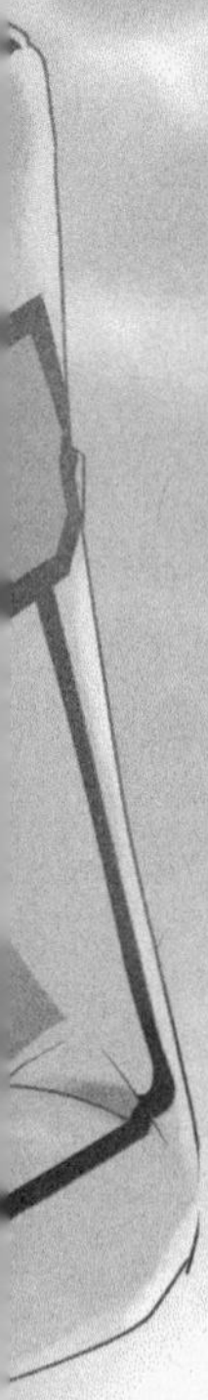

Postscript

The Honor Student at Magic High School has come to its fourth volume and thus the end of the Enrollment arc. I was able to come this far because of everyone's support. Thank you from the bottom of my heart.

The anime began its broadcast this spring too. I watched every week, moved at how subtle details in the series' setting were beautifully rendered in animation! I consider it a great honor to be involved in this work.

Honor Student will get into the Nine School Competition arc starting next volume. In it will appear Miyuki-san, Honoka, and the other students from First High, as well as honor students from other schools. I'll do my best to think about what kind of students they would be and how they'll relate to the story and other elements, so please continue to support me in the future.

Yu Mori

◎ Special Thanks ◎
Sato-sensei
Ishida-sama
Jimmy Stone-sama
Ishimoto-sama
Kitaumi-sensei
Hayashi-sensei
Tanaka-sama, the editor
Tomiyama-sama, the designer
Endou-sama
Kaneko-sama
Maeda-sama

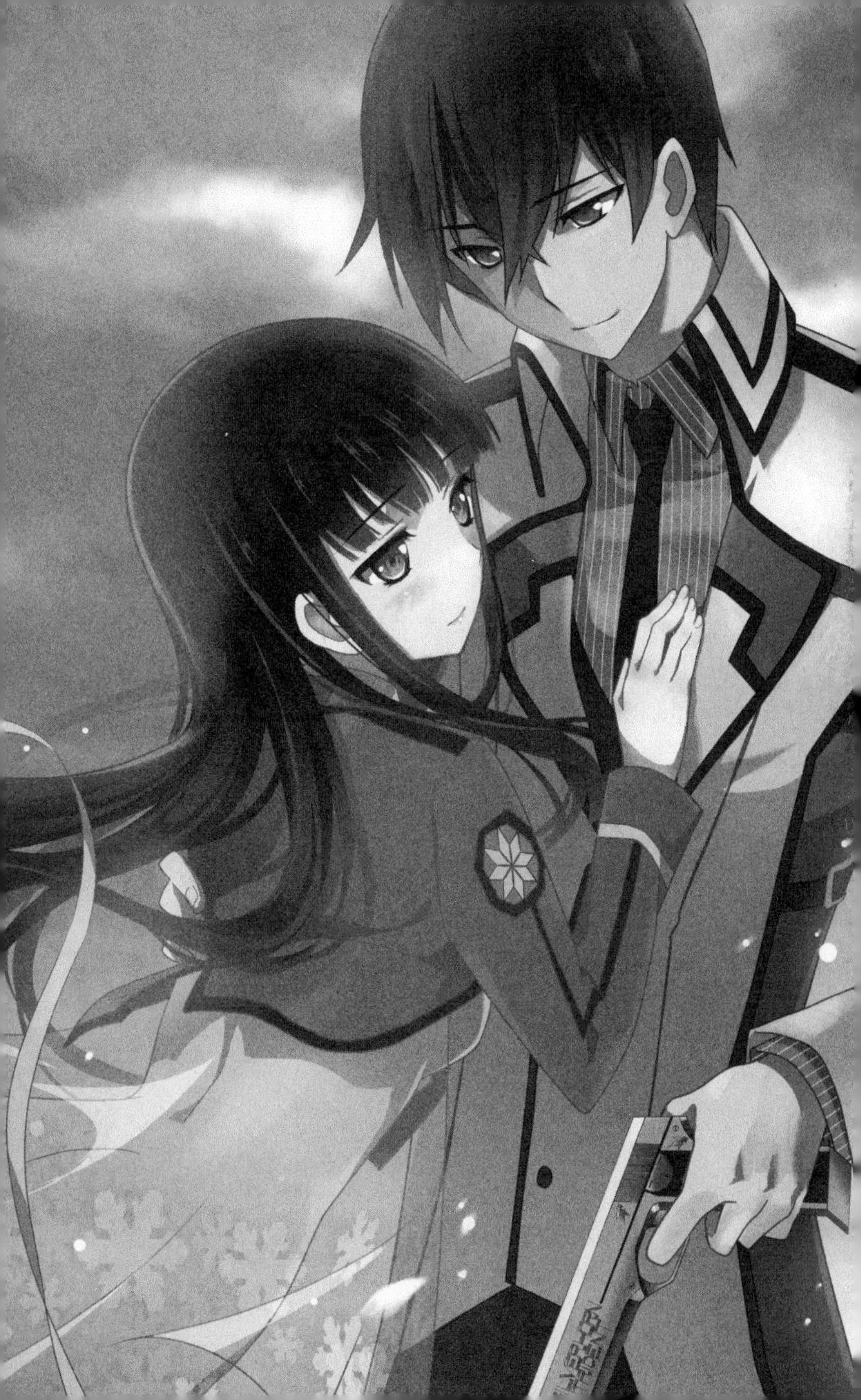

THE
HONOR
STUDENT
AT
MAGIC HIGH
SCHOOL

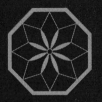

THE HONOR STUDENT AT MAGIC HIGH SCHOOL

SPECIAL CONTRIBUTION

Mori-sensei, congratulations on the release of the fourth volume of *The Honor Student at Magic High School.*

It's finally the climax of the Enrollment arc. As the original author, there were many psychological descriptions of Tatsuya and Miyuki in this volume that made me think, "Oh, I see!" In particular, I found myself in admiration over the passage about Tatsuya having "encountered this type of loneliness many times before......"

However, I feel that the joy of reading *Honor Student* comes from seeing what characters besides the Shiba siblings—namely, those who aren't depicted in the main story—are doing. Right from the beginning of Volume 4, Honoka and Shizuku were really putting on a show. Then we have the precious, diligent worker in Shun Morisaki. I also can't forget President Igarashi's gallant figure.

Personally, I'm looking forward to enjoying more of this other world of *Magic High School.*

佐島勤

Tsutomu Sato

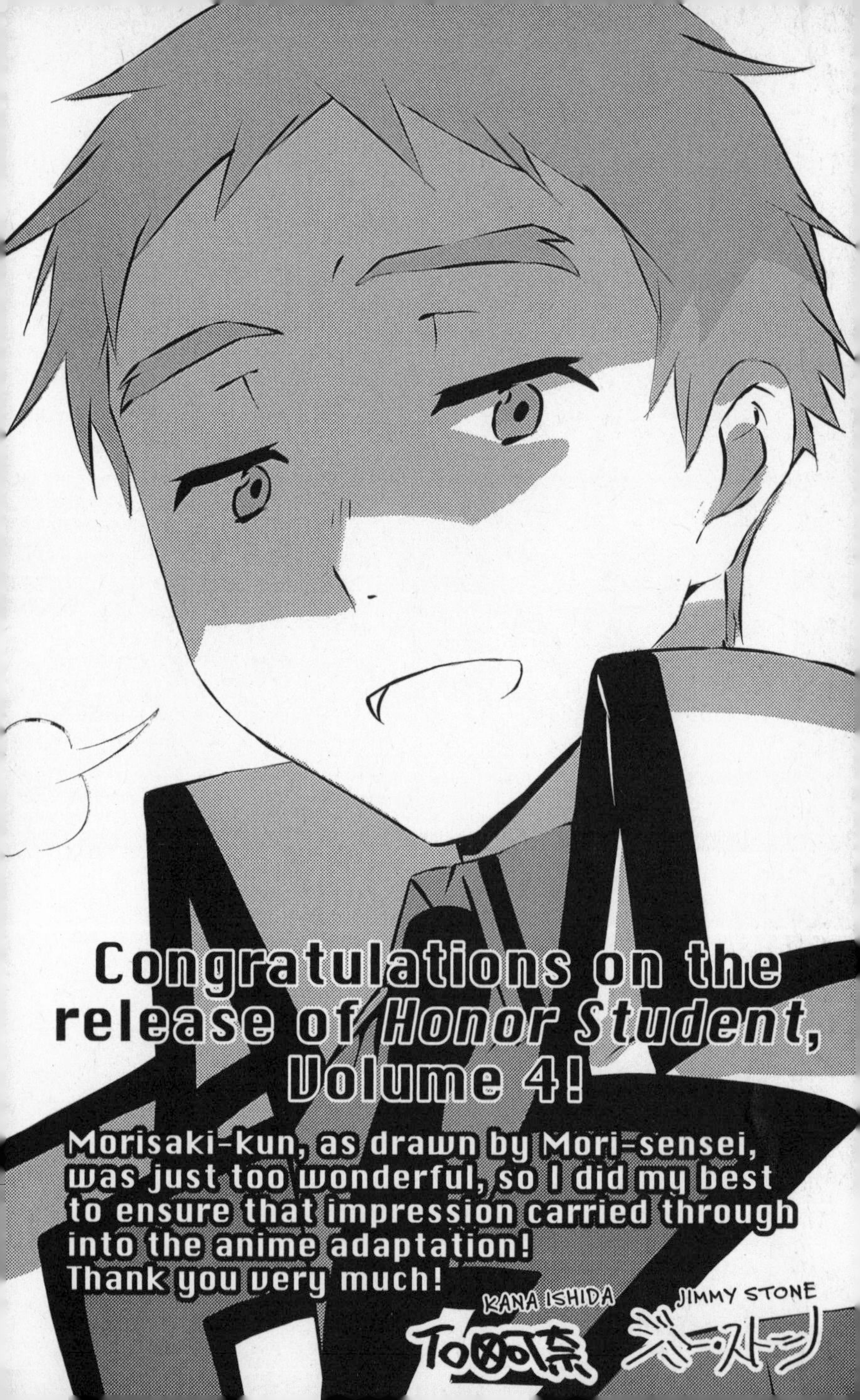
Congratulations on the release of *Honor Student*, Volume 4!
Morisaki-kun, as drawn by Mori-sensei, was just too wonderful, so I did my best to ensure that impression carried through into the anime adaptation!
Thank you very much!
KANA ISHIDA
JIMMY STONE

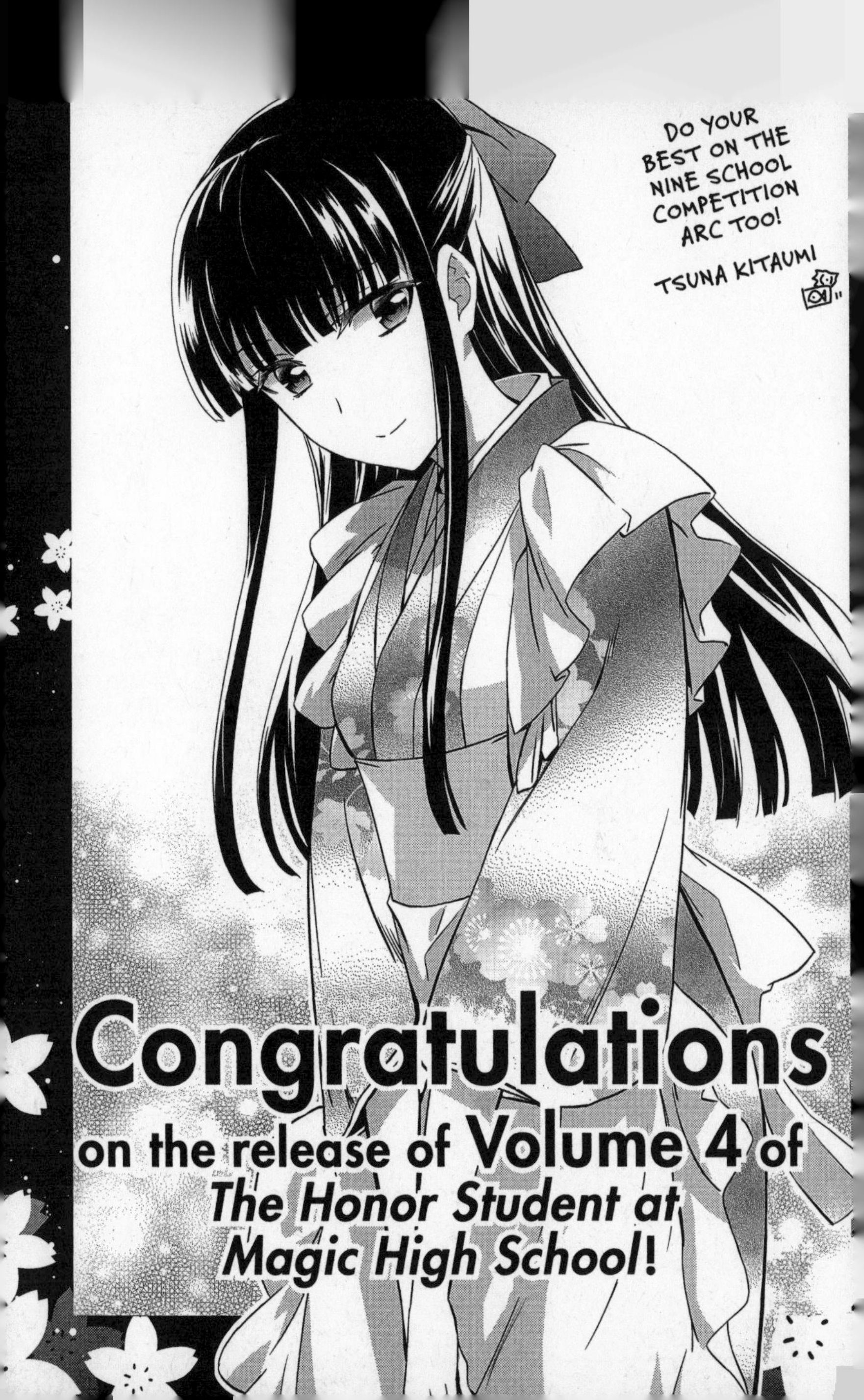
DO YOUR BEST ON THE NINE SCHOOL COMPETITION ARC TOO!
TSUNA KITAUMI
Congratulations
on the release of Volume 4 of
The Honor Student at Magic High School!

Next Issue

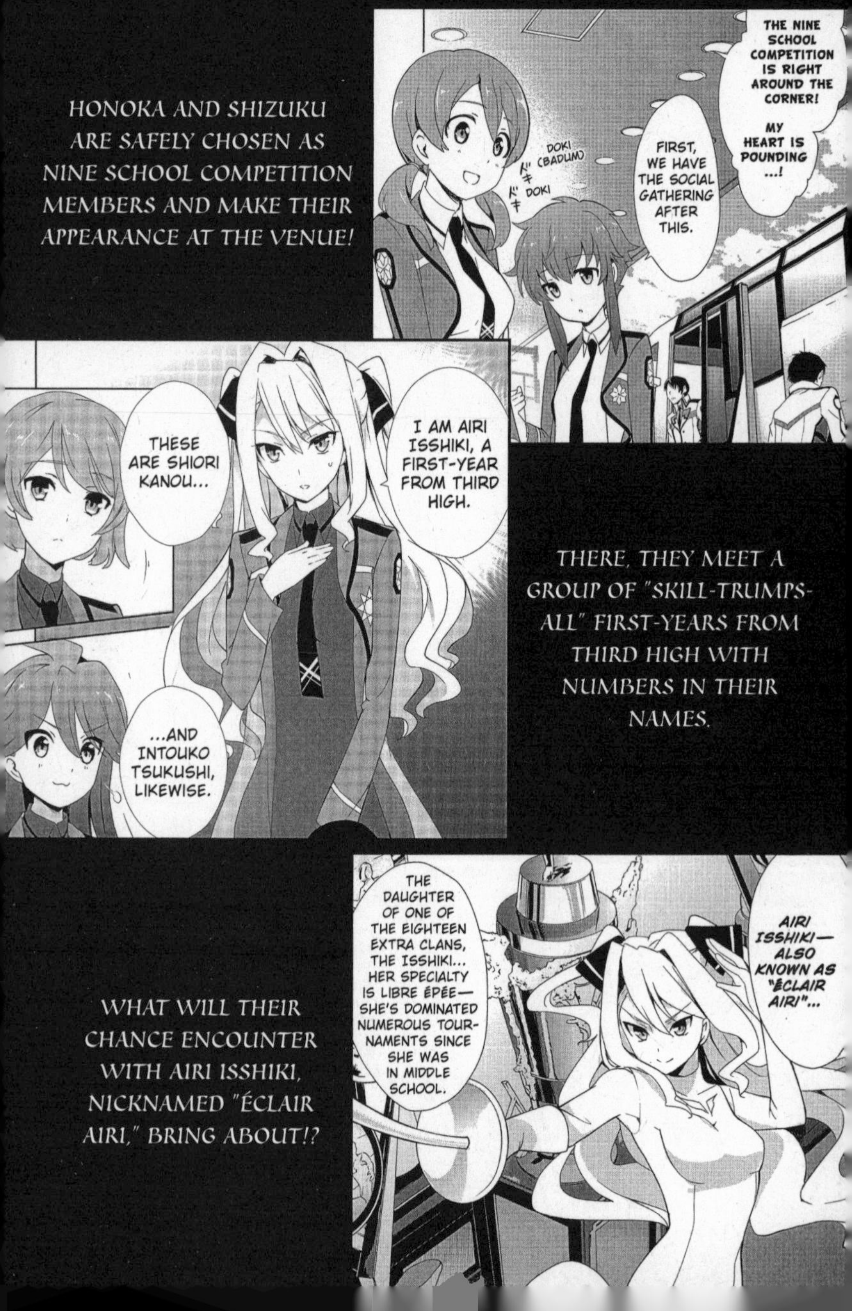

THE NINE SCHOOL COMPETITION IS RIGHT AROUND THE CORNER! MY HEART IS POUNDING ...!
FIRST, WE HAVE THE SOCIAL GATHERING AFTER THIS.
DOKI (BADUM) DOKI
HONOKA AND SHIZUKU ARE SAFELY CHOSEN AS NINE SCHOOL COMPETITION MEMBERS AND MAKE THEIR APPEARANCE AT THE VENUE!
THERE, THEY MEET A GROUP OF "SKILL-TRUMPS-ALL" FIRST-YEARS FROM THIRD HIGH WITH NUMBERS IN THEIR NAMES.
I AM AIRI ISSHIKI, A FIRST-YEAR FROM THIRD HIGH.
THESE ARE SHIORI KANOU...
...AND INTOUKO TSUKUSHI, LIKEWISE.
AIRI ISSHIKI—ALSO KNOWN AS "ÉCLAIR AIRI"...
THE DAUGHTER OF ONE OF THE EIGHTEEN EXTRA CLANS, THE ISSHIKI... HER SPECIALTY IS LIBRE ÉPÉE—SHE'S DOMINATED NUMEROUS TOURNAMENTS SINCE SHE WAS IN MIDDLE SCHOOL.
WHAT WILL THEIR CHANCE ENCOUNTER WITH AIRI ISSHIKI, NICKNAMED "ÉCLAIR AIRI," BRING ABOUT!?

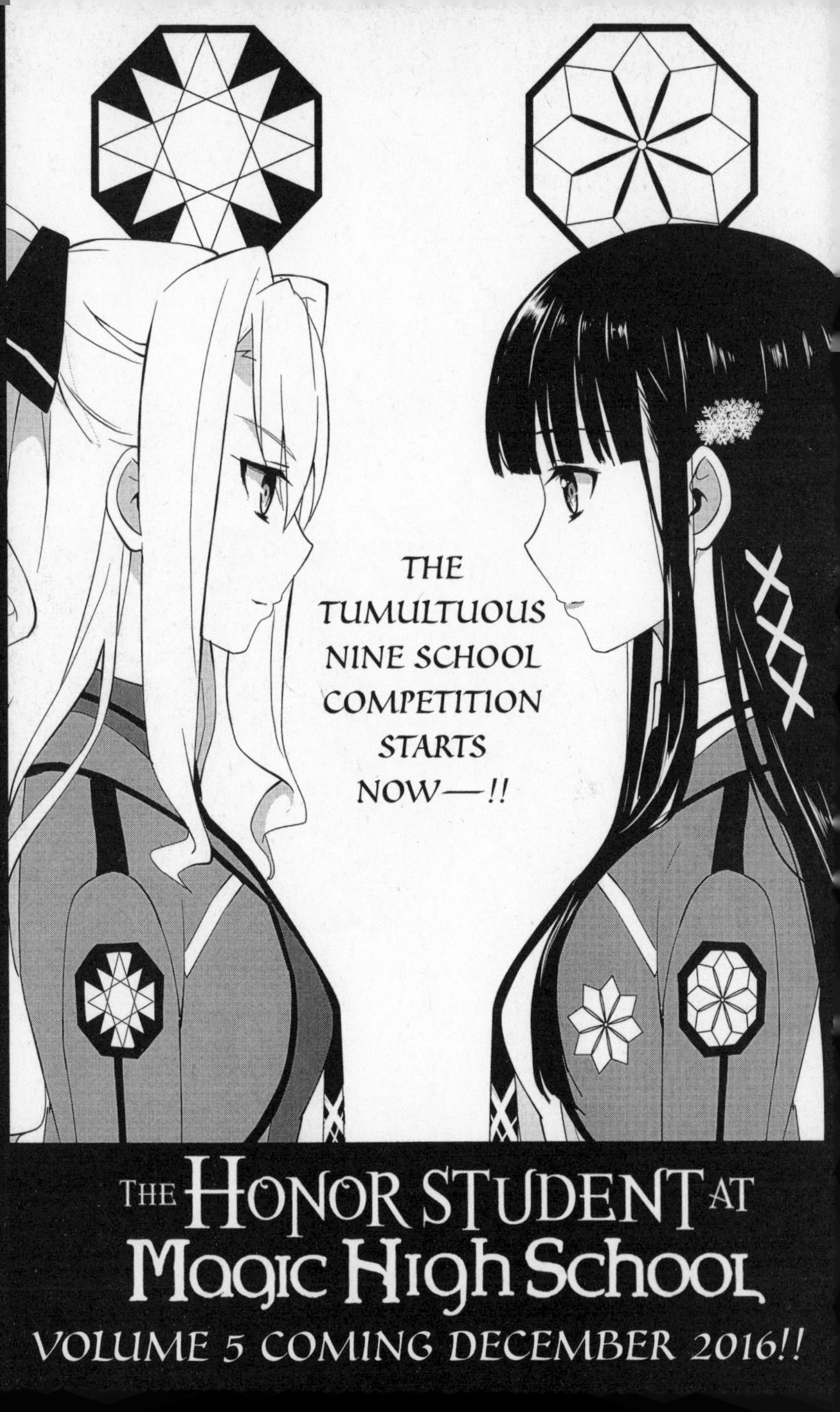
THE TUMULTUOUS NINE SCHOOL COMPETITION STARTS NOW—!!
THE HONOR STUDENT AT Magic High School
VOLUME 5 COMING DECEMBER 2016!!

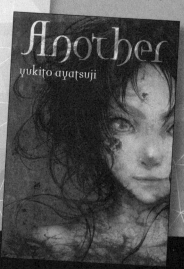